PAWS ON THE PLAYBOOK

MILE HIGH SPORTS SERIES
BOOK 3

JENNIFER J. WILLIAMS

JJW PRODUCTIONS, LLC

This one is for all of my fellow AuDHD girlies.
Jamie Wahlberg is for us, because we deserve a 6'3" NFL quarterback who clams up in social situations, but calls us his dirty little slut in the bedroom.

A NOTE FROM JEN

Hi Friends!

This book is near and dear to my heart. As a neurodiverse woman myself, I know how challenging it can be to read elements of yourself in a character. As both main characters are autistic, I want you to know there will be conversations in this book about anxiety, sensory issues, social cues, executive functioning, fears about public judgment, and many other autistic traits. No autistic person is the same. We are all beautifully unique in how we see the world. I've written this wonderful story as closely to what my day-to-day life is, including being married to a neurodiverse man, and raising two neurodiverse children. Life isn't perfect, and we have many struggles in our lives. But we're human, and we deserve love too.

Some other triggers you should be aware of:

- Animal cruelty/abandonment (off page)
- Mental health discussions
- Family abuse: emotional and physical

As always, take care of yourself first if you feel this book may be upsetting to you. You can reach out to me at jennifer@authorjenniferjwilliams with any questions or comments. Happy reading!

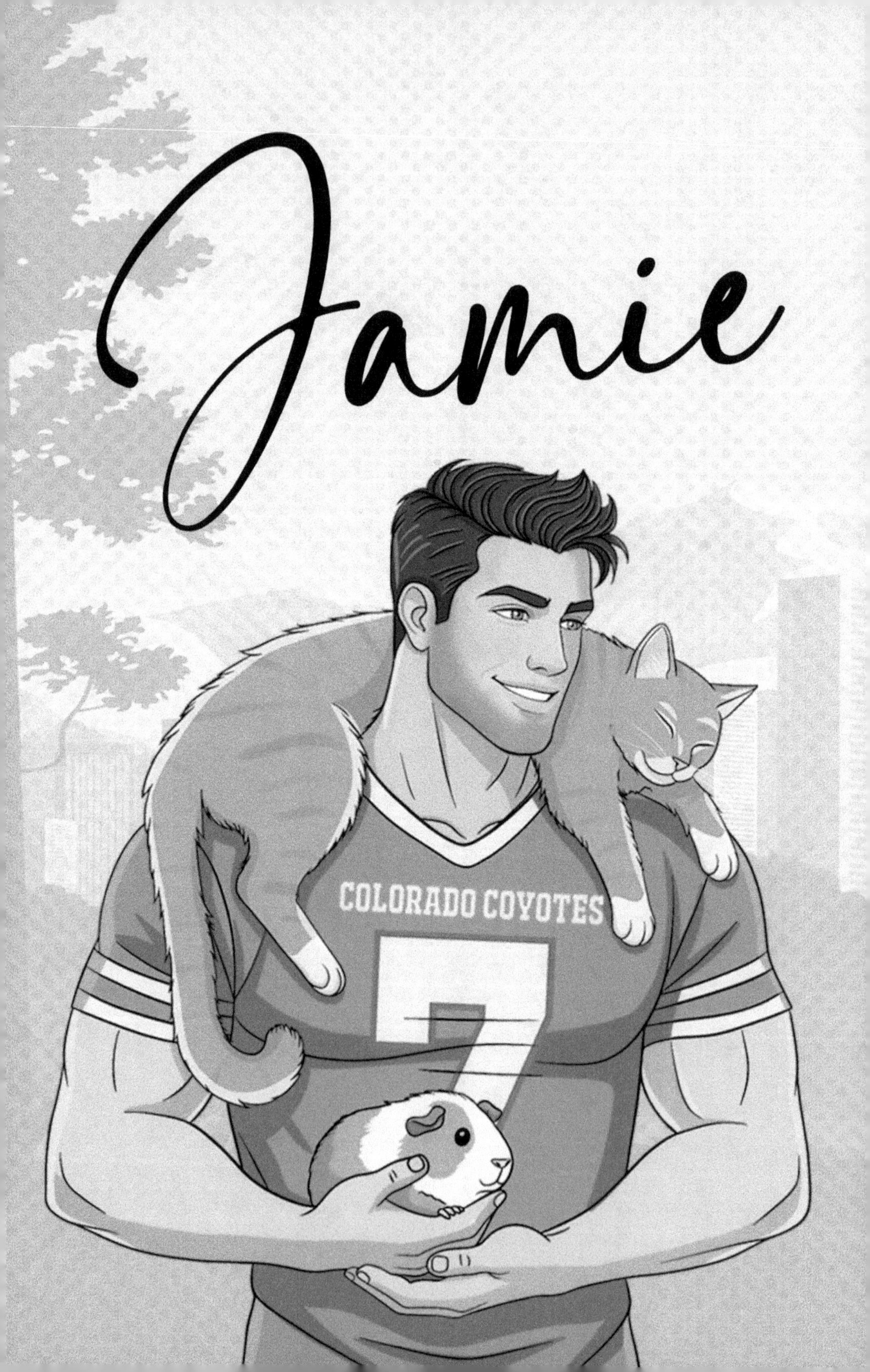

Jamie
COLORADO COYOTES
7

CHAPTER 1

"What the hell is wrong with you?"

I'm assuming that's a rhetorical question. If not, well. We could be here a while. But considering I just met this woman, I doubt she wants a list of my more unique qualities.

What set her off? It was probably when I said something about how the heel of her foot scratched my leg, and I gave her the name of my podiatrist. While we were in bed. She'd made it clear she was a sure thing, and I'd gone against my better judgment by agreeing to accompany her back to her place. I'd made the comment before anything really happened, so at least I can be thankful for small miracles there.

Was I eloquent? No. Considerate? Well, I thought it was.

Apparently, Monica … Maven? Moira? Crap. Whatever her name is, she kicked me out of her apartment before I even had my shirt on.

This is why I rarely date. Or have sex. Ever.

Because they think they're getting Jameson Wahlberg, NFL superstar quarterback, two-time Super Bowl MVP, but in reality, they're getting the guy who hyper-focuses on sensations way too much, and has the ability to read signals from women about as well as a rock. I can read signals on the football field just fine. But if the other team were amassed of all women, asking something of me? I'd run the other way, screaming, with my tail tucked between my legs.

"Dude, you're —" a guy says as he rounds the corner by the stairs, but I interrupt him.

"No, I'm not."

He laughs awkwardly. "I'm pretty sure you are. Were you at Misha's apartment? Better get checked for everything, man. That girl gets around."

Well, isn't that just great. I can't get an STD if my pants were still on, can I?

I nod as I shuffle past the guy, yanking my shirt over my head. The minute the fabric hits my skin, I shudder. It's on inside out, and I can feel every letter of the emblem rubbing against me. It's like I'm being slowly electrocuted under each letter, and I can't focus on anything else until I remove the shirt, flip it around, and put it on in its proper position. I pop on my Coyotes hat, pulling it low over my brow, hoping no one else notices me.

As I exit the high-rise apartment building south of downtown Denver, I pull out my phone and open the Notes app. I'm totally adding this building to my 'Don't Ever Come Here Again' list. It's a list of places that have bothered me in one way or another. While not necessarily a list of places to avoid because of specific people, it has definitely served its purpose in that way. I have the entire Denver metro area memorized, and I know where to avoid. Maybe it's because lots of athletes live in a certain area, or a place I got food poisoning. Honestly, once you've thrown up for forty-eight hours due to undercooked chicken at a Chinese restaurant, you pay closer attention to the department of health and what they rate restaurants.

Had I known that specific Chinese place scored a C, I'd probably have steered clear of it. Oh well. Live, barf up a lung, and learn.

Walking the two blocks to the closest RTD station, I grab the E train to head home. At this time of night, I'm alone in the train car. Looking at my watch, I let out an exhale of relief. I'm on the last train heading toward my neighborhood. While I know I could easily get a rideshare, I'd rather not put myself in a position where someone has control over where we're going, *and* finds out where I live in the process.

It took me quite some time to figure out where I wanted to live when I moved to Denver. Many of my teammates and friends like living downtown, not only for the proximity to the stadium and arena where we all play, but also for the restaurants and nightlife. I'm the exact opposite: I wanted to be as far away from the crowds and chaos as possible. I must have looked at over one hundred properties before I finally chose one. My previous coach suggested Cherry Hills Village, but checking out one house there made me veto the entire area. Way too snobby. Old money. Median home prices over three million. I hated it the minute I got out of the car, and that feeling only continued when my realtor and I stopped for lunch at a popular — but by invitation only — spot in town. I felt like I was cattle, being led out in front of a line of farmers, ready for one to bid on me. But instead of farmers, it was married women with nothing better to do than spend their husbands' money and have quiet affairs.

What goes on in someone's marriage is their business, until it involves me. Since I was raised in a home where infidelity ran rampant, and watched my mom slowly drink herself into a stupor every night because she actually loved my dipshit father, I will never participate in breaking up a marriage. Don't even get me started on my own volatile relationship with each of my parents. It's no wonder I've been in therapy for the last decade.

So, I settled on a neighborhood that borders Highlands Ranch and Greenwood Village, suburban areas south of Denver, known for good schools, outdoor activities, and family-friendly areas. Could I have picked an even more upscale part of the Denver metro? Of course. But I like the fact that I can blend in here. My home is my safe haven. The place where I can be me, with no judgment from anyone.

I mean, my two cats enjoy judging me, but they'd do that no matter where I lived. Maverick and Goose were a bonded pair of tuxedo cats I happened upon one day while dropping off some donations to one of the humane societies here. I don't know why I decided to go into the cat room that day. But as soon as I saw them, I knew they had to be mine. Who wouldn't want a pair of cats named after the dynamic duo from *Top Gun*?

Maverick is the more affectionate of the pair, while Goose is the more vocal one. After every road trip, Maverick happily makes biscuits on my chest, whereas Goose bitches at me from at least ten feet away. I'd never known the sound of a yowl before I brought him into my home. It's much louder than I ever thought possible. Thankfully, I have a pet service that checks on them every day whenever I'm out of town, and I have cameras set up all over my house so I can check in as well. I even have this fancy device that will toss out treats when I want it to.

Whenever I've had a bad day, it's calming to see them lounging on the massive cat tree located in my loft. Even though they know the camera is there, every time I speak into it, my voice scares the hell out of them. Can't help but laugh at that.

I haven't been back inside any adoption centers since I brought my two cats home, which I'm sure suits them just fine. I make donations around the city once a week when I can, and I have a spreadsheet to track where I've donated, what I've donated, and which locations are in dire need of specific items. Animal well-being is a passion project of mine, and I even have a foundation linked to a nondescript LLC where I'm able to make large donations to organizations across the country.

As I step off the train, I begin a steady jog west toward my neighborhood. Serves me right for listening to Jax Mitchell and leaving my car at home. Jax is one of my closest friends in Denver. We're quite opposite, with him being the extroverted hockey player to my quiet quarterback, but we balance each other out. He convinced me to head out tonight, determined to get me to break out of my shell.

"You're grumpier than normal, QB," he'd commented.

"Really?" I'd asked. I wasn't acting any differently than usual.

"Yeah. You've got this surly expression. Like you're already pissed about how tonight will go."

I shrugged. "Just tired, I guess."

"It's March. You don't have football for four more months."

"So? I can be tired in the off-season too, you know."

"What's really going on, Jamie? I know you. This ain't normal," he'd said.

I sighed, lost for a way to explain my thoughts. "I don't know. Kind of feeling stuck, I think. Wondering how much more I have left in me."

Jax nodded, understanding my thoughts. Hockey and football are brutal on the body, but for somewhat different reasons. In football, a player is more likely to get head injuries, whereas in hockey, players are subjected to pucks traveling upwards of eighty miles per hour. And the whole skating on a blade thing, which is why I was never meant to be a hockey player. Jamie and ice don't mix.

"Whatever happened to that last girl you were dating?" Jax asked, jarring me with how quickly he'd changed subjects.

"Susan? Nothing. We just stopped talking. Never really ended things."

"And that was, what? Six months ago?"

I did the math. "Closer to nine."

"'Bout the time I met Becca," he'd said, a lovesick expression covering his face.

"I guess."

"Is that the last time you got laid?"

"Jesus, Jax. You ever heard of the expression 'don't kiss and tell?'"

"I'm trying to figure out if part of your crabby-ass mood is because you need to get laid. There's a girl who hasn't taken her eyes off of you since we sat down, but I'm not gonna play Cupid if I don't need to. I know you're pretty particular about women."

Once Jax realized it had been nine months since I'd gotten laid, he played matchmaker anyway. Which is how I'd ended up at Maven/Moira/Monica's apartment. And how I ended up running home, dodging snowdrifts and piles of sand leftover from recent winter storms. And yes, I mean sand. The plow trucks dump a mixture of salt, sand, and other chemicals. Salt alone will corrode asphalt. Did I know this before moving to Denver? Nope.

Once in my neighborhood, I slow to a jog as I pull my phone from my pocket. Opening the security app, I open the gate at the end of my driveway as I approach, then quickly close it behind me. I'm not dumb. I know there are probably thousands of Coyotes fans out there who know exactly where I live. I protect myself with twenty-four hour surveillance, a six-foot privacy fence, and a film on every window that provides a layer of reflection, as well as a security measure that strengthens the glass.

I unlock a side door that leads directly into my spacious mud room, toeing off my shoes as I pspsps to let my cats know I'm home. I hear Maverick meow in return, then a guttural yowl sounds from somewhere upstairs. "I was gone for all of five hours, Goose. Chill."

Another yowl. Sounds like he's looking through the metal spindles on the walkway that overlooks the two-story foyer and great room. As I walk into my large gourmet kitchen, I can see Goose with his head through the spindles. Shaking my head, I grab a can of soft food, pulling the tab until the lid opens. A loud slam echoes throughout the house, followed by a disgruntled meow, and Goose gingerly walks in from the great room. "Jesus! Did you jump?"

He stares at me in response, but I swear Maverick shakes his head in disgust. Chuckling, I separate the food onto two plates, setting them on the ground next to my cats. I know they'll happily ignore me until they're done, so I head upstairs to my bedroom.

I love my house. But it's big and empty. I pass three empty bedrooms before walking into the primary bedroom, thinking about how I figured I'd be married with a couple of kids by now. While I'm sure I could have married a model, or influencer, who would blatantly use me for my name and bank account, I couldn't stomach that. I don't want to be with someone who doesn't actually like me for me. And once women get to know me a little better, they usually run for the hills. I'm incredibly type-A, and everything in my life has its place. I don't deviate from most things that are part of my everyday schedule.

I take a quick shower, washing off the night. It felt off from the moment I stepped into that girl's apartment. I should have left right then. Should have faked an emergency text, or just barreled out of there. My mind was elsewhere, and I wouldn't have been able to come without fantasizing about someone else. As I watch the suds cascade down my legs and into the tiled drain of my too-large steam shower, I'm acutely aware of how alone I am, and how I don't want to be anymore.

But I don't know how to be any other way.

Audrey

CHAPTER 2

I was raised to be soft, with an elegant demeanor. Don't raise your voice, Audrey. Represent the Carrington family. Marry a family-approved man from a respectable family. Never get involved in drama, online feuds, or participate in any activities that sully our name. We are Carringtons. Respect us.

I'm not valuable to my family unless I add to their connections or wealth.

"We participate in this charity for *you*, Audrey Michelle," my mother says through the phone, her voice somehow loud and soft at the same time. Her nasally whisper gives me an immediate headache with childhood flashbacks of her holding her wine glass, most likely filled well past halfway with an aged Bordeaux that cost hundreds. Glancing at the clock, I see that it's just past four. Knowing my mother, this is already her second glass. Hell, it might be her second *bottle*. The subtle dig at their involvement in a local charity that provides assistance to pet owners who are financially struggling? It's not the first time my mother has attempted to demean me this way, and it certainly won't be the last. Heaven forbid they donate their money to a good cause.

My family is a mixture of old and new money. My great-great

grandfather came to Colorado during the gold rush, but he was already considerably wealthy courtesy of hitting it big in Texas when he tapped into oil. My parents have no problem reminding me of the legacy our family has built in Colorado, and how important it is to keep up appearances within our snobby little community of who's who in the area.

Barf.

There was a time when I envisioned being the prim little princess my parents wanted. Following in the footsteps of my older brother and sister in how they always seemed to please our parents. My brother has been molded into a fine successor for my dad at REC. Real Estate Consultants is the company my father and grandfather founded in the seventies, and it's grown faster than anyone could have predicted. My brother, Preston, has known since he was a kid that he'd take over REC, regardless of whether or not he was the most qualified for the job. Probably why he has never shown any ambition, choosing instead to spend time partying and sleeping with anyone he comes across — both male and female. Our parents turn a blind eye to his shenanigans, only getting involved when his actions show up on the news or gossip websites.

My sister, Paige, also has no professional goals or ambitions. If this were one hundred years ago, she'd have happily attended a finishing school, ready to get married to any rich man she could find, and have a kid or two. Actually, there's hardly any difference to her life now. Married to an assistant district attorney for the county, she has one child, a snobbish and entitled brat named Daughton. I don't enjoy spending time with him. Even at the ripe age of nine, he's mastered a sneer as he judges me for a variety of reasons. I rarely see him, as a nanny spends the most time with him. Paige lunches with her equally as stuck-up friends often, then comes home to get railed by the man in charge of their landscaping. Her husband routinely stays late at work, and has bagged many interns for some extracurricular activities.

It boggles my mind how my parents find these behaviors acceptable. Yet somehow, me being a veterinarian is a punishable offense. Heaven forbid a child of Charles and Emmanuelle Carrington have a job. Even worse: it's a job that doesn't pay that well, and I work with animals. Gasp.

Pets were a no-go my entire life. From as early as I can remember, I've wanted any kind of animal. I'd have been happy with fish, hamsters, or even a rat. My mother could never hide her disgust when faced with a critter, regularly referring to it by its domesticated name. "Hello, dog. Oh, there is that cat." Honestly, that was my first sign that my mother lacked the necessary maternal instincts to parent well.

My parents also despise where I live. I had the audacity to leave our wealthy neighborhood of Cherry Creek Hills, the community I'd been raised in, and live in a small townhouse on the southwest side of Denver, in the Englewood suburb. How can they keep me under their thumb if I'm not under constant surveillance by them and their neighbors? Then I did the thing that basically put a nail in the metaphorical coffin: I adopted a dog. A handicapped dog, no less.

I fell in love with Flash the moment a passerby brought her to me after seeing her get hit by a car. The accident caused damage to Flash's spinal cord, paralyzing her from her belly to her hind legs. Corgis are known to have temperamental personalities, disliking other animals, and being somewhat difficult to have, and Flash was no different. Once I'd trained her in a specialized wheelchair, she happily zoomed all over my home, but she has never been social and friendly to anyone. She despises my parents, and the feelings are quite mutual.

Needless to say, my relationship has mostly stayed tentative with my parents. They've made it clear they expect me to participate in a variety of functions to keep up appearances, and in appreciation for my cooperation, they donate to my favorite charity. It raises tons of money each year, benefiting the Humane Society, a handful of trap and release programs, quarterly spay and neuter clinics, and providing free medical care to those who can't afford it for their pets. I absolutely love the program, but I don't care for the man who started it.

Jameson Wahlberg is the golden boy of Denver. The starting quarterback for the NFL's Colorado Coyotes. He's perfect and he knows it. The only reason I know he owns the LLC that the charity is under is because I saw an interview with him where he referenced the name, almost in an afterthought. I did a little digging into the LLC, finding a connection to his agent. Since I've seen both of them at a couple of adoption events in the city, I figured he was the proprietary owner. Do I absolutely know this? No.

But of course he is. Perfect golden boy with his good looks and a ridiculously chiseled body. Dark brown hair that always seems deliciously unkempt, like someone had their hands gripping it and held on for dear life. It's his blue eyes that really unnerve me, though. I feel like I wouldn't be able to look him in the eyes without feeling he's seeing straight into my soul. Knowing me, I'd have one conversation with him, scaring him half to death with my awkwardness and discomfort. It's a tale as old as time: brilliant Audrey Carrington puts her foot in her mouth yet again, scaring off potential love interests. Or friends. Frankly, my inner circle is about two feet in diameter.

"Paige said Dexter is prepared to take off work for the evening to show family support. You will be on your best behavior, Audrey. I will accept nothing less."

"You act like I routinely get on the table and take off my shirt," I remark dryly.

My mother gasps audibly, and I can imagine her hand resting on her sternum in faux shock. She's an excellent actress, a proper woman of money and good standing who can deliver remarkable empathy and caring, then turn around and rip someone to shreds. It's disgusting to watch, and I'm so glad I'm nothing like her.

"Audrey, I do not appreciate your jokes."

"Then don't call me." Even I'm surprised at my audacity, realizing an internal thought became verbal, courtesy of an intrusive thought winning.

"Audrey Michelle, I did not raise you to speak so abruptly to me," she chides.

"You didn't raise me. The nannies did."

She scoffs. "As if it matters. You were taught not to be so disrespectful."

I don't answer. She is correct. It was drilled into my head from as early as I can remember that I was not to backtalk to my parents, or any adults in general.

"Wear one of your black dresses. They're slimming."

"Mom."

"What?" she says breezily. "We don't want a repeat after that hospital gala from a few years ago."

I don't know how it became *my* fault that she forced me into a too-small dress, and when I bent over to pick up a napkin I'd dropped after getting an amaretto sour from the bar, the dress ripped right down the seam from mid-back to mid-thigh. It was horrid, and I refused to speak to my mother for six months.

I'm a plus-size woman. Not curvy. Not voluptuous. I'm big. Typically around a size eighteen or twenty. No matter how much I diet, or what exercise fad I try out, I can't seem to lose the weight. Getting under two hundred pounds has been a challenge, and I've been flirting with that number for a few months. I'm on a plateau I'd love to jump off, but it's been much more difficult than I thought possible.

Everyone in my family is skin and bones except for me. I take after my dad's family, where all of my aunts have struggled with their weight. It never really bothered me until I entered veterinarian school, and I had my first real crush on a man. I was a late bloomer, and didn't have my first kiss until I was in college. But meeting Sean was the first time I truly saw a man. Where I could barely focus because I daydreamed about him. At first, I thought Sean returned my feelings. Until I heard him ragging on me behind my back one afternoon. We'd been studying together for weeks, and he admitted to his friends that he was only using me to get ahead with our classes. He was truly befuddled when I refused to talk to him after that, only confronting him when he jokingly said he'd fail the next test if I didn't help him study.

He did fail. He failed out of the program completely.

And I didn't feel even a moment of regret.

Maybe that's the first time I truly stood up for myself. A turning point in my life, when I realized the only person who can bring me happiness is me.

"I'm sending over a variety of dresses for you to try on. You will not show up in something else."

"I will absolutely show up in something else if you send all of the wrong sizes again."

"Audrey," my mother warns.

"Mother," I reply, my voice replicating hers. "You can't send me a size fourteen dress and expect it to work. All the Spanx in the world won't even help that."

"The event isn't for three weeks, Audrey. You can lose at least twenty pounds by then. Write yourself an Ozempic prescription."

"Wow," I breathe, only slightly surprised at how easily my mother expects me to commit fraud. "I'm sure it'll be easy to explain to my pharmacy why my name is both the issuing doctor and the patient, not to mention the fact that veterinarians don't prescribe weight loss medications, Mother."

She tsks, effectively ignoring everything I've said. "You need to make better choices. How do you expect to ever find a husband in your current situation?"

And with that, I'm done. "I have to go, Mother. I have a patient."

"It's Sunday."

"It's an emergency case," I lie, before ending the call. Some might think it's rude to essentially hang up on my mother, but she's been doing it to me for years. I began doing the same a few years ago, and when she never commented on it, I continued. While a little juvenile, I don't care. I'm giving her the energy she gives to me. It's only fair.

For just a minute, I let myself dream about moving away from

Denver. From the only city I've ever known. Moving somewhere I'm not a Carrington. Where I'm Audrey, or Doctor Audrey. A place I'm valued for me, and not a placeholder for someone my parents want to add to their empire when they marry me off.

I fantasize about meeting someone who actually likes me, and isn't there because he is forced to be. A man who sees my value, likes me with all of my quirks, and doesn't let my parents steamroll over him. A man who won't expect me to turn a blind eye to his lifestyle like my sister and her husband, or one who ignores me for who I am.

I'm so tired of being ignored, and expected to be less. Expected to be invisible.

As my best friend Chelsea always tells me: I'm a fucking delight, and the right man will come along and see all of my quirks as strengths. Easy coming from my office manager, as she's a petite beauty with all-American good looks of blonde hair and bright blue eyes. But she's right.

The right man will come along, and accept me for me.

A brilliant veterinarian with zero game, somewhat lacking social skills, and borderline crippling anxiety.

And also autism.

Jamie

CHAPTER 3

"The foundation wants you to take a bigger role at the next event," my agent, Troy Brown, tells me. We're meeting over lunch at one of my favorite hole-in-the-wall taco places. I've never been one to lean toward five-star cuisine or trendy places. Give me comfort and anonymity any day. Fortunately, Troy is used to my choices, and doesn't give me any lip. Frankly, that's what I pay him for.

"What does that mean?" I ask warily, picking up my fourth barbacoa street taco. I'll probably eat seven or eight total. Fuckers are tiny, but delicious.

"The last event only raised half of the previous year's revenue, and the board members are nervous. Costs are rising, and they're afraid they'll have to make some cuts to funding."

Shit.

Playful Paws was a dream of mine from childhood. My grandmother used to tell me she thought I was the animal whisperer, because animals always seemed to show up wherever I was. I began volunteering in an animal shelter in high school, and continued in college whenever I could. As soon as I got my first contract with the NFL, I started the process of creating the charity.

"If we announced you as part of the board, and the one who founded the charity, I bet we'd get a massive increase in donations," Troy says nonchalantly. "People have to know already. You slipped that one time and mentioned the charity by name in an interview."

"I know," I snap. I felt awful afterward, like I'd just dropped a major bomb on my own damn life. "I don't want to be the face of the charity. You know this."

"What about if you just participated this year? Like a special guest. It would gain more exposure, but still keep the foundation covered."

I hesitate, thinking about the option. I'm incredibly private. Probably more than needed. But I want people to *want* to donate to a good cause. I hate knowing they'd do it just because they want to meet me. Who wouldn't donate to a charity helping animals? Now you're going to do it just because I'm connected to it? Fuck right off with that bullshit.

"What's the event this year? Hoity-toity gala? Silent auction? Car wash for the rich and famous?" I ask, irritated.

Troy chuckles awkwardly. "They've thrown out a couple of ideas. One is a celebrity calendar with adoptable animals —"

"All male athletes, I bet."

"That detail hasn't come up yet. They've discussed doing an old-school telethon as well."

"I don't know one person who would watch something like that. It's a waste of money and resources," I reply.

"I agree. I suggested having a hybrid event for everything."

"How would that work?"

I see the glint in Troy's eye when he realizes he's hooked me. "It would be a somewhat formal event where celebrities could mingle. Maybe each person would walk around with their adoptable animal. They've also brought up the concept of a win-a-date auction —"

"Absolutely the hell not!" I shout.

Troy's face reddens as multiple tables of patrons turn to stare at me. "Jesus, Jamie. I didn't say you had to participate. I mentioned I'd talk to you about being the MC."

My heart hammers against my ribs. "You know I can't — no. I'd have no control over who might bid, and it would end so fucking badly. Jax talked me into going home with this woman the other night, and Jesus, it was awful."

"You can't trust Jax with anything, man. He's a lovesick puppy who only sees sunshine and rainbows," Troy says with a laugh. He's not wrong.

"Is the board set on anything right now?" I ask.

"No. They're making final decisions in the next few weeks, with the event slated for right before training camp begins."

"Don't they usually plan this shit a full year in advance?"

Troy nods. "They scrapped everything due to costs and lack of volunteers. The usual donors, the Carrington family and their real estate business, were demanding more control over the event. The board pushed back."

"Good," I state, pushing my plate away. "I think I've met them once, and I'm cool with never meeting them again. The guy had the nerve to ask me if I wanted to meet one of his daughters within a couple minutes of introducing himself. I don't have any respect for a man who pawns his kids off on me."

"He has two daughters," Troy says. "One is married, and a vapid, narcissistic bitch. I've heard through the Denver grapevine that the parents don't speak well of the other daughter. Apparently she's a mess."

I grimace. "Is she actually a mess, or just someone the parents don't have control over?"

Troy shrugs. "Who knows. I've never interacted with any of the children. Once rich people realize I'm not going to introduce them to my clients just because they're wealthy, they leave me alone."

If only that were the case with me. "Do I have to give you an answer about being the MC now? Can I get them to make any concessions?"

"They'd like to know by the end of the week. I can ask about anything. Obviously you're the founder of the charity, Jamie. You don't have to do anything you don't want to do. The only thing they seem to be pretty set on is having you partner with a local veterinarian to do some of the planning, as well as marketing for many of the shelters in the area. The vet is apparently very involved with the Humane Societies around Denver, and provides supplies to trap-and-release organizations all along the Front Range."

"Who's the veterinarian?" I ask, wracking my brain to think of who it might be. The Denver metropolitan area has well over three million residents, so it's likely someone I've never heard of.

"They referred to him as Dr. A. That's all I know."

"Would he be an MC as well?" I ask hopefully. The thought of being front and center anywhere but a football field is nauseating.

"No, he'd be behind the scenes." Dammit. Troy gives me a sympathetic smile. "I can ask if he'd be willing to help out. To take some of the limelight off of you."

I shake my head. "No. I'm sure he's not used to being in the public eye. It's probably better if it's only me. Maybe it'll bring more money that way."

"Do you want me to tell the board you're a go?"

I sigh before nodding. "Fine. But I want to get a correspondence going with Dr. A before we meet. Before he finds out who I am."

Troy nods. "Alright. The usual incognito email?"

"Yep."

I'm not sure if other athletes also have an alternate email with a fake name, or if it's just me. I know tons of guys use fake names when they check in at hotels, or when they have dinner reservations. Lots of us have private social media accounts for just close friends and family.

I'm pretty sure I've taken it a little further with my James Young email, though. It's been so instrumental in allowing me to schedule donation drop offs, working anonymously at shelters, and even working out times I can stop by Colorado Children's Hospital to visit when it's not going to be a news story.

I can't use Jameson or Jamie. But James is a common enough name that people don't question it. And I chose the name Young after my favorite NFL quarterback growing up, Steve Young. I'm not even sure why I felt such a connection with Steve Young, considering I wasn't a San Francisco fan growing up. I'd never been to California until traveling there for college. I'd seen multiple interviews with Steve as I began my football career in the nineties, right as his career was winding down.

I think the thing that really struck me about Steve was how much he fought for his job. It wasn't easy. He didn't have perfect seasons back-to-back. He was resilient and determined. Even after injuries and multiple concussions, he never gave up. That was the kind of quarterback I wanted to be.

I knew I loved football from the first moment my little hand touched the pigskin. I loved how it felt. How it smelled. The sound it made when I threw a perfect spiral. I only lasted one season playing flag football, before I begged my parents to let me switch to a tackle team. Every sound, from the harsh breathing on a cool October morning, to helmets crashing together, was like music to my soul. I loved every note.

Growing up in the panhandle of Florida, I was surrounded by amazing prep sports programs. High school football is huge in Florida, and I was expected to follow my dad to his alma mater, Florida State. I know they meant well, but my parents were a little too pushy about wanting me to do things the same way they did. They met at FSU when my mom was the 'sweetheart' for my dad's fraternity, Sigma Alpha Epsilon. My mom was a member of the Zeta Tau Alpha sorority, and she has always said her year as the SAE sweetheart was one of the best of her life, because it introduced her to my dad.

She undoubtedly still thinks that, even though they're divorced. She stayed with him through countless affairs, and I know their divorce was much harder on her than him. Could be why she chose to make such a colossal mistake, engaging in an affair of her own. Of course, her affair was huge. Monumental, and national news.

The idea of participating in a fraternity practically made me break out in hives. It shouldn't have. Being part of a football team is similar to a fraternity in a lot of ways. I knew what to expect with football, though, and couldn't take on the idea of a frat. College itself was enough of a new life for me.

My dad waxed poetic about his time at FSU. Told me fond stories about almost getting alcohol poisoning, how much enjoyment he got out of hazing new pledges, and how a different fraternity chapter got expelled after a student reported being sexually assaulted by four members of the frat. The fact that my dad believed the frat over the girl was enough to tell me I wanted nothing to do with Greek life at FSU, and I wasn't too sure about attending there at all.

Instead, I went as far away as I could possibly go, accepting a scholarship at the University of Oregon. I knew if I stayed anywhere in the Southeast, my parents would be way too involved in my life, and I wanted to get out from under their suffocating umbrella.

For the most part, I understood some of their concerns. I'm their only child, and they didn't want to give me up yet. Plus, they knew my struggles with having difficulty recognizing social cues. But instead of being proactive and using any means necessary to help me develop, they pulled me tighter into their circle. My childhood consisted of school, football, and them. It wasn't until I was finally at Oregon that I could ask for help.

If it wasn't for one of my assistant coaches, I'd still be struggling. He recognized my quiet cries for help. He saw the similarities between his son and me, and pointed me to a developmental psychologist. Which is how I was finally diagnosed with autism at the ripe old age of twenty.

Getting the diagnosis didn't correct anything, but it helped explain so much. My hyper focus. Issues with textures and tastes. Inability to recognize correct social cues, and not realizing when I've hurt or offended someone. Psychosomatic reactions to situations that stress me out. It was like I'd been living my life in a darkened room, and suddenly the lights were turned on.

There's no cure-all medication for autism. No get-rich-quick scheme that could instantaneously make me 'better' or 'normal'. But I began working with a therapist, identifying every area that I struggled in, and developed a plan to help me to continue growing as an autistic adult. Using my wonderful fake name and email address, I got involved with a few online autism communities, and found out I was nowhere near the only adult who'd gotten a late diagnosis.

I immersed myself in all things autism: blogs, community groups, podcasts. I learned about masking, which immediately became a key part of surviving life. Controlling how sensations impacted me was huge. Many athletes walk around with noise-canceling headphones, and I became one as well. I watched a movie called *For Love of the Game*, with Kevin Costner, where he's a Major League pitcher. Whenever he was on the mound, he'd say, "control the mechanism." He taught his brain how to drown out all the noise so he could completely focus on the task at hand. I was able to do that, drowning out everything in the stadium except for my teammates in the huddle with me, and the radio in my helmet where my coach gave me the plays.

But every now and again, I get lost. Where something that's always been easy to handle is suddenly … not. For no real reason, it's like I hit a wall, and can't find my way around it.

Today, that wall is messaging Dr. A.

I have to get the ball rolling for this event, and the first thing is establishing a partnership with the veterinarian. I have no idea why this seems so monumental. It's a conversation. Something I routinely do. Instead, every single thing I want to say sounds weird.

Hello, I like animals.

I really don't want to do this.

Dr. A., I'd like to know your real name because calling you Dr. A is weird.

I really don't want to do this.

Is there a way to be an MC without actually being seen? Like the wizard behind the curtain in The Wizard of Oz?

Is there a name for a man who'd rather be with his cats? Can a thirtysomething year old man have too many cats? What's the male version of spinster?

I really don't want to do this.

Not exactly sounding like an award-winning NFL quarterback right now, am I?

Goose meows at me from his perch on the massive cat tree I had custom made for my bedroom. When his eyes meet mine, I swear he nods in agreement. Yep, I sound like a wimp, and even my cat agrees. Maverick head butts me, then proceeds to make biscuits on my chest. "Well, at least one of you doesn't think I'm a chump."

Audrey

CHAPTER 4

Hello, my name is James Young. I'll be the MC for the Playful Paws event. The board wanted me to reach out to you so we can begin planning.

Flash yips excitedly as I stare at my phone in confusion. Who?

How did you get this number?

The board?

I was unaware I'd be working with someone on this year's event.

It was sprung on me this week.

Is the board worried I won't be able to do it alone?

UNKNOWN

> No, I think they're more worried about financials. They want to make the event as big as possible, to bring in as many donations as they can. Last year's event wasn't as successful as they'd hoped.

Damn. I was part of the planning team then too. Granted, I definitely noticed a decrease in attendance at the event, a black tie gala with a silent auction. I'd felt out-of-place with the team of event planners hired for the gala, and held my tongue on a variety of issues. It was my first year actually helping to plan and implement the event, but I wasn't sure where I should step in with my thoughts. I wish I had, because the hired band was lackluster, the hotel ran out of liquor within the first hour, and I counted a handful of older men asleep at their tables by the end of the night. I have no idea who James Young is, but he seems legit, so I change his contact info in my phone.

ME

> Okay. I assume they want to make changes for this year. They must have some ideas.

JAMES YOUNG

> Yes. Some ideas I think will be great, and some I don't like.

ME

> Like what?

JAMES YOUNG

> One idea I agree with is having a variety of animals at the event who are available for adoption.

ME

> I think that's a great idea. I've participated in quite a few adoption events around Denver, and donations almost always increase the week after an event. What else?

JAMES YOUNG

Can we meet in person to discuss the other ideas? Texting takes too long, and I think we'll be able to sketch out a plan faster in person.

ME

Alright. I'm only available after six in the evenings this week, and Saturday after four. I'm doing a spay/neuter clinic with a colleague all day.

JAMES YOUNG

I'm only free tonight, unfortunately. What part of town are you located in? I'm in a suburb on the southwest side.

How very vague. Flash growls at me, and I realize she's been patiently waiting for me to open the door. As soon as I do, she zooms down the ramp I installed at the front door of my clinic, one wheel catching air as she rounds the corner toward my car.

ME

I'm on the south side as well. I just finished work and intended to grab dinner at one of my favorite places. Are you familiar with The Red Llama in Lonetree? It's a Peruvian restaurant.

JAMES YOUNG

I am! I love that place!

ME

I have to drop my dog off at home, then I can meet you there. Is seven-thirty too late?

JAMES YOUNG

No, that's fine. I'll arrive a little early and get a table. Tell them you're with me.

ME

They'll know who you are?

JAMES YOUNG

Yeah, they'll know. Tell them you're with
Jamie.

A pit settles in my stomach. I'm not a huge follower of football, but I'm pretty sure Jameson Wahlberg goes by Jamie. I'm almost positive he's the founder of Playful Paws. Is there a chance he's who I'll be working with on this event?

Crud.

After dropping Flash off at home, and actually putting on makeup for the first time in a while, I arrive at The Red Llama feeling like I might actually vomit. In most aspects of my life, I can hold my head high with dignity. For some reason, I'm more nervous than I've ever been. Well, I know the reason. It's because if the man I'm meeting is Jameson Wahlberg, I'll undoubtedly be stupidly tongue-tied and embarrass myself.

Looking around the parking lot, I don't notice any obviously expensive vehicles, but that doesn't mean anything. I'd quickly Googled Jameson as I waited for Flash to pee before removing her from her wheelchair to give her a rest in her crate. I follow football, on and off, and am a fan of the Colorado Coyotes, but I haven't done a deep dive into any of the players until now. The information I discover is enlightening, and I quickly realize I may have misjudged him based solely on his appearance, as well as his interview skills.

Jameson Wahlberg is not, nor has he ever been, flashy. According to multiple interviews, teammates have teased him for his lack of fashion sense. There also doesn't seem to be much bad publicity about him at all. From all appearances, he seems to be quiet, and keeps to himself. But there's an air of confidence and superiority that emanates from him. He knows how to flash those pearly whites and draw everyone's attention. Yet there's something familiar in his stance during interviews. His posture is stiff, even though his eye contact seems engaging.

It's like he's masking.

For me, I mask when I'm in unfamiliar situations that increase my anxiety. It's also a very important facet of how I survive public events. When I mask, I'm basically hiding any autistic trait so I can seem more 'normal' and less neurodiverse. I hate thinking of it that way, because I know I'm not abnormal. But it's just the way it is: neurodiverse people are expected to blend into the neurotypical world, and not the reverse.

I take a deep breath in through my nose, holding it, and counting to five, then release it slowly through my mouth. Focusing on my breathing helps to regulate my heart rate, and within a couple of minutes, I'm finally feeling comfortable enough to open the car door. One foot in front of the other, I feel like my feet weigh fifty pounds each as I slowly make my way to the front of the restaurant. I don't like meeting new people this way. It's why I've never done online dating. I know this isn't a date, but the concept is the same.

As soon as I open the restaurant door, the hostess smiles warmly at me. "Audrey! I didn't see an order for you. Are you dining in? You never eat inside!"

God. Even a hostess I don't know recognizes I'm weird. I could never eat alone in public. I don't take offense to the hostess noticing this, but it makes me sad that someone recognizes such a minor thing about my life. "Oh, I'm meeting someone. James Young. Jamie?"

Her eyebrows rise. "You're meeting someone. Here?"

I nod. "We're working on an event together. It's not a date. I'd never meet someone here that I didn't know at all for a date. I mean, there's nothing wrong with that, but I could never do it. Blind dates. Online dates. Well, basically any dates at all, but that's beside the point."

Brows furrowed in confusion, with a little bit of pity featured in her eyes, she nods sympathetically. "I don't have anyone here that is waiting for someone, and definitely not anyone named Jamie. Why don't I get you seated, and I'll bring your party to you when they get here?"

Oh my God. Am I honestly getting stood up for a work meeting by someone I've never met, *and* at one of my favorite restaurants? I'll never be able to show my face here again. Heat floods my face, and I can only imagine the shade of red my cheeks must be. "Oh. Okay. That's fine."

I follow behind the hostess as she cheerfully takes me to a back table. I quietly sit as she places a menu in front of me, which is silly because we both know I have the thing memorized. "Yuca Fritas while you wait?"

I nod. "Yes, and a glass of ice water, please."

Might as well enjoy some of my favorite foods before I leave this place forever. I make a mental note to see if they deliver, because I'm just not sure I can go without Ceviche for the rest of my life.

While the bones of the restaurant are fairly standard, it's the way the owners have livened up the space that has always spoken to me. Colorful strings of pom poms cascade down the front windows, as well as one wall, while another wall features a beautiful floral backdrop perfect for selfies. Lights with red shades drop from the ceiling over a handful of tables, and they have the most amazing type of glassware. I know many people talk about the autism spoon or fork, but for me, it's always about the type of glassware. The Red Llama has a beautiful set that has me tracing each line of bumps as I await my possible dinner companion, and my possible last appetizer.

Yuca Fritas are the Latin American equivalency to French fries, but have a sweeter and nuttier taste. I love the yellow chili sauce served with them, and could probably drink the sauce if needed. Pulling out my phone, I keep my head down while I scroll through a listing of professional journals I want to read this spring, and I enjoy my wonderful appetizer.

Thirty minutes later, I'm slowly eating my fritas, aware that I've been stood up. Is it considered being stood up if it's not a proper date? Whatever the case, it's obvious the person I'm supposed to work with on this event is a disrespectful jerk. It's well past eight o'clock, and I have a long day tomorrow. Sighing, I motion for the server to bring me my check. As I wait, I fire off a response to James Young.

ME

Mr. Young, since you clearly do not respect my time, any correspondence moving forward can be done over email or text, but I'd prefer to work with someone else the board recommends. You may not feel a charity benefiting animals is important, but it is to me. I'll be letting the board know you aren't a suitable person to plan the upcoming event.

JAMES YOUNG

I have no idea what you're talking about, Dr. A. I've been waiting for you for thirty minutes. And this charity is important to me. Much more than you would ever understand.

ME

I'm at the restaurant, Mr. Young. You aren't here. Unless there are two The Red Llama locations?

JAMES YOUNG

Not that I know of. The restaurant is almost completely empty, and I'm the only guy in here. I definitely don't see you.

Wait. What does he mean by that? Raising my gaze, I look around the space. An older woman sits quietly at a table by the door, and a couple with an infant eats by the pom-pom wall.

Craning my neck, I see the top of a head, facing the door, but I can't tell if the person is male or female. A hoodie covers the person's head, with the brim of a cap sticking out, only barely. Is that him?

ME

What do you mean by "I'm the only guy in here?"

JAMES YOUNG

Unless you're also with your partner and a baby, I'm literally the only man here.

ME

Did you automatically assume I'm male?

JAMES YOUNG

You aren't?

ME

Last time I checked, no.

JAMES YOUNG

I've watched the door for the last thirty minutes, Dr. A. No one has come in.

ME

I've been here longer than that, Mr. Young. Perhaps you should turn around.

The person in the hoodie straightens, slowly turning until our eyes meet.

Shit.

Jamie

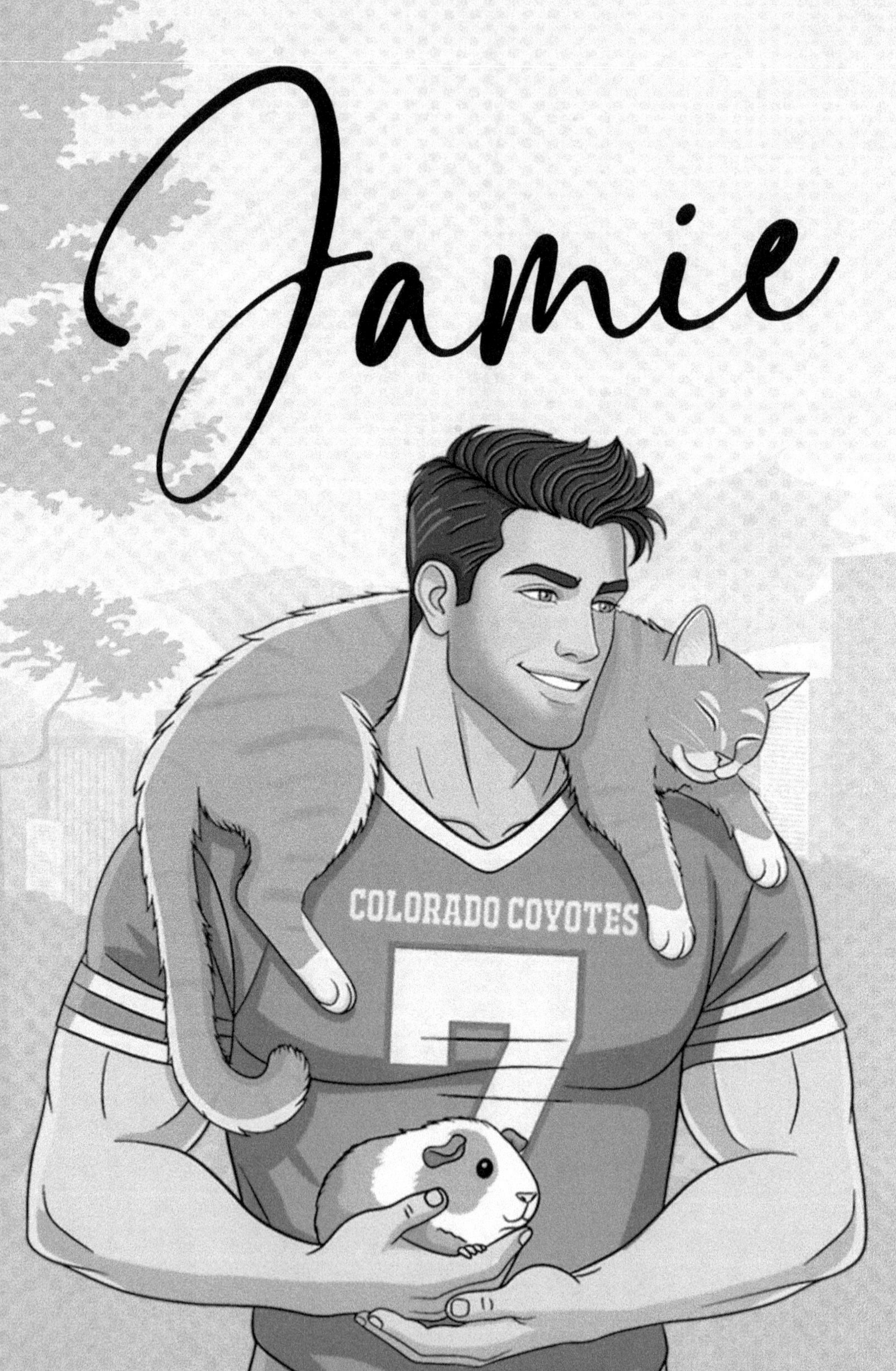

CHAPTER 5

Shit.

Dr. A is a woman? And an absolutely gorgeous one at that? I'm truly screwed.

I saw her when I stepped in. We didn't make eye contact, but I definitely looked. Gorgeous dark brown locks, and a smattering of tattoos on her arms. Hair up in a thick bun, I wonder how long it is, and how it would feel wrapped around my fist. But most of all, I notice her curves. Good God, I want to drag my tongue along every breathtaking inch of her.

It's pretty rare for me to have such a visceral reaction to someone the instant I see them. I've always been more attracted to personality than looks, so I'm perplexed at my reaction here.

There was a time when I allowed my agent to find me women who could accompany me to big events. Early on in my career, after really bad advice from an assistant coach from a previous team. I was drafted to play in Nashville, and signed a four-year deal there, but it wasn't a good fit. The coaching staff disregarded my neurodiversity completely, instead choosing to tell me to "man up" whenever I had challenges. Needless to say, I was thrilled when a trade to Denver was offered, and I've been happily playing here since.

My agent quickly realized hiring out arm candy was an even worse idea than me attending an event solo, as it made me so uncomfortable and awkward that the women typically snuck out at one point or another. There was a five-year period where gossip rags were convinced I was in the closet, due to my lack of high-profile dates. Not gay. Just hopeless, somewhat off-the-wall, and most definitely one hell of an unorthodox NFL quarterback.

Now I have to approach a woman. One that I find profoundly attractive. A woman I'll need to work somewhat closely with over the next few months and try not to frighten her away with my idiosyncrasies. Taking a deep breath, I slowly rise from my table, the chair legs squeaking loudly as they scratch along the tile flooring. I see multiple people in the restaurant glance at me out of my periphery, and I wince. I'm trained to handle attention on the gridiron, and even with reporters before and after the game. But this kind of situation makes me feel like I'm naked on stage at a middle school band performance, and my balls haven't dropped yet.

Turning to walk behind me, I take a chance by looking through my lashes at Dr. A. Assuming I'll find an expression of realization, or excitement at the prospect of working closely with a professional athlete, I'm surprised to find what I can only describe as complete terror on her face. Well, that's new.

"Uh, hi. Sorry I made the presumption you were a man," I say sheepishly. "Is it okay if I join y —"

"Your name isn't James!" she shouts, the sound reverberating off the walls. "It isn't even Jamie! What kind of game are you playing?"

Her voice has risen comically, her eyes so wide I imagine they might completely pop out of their sockets like in old cartoons. Instead of waiting for her to motion that I can join her, I slam down into the chair across from her, leaning over the table. "Look. I'll explain if you agree to listen, but I'm going to need you to lower your voice a little. Alright?"

She shakes her head frantically. "I knew this was your charity. I knew it! What's with all the damn secrecy? And a fake name and email account? Does the board know you're doing this?"

"Of course they know … wait." I stare at her incredulously. "How did you know it's my charity?"

"You mentioned the charity in an interview once, and I've seen you at different events. I put two-and-two together," she whispers, her eyes darting around like she's giving out state secrets, and she's worried who might be listening. Well, part of that is correct.

"Y — you know who I am?" I ask uncertainly, my voice cracking.

She nods. "I do."

"What's your name?" I ask.

"Audrey."

Oh. "The A is for Audrey."

Audrey blushes as she twists her hands together. "It's the name I put out there for anything that involves me going into the community. I'm a really private person, and usually once people find out my last name, there are … questions."

Now I'm intrigued. "That I completely understand. I won't ask any questions if you don't ask me anything."

"Do you get asked a lot of questions by people you barely know?"

I laugh with a huff of breath. "Oh yeah. People have no shame, asking me the weirdest shit."

Audrey cocks her head to the side. "Is it wrong of me to wonder what the most outlandish and off-the-wall question you've ever gotten is?"

I can't help the smile that covers my face. "Typically it's whenever a kid interviews me. They'll ask questions like making me choose between uncooked Ramen noodles and a charred marshmallow, or ask me the last time I cried in a movie theater."

"I'll need answers to both."

"Charred marshmallow and I believe I told the kid I've never cried in a movie theater. But I'm pretty sure I cried at the end of *Marley and Me*."

Audrey gasps. "Anyone who didn't is a heathen! Now tell me the weirdest question an adult has asked you."

Tapping my chin I think for a moment. Probably eighty-five to ninety percent of questions reporters ask me are about football or dating. A reporter down in Colorado Springs routinely asks me random things about my childhood, though. "One guy asked me what my favorite subject was in elementary school, then wanted to know if I remembered what grade I got in it."

"What subject?" Audrey asks.

"Science."

"Why?"

I shrug. "I like cause and effect. Manipulating one variable can change an entire experiment. I think that's pretty cool. It's messy, though. I'm not a big fan of mess."

Audrey nods in agreement, her eyes sparkling beautifully. "There's a time and a place for messiness. I don't like getting different textures on my skin, so I have boxes of surgical gloves everywhere. It makes dealing with messes slightly less traumatic."

Fucking hell, I think I just fell in love with her a little bit. "Alright, now it's your turn. You don't have to tell me your name, but give me one unhinged question you've been asked."

I watch as her eyes dull slightly. "A new client asked why I was a veterinarian when I could just marry a friend of my father's."

My mouth drops open. "Jesus. Was the client male or female?"

Her nose scrunches up. "A woman."

"That makes sense. I suppose a man would probably proposition you, or ask if he had a chance, whereas a woman will see you as competition."

Audrey harrumphs. "This is why I don't understand women. Why see me as competition? Why aren't we building each other up, and celebrating our successes?"

I shrug. "You're asking the wrong person. I don't understand women either."

Audrey rolls her eyes. "Please. An NFL quarterback? Women

are beating down your door. You don't *have* to understand us because you have a line waiting to get their shot with you."

"Not true," I murmur, my eyes dropping to study the swirls of colors on the table. I love how colorful The Red Llama is. Except for the bathrooms. Red bathrooms actually weird me out.

"You don't have a line of women?" Audrey asks.

I shrug again. "Maybe. But once they get to know me, truly know me, they're not interested."

I expect a look of sympathy, or even a somewhat fake answer about how she'd never do that to me. Instead, Audrey surprises me again. "I totally get that. I have that issue too. It's even worse with friendships because a lot of time, they'll be so excited about our bond, and then they suddenly rip it away. It's like friendship love bombing."

Stunned, I stare at her incredulously. Who the hell is this woman? "I've never heard of love bombing."

"A friend has experienced it. I haven't." She snorts. "No one would ever love bomb me. But it's basically where someone showers you with gifts, words of affirmation, and anything else that makes you believe you've found *the one*."

"Fascinating," I murmur. "Why don't you think anyone would love bomb you?"

"Oh," she replies with a nervous giggle. "I'm too analytical. I have questions. Why all the gifts? Where are they coming from? Did you do something you feel the need to apologize for? Are you trying to buy affection, or cover up something dastardly?"

"Dastardly is such an underused word," I muse, tapping my forefinger to my chin. "I love using old words that need to be revived again."

"I have a word-a-day calendar. Two, actually. One at home and one at work," Audrey says shyly.

"Nice! What were today's words?" I ask.

"Jovial, which means good-humored, and fugacious, which means lasting a short time."

"Huh. I'd never be called jovial."

"Me neither. My best friend told me I'd be the grump in one of the romance books she reads," Audrey tells me.

"There are romance books specifically about grumps?"

She nods. "Evidently, there's an entire category about grumps falling for jovial people. I don't read many romance books, so I'm taking her word for it."

"So basically, it's an opposites attract scenario."

"I guess. She tries to get me to read some, but it's not my cup of tea."

"Why not?" I ask.

Audrey sighs, her eyes drifting off to look over my left shoulder. "Because I'm a realist, probably to a fault. Romance books aren't realistic. The men are over-the-top. I prefer to keep my feet on the ground instead of living in the clouds."

"I can understand that," I tell her with an emphatic nod. "I'd say I'm also a realist, but anyone who knows me would probably say I'm a pessimist."

Her eyes meet mine, and I can see a tentative layer of trust simmering in her gorgeous hazel eyes. It makes me wonder if certain colors bring out the green tones, and when she gets excited, if the speckles of gold I see might shine a little brighter. "Really?"

"Yeah, really. I understand. I'm pretty calculated in everything I do. A lot of football is a game of numbers. Plays. Go where you're supposed to go. Don't overthink things, and don't deviate from the plan. Granted, there are tons of times I make split-second decisions on the field, but the foundation of football is pretty black and white."

Audrey clears her throat. "Speaking of black and white, that was the color palette for last year's gala. I don't recall seeing you there."

I scratch the back of my neck sheepishly as I feel heat creep onto my cheeks. "I, uh, try to keep a low profile. A black tie gala isn't a good fit for me."

"I don't understand. Why found a charity if you don't want to show your face?" Audrey asks quietly.

"Because I want people to donate because they're good people, not because they want to get near me. This is about the animals, not the quarterback."

"When did you establish the charity?" she asks.

"Ten years ago, but it's been on my mind since I was a kid."

Audrey hums, and I wait for the inevitable question. Why? Why did I want to have a charity for animals? I don't want to get into that, and I see the moment Audrey realizes it. "You don't want to tell me why. And that's absolutely your right."

"Seriously?" I blurt out.

She giggles as she nods. "It's perfectly acceptable to establish boundaries, Jameson. People aren't entitled to every piece of you."

"Thank you. Most people don't understand that. They seem to think since they cheer for me on the field, they're entitled to all the details about me off the field too."

Audrey shudders. "I could never. I'm way too private. I live over thirty minutes away from my clinic just to ensure I don't run into clients anywhere. I can't even imagine what you must go through."

"Unfortunately, I'm used to it now. But I've learned how to deal with it. Can't say I'm sad about how much can be delivered nowadays, but I also have an assistant who does a lot for me to guarantee I'm not in a compromising position in public."

"Compromising position?"

I nod. "Believe it or not, I've been surrounded in a grocery store. Right up against the meat counter. And before you ask, no. They weren't asking for autographs. They were all pissed at a shitty pass I'd thrown the prior weekend that was a pick-six, and that knocked us out of playoff contention."

"Oh, that was five years ago. I remember that game. Baltimore, right?"

"Uh, yeah. It was Baltimore."

Audrey's lips twitch. "It was indeed a shitty pass."

I throw back my head with a bark of laughter. "It was."

Audrey

CHAPTER 6

"Excuse me, but we're getting ready to close ... oh, that's who you meant by Jamie!" the hostess says with an audible gasp. "We always call him Señor Wahlberg."

"It's okay, Marisol." Jameson looks somewhat embarrassed, a slight pink hue covering the back of his neck. His eyes dart between mine and hers, as I notice has happened quite often tonight. Maintaining eye contact is either a challenge for him, or he's very uncomfortable in my presence. Honestly, it's a toss-up which one it might be.

"Can I order something to go?" I ask the hostess.

"Sure."

"I'd like the arroz chaufa, please."

"Oh, that's my favorite as well. Make that two, Marisol."

"Coming right up!"

"Why James Young?" I blurt out as the hostess walks away.

Jameson smiles. "Well, James is a play on my actual name. And Young is after my favorite quarterback growing up, Steve Young."

"What should I call you? You seem to have a lot of names."

"Jameson or Jamie. My friends call me Jamie, or QB if they're being scrappy. If we're going to be working closely together, I'd like to think we'll become friends, don't you?"

It's incredibly hard to put a lid on the internal squeal just begging to be let out. "Jamie it is."

Once we have our to-go containers, we set off toward the parking lot. As we approach the front door, I can see our reflection in the glass. I watch as Jamie begins to place his hand on my lower back, then hesitates. He runs the hand through his hair before dropping his arm against his side. I'm not sure what to make of that.

As I walk in the direction of my car, Jamie falls in step beside me. "I'll be out of town the remainder of the week for a sponsorship deal. Next week I have some team things in the mornings, but I can meet again to begin actually planning the event. Will any night next week work for you?"

"I'm flexible." I'm not flexible. I'm wide open. Other than work and a dress fitting for the charity event my parents guilted me into attending, I have nothing to do. My social calendar is a travesty.

"I'll, uh, get in touch with you soon." Jamie looks at me expectantly, jolting in my direction. Lunging toward me, he suddenly plants a kiss against my cheek, and I'm too stunned to respond. "It was really lovely meeting you, Audrey. I wasn't looking forward to planning this event, but I certainly am now."

I assumed I wouldn't hear from Jamie for a few days, so I was undoubtedly surprised to find a text from him the following morning. Seeing the name James Young makes me giggle, and I immediately change his contact info.

QB

I need to know what the word of the day is.

ME

Polyglot.

QB

What the hell does that mean?

ME

It means someone is fluent in multiple languages.

QB

Clearly that is not me. Do you speak any other languages?

ME

No, but I can understand a fair bit of Spanish. Just don't ask me to speak it, or I'll ask where the bus station is, and we'll end up at an underground rave.

QB

In your defense, an underground rave IS a ride.

ME

That is true.

QB

I have this natural interest in random facts, so I tend to be swayed into rabbit holes on a fairly consistent basis. Did you know the first rave was reported to have happened in the nineteen eighties in the United Kingdom?

ME

I can honestly answer that I didn't know anything about raves before this conversation.

QB

No hardcore partying in college?

ME

No. I was determined to graduate in three years so I could move on to vet school quicker.

QB

Why?

ME

Long story.

QB

Is this your version of me not wanting to talk about why I founded my charity?

ME

Yes.

QB

Noted. I'll honor your boundary just as you've respected mine.

ME

Thank you.

QB

You should know something, though.

ME

What?

QB

I bought my own word-a-day calendar. My word for today is reify.

ME

I don't think I know that one.

QB

It means making something abstract more concrete or real.

ME

I will, without a doubt, never use that word in a sentence.

QB

I realize you're right.

Also, realize is a synonym for reify.

I like words.

Have I scared you off a little?

I reify my personality is a lot.

That does NOT roll off the tongue as easily as realize.

Kinda feeling like you blocked me, Audrey.

ME

Sorry. Someone dropped off a box of guinea pigs they found in a park nearby. I was helping my office manager sort it all out.

QB

Oh, shit. Are they okay?

ME

Seems like they are, but my knowledge of guinea pigs is pretty limited.

QB

Want me to call my friend Jax? He has a billion of them.

ME

A billion?

QB

That may be an exaggeration. I think it's six or eight. Has an entire room devoted to their cages and everything. It's elaborate, and pretty neat.

ME

Would he be interested in fostering them?

QB

I don't know. He's in and out of town with the Denver Wolves, so any care would fall to his wife. I won't answer for her.

ME

Jax? Jax Mitchell? The hockey guy?

QB

You know who he is?

ME

I do. I don't pay attention to hockey as much as I do football, but I can follow the game. I only became aware of him after he married his wife, though. I always thought she seemed like a neat person when I watched her forecasts.

QB

I cannot wait to tell Jax that you like his wife better than him.

ME

That's not exactly what I said …

QB

I paraphrased.

ME

You already told him?

QB

Yup. He said he'll stop by your clinic after lunchtime. If I had to guess, it's because he'll be bringing his wife.

ME

I just did a little happy dance. Thank you!

QB

My pleasure. But next time, record the
happy dance, please.

ME

I'll take that into consideration.

It's probably good Jamie didn't see me react when he said he'd send Jax Mitchell my way. I may not follow hockey too much, but I know who he is. He's incredibly handsome, and has the most amazing Texas twang. But, as a woman with an affinity for science and technology, I may have a little bit of a girl crush on Becca Stephens. Or is it Becca Mitchell now? Is there an eloquent way to ask if a woman has taken her husband's last name? Hello, I'm Audrey. Have you decided to continue on in the antiquated tradition of losing your own identity?

Well, that probably isn't the best way to put it.

I peer into the cage at the five frightened guinea pigs. I had a small plastic hut that I put on top of a bed of hay, and four of them managed to squeeze inside. The fifth one only got its head inside, choosing to burrow as far into the hay as possible to hide its body. Poor things. I can only imagine what they must be thinking.

I quietly leave the back room, walking down the long hallway of my clinic. When I purchased the clinic years ago, I immediately changed the name. My predecessor had chosen a name based on location, and I wanted something cuter. I settled on Precious Paws Veterinary Clinic. I decorated the space with pops of blue and yellow, because those are the two colors dogs and cats primarily see. I added extra insulation between my exam rooms, because I've always hated how paper-thin walls seem to be in clinics of all kinds. An anxious dog doesn't need to be made even more frantic because of every sound reverberating off the walls. It's bad enough that they're at the vet. I want my space to be as calming as possible for them, and I'm pretty damn proud of the environment I've curated.

When I hear a very loud gasp, I look up to find Chelsea staring wide-mouthed out the window. I may not consider myself lucky in a lot of ways, but I know how lucky it is to have my best friend working as my office manager. "Aud, why is there an absolutely gorgeous woman walking toward our door with a man who bares a remarkable resemblance to Jax Mitchell?"

Leave it to my lesbian best friend to explain Jax and his wife like that. "They're coming to give me advice on the guinea pigs."

She turns to me, brows furrowed. "You know you're the vet here, right?"

"I know. But I don't get a lot of rodents in here. Jax is apparently pretty knowledgeable about them, and …" I break off, trying to figure out how to explain how I know Jamie, "…a mutual friend suggested he come to help."

"Mutual friend?" she asks, as Jax and Becca open the door. She glares at me as she hisses, "You're not off the hook, ma'am. We'll discuss this later."

I nod as Jax approaches, a friendly grin stretched across his handsome face. Arm around his wife, he's wearing fitted jeans, a blue henley that perfectly matches his eyes, and a worn Denver Wolves baseball cap. Becca smiles warmly at me, and I immediately notice her tee shirt, which says 'women belong in all places where discoveries are being made.'

"I love that shirt," I gush.

"Thanks! I'm pretty partial to women in STEM," she says with a laugh.

"Me too! Well, duh. I mean, that's obvious. I'm a vet. It technically falls under science. I guess it sort of falls under engineering as well. Maybe even math? Vets are jacks of all trades, really. But I guess meteorologists are too. You definitely get the technology aspect of STEM. Did you know that they've now added the A for art to the category? Now it's STEAM. I guess neither of us gets to say we regularly use art in our jobs. Well, maybe you do, a little, if you do any projects when you visit the elementary schools. That must be fun, right? I'd probably freak out and I become a chatterbox —" I break off, horrified.

"You two are going to be great friends," Jax says with a chuckle. "My lovely wife here also likes to monologue."

"Jacob!" Becca says, eyes wide as she lightly slaps his chest. "That isn't something you tell people!"

"Why not? She just said she does it too, so I know y'all are gonna be comfortable with one another." Jax shrugs as he glances at me. "Apologies if that made you feel awkward. I love when Becca gets going, especially when she talks weather to me. I know it can be hard to find female friends who understand the plight of a woman in a male-dominated career."

"Actually around sixty-eight percent of veterinarians are female," I blurt out.

Chelsea whips her head to stare at me. "Seriously? You know the statistics of that?"

"I got curious one night. The numbers are slightly increasing. It was sixty-seven percent a year ago."

"The numbers are going up in meteorology as well," Becca pipes up. "Twenty-nine percent not even ten years ago, and now it's around thirty-eight percent."

"See?" Jax says proudly, squeezing Becca into his side. "Like-minded women who think statistics are sexy."

I glance at Becca, who shrugs. "He's not wrong."

"Great. You both can exchange numbers in a bit. Now show me the piggies!" Jax says enthusiastically.

I motion for them to follow me down the hallway to the procedure room. "They seem to be adolescent age, I think. Not fully grown, but definitely not pups. I'd say around four months old."

"I bet they're adorable," Jax gushes.

"Rein it in, hockey boy," Becca mutters. "We have enough."

"Party pooper," Jax mutters. As we approach the cage, he leans toward me and whispers, "I bet I can talk her into at least one."

"Nope. I know you'll want an even number, which is why we're leaving with zero."

A cacophony of squeaks interrupts their odd quarrel, and we all peer into the cage. The pig who couldn't fit into the cage earlier has now wedged itself on top of the others, and a different pig is on its back, all four paws flailing as it attempts to right itself.

"Spitfire, you got the veg?" Jax asks, holding out a hand.

"Oh, right." Becca opens her handbag, pulling out a Ziplock bag of fresh mixed vegetables. She opens it, pulling out a handful of spinach, and gives some to Jax. "Our girls love spinach. Let's see if these lovelies do as well."

I carefully remove the top of the cage as we crowd around. Jax puts a leaf next to the hut, and we watch as two pigs immediately begin sniffing in the direction of the vegetable. Quickly all five turn toward the offering, and Becca puts down two more leaves. I watch, quite transfixed, as all five pigs surround the food and begin to nibble. Becca then places strawberries sporadically throughout the cage.

"I bet that one with the white fur immediately goes for the strawberries," Jax comments quietly. He looks at me and winks before continuing. "Out of our six pigs, it's only the ones with white fur who love strawberries. Makes 'em look like murderers."

I choke out a laugh. "Oh, wow. I hadn't even thought about that."

"So, what do you want to know?" Jax asks. "You're doing great with a cage. Five pigs is tight for this size, though, so you may want to get a second cage or something pretty big for all five of them. They love most fruits and vegetables, but there are all kinds of treats and toys for them you can find online."

"Oh, I didn't intend to keep them all," I answer hurriedly. "I know if I send them to any of the humane societies here, they'll likely be euthanized. I was hoping to find a foster for them until I can find homes for them."

Jax stares at me. "Did Jamie tell you I'd foster them?"

"No, he specifically said he didn't know, but that you traveled a lot, so the care would fall onto your wife, and he wouldn't answer for her."

"I think Jamie is my favorite of your friends, Jacob," Becca says with a smile. "I love our girls, but I don't think I can take on five more. Plus we have a dog, too."

Jax turns to her. "You know I'd never ask you to care for all of them. I was only teasing about bringing one or two home. Mostly."

She cups his cheek lovingly. "I know. And as cute as they are, it pains me to say no. I don't want to overextend myself."

"It's fine, darlin'. I'd never ask you to. I'm sure we can help Audrey find homes for them." He smiles adoringly at his wife, and the pang of jealously I feel is instantaneous and immense. They're such a beautiful couple, and to bear witness to it is remarkable.

"So I should probably buy some other kind of cage in the meantime?" I ask, forcing myself to look away from Jax and Becca before I either begin to ask them inappropriate questions about their life together, or I make an even bigger embarrassment of myself by starting to cry.

"You know what? I'm pretty sure I have a spare caging system that we aren't using. You're welcome to it if you'd like. It's not put together currently, but I still have the directions. I can have it sent over to you tomorrow." Jax's expression is odd, and Becca looks confused. What is going on right now?

"Uh, okay. Yeah, that would be great. Can you send it to my house instead of here? Today is a quiet day, but most days we have at least one loud dog in here. I'd hate for them to be frightened. And I don't want them to be alone during the weekends."

"Sure. As soon as Becca gets your number, you can send her your address. Once I know when the cage can be delivered, I'll let you know."

"Are you taking new clients, Audrey?" Becca asks suddenly. "I have a vet, but I'd prefer to use someone I know, and you give off good vibes."

Touched, I beam as I reply. "I'm always accepting new clients. I'd be honored to take care of your pets. What do you have?"

"A ball of fluff with five working brain cells," Jax quips.

"Be nice! A golden retriever named Thunder," Becca explains.

"A meteorologist with a dog named Thunder? That's amazing." I jump when I realize Chelsea is right behind me. "Sorry, Aud. Didn't mean to scare you."

"It's fine. Oh, if you get more pets, I hope you keep with the weather names! You could have a cat named Nimbus, or a rabbit named Cyclone."

Becca smiles widely. "I don't think we'll be adding any more animals to our menagerie anytime soon, but I do love Nimbus for a dog name. Maybe for our next golden?"

Jax looks at her, deadpan. "Baby, I'm gonna need a dog with a little bit more working memory next time."

"Goldens may not be the smartest dog out there, but they're one of the most loving, and they're one of the best for living with kids. You know, if you ever think about having children, I mean." Good God. I need a filter.

Becca looks triumphantly at her husband. "See? If you want a basketball team of little Jax Juniors, we're sticking with goldens."

Jax groans, but the smirk on his face tells me he'll do whatever it takes to keep Becca happy. If she wants a dozen golden retrievers, he'll make it happen. They're so cute together.

As they're heading out, Becca reminds me to send her my address. "I can find a cage. I don't want to be an imposition."

"Nonsense. It's not being used, Audrey. I'd love to donate it to some piggies that need it," Jax says with a wink, then waves as he guides Becca outside. Not being used? His inflection hints this isn't what I expect. Something tells me that Jax Mitchell doesn't do things lowkey and basic.

And the next day, when a brand new four-level wooden cage that's taller than me and a massive box of every kind of toy and treat imaginable shows up at my house, I'm not even remotely surprised.

Jamie

CHAPTER 7

While I didn't hear from Audrey for a few days, Jax supplied every minute detail of his visit to her clinic. Not only that, but he continues to give me his thoughts to this day.

JAX

Did I tell you how well she got along with Becca?

ME

Yep.

At least half a dozen times.

JAX

Nah. Couldn't be that many.

ME

I don't delete texts, man. I can go back and count if you'd like.

JAX

That's okay. Let's move on.

I snort as I buckle my seatbelt. It's been a long five days in New

York City, and I'm anxious to get back home. Brand deals are a necessary evil in professional sports, and while they definitely pad my bank account, it's a tremendous amount of peopling for my neurodiverse brain.

JAX

Audrey suggested we name our next dog Nimbus.

ME

Like the cloud?

JAX

Yeah.

ME

You should get one of those big white malamutes or something. Then it would actually look like a cloud.

JAX

Holy shit, that's a fantastic idea.

Disregard. Becca is not on board with the floofy cloud idea.

ME

Floofy cloud.

JAX

A floofy cloud dog is a better way of describing a white ball of fur than calling it a cotton ball. Both are accurate, but one is more appealing.

ME

We've been friends for too long, because I'm starting to understand the way your mind works.

JAX

Only uphill from here, my boy.

Laughing, I close out of his text exchange to open the one I had with Audrey before I left. I'm tempted to text her. Ask how she is, and if the guinea pigs are doing well. What her word for the day is today. If she's had any brilliant ideas for the charity event that could possibly replace a bachelor auction. Shit, I don't think I even told her that was the main idea the board was behind. I hate all of this.

"Mr. Wahlberg, we'll be taking off shortly. Would you like a drink?" Allison, the only flight attendant on this private jet, asks me sweetly. She leans in just enough so I can see partially down her blouse. I'm sure for most flights, she has each button secured perfectly. But for me, she's giving a very clear indication of what services she's willing to provide. I may miss a lot of social cues, but even I don't miss this one.

"No, I'm fine, Allison. Thank you." I grab a paperback I've been slowly reading through, effectively dismissing her. The saying 'don't shit where you eat' comes into play here. Since I use the same company to charter jets when I need them, I'd undoubtedly have awkward run-ins with Allison after sleeping with her. Since I have no desire to attempt a relationship with her, no sex is worth months — or years — of discomfort.

Which is precisely why I shouldn't be thinking about Audrey in any capacity other than an acquaintance. A peer I'll be coordinating an event with. So what if she seems to understand a lot of my idiosyncrasies? Could be just a coincidence. She doesn't know me. I don't know her. The weird pull I feel towards her is just that. Weird.

Reclining my seat, I let my eyes flutter closed. It's an over four hour flight from New York City to Denver, and I know if I look like I'm asleep, Allison will leave me alone. Typically, my mind whirls, forcing me to complete a series of steps to empty my brain and relax my body. But the last four days have been nonstop, and I'm exhausted.

My mind wanders to more personal thoughts of Audrey. I wonder if she has trouble falling asleep, or if she's one of the lucky ones that goes unconscious as soon as their head hits their pillow.

Does she let her hair down, or is it up in that bun? Would she let me hold her to fall asleep? I wonder what her hair smells like, and if she makes cute little noises while sleeping.

And that's how I fall asleep: dreaming about a woman I barely know, and one I probably won't ever get an opportunity to have.

Another week goes by with no word from Audrey. I'll admit, I'm struggling hard. I can't decide if I should reach out to her again. Google was no help on the matter, and basically told me to 'match her energy,' but I don't know what the hell that means! I found forums that revolve around dating rules, and everything contradicted each other. The man should do all of the wooing. It should be even between the pair. The woman controls the conversations. Contact the woman the day after meeting. Three days. One week. Don't appear too interested. Show her minor interest. Suffocate her with love immediately.

I'm analytical to a fault. I like knowing the steps of things. A plus B equals C. Black and white. Dating is so deep into the gray that I don't know how to move forward.

Jesus Christ. I'm not dating the girl.

I need to get that through my thick skull. I only need to contact her about the event.

Mind made up, I fire off a semi-professional text and hope for the best.

ME

Hello, Audrey. I hope you're doing well. I'd like to schedule a time we can meet to discuss the event. I have some new marketing images I can share with you, and tell you about what the board wants to do. This week, I'm available any evening.

I'm surprised when I see the dots immediately moving, telling me Audrey is responding.

AUDREY

Hello, Jamie. I wondered when I'd hear from you again. Is there any chance you could come to my home to meet? My dog just had surgery, and I don't want to leave her alone in the evenings.

ME

Of course. May I ask what she had surgery for?

AUDREY

She was hit by a car a few years ago before I adopted her. Her spinal cord was severely damaged, paralyzing her. Surgery today was a follow-up to reduce pressure.

ME

Wow. You have a paralyzed dog.

AUDREY

Yes. And five guinea pigs.

ME

Now I really want to come to your house, just to experience the zoo.

AUDREY

It feels like that sometimes, especially when Flash gets the zoomies.

ME

Flash? Like Flash, Flash, hundred yard dash? From Zootopia?

AUDREY

Yup!

ME

That is absolutely amazing. I can't wait to meet her.

AUDREY

She's pretty opinionated, so don't take it personally if she doesn't like you. Corgis are notorious for being brats.

ME

I'll keep that in mind. Is tonight okay? Are you alright if I bring dinner?

AUDREY

As long as I can reimburse you for half.

ME

That's fine. Any allergies or foods you won't eat?

AUDREY

No allergies. I don't like to eat much with my hands, and slimy food freaks me out.

ME

One time I had natto, which is fermented soybeans. I was unprepared for how slimy, yet sticky, it would be, and I immediately threw up, so I'm with you on the slimy food thing. Chinese food okay?

AUDREY

I'm going to ignore the comment about natto, because I actually like that dish. But my favorite Chinese dish is beef and broccoli.

ME

Mine too! And I'm ignoring your comment about liking natto.

A few hours later, I'm in front of Audrey's small townhome, which is only about twenty minutes from my house. Over three million people in this city, and we're this close to each other. It makes me wonder if I've ever seen her before. I have to think I'd have looked twice if I had.

I can't help but notice the massive disparity between our neighborhoods. Mine is full of palatial estates, with tons of space between each home. I haven't even met one of my neighbors. Audrey's neighborhood is quaint, but old. Large trees line the quiet road, still bare from the winter, but I imagine how beautiful the street must look in the summer and fall. I pass a young family pushing a stroller, and a gentleman walking his large Labrador retriever. I bet Audrey knows many of her neighbors, and is probably well-versed in the gossip of the neighborhood.

I snag a parking spot right in front of her house, noting the fun wreath on the door that includes figurines of a variety of animals. The center one is a dachshund holding a four-leaf clover, obviously for Saint Patrick's Day. Undoubtedly Audrey has figures for every holiday of the year, which I find completely adorable.

As I step out of my Maybach SUV, I realize how out of place I look. Not only is my car at least double the price of every car around, but it didn't occur to me to clean myself up at all after my workout today. I've arrived in a worn Colorado Coyotes long-sleeve shirt, a backwards cap to cover the hair that is badly in need of a trim, and mesh joggers. Not exactly the greatest way to make an impression.

I wonder if Audrey's hair is down. I'm desperate to see it. Is it curly, or stick straight? Does she like it when someone plays with her hair? I have a feeling it would be incredibly calming to drag my fingers through her tresses. Wind it around my fingers to feel its softness. Or around my fist as I pound into her from behind.

Dammit. No. Get it together, man.

Knocking on Audrey's door, I take a couple of deep breaths, trying to calm my nerves. When I get anxious, it can go one of three ways. I might be able to calm myself down. Or, I could get incredibly overstimulated, needing to get the hell out of here fast before I embarrass myself. But worst of all, I might actually puke.

My first two years in the NFL, I puked before every game. It became a running joke with my teammates. "Sorry, Coach, you can't give us your inspiring Ted Talk just yet. Wahlberg's barfing again." I'm honestly thrilled it didn't make the evening news, although I'm not sure how.

Unfortunately, as soon as I hear Audrey unlock the door, I know I'm going to hurl. She barely has time to smile at me, after opening the door, before I rasp, "Where's your bathroom?"

She doesn't speak, just points. I bolt inside her home, shoving the takeout bag of Chinese into her hands, and barely make it into the tiny bathroom before slamming the door shut. I don't have time to turn on the water or overhead exhaust fan to cover up the sounds I'm going to make, because I'm already making them. I'm a violent puker. It's appalling. There's no covering up what I'm doing right now. Pretty sure I barf up a pizza I had three or four years ago.

Once done, the wave of humiliation comes over me. I'm an MVP-winning NFL quarterback, and I puke when my anxiety gets too high. I don't know what I'll have to promise this girl not to leak it to the press, because it honestly could be career suicide if the team finds out. I'm supposed to be a leader. A take-charge man who carries the team on his back. But the thought of a pretty girl, and what her hair might smell like, and suddenly I fall apart.

"Jamie? Do you need anything?" Audrey asks softly, her voice noticeably even-toned and pleasant.

"A spare toothbrush or some mouthwash would be great," I admit, taking a long look at myself in the mirror. The only advantage to the anxious barf is I now feel incredibly regulated.

"There are both under the sink," she replies. Opening the cabinet door, I find perfectly organized packages of a variety of items, most travel-sized. Soaps, lotions, toothpaste, even floss and hairspray. The items are organized by size, smallest in the front, and I feel such a sense of peace come over me at how meticulous it all is.

I grab a new toothbrush and travel mouthwash, doing the best I can to clean myself up. When I step out of the bathroom, I find Audrey nervously wringing her hands. "Uh, thanks for the toothbrush. I'll get you a replacement."

"It's okay," she says, shaking her head and waving a hand in dismissal. "You probably can tell that I have a lot. I like to be prepared."

"It's quite the setup you have in there," I comment.

"I like things tidy. And organized. Well, at least in here. My closet is a disaster," she jokes. I honestly find that hard to believe. Taking a quick glance around the space, I find everything in perfect order. It seems Audrey has a favorite color, as the only splashes of color in her house are shades of purple. I appreciate the subtle tones, as everything in my house falls in the beige and gray scheme. I'll fully admit I hired a professional interior designer to set up the entire thing, literally approving and vetoing mockups before she was allowed to step foot in the place.

"Are you sure you're okay? We can reschedule," Audrey says hesitantly. She chews on her bottom lip when she's nervous, just like I do.

"I'm fine. Just swallowed wrong, I guess," I lie. Fuck, I hate lying. Not only am I awful at it, I find that I really don't want to lie to Audrey. But I can't fathom admitting that my anxiety was through the roof either. "I'll wait to eat, though. Just to be sure. But you can go ahead."

"Oh, I'm good with waiting too. Please, sit wherever you'd like. I'm going to grab my dog and bring her out here so I can watch her." She turns to head into a hallway, and I hear an immediate squeak.

"Can I see the guinea pigs?" I blurt out. "I've been to Jax's enough to recognize the sound."

"Oh, sure. Come back here. I put them in a small room because

Flash wouldn't stop barking at them." I follow Audrey deeper into her townhouse. Usually when I'm at someone's home for the first time, I'm acutely aware of how different our spaces are. But Audrey's home is very similar to mine. As we pass through the kitchen, I note hardly any clutter on the counters, except for a small air fryer, and a bowl where she keeps her keys. A container of wooden spatulas sits beside the stove, and a picture of a puppy, overlaid with script that says, 'the best therapist has fur and four legs.' I tend to agree, but my actual therapist probably feels otherwise.

Audrey pauses to pull a container from her fridge before we continue into another room. "This is my guest bedroom. Well, I haven't had any actual guests stay here. But the guinea pigs are technically guests, so it still counts. Right?"

"Sounds good to me," I say with a chuckle. As we enter, I'm greeted by a massive enclosure that has to be six feet tall. "Woah. That's intense."

"It took me an entire day to put it together. The delivery guy said he would put it together, but I like that sort of thing. I had to get creative with it, though, since it's taller than me. I haven't quite figured out which of them is going all the way to the top to kick poop across the room."

I cough as I swallow. Not what I expected her to say. "What now?"

She looks up at me with a nod. "I keep finding poop by the door. Unless one of them has a sphincter powered by fuel, I have to assume it's kicking the poop out."

"That's really … not something you hear every day," I finally say.

"There has to be some element of gravity at play here. Maybe I should ask Becca if she has any memories of physics equations. Speed plus distance or something. I don't find any poop on the floor beside the hutch. Just across the room."

I hum noncommittally. What the fuck was Jax thinking sending her this? I told him to get her a medium-sized cage, and that I'd pay for it. "I think Jax misunderstood the assignment here."

Audrey snorts. "If he thinks I'm taking this apart if the pigs get adopted, he's out of his mind. Someone is going to need to remove an exterior wall to get this thing out of here."

I chuckle, then still as her words marinate. *"If* they get adopted?"

An adorable pink hue creeps up her neck and onto her ears. "I mean, I haven't exactly advertised them yet. And Becca told me how Jax will watch on a camera when he's on away trips because he finds them comforting. I completely understand it now. I've found myself in here most nights, watching them eat dinner as I eat mine."

"You don't have to give them up for adoption if you don't want to," I say quietly. One look at Audrey's profile tells me she's struggling with the decision. "When I adopted my cats, I only intended to adopt one. The shelter said the pair were bonded, and they only figured that out because they were initially separated when they came in, and both cats became depressed. So I adopted two cats instead of one."

"You adopted two cats because they were sad without each other."

"Yes." Jeez, when she says it like that, it makes me sound like a pansy.

"That's incredibly sweet, Jamie. If you hadn't stepped in, the cats may not have been adopted. Most people don't want to take on two animals, especially rescues, because they think it'll be too much work. Plus, the sadness could have made them stop eating. It's hard to believe that animals can suffer from depression, but they can. Most animals do better with a playmate anyway."

"I was worried the rescue might have been forced to euthanize them," I admit.

Audrey nods. "It's possible, although rescues are less likely to do that. It really depends on a variety of factors. But I'm glad your two are safe and happy with you."

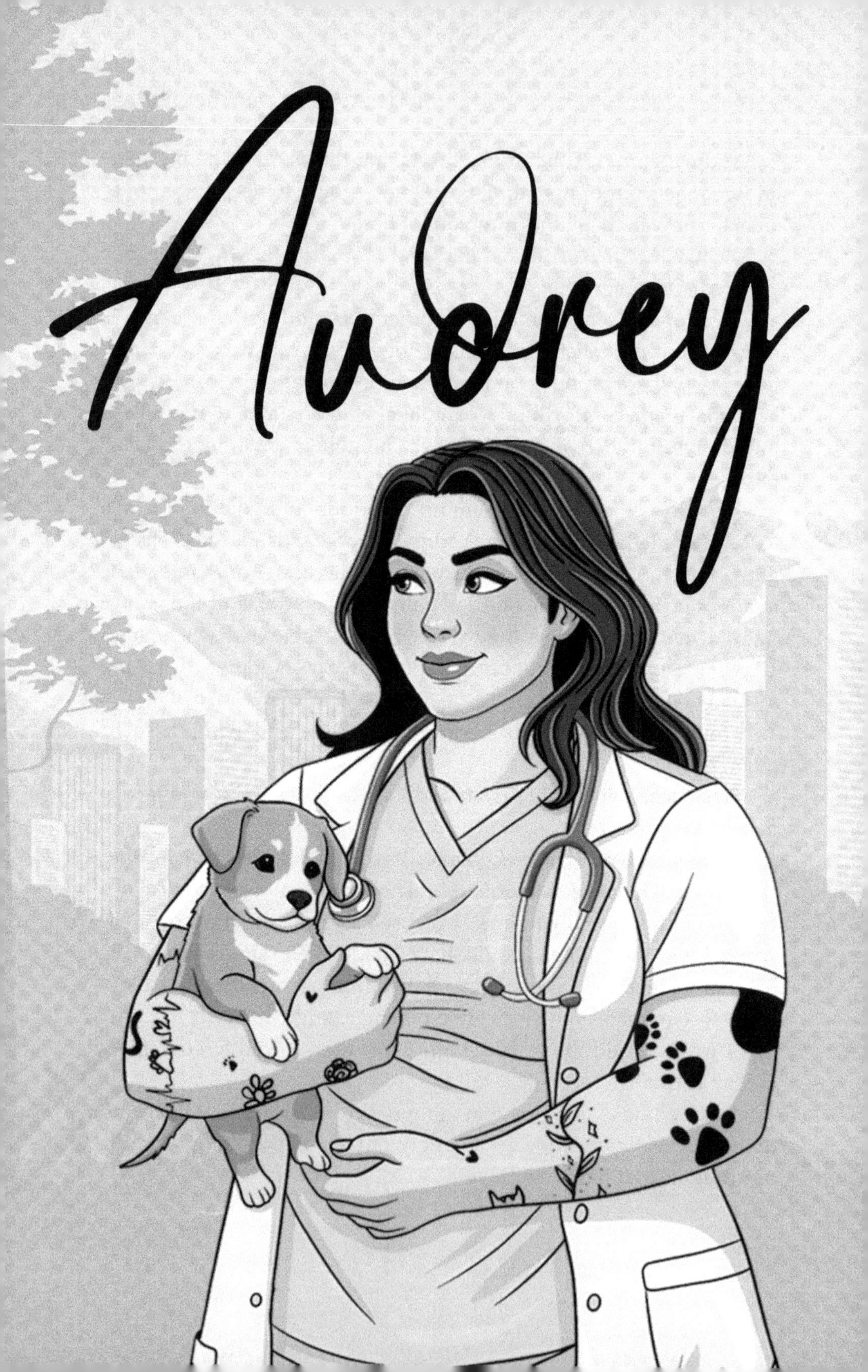

Audrey

CHAPTER 8

It amazes me how quickly my opinion of Jamie is changing. I called him the golden boy. Perfect in every way. And while things I learn about him aren't necessarily taking away from that persona, I realize he seems to be a genuinely nice person. He doesn't give off a fuck-boy vibe.

As he peers into the massive cage Jax sent over, he sheepishly grips the back of his neck with a lopsided smile. "I told Jax to get a medium-sized cage."

"If he thinks this is medium, I'm afraid of what he thinks is large," I comment.

Jamie whips out his phone. "I have a picture of his pig setup. It's pretty elaborate. I guess I should have been more specific."

He scrolls for a moment, then turns his phone toward me. I gasp when I see the wall of cages, tunnels, and enclosed staircases that eclipse an entire wall. "So I guess this is a medium-sized cage."

"When I saw the charge, I vaguely thought about asking him for clarification. In today's economy, you never know how expensive things are, and clearly I've never bought a critter cage before. So I didn't ask."

"Wait a minute. You bought this?" I stare at him, mouth agape in shock.

"Uh, yeah. I did."

"He told me he had one lying around."

"I told him I'd cover whatever you needed. Evidently, he felt he could stretch the truth a little."

"I should reimburse you," I say hastily, pulling my phone from my pocket. "I can send you some money."

"It's not necessary. I like helping out, and being able to give a home for a box of guinea pigs is a reward in itself."

"Tell me how much I owe you."

"No."

"Jamie!"

"I don't want your money, Audrey. I have an entire charity devoted to helping animals in need. Now I've helped five of the smallest animals," he says with a shrug.

I shake my head, going to Google. "No. I don't like that. I'm at least going to donate to your charity then. I'm sure I can find the cost of this hutch — one thousand dollars? Why the heck is this so expensive?"

"Jax has expensive taste, and he very much loves to spend his money on the people around him. You should see how many shoes and cowboy hats he has."

I look up at Jamie. "That's just the cost of the cage. A huge box of supplies showed up too."

"I know, Aud. I paid for that as well," he says with a hint of a smile. Oh boy. Why did my heart just jump when he shortened my name?

"I don't feel comfortable taking all of this. It feels odd, and I don't like it."

His gaze is intense as he studies me. "Can you elaborate?"

"I —" I close my eyes, struggling to find the words. I'm not sure how to express that my family's money has changed how I view relationships, both on a personal and professional level. "My family has money. It's impacted every relationship I've had my entire life, even just friendships. I don't like feeling as if power has shifted. I don't want this held over my head."

I wait for Jamie to reply, nervously tapping my fingers to my thighs.

"Have you experienced someone holding a similar situation over your head?" he asks quietly.

I sigh. "Not exactly the same, but yes. And my parents always bring up money. 'You have to do this, because we donated to this charity, Audrey.' Or 'why did we bother to pay for your undergrad if you won't even do such-and-such, Audrey?' I don't like feeling beneath someone because of money."

"I can understand that. I guess I feel something pretty similar. I hate it when I realize someone is taking advantage of me because of my money. Pretty hard to determine who truly wants to know me for me, and who wants access to my bank account."

I open my eyes to see Jamie staring into the distance, his blue eyes stormy. "You must get that a lot."

"I used to. My first few years in the league really toughened me up. It was trial-by-fire figuring out who I wanted in my circle. Every year it feels like it gets a little smaller."

As I'm about to ask more questions, Jamie's stomach quite audibly growls, making us both laugh. "Is that a sign you can eat now?"

"I'd say so. Where's your dog? I want to meet Flash."

"I'll grab her and meet you in the kitchen."

Two hours later, after a quick introduction and a great meal, Jamie and I settle onto my couch to discuss the event. Flash is on her favorite dog bed, completely passed out courtesy of some intense pain medication. Jamie asked a lot of questions about Flash's wheelchair, and seemed genuinely interested in her recovery, as well as her chance at regaining feeling and function in her hind legs.

Ready to get down to business, I pull out my favorite notebook and pen. Yes, I have favorites, and no, I won't share them.

"Every year, we've chosen the name of the event depending on the overall theme. Since last year was a black tie gala, it was Tails and Tuxedos. The year before that was a silent auction, and we titled the event Paws and Proceeds. With this year being a win-a-date, I'm really drawing a blank on what to call it," Jamie explains.

Excuse me? "Did you just say win-a-date?"

"Oh, shit. I forgot to explain that. Yeah, the board decided it'll be a bachelor auction. They plan on having each guy feature an adoptable pet, and while they definitely want the pets to be adopted, the main draw will be the men."

"How many men?" I ask.

"A minimum of twelve, but they'd like twenty-four."

"That's a random number," I muse.

Jamie scratches his neck. I'm beginning to recognize he reaches for his neck when he gets uncomfortable. "There may have been talks of a calendar, so I assume they'll want bachelors in units of twelve."

"How do they intend to pick bachelors?"

"They're asking all the major sports teams in town, plus some local influencers, content creators, and some guys who are pretty well-known. The shortlist I saw included a few realtors, a CEO of a bank, and a couple chefs. It's a random group for the most part."

Before I can think otherwise, I blurt out, "Will you be auctioned off?"

Jamie's eyes widen comically. "What? No! I told them no. That's how I've ended up as the MC."

"Oh, okay. I didn't know that you're in a relationship."

"I'm not. I don't want to be in the auction regardless."

"Why not?" I ask, thoroughly confused. The man is gorgeous, he's an NFL quarterback, and he'd no doubt get the most donations. "I'm sorry. It's none of my business."

"I don't want to be the center of attention."

"Aren't you the focus whenever you're on the football field?" I ask.

"I know. It sounds ridiculous. I get it. But I've spent my entire life learning how to be on the field. I know exactly what I'm supposed to do, and I'm surrounded by a bunch of guys who will protect me at all costs. You slap me on a stage in front of a thousand strangers, where I'm supposed to strut around? And then some random person wins, getting access to me? Absolutely not. I'm incredibly careful about who I let into my private life."

"I figure if you were in it, you'd get the most money. But I don't know who else is attending. Do men actually like doing this kind of thing?" I wonder aloud.

Jamie shrugs. "I assume some do. Jax would have been fine with it before he met Becca. Occasionally a coach will participate, but I don't think my coach will. He's kind of a stick-in-the-mud. One of the wide receivers on my team is doing it, and my center is as well."

"Oh, the center will get a lot of attention."

"You think so?"

I nod. "He's extroverted and has a dad bod. My best friend explained how similar he is to Jason Kelce. Same position and all."

Jamie chuckles, shaking his head. "I can't wait to tell him that. He'll hate it. He's from Cleveland, and knew the Kelce brothers growing up. He never played against Jason, but did play against Travis right before Travis graduated."

"How odd it must be to still hate someone after all these years," I comment.

"Oh, he doesn't hate Kelce. It grates on his nerves to constantly be compared. I get it all the time with Tom Brady. It's exhausting feeling like you have to live up to the best that ever played your position."

I'm silent for a moment, thinking about my high school days. I mostly kept to myself. Sure, there were some individuals who were more likely to harass and bully me those years, but I didn't hate them. But I certainly haven't been compared to them as an adult. I was, however, almost always compared to my sister. It never mattered that I was smarter, worked harder, and got way better grades. All my parents ever cared about was connections. Paige married into another wealthy Denver family, thus making her so much better than me in my parents eyes.

"What about calling the event 'The Paw-suit of Love?'" Jamie asks suddenly, jolting me from my trip down memory lane.

"Paw-suit? I bet people think it's a misspelling."

Jamie frowns, his brow furrowed in concentration. "There are so many neat names I'm thinking of that my teammates will completely destroy. I can't use anything with the word 'ball' or 'balls' in the title. I thought using the word 'collar' could be neat, but then at least one guy will comment about BDSM, so that's out."

"What about just calling it 'The Perfect Catch?' I ask. "It implies finding a romantic love interest, but also a play-on-words with a game of fetch. I don't think there are any euphemisms your childish adult teammates could run with."

"For the most part, they're incredibly professional and respectful. But the locker room talk can get a little out of control."

"That would make me so uncomfortable," I confess. When Jamie's eyebrow lifts, his blue eyes locked on mine, I continue. "I think there's a time and place for discussions like that. At work isn't where I'd choose to chat about BDSM."

A hint of a smile ghosts across Jamie's face. "I don't think there are many places where I'd feel comfortable talking about that."

Oh, thank God. For a moment, I worried I'd stepped in a metaphorical landmine. "Let's move on."

Jamie's breath whooshes from his lungs. "Good call. So we'll call the event 'The Perfect Catch,' and add a subtitle about it benefiting the charity."

"Sounds good. What else do we need to do?" I ask.

Jamie pulls out his phone, opening his notes app. "The board already approved the location, but they'd like us to finalize a menu. A DJ has signed on, waiving his normal fee if we allow him to leave flyers and business cards around the room, and the board agreed. They have asked us to look through a long list of songs the DJ typically plays at events and veto some of the ones our more esteemed guests may disapprove of."

"So anything with foul language or raunchy lyrics? I guess no BDSM talk then," I joke.

"Such a shame. I fully intended to offer up collars to each winning woman."

"How have I never noticed a woman wearing a collar in public? If they're so popular, why don't I notice any?" Before I have time to feel embarrassment at my innocent question, Jamie answers.

"A guy I went to college with was big on the BDSM scene, and he collared his college girlfriend. I couldn't get it out of my head, so I did some research. I don't know about you, but once a topic gets imbedded in my brain, it's incredibly hard for me to move past it without some kind of closure or redirection."

Wow. He's pretty much describing me. "I'm the same way. I suddenly remembered a vacation to New England years ago, where I had the best clam chowder of my life. I couldn't sleep because I didn't know the recipe. I stayed up all night trying to find it."

"Did you find it?"

I shake my head. "Not the exact one, but I found a good substitute. I always make it on the first snow of the year."

"I bet it was good."

"It was. I'll send you the recipe, if you want it."

"I'm actually allergic to shellfish, but thank you for the thought."

"Oh, wow."

"Yeah. Typically my reactions aren't too bad, but I have an EpiPen just in case."

"I'm so sorry. You've accidentally ingested some seafood? That's awful." Without thinking, I reach over to rest my hand on his forearm. The movement stuns me, and my eyes drop to stare at where my hand meets his skin. While I'm not averse to physical touch, I never make the first move. I don't reach out to hold a man's hand, or initiate a hug. I've never leaned in to kiss someone, and I've certainly never felt sparks just by touching a forearm.

Until today.

By Jamie's quick intake of breath, I wonder if he's as shocked as I am. I quickly glance up, finding his gaze locked on my hand as well. Did he feel the sparks too?

But then the anxious side of my brain takes root. Maybe he wants to recoil. Or throw up again. What if I truly offended him? Perhaps I invaded his personal bubble, and I should apologize. Would this be considered flirting? When is physical touch okay in a neutral setting? While we are alone, this isn't a date, and I'm not touching anything that could be called an erogenous zone. Reading social cues has always been a challenge for me, no matter what I do.

And then Jamie's hand covers mine, and it's like a million bees are buzzing against my skin. His eyes are intense as he watches me. "Thank you, Audrey."

He shifts slightly, lessening the distance between us, and for a euphoric moment, I wonder if he's leaning in to kiss me. His eyes dart down to my lips, and butterflies erupt in my stomach.

We both jump when Jamie's phone rings. "Shit. It's my coach. I need to take this."

"Of course," I reply, watching as he stands from the couch, quickly striding across the room to exit my townhouse. Flash whimpers in her sleep, then sighs loudly. I feel the same way, girl.

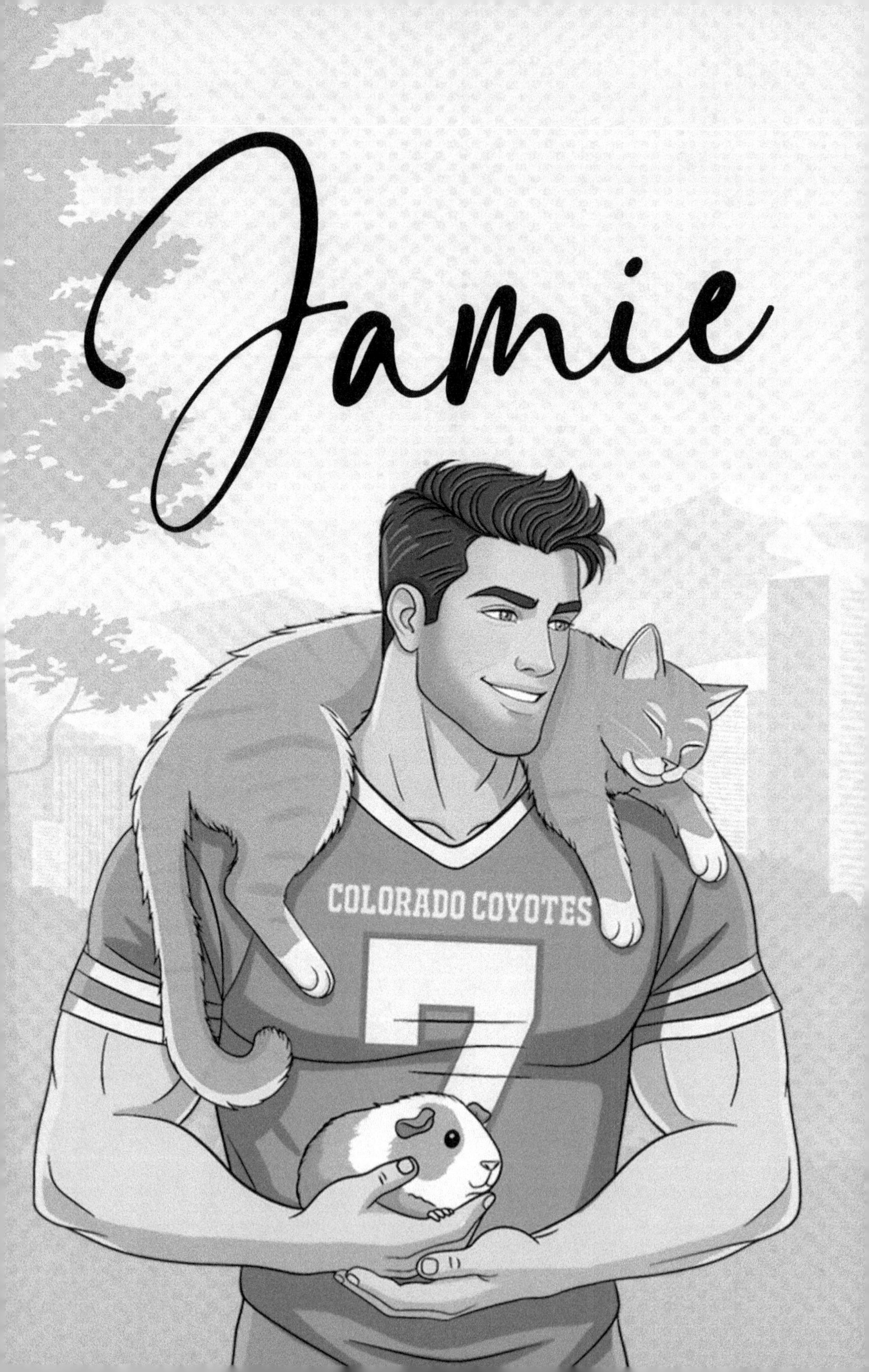

Jamie
COLORADO COYOTES
7

CHAPTER 9

"Coach." I say as I answer the phone, quietly closing Audrey's storm door behind me. I probably didn't need to come outside to take this call, but I need the fresh air. I was a split second away from kissing her, simply because she seemed so genuinely compassionate about my seafood allergy, and then she touched my arm. What the fuck is wrong with me?

"I made a bet with Bennett Davenport of the Wolves, and I lost." Bennett Davenport is Jax's coach. While Jax hasn't had anything truly negative to say about Bennett, he also hasn't spoken very highly of him either. Then again, no one except for me seems to be on a first-name basis with Silas Youngstown as he begins his second year as the Coyotes head coach.

"Okay?" I ask, confused. All kinds of bets are made in sports. Usually it's dumb things like wearing the same underwear for a straight week, or eating a specific thing right before practice. I don't know why this impacts me.

"We played golf today, and I lost."

"And if you had won?"

"He'd have to buy me season tickets for the Wolves in one of the suites."

"And since you lost?"

Silas growls audibly, and I stifle a laugh. Coach is pretty gruff. Rough around the edges. He glowers on the sidelines, hates doing post-game interviews, and keeps an incredibly small circle of friends. In his late forties, he has no idea that there are hundreds of forums and groups based solely on how attractive women think he is. Or if he does know about them, he keeps that to himself. About an inch or two taller than me, his salt-and-pepper hair has just enough silver to give him a distinguished quality, and an ever-present five o'clock shadow makes him look even rougher.

"I have to participate in your stupid auction."

"What?" I shout, loudly laughing.

"We were tied on the ninth hole, and a fucking gust of wind took my ball all the way across the green. Davenport is convinced it was meant to be. I call bullshit."

"Should have said you had to play eighteen instead of nine holes."

"We couldn't. He had something to get to. Or maybe he made it up, because I was ahead the whole damn time."

"You understand what the auction is, right?" I ask, unable to withhold the smile that is evident in my tone. The women are going to go absolutely nuts for him, and he'll hate every minute of it.

"I know it's a date with me. Am I allowed to set the parameters? Like we meet for a thirty minute coffee?"

"Uh, we haven't decided that yet. I'll get back to you." I'm totally going to add a minimum time to the rules now.

"Jamie," he growls. "I don't want to fucking do this."

"I didn't make the bet, Silas. You did. This is all on you."

When he doesn't respond, I check my screen to see the jerk hung up on me. I'm not surprised.

Knocking quietly on Audrey's storm door, I open it to find her on the floor next to her dog, speaking softly. I can only imagine what she's telling Flash. I bet she's explaining how the medication works, any side effects Flash might have, and how hopeful she is that Flash regains the use of her legs.

"Hey," I say quietly. Audrey jolts, rolling over to face me, and I have to force myself not to groan. Spread out on the floor, she looks like a present I wish I could unwrap.

"Everything okay?" she asks as she quickly stands up. Her hair, no longer perfectly coiffed in her bun, makes her look even more perfect. Small tendrils fall against her head in haphazard directions, and I love how she looks approachable and innocent. Stunning.

Mine.

For fuck's sake. I have got to get a hold of my emotions here.

"Yeah, it was my coach. He lost a bet with the Wolves coach, so now he has to do the bachelor auction," I tell her, grinning widely.

She gives me a hesitant smile. "And we're … happy about this?"

"Hell yes, we are! Coach has no idea how feral Denver women are for him. Or if he does know, he never brings it up. But they love him. I think he'll get the highest number of bids."

"I still think you'd get the highest number of bids. Certainly the largest amount in winnings." Audrey looks down at the carpet, and I almost ask what she's thinking.

"I won't feel comfortable up there. I puked just coming here, Aud. I'm likely to spew all over the guests at an event of that magnitude, and I don't think I can come back from that kind of display." Besides, I don't want to go on a date with just anyone. Tonight has made me acutely aware of the fact that I want to date *her*.

"You puked because you were coming here?" she asks quietly.

Shit.

"I thought it was a bug or something," she reminds me.

I sigh. "It wasn't. I was nervous. I'm freaked about planning this, and you're a cool woman, and I'm me. I got in my head."

Mouth agape, Audrey stares at me. "You — you're *you*. And I'm cool? You're an MVP-winning quarterback, Jamie. If either of us should puke from anxiety, it's me. I'm not an anxious puker, though. When I have an anxiety attack, I cry, then typically pass out."

Woah. "You have anxiety?"

Audrey nods. "Someday, I'll explain the dynamics of my family. Honestly, they probably run in the same circles as you. I bet you've at least interacted with my parents once or twice. Ever heard of Charles or Emmanuelle Carrington?"

Why does that last name ring a bell … oh, shit. "Wait. My agent was just talking about your dad trying to marry off his daughter to anyone who will take her. Is that you?"

Audrey winces. "Yep, that's me."

"Shit, Aud. I'm sorry. That was incredibly uncouth of me."

She shakes her head. "Not really. If it's true, is it still considered to be uncouth? Oh well. It doesn't matter."

I hear a whimper, and look down to see Flash struggle to sit up. Audrey immediately crouches down, picking Flash up carefully. "I need to take her out before I can do all her before bedtime care."

"There's a whole routine?" I joke awkwardly.

Audrey giggles, making me exhale in relief. "For now, there is. I clean her wound, make sure she's clean after urinating and defecating, and give her all her medications. I kennel her at night, so I put an inflatable donut around her neck so she doesn't attempt to somehow get at her wound. She doesn't very much care for the kennel, so I usually end up falling asleep on the floor as she does."

"Impressive. Sounds like Flash has the perfect human mom."

"I hope she thinks that. I love her so much. And somehow I've ended up falling for those fluffy little rodents, too."

I bark back a laugh as I walk toward the door. "They're pretty easy to fall for."

The following day, I'm at spring practice. Every NFL team has a spring schedule. It is nowhere near as intense as training camp, but it keeps everyone aware of what they need to work on, if they've gotten really out of shape, and allows us to spend time with one another. While I can genuinely say all of these guys are my friends, I have a couple of really good friends on the team. Best friends, even.

"You ready for this, QB?" My most used wide receiver, Maddox Lawson, says as he falls into step beside me. We're walking into our indoor field, as the outdoor fields are still too icy for us to use.

Colorado loves its sports teams, and they love new state-of-the-art stadiums, practice fields, and everything our players need to stay in tip-top shape. It never ceases to amaze me that I get to play here. There are some teams that play in thirty-year-old stadiums, with the owners unwilling to put one extra cent into the team. The Coyotes are incredibly lucky to be represented by an owner who recognizes the need of high-cost products, and he put his money where his mouth was when he campaigned for our new digs.

Our brand new stadium, with a retractable roof and every technological advancement known to man, came at the bargain price of two billion dollars. Partially funded by taxpayers, fans expect the most out of us. It will be an honor to step foot on the turf in a few months when the stadium is fully open.

"Yo. QB. You with me?" Maddox says, slapping me on the back. While we occasionally have pads on for spring practices, it's rare. Today we'll be in our practice uniform and pants, with helmets, of course.

"Yeah, I'm ready. Excited to be that much closer to the season starting."

"You typically fill up the offseason with a lot of charity things, right? And you're the MC for the animal charity event? I'm hoping the ladies dig the guns," he boasts, flexing his biceps with a massive grin.

"I'm sure you'll have no problem getting bids, Mad," I say with a chuckle.

"Are the bachelors allowed to make requests?"

"Like what?"

Maddox leans toward me conspiratorially. "What's the age

range for women bidding? Are men allowed to bid? What if it's a couple and they're hoping for a little group action?"

"Jesus, Mad. You know you don't have to sleep with them, right?" I rub a hand over my eyebrows.

He bursts into laughter. "It's too easy to rile you up, QB. I'm just fucking with you. I have no problem wining and dining an octogenarian widow. Hell, I'm cool to hang out with a guy who's just coming out of the closet. None of that shit bothers me. As long as the charity gets a ton of money, that's all that matters."

"I'm hopeful it will. Also thankful they're letting me MC instead of being up for auction," I say with an exaggerated shudder.

Maddox lowers his voice. "You gonna be okay with being on the mic? I know you've come a long way since our first years in the league, but this is a different situation."

There are no more than ten people on the team who know about my autism diagnosis, and I'd like to keep it that way. Maddox found out accidentally, but has been so supportive and instrumental in ensuring I'm always in a good situation. "I should be fine. I'll have a script to work with, and I've been paired with a local veterinarian who will assist me while the auction goes on."

"Oh? What's his name? Could be my vet for all I know."

"Audrey."

Maddox's eyes bug out of his head. "You got paired with a female vet? Is she hot? You like her. I can tell. You have to be smart to be a vet, right? They, like, have their own medical school. And she loves animals. This may be your perfect woman."

I can feel embarrassment creeping up my neck, and I turn slightly away from Maddox. He's been my best friend for over a decade, and he'll see right through me if I lie. "She seems very intelligent, yes. And she definitely loves animals. Someone dropped off a box of guinea pigs at her clinic, and she's fallen in love with them."

Maddox snorts. "Does Jax know?"

I nod. "I had him give her advice. It turns out she's a big fan of his wife."

He chortles. "Fucking love that for him. The pretty boy of the NHL getting knocked down a notch because of his hot and nerdy wife."

"Nerdy?" I ask, raising an eyebrow. I happen to know that Maddox is a closet nerd, even playing in a World of Warcraft group online when he has time. He's one of the few who actually enjoyed college, choosing to stay all four years to complete his bachelor's in electrical engineering.

He smiles. "You know I think being a nerd is a plus. Just so happens she's pretty damn hot too."

Becca is definitely attractive by society's standards, but she's not my type. Mine just so happens to be a foot shorter than me with curves for days.

"So," Maddox says as we walk onto the field to stretch, "you put the moves on this Audrey chick yet?"

"What? No!" I yell, making everyone turn to me. Maddox waves his hand nonchalantly.

"He's fine. I just dropped a *Grey's Anatomy* spoiler he wasn't ready for," he lies. When I look at him questionably, he shrugs. "I know you watch that show."

"I'm a few seasons behind," I admit with a laugh. "But I'm not putting any moves on Audrey. First of all, I don't even know if she's interested. And secondly, we have to work together for the next couple of months to plan this event. If I put the moves on her now, and it goes badly, it's going to make for a horrendous time for me."

"Or, you could be having fun sex with a woman you're attracted to, and then you'll be done with the auction, and you can date her for real," he says casually.

I shake my head. "I don't think she's interested. She hasn't given any vibes that she's attracted to me."

"With all due respect, Jamie, your ability to decipher vibes is nonexistent. She could have a neon sign pointing straight to her pussy that says, 'get it here' and I still don't think you'd recognize the invitation."

He's not exactly wrong. "I hate that I don't see these social cues, and that I'm way too used to women basically throwing themselves at me. I don't know how to pinpoint a valid interest."

"If she looks at your lips, bites her own lips, or her nipples get hard enough they poke through her shirt, she's interested."

"Seriously? It's just that easy?"

"Yep. You wanna know the surefire way to determine interest?"

"Obviously," I answer, on pins and needles waiting for Maddox to school me.

"Casually look at her lips, then tuck a piece of hair behind her ear."

"Her hair is almost always in a bun."

"Act like there's a piece out anyway." He looks at me smugly. "Just do it as an excuse to touch her. I bet she looks at your lips right after. Or she sighs all romantically."

I'm in my head. "Tuck a piece of hair. How far behind her ear? What if she knows there isn't even one strand of hair loose from her bun? What do I do if she doesn't react at all?"

"For fuck's sake," he mutters, coming to stand in front of me. He's only an inch or two shorter than me, with dark brown hair and green eyes. Reaching up, he pretends to push a piece of hair behind my ear, his finger dragging across my skin.

Like some fucked up version of Pavlov's dog, my gaze immediately drops to his mouth. "What the actual fuck? How did you do that?"

"Honestly, it's a gift."

"You ladies about done?" Coach shouts from the sideline, and I realize Maddox's hand is still against the side of my face. He doesn't look thrilled.

"Just teaching QB about the 'hair behind the ear' trick," Maddox answers. "You know, to tell if a woman is interested. You wanna learn, Coach? I can give you some pointers."

"I don't need pointers from you, Lawson. Now get back to stretching," Coach growls.

Maddox lowers his voice so only I can hear him. "Sure would be nice if he got laid sometime soon. Then maybe he wouldn't be such a jackass."

"I heard that," Coach shouts. "Don't worry, I got laid last night."

"Oh yeah?" Maddox asks.

Coach nods. "And your mom made me breakfast this morning too."

As the team howls with laughter, Maddox chuckles. "Guess I had that coming."

Audrey

CHAPTER 10

It's been a few weeks since I've seen Jamie, but we text often. At first, our conversations were solely about the event. Picking out the centerpieces, table linens, and other small details. Jamie is surprisingly involved in every aspect of the event. He never excuses himself, or tells me to just pick something. He's present and alert for every decision. As if I needed another reason to find him attractive.

Over the past week, though, our texts have become less about the event, and more about ourselves.

QB

Where did you go to college?

ME

CSU.

QB

I would have thought you'd go somewhere
far away.

ME

CSU has one of the best veterinary medicine programs in the country. I couldn't turn it down. Plus I really like having a mountain view, and state tuition is an added bonus.

QB

Your family didn't pay for it?

ME

There were addendums to paying for my tuition. I feared they'd suddenly stop paying, and I wanted to ensure it was as low as possible if I needed to take over the payments.

QB

I really kinda hate your parents.

ME

I hate them sometimes too. But I've had years to come to terms with the fact that I'll never be the daughter they expected, and they'll never love me the way I need. I have friends and animals that fill any void left by my family, and I refuse to spend even one more minute feeling bad for a shitty relationship with them.

QB

You're a better person than me. I'd want to be petty.

ME

A few months ago, pictures were posted at a society event. It was an incredibly bad angle of my mom. She was roasted online. I don't know if I've ever been happier.

QB

I'd like to think my pettiness would involve me taking the photo, then sending it to the news source for publication. THAT would be perfectly petty.

ME

If a situation arises where I need to be petty, I'll definitely come to you.

QB

I'm great with ideas. But actions? Nope.

ME

What do you mean?

QB

I have to be perfect. Set a good example for the younger guys on the team. Be a leader. A role model. Have to say all the right things and have no weaknesses, because the press can smell it. They'll pounce, and they take no prisoners.

ME

That sounds awful. I'm so sorry you have to go through that, Jamie.

QB

I've been a quarterback for twenty years. It's become second nature, unfortunately. It's fine. Just another mask I put on.

ME

I hate that. You should have the opportunity to be YOU, and everyone should accept that.

QB

Thanks. I appreciate that.

ME

Can I ask you a personal question?

QB

Sure.

ME

Do you wear a mask when you're talking to me?

QB

Yes, because puking in your house was the best mask I have in my arsenal.

Or assuming you were a dude.

Or buying you a massive guinea pig enclosure, but not thinking about how you'd have to put the damn thing together.

Honestly, no. I don't have any masks with you. You're a rare exception to my everyday life, Audrey. You've become a genuine friend.

ME

Thank you. That makes me happy.

And I didn't mind putting together the enclosure. Which they still love, by the way.

But I'm cool if we do away with the puking mask. That was kinda gross.

QB

Dammit. There goes my plans for our next outing.

"Aud, if you don't get some actual booze here, I'm never coming over again," Chelsea calls from the kitchen.

"There are two bottles of wine in the back of the fridge," I respond. Squeaks ensue as I continue to clean out the pig enclosure. "Frank, you need to stop kicking your poo everywhere. It's disgusting, and Flash keeps eating it."

I finally named the pigs when I realized I wouldn't give them up for adoption. Frank is mostly white with brown and black splotches. Norm is all white. Jax was right, he's feral for strawberries and looks like a murderer after finishing one. Desmond is fluffier, and mostly brown, while Burt is almost completely black. Finally, Bill is light brown with black ears.

Five boy guinea pigs. Honestly, I lucked out. A mixture would have made me separate them to ensure they weren't constantly making little piggies. As cute as that would be, I don't have the time or the desire to add to the guinea pig population.

I'll admit, I set up a camera to figure out which one was kicking the poop out. Frank legitimately looked directly at the camera, turned around, and started kicking. I fear he's the ringleader. He may also be my favorite.

"Oh, it's the good Chardonnay! I forgot you had them. You sure you're okay if we drink these?" Chelsea asks.

"Yeah. I'm not entirely sure why I've saved them this long." I bought one bottle after opening my clinic, with the thought that I'd celebrate when I'd accrued one hundred clients. But when I flew past that number, I couldn't seem to open the bottle. The second one was a gift from a client, after her beloved dog passed away. I'd gone to her house to be with her family as the dog was euthanized. Her two children have special needs, and saying goodbye in a stark veterinary clinic would have been incredibly difficult for them to comprehend. I didn't mind the change in procedure, and may offer it in the future if needed.

After handing me a glass of wine, Chelsea plops down on the couch, giving me an expectant look. "So. Tell me about the quarterback."

Without maintaining eye contact, I say, "There's nothing to tell. We're planning an event together. He's a nice guy. That's all."

Chelsea is silent for a minute, before she bursts into laughter. "You are so full of shit."

"What? I am not. Nothing is happening with him."

"But you want something to happen, don't you? He's a cutie."

"You're not much help, you know. You're attracted to everyone."

"No, I'm not. Just because I comment that someone is cute doesn't mean that I'm automatically attracted to them. I can look at someone and recognize societal standards of beauty. Your quarterback is hot. And I'll have you know I've only ever really felt attraction to a man a couple of times. Then when the dick gets involved …" she shudders. "Hard pass. I prefer the V."

I can't help but giggle. "I know you aren't attracted to everyone. And I know Jamie is quite handsome. But he's shown absolutely no interest in me whatsoever. I'm sure he can have his pick of any woman in the world, so it's hardly likely he'd choose me."

Chelsea sits up straight as I take a sip of wine, her face defiant and angry. "And why the hell not? Why wouldn't an NFL quarterback want to be with my amazing best friend? You're gorgeous. And smart. You're insanely talented, and you have such a big heart. You're a fucking catch, Aud. I really wish you could see that."

I sigh. "It's not that I think I'm unworthy of him. I like to say I'm realistic, but I can see how that could be perceived as pessimistic. But look at every NFL quarterback out there. Not one of them has a curvy woman. I bet a good chunk of them are models and influencers. Comparatively speaking, I'm quite different."

I'm a fairly confident woman. No, I'm not a sample size. Far from it, in fact. But I like my curves. And while there may be a pudgy layer between my skin and muscular system, I'm actually in fairly good shape. And I refuse to starve myself to please someone else, so a man better take it or leave it.

"Okay," Chelsea says. "I'm going to word this differently. Are *you* attracted to him?"

"Well, I mean, attraction is such a broad term, and we're essentially colleagues —" I stammer, until Chelsea holds up a hand.

"Nope. I don't need to know all the reasons you've convinced yourself that you can't find him hot. Answer the question, Aud. Are you attracted to him?"

"I, well, I'm not …" I trail off, frustrated. Sighing, I give the answer she already knows. "Yes."

She claps her hands gleefully. "I knew it!"

I roll my eyes. "It still doesn't matter. He's not attracted to me, and we have to plan this event. Can't start something with him now."

"You don't know if he's attracted to you. That's an assumption you're making. And we both know your ability to recognize social cues isn't the best. Do you think you'd understand if he flirted with you?"

"Define flirting."

Chelsea exhales, a sound so resigned and flat that I giggle. I know I frustrate her, but she takes it all in stride. "If he compliments you. If he seems giddy around you. If he touches you in any way that doesn't seem needed, like pushing your hair behind your ear. If he teases you, and if he texts back right away. Obviously not when he's at something football related, but if he answers you immediately, he's interested."

"I don't think I've seen any of that —"

Chelsea interrupts me again. "Now, if a guy isn't interested at all, it's a little more nuanced. If he ever calls you 'bro', he's not into you. If he's constantly trolling you or trying to one-up you, it's a no. If he's really short with you, and doesn't care about your opinion of him, he's not interested."

"Well, I don't think Jamie has done anything on either one of those lists. Now what?" I ask exasperatedly. I don't have any desire to try and discern what possible sign a man may or may not be throwing my way.

"Now, we set a trap." Chelsea's smile is wicked.

"I don't want to trap him."

"Trap may not be the best word. We're going to tease him a little bit, and see how he reacts. We'll know if he's interested or not."

"Or he won't react to anything, and I won't have an answer."

She shrugs. "I doubt it. Men typically think with their dicks. If he's into you, we'll know."

"We?"

"Yes, we!" she yells. "I'm invested now! I want to see him in action. Hell, I want to see *you* in action. I'm not sure if I've ever seen you all twitterpated over a boy."

"I'm not twitterpated. I have never been twitterpated." I stare blankly at her, crossing my arms in frustration and defiance. Emotional attachment was never okay growing up, and I'm not starting it now.

Chelsea comes to sit next to me, placing a hand on my shoulder. "It's okay to say you like a guy. It doesn't mean you're stupid, or immature, or any other bullshit your parents told you. It means you're human. We have thoughts, feelings, and we're naturally destined to gravitate toward one another. You're doing exactly what you're supposed to do."

I hate how she zeroed in on everything I was thinking. How I was raised to think emotions were inferior, and crying definitely wasn't allowed. Any fighting amongst family members was done in private, because we had a reputation to protect. The name comes first, above all else.

"I really don't think he's interested," I confess softly, dropping my eyes to my lap. Wringing my hands together tightly, I continue. "I'm afraid it'll hurt me more when I get confirmation of that. Right now, I can live in blissful ignorance that it doesn't matter. That we're just peers, working together for charity. But the moment we initiate any kind of plan to find out if he's interested, I have to acknowledge that I *do* like him … and that he quite possibly doesn't return the sentiment."

"I have a back-up plan if that happens," Chelsea announces. "It involves a donkey, goose feathers, glitter, and a lot of old fish."

"A donkey?" I sputter, laughing loudly.

"Yup. Probably a baby or a miniature one. They have small

donkeys, right? It'll need to fit in Jamie's car. Because there's no way he'd expect a donkey in his car."

"I think the fact that I'm a vet means we probably shouldn't use animals in any sort of revenge plan."

Chelsea huffs. "You're no fun sometimes."

We spend the evening watching *Love is Blind*, and I shoot down idea after idea from Chelsea about how we can figure out if Jamie likes me or not. It was a surprisingly fun night, and it makes me wonder if this is what typical girlfriends do. I didn't have many friends growing up. I was awkward and uncool, and my parents vetoed any potential friendships they didn't approve of. By the time I got to college, I didn't know how to establish a bond with other women. The first time I met Chelsea, she point-blank told me we were going to be best friends. And that was that.

Monday morning, I enter my clinic to see Chelsea with an evil glint in her eyes. "What did you do?"

"Nothing … much," she replies sweetly.

"What on earth does that mean?" I shrug off my coat, hanging it on the hook behind the front desk. Some places might consider the beginning of May to be the start of summer, but in Colorado, we still get cold stretches — and sometimes snow — into the middle of the month. It's cloudy and raining, with a temperature in the upper forties, and that cold just soaks into my bones.

"Well, I may have reached out to our favorite quarterback to request he help move some boxes this morning. You shouldn't leave your phone unlocked when you know I can memorize phone numbers so quickly. And saving him as QB in your phone? So adorable! But it'll help having him here to organize the boxes. You know, because he's so tall. And built. And Jesus — so much better looking in person!" she gushes, her eyes locked on someone behind me.

"Uh, thanks, I guess?" I hear Jamie answer, and my heart skips a beat. While we've certainly kept in touch the last few weeks, I haven't heard his voice. The deep timbre of his voice flows slowly over my skin, and goosebumps pop in its wake. Turning, I almost lose the ability to speak. He's wearing a backwards baseball cap, and glasses. It's simply unfair how hot he really is.

"Hi, Jamie," I say, and his answering smile makes my knees weak.

"Hey, Doc."

"Jesus Christ, I think I just came," Chelsea murmurs behind me, before clearing her throat to speak up. "Thanks for coming in to help. I'm only a couple of inches taller than Audrey, so it's very helpful to have someone a billion feet taller than us."

He chuckles, then winks at me. What the fuck? He winks at me!

"It's no problem. I didn't have anything to do this morning anyway, so it got me out of the house. My cats were beginning to think I'd become one of them," he jokes. "What do you need help with?"

Chelsea points up, and my eyes slowly lift to find box after box of supplies jammed on top of the cabinets. Boxes that absolutely were not up there when I left Friday afternoon. She must have spent all weekend moving things around.

"Why'd you put this stuff up here in the first place?" Jamie asks, grunting as he grabs the first box. An inch of perfect skin is visible as his shirt rides up, and I find myself gaping.

"Close your mouth," Chelsea hisses, but I find her staring as well. A sliver of his underwear is visible, and Chelsea whispers, "Calvin Klein."

I raise one eyebrow at her. How the hell does she know the brand of underwear Jamie is wearing based solely on a tiny bit of fabric?

"You think I've never dated someone butch before? I know male underwear." I can't help the snort that escapes. Chelsea is girly and feminine, always sporting shades of pink dye in her hair and a plethora of nose rings depending on her mood. I've only met a couple of her girlfriends, but I know she enjoys playing the field. Chelsea is a true romantic, and feels when she meets 'the one,' she'll know immediately.

My analytical brain thinks true love is an absolute myth, but who I am to shoot down her hopes and dreams?

"Where do you want the boxes?" Jamie asks, grabbing the last two.

"Oh, uh, over there," Chelsea responds, pointing to the empty space right by the cabinets. Where the boxes originally were.

"Huh." Jamie peers down at the floor, obviously noting the subtle discoloration. "Kinda looks like boxes were already here."

Chelsea laughs loudly, then jumps when the phone rings. "Saved by the bell! Err, phone."

As she dances off to answer the phone, Jamie walks to stand in front of me. He gives me a lopsided smile. "Wanted to see me again that badly, Doc?"

Okay. The nickname should not make me wet, but it does. "I swear I had nothing to do with that. Chelsea must have been in here over the weekend, because that's not where I left the boxes."

His smile dims slightly, then perks up again. "How'd she get my number, anyway?"

"I really have no idea. It's possible she stole it out of my phone Friday night. There was wine involved, and I'm a lightweight. I'm sorry she contacted you out of nowhere. That's such an invasion of privacy, and I know you value your personal life so much."

He reaches up, dragging a finger around my ear, seemingly tucking in a loose strand of hair, and my sharp intake of breath is audible. "It's okay. I'm guessing it was because of something you said. Do you ever wear your hair down?"

"Sometimes," I whisper, captivated as his finger slowly traces down the side of my neck.

"I really want to see it down," he says softly. "May I?"

I nod, aware my tongue has gone numb, and I've lost the ability to speak. As I'm reaching up to take apart my bun, Jamie beats me to it, and I bite back a groan. Every follicle on my head is standing up, screaming for attention, as he slowly unwinds the hair tie. He places the tie on his left wrist, then pushes both hands into my hair. When his fingers hit my scalp, I whimper. I love having my hair played with. When I have trouble sleeping, I watch ASMR videos on social media to relax. But this? This moment beats any sensation I could possibly get from watching a video.

"It's fucking gorgeous, Audrey. You're gorgeous," he whispers, dragging his fingers along the tresses, then slowly wraps the ends around his hands. If he pulls my hair right now, I will beg him to take me somewhere. Anywhere. The damn closet in my office if need be. I am two seconds away from orgasming in my clinic, just because this beautiful man touched my hair.

My eyes dart to his lips, and I watch, captivated, as his tongue slowly sneaks out to lick his bottom lip. Good God. Everything he does is sexy. Does he even realize it? I look at his eyes again, assuming I'll find some kind of victorious or smug expression, but it's not that way at all. Instead, Jamie is looking at me like he wants me, too. Like if I asked him to take me in the closet, he'd gladly do so.

This so complicates things.

"Dr. Carrington?" Chelsea's voice permeates my lust-filled mind, and I recognize the tone. "I'm sorry for the interruption, but we have an emergency."

I look up at Jamie, and he gives me a tender smile. "Go save the world, Doc."

I'm unprepared for him to lean in and place an absentminded kiss against my forehead.

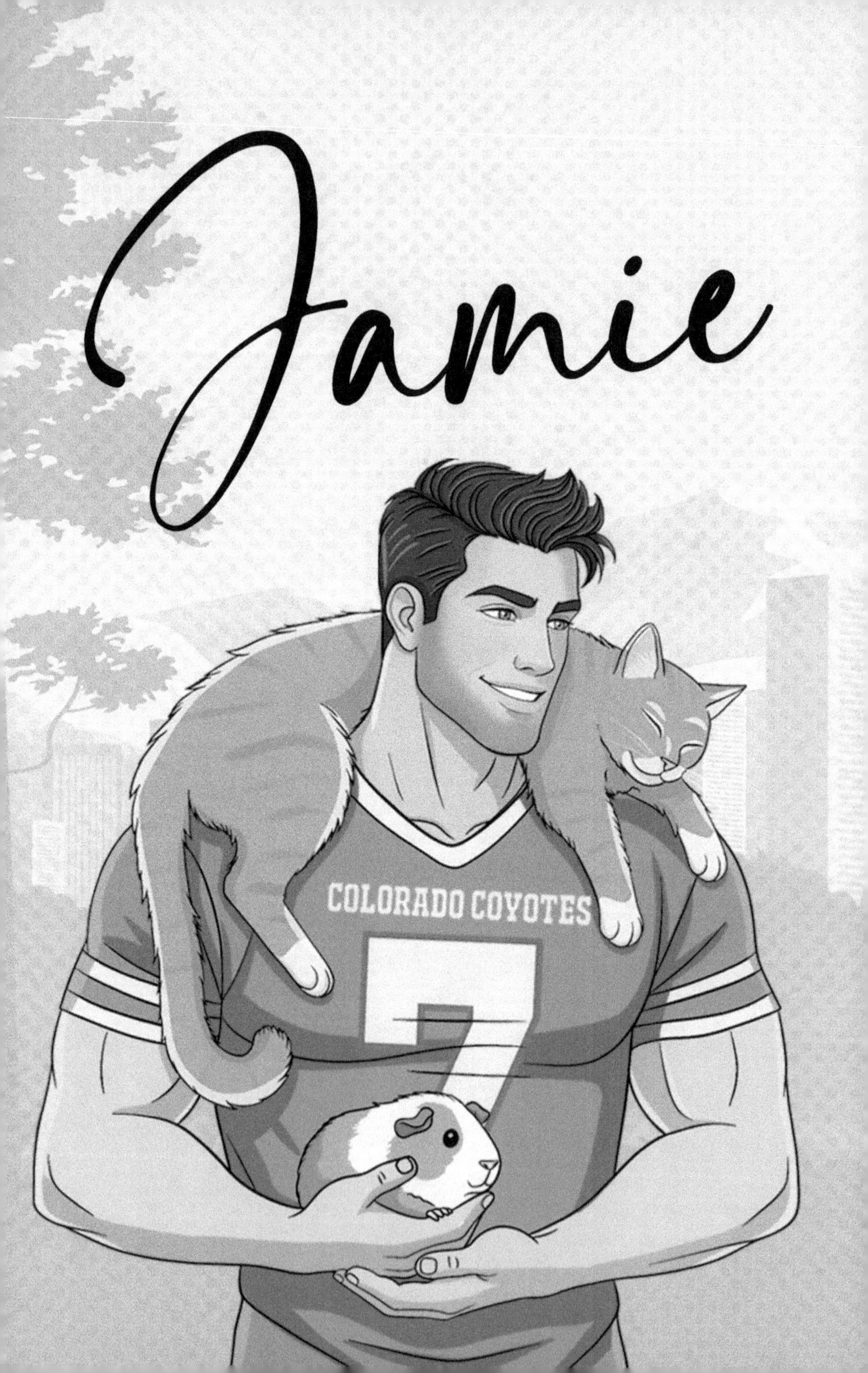

Jamie

CHAPTER 11

I'm thirty-six years old, and I've never kissed a forehead in my life. But I had to kiss … something. I just had to. Holy hell, that was intense. The lust I felt wasn't solely from me. It permeated the air, enveloping us. I'm not sure if Audrey knew she moaned out loud, but I'm sure glad she did. It was incredibly hot.

And even I know that meant she was turned on. Which means she is attracted to me.

I pull up Maddox's contact information as I climb into my car. I don't even give him the time to speak before I shout, "She's into me! She's fucking into me!"

"Christ almighty, QB," he rasps, his voice thick and gravelly. "It's eight in the morning. How the fuck do you know she's into you at this godforsaken hour of the day?"

"I was at her clinic. I did the hair over the ear thing. Then I asked if I could take her hair down from her bun, and she said yes. As soon as my fingers hit her scalp, she moaned. Loudly, I might add. It was hot."

"You're sure it wasn't just a response to physical touch?" he asks.

"I'm sure." I pause. "At least I think I'm sure. Her pupils were blown out. I swear I read somewhere that it means a person is turned on when that happens."

"Or they have a brain tumor," Maddox mutters.

"Let's just stay on the optimistic side and assume it's because she's attracted to me."

"I'm sure that's the reason, man. Who wouldn't be attracted to you? I'm confident enough in myself to say that you're a damn good looking guy. And with that bank account, it would be more concerning if she weren't into you."

"That's the thing, though," I say, turning out of the clinic parking lot as I head toward the Coyotes facilities. "She's not into me for those reasons. I'd even venture to say me being a rich, professional athlete is a negative to her."

"Alright. Well, now what happens? You've still got a few months until the charity event. You gonna put the moves on her, and risk making things awkward for a bit? Or wait it out?"

"Shit," I mumble. "I was so in the moment, I forgot about that. I hate how complicated this is. What should I do?"

"Don't know what to tell you," Maddox says through a yawn. "But I am going to implement a new rule for our friendship, QB."

"What?"

"No relationship breakthroughs before lunchtime. I'm going back to bed." He ends the call with no fanfare, and I chuckle as I head to get an unplanned workout in.

"No."

"I hate that I have to ask you, but my daughter invited me to her graduation party. I've never been truly close with her, so this means a lot that she extended the invitation. But I was already scheduled to attend that gala this weekend. You'd be doing me a huge favor if you went in my place," Coach says, his eyes pleading with me.

I'm regretting coming in for a workout. The high that I felt after leaving Audrey's has dwindled to a flat feeling of nothingness. If I hadn't been here, Coach wouldn't have seen me, and I could have avoided all of this. Because he wants me to escort his niece to the gala.

"I don't feel comfortable with this at all, Coach."

"I know. If I hadn't promised her, I'd send the tickets back."

I sigh, letting my head fall back in frustration. This is only my second season with him. Is he the kind of coach that holds grudges? Would he take it out on me, or the entire team? How can I get out of this without repercussions?

"Can you ask anyone else?" I finally say. "I'm not the best in social situations where I don't have time to prepare. And you're asking me to go with someone I've never met, which means I'll be even more uncomfortable than I already am."

Coach nods. "I know. If it helps, I didn't want to go either. But when Mr. Sanderson hand delivers tickets, I don't think we get a choice."

Martin Sanderson and his family own the Colorado Coyotes, as well as the Albuquerque Scorpions NHL team, and two baseball teams in California. Mr. Sanderson only visits a few times a year, choosing to reside in San Diego, near the San Diego Surge baseball team. His granddaughter, Jordan, manages the day-to-day operations here in Denver.

"Shit," I mutter. "I really don't have a choice, do I?"

Coach exhales loudly, rubbing a hand across his forehead. "I'm choosing to view it as an opportunity for you to grow as a leader, Wahlberg. I'll text you the details, and where you'll need to pick up my niece."

"How old is she?" I ask, visualizing a teenager with braces and acne.

"She's twenty-seven." Great. I can already see how this is going to go, and I want to lay down the law right now.

"You need to make it abundantly clear to her that absolutely nothing will happen between us. We will be cordial and respectful, but there will be no touching, kissing, or anything else."

"Of course not, asshole. I don't want her hooking up with an athlete anyway."

"Alright. Just so we're on the same page. What's her name?"

"Tessa." Coach looks around before stepping closer to me. "Listen. Don't let her drink. She has, on occasion, gotten a little wild when she's been under the influence."

"Dude, I am not babysitting your niece. Tell her not to drink, or I'm leaving her ass there alone."

His eyes widen as his nostrils flare. "I don't appreciate a threat, Jameson. Watch your fucking tone. I'm still your coach, and you better show me some respect."

"Then show me the same respect!" I hiss, anger coursing over me in palpable waves. "You pulled the owner card. That's so messed up. I literally *just* started talking to a woman, and now it's going to look like I'm taking someone else out to a fancy event."

Coach steps back as he studies me. "Really? You've got a girl? Honestly wondered if you were gay, not gonna lie."

I roll my eyes. "You're a funny guy while asking for a favor. Not gay. Just very selective." I begin to walk away from him, wanting to get as far from this conversation as possible. I feel my anxiety rising, and if I don't get out of here, it could spiral into a full-blown panic attack.

"She know you're autistic?" he asks, and I stop dead in my tracks.

"What?" I growl, still facing away from him.

Coach walks around me, lowering his voice. "Does she know you're autistic? And what to expect when you're spiraling? Or when you're overstimulated?"

My body shakes as I struggle to maintain my composure. "As I said, I just started talking to her. So no, my mental health and medical diagnoses have not come up in conversation yet. At this moment, I'm a little more concerned with the fact that you just spewed that out in the middle of the facility, when you know I keep that shit private."

Coach puts up his hands in a defensive stance, his eyes darting around. My gaze follows his, and I should be relieved there's no one around, but I'm not. His eyes are full of pleading, and he scratches at his beard as he leans toward me. "I know. I didn't mean to upset you. I know there are only a few people within the organization who know. I'd *never* blast that out. When you're ready to tell her, we can sit down to work out a plan."

I bleakly nod, suddenly so overcome with fatigue and emotional exhaustion. "It's not cool to announce that shit."

"I apologize. You're absolutely right. I'm sorry, man. I just don't want you to get in over your head with this girl. You're the first genuine person who welcomed me in Denver, and I want to be sure you're surrounded by people who value you like I do." I can hear the sincerity in his voice, but I'm still ticked.

"She's different. I can feel it. If I need your help working out a strategy, I'll let you know. In the meantime, keep my personal business to yourself. You want me blurting out your private business, old man?"

"Noted. But if you call me an old man again, I'll force you to run suicides against me next practice," he calls out as he walks away. "We'll see who the old man really is then."

I'm not dumb. He's in excellent shape, and would beat me by a mile.

I felt drained and out-of-sorts all week. Mentally preparing for this stupid gala with Coach's niece has me stressed and tense, while attempting to maintain composure and not blurt everything out to Audrey is exhausting the hell out of me. How do I explain to someone that I'm escorting a woman I don't want to be with to an event that I don't want to go to? It might sound easy, but I have an unfortunate habit of rambling when I'm extra nervous. It's why I plan responses for everything. I know what reporters will ask. What they'll focus on. I have no idea what Audrey might say, and that scares the hell out of me.

I was close to showing up at her townhouse and confessing, but Maddox talked me out of it. Everything he said was fact. I'm not dating Audrey. We haven't had any discussions about interest on either side. Furthermore, according to Maddox, if we were only dating, I still wouldn't owe her any information unless we'd discussed being exclusive. Besides, he said, it's only one event. I'm definitely not interested in Coach's niece, so I can do my team duty and move on.

But as I'm in the car with Tessa while she talks animatedly about how all her friends are 'so jealous' she's on this 'date' with me, I feel like my head is going to explode.

"This isn't a date," I snap for the third time.

"Hmm?"

"Tessa. This isn't a date. I'm helping your uncle out, and that's it." My driver, Tony, looks back at me through the rearview mirror with a questioning look. I've used him for the last five years for any event where I might have a drink or two. In this instance, I think keeping Tessa out of any of my vehicles is also a good idea. She seems like the type to either memorize my license plate, or put a tracker in my car somewhere.

She lays her hand on my knee, making me recoil. "Jameson, it's fine. I won't tell my uncle we hooked up if you won't."

"Remove your hand," I say quietly through clenched teeth. Her eyes widen, but she does what I've asked. "You will keep your hands to yourself tonight, or I will talk to Coach about how disrespectful you were. This is not a date. There will be no hooking up. Are we clear?"

"Jeez, fine. God," she grumbles. "Would have been nice if he'd asked a player without a giant stick up his ass, but okay."

As we pull up to the venue, I turn to her. "I don't have a stick up my ass. You don't know anything about me. I just prefer to have consent when interacting with a woman. If I touched you when you didn't expect it, or didn't want it, I'd be crucified. Same should be true for me, right?"

"Oh, come on. You're being ridiculous," she scoffs, rolling her eyes. "No professional athlete says no to a hot girl. Not even the married ones."

"That's where you're wrong," I say, as I open the door. "I don't know any married athletes that would say yes to another woman."

A venue employee waits beside a side door, motioning for us to walk through. I had the foresight to call ahead and request we not enter through the front. Many of these events will have some kind of red carpet where local news, and sometimes national publications, will take photos. Not a chance in hell am I allowing one damn picture to be out there of me with this woman. I can already tell Tessa would love her fifteen minutes of fame, probably do interviews herself, and blatantly lie about the entire night.

"Where are the paparazzi?" Tessa asks, proving my point.

"In the front," I answer.

"Why didn't we go in that way?" she pouts.

"Because we aren't here for that. Again, this isn't a date. You clearly aren't here for the charity. I'll introduce you to some teammates once we're inside."

"Really?" she says, her voice much perkier. "Do I get to veto anyone?"

"Nope."

"You know, this is exactly why my uncle chose you. You're boring as fuck."

As we're guided into a large ballroom, I turn to Tessa, lowering my voice. "I won't introduce you to any of my married friends, or anyone in a relationship. I'll introduce you to the single ones who will be fine with a one night stand. Sound good?"

"Maybe I'm interested in a relationship."

I raise an eyebrow at her. "Are you?"

Tessa huffs as she visibly deflates. "No. But I don't like you insinuating I'm a slut."

"You said you wouldn't tell your uncle that we hooked up. At that point, I'd barely said two words to you. You knew nothing about me except for my job, and how I look."

"Well, I'm not a slut." Chin up in defiance, her eyes have a sheen of tears in them, and I immediately feel awful.

"Alright. In the future, don't suggest sex right when meeting someone. And make sure the man shows interest before you touch him." Then I say something I'm even surprised comes out of my mouth. "I don't like being touched unless I know it's coming."

Tessa's mouth drops open. "Seriously? How do you play football? It's all touching!"

"Because I know what to expect then. And I'm desensitized to it after playing it for thirty years. It's a sensory thing."

"Wow. Um, I'm sorry. I didn't know. You're right, I should have been more cognizant of how you might feel about things." In my periphery, I see her chewing on her lip, and her hands are clasped tightly against her abdomen. The facade she wore in the car is gone, and I finally see a young woman who got a little too excited about tonight.

"Thank you for apologizing. Now let's get in there. Coach said there was a silent auction. Did he at least give you his credit card?"

She giggles. "He did. He told me to try and be practical, but that seems like a subjective word. What does practical mean? In the eye of the beholder and all that."

I chuckle as I beckon for her to lead the way. "Let's go spend your uncle's money."

Two hours later, I'm slightly buzzed as I hang with Maddox. Tessa has flitted all around the ballroom, making friends wherever she goes, and has bid on just about every item available. She bid on a Michelin starred restaurant meal for two, a weekend trip to Vail, a hot air balloon ride in Colorado Springs, and a behind-the-scenes brewery tour. I bid on a suite for Wolves games, a vacation home in Aspen, snowboarding lessons, and a set of cooking lessons in your home.

"Does Coach know his niece gets around?" Maddox asks.

"Doubtful. He told me he didn't want her getting with an athlete, but she insinuated I'm not the first one she's been around." I take a long pull off my beer as I relax back against the wall.

"Murray told me about her," he says, referencing one of the defensive ends on our team. "Said he met her out clubbing one night. She only dropped Coach's name after he'd already taken her home."

I wince. "How do we handle this? Tell him point-blank that she's trouble?"

Maddox shrugs. "I don't know. Sure am glad I'm not you, though."

Another one of our friends joins us where we're leaning against a wall. Max Callahan, a recent trade to the Major League Baseball team here, the Rocky Mountain Raptors, sighs as he surveys the room. All glower and growl, Max and I met through our shared agent. "I fucking hate these things."

"Why are you here then?" I ask.

"Because Troy told me to go. The season just started, and fans don't seem to like me."

"Shocking," Maddox drawls, and Max snarls at him. "What? You mean this sunny disposition isn't sitting well with fans?"

"Guess not. It's all bullshit. Fans back in San Diego loved me."

I laugh. "No, they didn't. But they put up with you because you kept hitting home runs."

"And you haven't hit one here yet," Maddox adds, before looking at me. "Isn't there some kind of thing about balls going farther in high altitude?"

"That is true," I answer. "But our boy Max here hasn't actually made contact with the ball yet."

"Dayum," Maddox whistles. "You ever gone a month without an RBI, Maxy?"

"No," Max growls, "and don't even think for one second you can call me Maxy."

I hear a high-pitched cackle, and turn to see where it came from. "Crap. Does she look drunk to you? I told her not to get wasted. Coach even told her not to drink."

"This isn't a good look," Maddox murmurs. We all push off the wall, silently on the same page as we stride toward where Tessa hangs on Damian Scott, a rookie on the basketball team. Damian looks less than thrilled with the situation, but Tessa is blissfully clueless. Multiple empty glasses are scattered on the table, but Damian holds a longneck bottle of Coors in his hand. My assumption that Tessa is drunk is most likely correct.

"Tessa," I say sharply, when we reach them. Her glazed eyes slowly meet mine. "Remember what I said about confirming consent before touching someone?"

"Oh, Heyyyy! It's my favorite ass stick!" she exclaims happily.

Brow furrowed, I stare at her. "Your what?"

"Ass stick. Stick ass. Something. I don't know. You got something so far up your butt you can't loosen up. Hence, the asssss stick." Suddenly, she gasps. "Oh my God! Are you gay? Do you *like* the ass stick?"

"Jesus Christ," Maddox mutters behind me, as Damian muffles a snicker.

I am not amused. "Not gay, Tessa. Just not interested in you."

"Well!" she harrumphs. "I'll have you know I'm a fucking tiger in bed, Mr. Ass Stick Ass. You wouldn't even know what to do with me. I could rock. Your. Fucking. World." She pokes my chest hard with every word, her entire body swaying.

"Okay, I think it's time for you to —" I say, but I'm interrupted.

"Excuse me."

I look over my shoulder to find a couple looking very displeased. "I'm getting her out of here."

"Yes, well, you should leave too. We don't need your kind making a mockery of this entire event," the man says with a sneer as he glares at us. How a man five inches shorter than me manages to look down his nose at me, I'll never understand.

"Our kind?" Maddox growls.

"The fuck?" Max adds.

"Yes. Your kind. Please leave."

Tessa takes the opportunity to grab onto the lapels of my tuxedo jacket. "Oh, please. The only reason there are cameras here is because of these guys, you dusty old fuckers."

The couple gasp in outrage. "The disrespect!"

Tessa cackles again, and I notice many heads turning our way. "We'll leave, it's fine."

"No!" Tessa shouts, teetering in her stilettos, and she grabs onto my shirt. "They are the dissspectful ones. They need to 'pologize to *you*. No one dissspects my man!"

Fuck me.

Can this get any worse?

Yes. Yes, it can.

Because the next thing I hear absolutely stops my heart.

"Jamie? You have a girlfriend?"

Audrey

CHAPTER 12

I'd just been thinking about him. Wondering what he might be up to tonight. Imagining what it might be like to attend an event like this, with my family in attendance, on his arm. I should know better than to allow myself even a moment of dreaming. My life has always been carefully held between my own realistic boundaries, and had I stuck to my guns, I wouldn't feel the way I do right now.

I know I have no claim to Jamie. He's a professional athlete. A celebrity. Way too many forums and websites devoted to ogling him. I'm just … me. Normal. Nowhere near as tiny as the stick figure hanging on him. If that's his type, then I'm definitely not.

"Audrey," he whispers, a panic stricken expression covering his gorgeous face. The perfectly fitted black tux seems to make his blue eyes even brighter, and I so desperately want to know how his scruff feels against my skin.

"Do you know this man?" Mom asks, a sneer on her overly made-up face. While she definitely wears too much makeup, my mother has always known how to dress. Her gold-beaded Oscar de la Renta dress only offers a hint of cleavage, and it pops against my father's burgundy suit. I don't know many men who can get away with burgundy, but my dad can. Then again, it may just be the fact that he can pay virtually anything for designers to outfit him. Anything for appearances.

Between the two of them, I look like an adopted child. While I know I look remarkably good tonight, after finding the most amazing Alexander McQueen silk taffeta dress in a deep navy color that suits my complexion perfectly, I stare at Jamie's date in sheer awe. Bronze skin on mile-long legs. A pale blue dress with a slit up to mid-thigh … and her arms tightly around Jamie's waist. That's the part that I can't rip my eyes away from.

"Audrey," Mom snaps, finally drawing my attention away from the train wreck of my life happening right in front of me.

"I'm sorry," I answer automatically. Clearing my throat, I make the introductions. "Mother. Father. This is Jameson Wahlberg. He's the quarterback for the Colorado Coyotes football team, and we've both been tasked with organizing the charity event I help spearhead every year."

In most worlds, hearing that the man in front of you is a celebrated NFL quarterback would make most people light up. It seems to displease my parents even more. I can almost hear their internal monologues right now. An athlete? How gauche. Uneducated. New money. Beneath us.

My eyes dart to Jamie's face, and I find he still looks shell-shocked. "Are you okay? Are you going to get sick?"

My mother immediately retreats with a gasp. I hear her mumble under her breath, "Absolutely appalling behavior."

"Oh my God," his date giggles. "Can you even imagine? Don't you dare puke, Jameson. My shoes are Louboutins."

I can't help but screw my face up in distaste. I can clearly see Jamie is incredibly uncomfortable. Then again, I guess I don't know him well enough at all. Not even a week ago, I thought he might kiss me, and he's been dating someone all along? Typical.

"Audrey," he whispers again. "This isn't — I mean, it's not what you think."

I chuckle sardonically. "Wow. That's the wonderful metaphor you're going with? Lovely."

"I swear. Please," he says, clearing his throat. "Please believe me. I've never lied to you."

I watch as his date tries to wind her arms around him again, but he shifts, taking a step toward me. I put up both hands, forcing him to stop. "No. Don't take another step. You don't owe me any explanation. We're nothing."

Jamie grabs the back of his neck in distress. "I don't believe that to be true. You know me, Audrey. You know *me*."

I shake my head as tears fill my eyes. As I turn away from him, I whisper, "I don't know you at all."

Head held high, I quickly walk from the ballroom, only hearing my father demand that Jamie and his date leave. I rush to the elevators, happy when one opens immediately. I hear Jamie chasing after me, but I only catch a glimpse of him as the doors close. His eyes are full of pain, but pain for what? For me? For being caught? For getting kicked out of the event?

I fall against the wall as the first tear cascades down my cheek. Bending down, I remove my shoes, ready to run to my room as soon as the doors open on the forty-third floor. I'd only agreed to stay in the hotel tonight because my parents paid for the room. At over two thousand dollars a night, it's not something I'd splurge on. I'm frugal to a fault, but even I can recognize the luxury of a beautiful hotel with breathtaking views of the Rocky Mountains. I didn't even realize I'd gotten a deluxe suite until I got here, and there was a note on the reservation telling me I'd been gifted a spa treatment as well. I never give myself things like massages or manicures, so I considered this weekend to be a perfect treat.

When I woke up this morning, a foreboding feeling swelled in my stomach. I'd felt off all week, and hindsight tells me it was because Jamie acted differently as soon as he left my clinic. I'd felt something with him. Something remarkable. Sizzling. Eye-opening. And while I thought I saw those same thoughts in his eyes, obviously I was wrong. His texts all week were more formal. Fairly distant. I chalked it up to me overthinking things, and allowed myself to dip my toes in the dreamland of what if's. What if he did feel attracted to me? What would it be like to kiss him? How would I feel dating him? Sleeping with him? Falling in love with him?

As I reach my room, I hear the ping of an elevator opening behind me, and male voices make me hurry to pull my key card out of my bra to scan it on the lock. I barely close the door before I hear the pounding of feet as someone jogs down the hallway. Tiptoeing from the door, I reach the bedroom as someone knocks. "Audrey? I know you're in there."

Wait. That wasn't Jamie's voice.

Turning, I stare at the door. I shouldn't open it. I know that. But curiosity is getting the better of me, and I slink back to peer out the peephole.

It's one of the men Jamie was with. I know he's a football player, but I can't remember his name. Mason? Marcell? Maceo? Something with an M. He looks down at the ground as his hands bracket the doorframe.

"I can hear your dress rustling around, Audrey. Might as well open the door." Well, shit. You'd think a luxury hotel wouldn't have thin doors where he can hear clothing movement, but seeing as how public restrooms in this country have huge gaps between stalls, I guess I shouldn't be that surprised. In any case, I stay still and silent, waiting for him to leave. It's a good five minutes before he speaks. "Listen. My name is Maddox. Jamie is my best friend. I've known him a while, and I can tell you with absolute certainty that you've got it all wrong. He really is a good guy, and you should give him a chance."

I can't help myself. "I know nothing about him, and we don't owe each other anything. We're just planning an event. That's all."

Maddox chuckles. "We both know that's not true."

"I don't know anything right now. Please just let me be alone. Don't tell him what room I'm in."

"I won't. That girl downstairs? Not his. It's our coach's niece. Coach was supposed to escort her tonight, but went out of town. He begged Jamie to bring her, mostly because he knows Jamie is the most stand-up guy on the team, and he wouldn't mistreat her.

But I think you should give him a chance. Jamie is … different. But not in a bad way. He's unique, loyal, and genuine. You'd be missing out."

"Considering he had a woman wrapped around him not even five minutes ago, I think we'll have to disagree on that one," I whisper. "Please leave."

A piece of paper whooshes under the door. "She's not his woman, but I don't think you're going to hear that right now. That's my number. Just in case you ever need it. I'll leave now. I'm sorry, Audrey. Think about it. He's worth it. Give him a chance to explain."

"Explain what? You just explained it all."

"Explain … him. There's a lot about Jamie you don't know."

I turned off my phone and took a very long soak in the massive tub in my suite. I almost ordered room service, but felt the best idea was for me to stay holed up in my room without opening the door again. Thankfully, I packed a couple of granola bars in my bag, and that was my dinner.

In the morning, I woke before sunrise, sneaking out to drive to Chelsea's apartment, where Flash spent the night. I worried Jamie would be at my townhouse, and just couldn't bear to see him. Yet. I know I'll have to eventually, but my mind is too jumbled up to handle a coherent conversation right now.

One problem I have with autism is the fact that I need two to three business days to deal with confrontations. I don't like them, and I struggle to prepare myself for the other person. Right now, my thoughts and emotions are all over the place. I need time.

Chelsea and I have keys to each other's places, and I quietly let myself in. She's not the best in the morning, and I figure I can butter her up with a fresh pot of coffee before I tell her everything.

I walk quietly into her kitchen, starting her coffee machine, then go to open Flash's cage. Yes, my dog has a kennel at my best friend's house. I trust her implicitly.

Flash yawns, then yips, as I unlock her kennel. "Hi, sweet girl. Did you miss Mommy?"

I know. I'm gross with animals. They're all my babies, even the ones that are only in my care for an hour.

I carefully pick her up, then pull her wheelchair over to strap her in. We quietly head to the door so she can go potty. Flash is very fortunate that she still has control over her bladder and bowels, although she has accidents at times. She loves to feel the grass under her paws, and the wind across her fur. I often find her sniffing the breeze, eyes closed, enjoying the moment. This morning is no exception.

I sense Chelsea before I see her. "Did I wake you?"

"It's weird when you do that," she says, her voice raspy. I look over my shoulder to find her rubbing sleep from her eyes, a robe haphazardly hung on her thin frame, but a steaming cup of coffee gripped tightly in her left hand. The mug she chose is black, with the words 'gay by birth, proud by choice' in a rainbow ombre, and it's one I gave her a few years ago. As soon as I saw it, I knew she had to have it. Chelsea's parents didn't accept her coming out, and it broke her for quite some time. I, however, wanted her to know I loved her exactly as she was. "I guess I shouldn't say anything, because I didn't hear you at all. Just knew you were here."

"What did you call us once? Platonic life partners?"

She nods. "I sometimes wonder if I am the love of your life. You can only be so lucky as to get a piece of this amazing ass."

"It's your modesty," I reply, deadpan. "It's so attractive. I can't fight the pull to you anymore."

Chelsea yawns. "Give me a few more sips of caffeine, then you can give me the gossip."

"Who says there is gossip?"

She gives me a look of disinterest. "You showed up here on a Sunday morning before sunrise. I know there's gossip. I'm not alert enough to think of which sibling of yours started something at the event."

"Neither of them did anything," I say with a sigh.

"Your parents?"

"Nope. Well, kinda. But not on purpose."

Chelsea studies me. "This can't be good."

"No, it's not," I reply, then watch as she takes a large gulp of the coffee. "I don't think that was a good choice."

"It's fine," she says hoarsely, pounding her breastbone a few times. "I'll be fine. Get the dog and get inside. I'm awake."

Thirty minutes later, Chelsea stares at me in disbelief. "Jamie. The quarterback? Who looked like he was ready to mount you in the exam room on Monday, had a girl wrapped around him on Saturday?"

I nod.

"And Martin —"

I interrupt. "Maddox."

She swivels her hand in the air nonchalantly. "Whatever. He said the girl isn't Jamie's girl, but some kind of good deed he was doing for their coach?"

"Yep."

"And you haven't spoken to Jamie at length about it yet?"

"No. You know I can't do that. I need time to decompress and work out all the details first."

"Do you think Jamie was on a date?" she asks.

I shut my eyes tightly, hating the image that pops into my head. Him looking so dapper and beautiful in his tux, and her climbing him like a damn spider monkey. "They looked perfect together. Like she was just his type."

"You don't know his type, Aud," Chelsea says softly. "You're assuming based on a lot of factors here, none of which come from the man himself."

"All I know is what I've seen with my own two eyes, and everything that Google has told me. A quick search of 'Jameson Wahlberg girlfriend' brings up quite a few women, and exactly zero of them look a thing like me. And I know it's ridiculous of me to believe Google, because the Internet isn't always the truth, but my own history says that men lie." I don't realize I'm crying until a tear drops onto my hand. I'm not the crying type, and I've cried more in the past twelve hours than I have in the past year.

"Aud," Chelsea says quietly, "I think you need to give him a chance to explain. If for no other reason than getting closure so you two can plan this event."

"I feel so stupid," I whisper.

"Why?"

"Because I let myself believe. That maybe we could be something."

"Why do you think you can't be something now?"

I shrug. "I don't think I fit into his world. The only reason I was there tonight was because my parents forced me to be there. Had it been for any other organization, I wouldn't have gotten an invite. But Jamie can show up wherever, and he'll be let in. He'll have an entourage, sign autographs, and every woman in the room will wonder what he's like in bed. I doubt myself on an hourly basis, Chels. I'd never be able to confidently be on his arm."

"Audrey," she whispers, pain and sympathy etched into her face. "I wish you could see how truly amazing you are. I hate that you think you'd just be an ornament for him, because I know you'd steal the show. I can only hope that Jamie is the guy that recognizes your worth too, and he'll patiently help you build up the confidence you need to walk beside him."

I shake my head. A quick moment, a blip in time, is bringing back every bad memory of my life. Ridiculed for my weight. Mocked for my love of animals. Mocked for misjudging a social situation. It's dumping on me, wave after wave of depression, sadness, and emotional trauma. "I'm not ready to face any of that."

"Okay, sweetie," Chelsea says patiently. "Why don't you take a nap? I know you, and I bet you didn't sleep much at all last night."

"I didn't," I whisper. She moves off the couch, handing me a blanket. "Is it okay if I stay here tonight? I don't want to go home. Just in case he — he knows where I live. I'm not ready to face him."

"Okay. Just sleep for now. We'll figure it out when you're rested."

Shit. The guinea pigs. "Wait! I need to go home. The piggies —"

Chelsea interrupts me with a devilish grin. "I'll go feed them this evening. I can be sneaky and quiet. The QB won't even know I'm there."

As Chelsea quietly walks into her kitchen, I ball up the blanket, holding it tightly to my chest. It relieves a tiny bit of the ache, but not much. I fall into a deep, dreamless sleep, but wake no closer to a resolution than before.

I sleep on and off throughout the day on Chelsea's couch, content to ignore the world from my own little self-imposed bubble. If I wasn't the only vet at my clinic, I'd be tempted to call in sick Monday, but I can't let my clients down. I've used a traveling veterinarian to fill in for me a couple of times, but it's always been for more valid reasons than now. Plus I'm pretty sure Chelsea would kill me if she had to handle everything in my absence.

Bright and early Monday morning, I head back to my townhouse. I need to shower and get ready for the day, and I want to spend some time with the pigs. I feel guilty for leaving them alone this long. I'm thankful I don't have any appointments for a couple of hours, so I can work on focusing my attention and emotions. Since I typically spend an hour on Sunday afternoons doing a little meal prep for the week, I guess this week's lunches will be a free-for-all.

As I turn into my complex, I have a perfect view of the front of my townhouse … and the large quarterback currently slumped against the front door.

Jamie

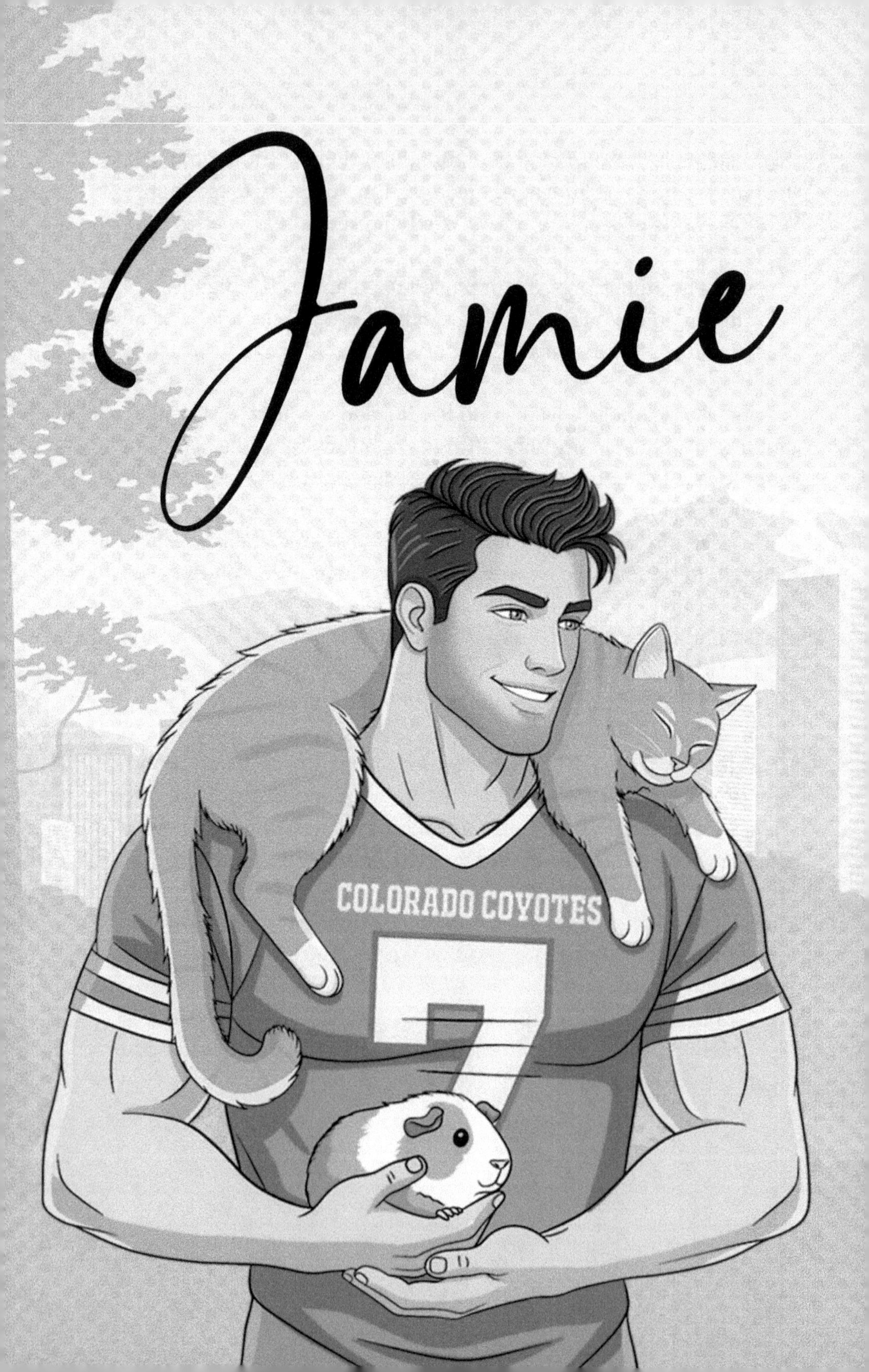

CHAPTER 13

As soon as I saw the headlights, I knew it was Audrey. I figured she went elsewhere to avoid me, but didn't know what else to do. So I've been sitting here for over twenty-four hours. I've gotten up occasionally, especially when my ass has completely fallen asleep, and to grab a delivery order of food. I also really hope Audrey doesn't have any hidden cameras anywhere, because I took a whizz in her shrubs. But if she does have a camera, oh well. It was pee in a bush, or leave, and I wasn't leaving.

I watch as Audrey drives around the building to her attached garage, holding a hand to the side of her face in an attempt to disguise herself. Great job, Doc. I really didn't know it was you.

I wait a few moments, listening hard to hear when she is inside her home, but there's hardly any noise. I suddenly hear a crash, a yip, and a muffled, 'shit.' I guess she's home now, so I begin ringing the doorbell. Incessantly.

More yips and barks ensue, and I can't help but grin. Looks like Flash is on my team. After a few moments of ringing the doorbell, Audrey yells, "Any chance you are going to stop?"

"No."

"At least you're honest."

"I'm not a good liar."

"Isn't that something a good liar would say?" she asks.

"I don't know. Maybe? I've never asked someone if they're a good liar or not." She's probably right. No one will admit they excel at lying.

"How do I know if you're telling the truth?"

I sigh, resting my head against the door. "I think it's a leap of faith. You're going to have to trust me."

It's a long moment before she responds, her voice much closer than before. "I don't like when things are up in the air. I want black and white."

"I know. I'd like to explain, if you'll let me."

It's silent, and my heart begins to beat so loudly I can't hear anything else but the sound of my own blood rushing through my veins and arteries. If Audrey said anything, I'm not sure I would have heard her, so I'm thrilled when she tentatively opens the door. Her beautiful hair is in a messy bun, and she's wearing an old Denver Wolves tee shirt and leggings. She has Flash in her arms, but I can't focus on the sweet pup, because Audrey's eyes are swollen and red.

I made her cry, and I don't know how to rectify that.

Waiting until she sits down on her couch, I sit beside her, but far enough away that I'm not crowding her space. It also keeps me from reaching out to touch her. I'm not a handsy guy, but my fingers positively itch to feel her skin. I want to know if her heart beats as fast as mine when we're near one another. I hear a muffled squeak, and my body tightens. "Were the pigs alone all weekend?"

"No," Audrey sighs. "Chelsea fed them Saturday night, and then she snuck over yesterday to feed them again. She came in through my garage."

"Okay," I begin, suddenly aware that I planned absolutely nothing to say. Sitting against her front door for twenty-four hours, and I should have had enough time to memorize a monologue. How unfocused was I that I didn't even hear Chelsea inside

Audrey's house? Jesus. And now I'm hit with the most intense wave of stage fright I've ever experienced.

"Yes?" Audrey prompts.

"Shit," I murmur. "Audrey, I'm really bad with words. I'm probably going to butcher this. But that girl Saturday night was my coach's niece. He went out of town to his daughter's college graduation, and his niece was hellbent on still going to the event. He asked me to escort her. I told him that he better make it clear to her there would be no romance at all, and I drilled that point in when she put her hands on me in the car on the way over."

"She put her hands on you?" Audrey asks, her eyes darkening. I have a moment where a spark of hope lights in my heart. If the roles were reversed, I'd be furious if someone touched Audrey without her consent. Surely this has to mean I still have a fighting chance, right?

"Yes. Well, probably not in the way you're thinking. She put her hand on my knee, but I put the kibosh on it immediately. I'm a big proponent of consent. It's why I asked you if I could touch your hair. I have … challenges with being touched when I'm not ready for it. When I don't expect it."

"That makes sense," Audrey replies slowly, her eyes darting between Flash and me. "What I don't understand is why she was wrapped around you, and why you didn't tell me immediately what was going on."

I rub my forehead, feeling a tension headache coming on. Snoozing on concrete on a cold May night probably didn't help. "I forgot that Coach told me to make sure she didn't drink. Evidently she gets …" I trail off, searching for the word to describe Tessa's behavior from Saturday night, "I guess she gets pretty wild when she drinks. When that old couple came over —"

Audrey interrupts me. "My parents."

I wince. "Yeah. You have the same nose as your mom, but other than that, you're nothing like them. I never would have expected that connection."

"How can you say that when you don't know them? You barely know me."

"I've met them a couple of times at events, Aud. But I know enough about you to know you're warm. And comforting. Your heart is full, and you want to bring joy to every animal you meet. You found a box of guinea pigs and ended up adopting all of them. You're a good person, Aud. And one meaningless interaction with your parents told me that they aren't the kind of people I want to be around. I'm sorry if that upsets you, but it's how I feel."

She tilts her head as she studies me, and I notice one corner of her lips has turned up the tiniest bit. "I guess that does tell me you're as honest as you claimed. I still don't know why you didn't tell me right then."

Bracing my elbows on my knees, I drop my head into my hands, closing my eyes as a bit of word vomit spews out. "For a variety of reasons. I'm not good with confrontation in public. I think I've been trained to be perfect in front of the media, and it's spilled over into my personal life. And I may not like your parents, but they still scare the hell out of me. Plus, I was definitely speechless because you looked so damn phenomenal in that dress that I couldn't breathe, and all I wanted to do was take you in my arms and kiss you."

When Audrey doesn't make a sound, I continue. "But it's not like I could kiss you in front of your parents, right? And then I've got this psychotic chick hanging on me, and I'm thinking about how my coach is probably going to murder me when he hears about everything. I'm trying to come up with a plan that allows me to drop the girl and throw you over my shoulder, all the while keeping your parents from also murdering me, but the thought of you being on my shoulder made me think about your ass, and I'm pretty sure all the blood went to my dick at that point, and I couldn't focus on much else other than trying to keep it from making an appearance."

For fuck's sake. Not many men would admit to a woman they're attracted to that they couldn't speak because they were willing a boner to go down, yet here we are. I wait for the inevitability of Audrey announcing that I need to get the hell out, and am therefore incredibly unprepared when she bursts into peals of laughter.

"My parents absolutely hated you," she cackles. "When I turned my phone back on before letting you in, I had at least fifteen texts from my mother complaining about you. You made a spectacle at our event. You're not invited back. It's all my fault, even though I didn't know you'd be attending."

My heart drops into my stomach as I lift my head to stare at Audrey. "Your event?"

"Yeah, I thought you knew. It's my family's gala."

"Your parents donate to charity?" I blurt out.

"Yes, but nowhere near as much as other events and non-profits. It's all for appearances. They donate what they have to. Gotta keep up the charade like they actually care about the less fortunate."

"I didn't even see what the charity is for. Usually I do a lot of research about events, but I didn't this time, because I was so pissed I even had to go. What's the charity for?"

Audrey snorts. "Homelessness! As if either of my parents would ever help the homeless in real life. I bet they'd run over someone for a hundred bucks."

We're both quiet for a few minutes, an awkward lull that makes me feel uncomfortable and unsettled. I rub two fingers together, hoping the stimming sensation will help to calm my rapid heartbeat.

"Audrey, where does that leave us?" I ask, my social filter apparently having left the building some time ago. "I'm laying it all on the line here. I want to date you. And kiss you. And tell my friends about you. But if you're not on the same page, tell me now."

Her eyes dart between mine as she bites her bottom lip, and I resist the urge to pull it from beneath her teeth. "I don't know."

Well, fuck.

"I like you too, Jamie. But our worlds are very different. If Saturday night was any indication of what you deal with fairly often, I'm not sure I'm strong enough to handle that. I made the mistake of Googling you —"

I interrupt her. "Please don't believe everything you read on the Internet."

She gives me a tentative half smile as she continues. "I didn't read anything, but the pictures spoke a thousand words. I'm nothing like the type you regularly date."

"I don't regularly date anyone. And I don't have a type."

"Almost every picture of you at events had you with a statuesque blonde, much like the girl from Saturday. It's pretty hard to imagine anything with you, when I look like … this," she says, dragging her hand up and down her body.

"I think you're stunning," I tell her passionately. "I want to memorize your curves. And most of those women? I probably met them that night, much like this weekend. My agent would work out agreements with models, influencers, and actresses to accompany me to things. It was good publicity for both of us. I'd never say I'm only attracted to blondes, or I only like thin women. There are so many different factors that go into attraction for me."

"I'm scared," she blurts out.

"Why?"

"People will talk. You'll get a lot of backlash, and I'm scared you'll ghost me when you realize how much bad publicity it brings. If you can bring a skinny girl to an event for good publicity, dating a fat one can be the opposite."

"I don't ever want to hear you call yourself fat again," I command, watching as Audrey stills completely. "You are the definition of voluptuous. You're curvy. Every inch of you is spectacular. Do you want to know what it's like hugging a tiny actress? Or fucking a model who only eats less than five hundred calories a day? It actually hurts, Doc. They're all sharp angles and bones. That girl this weekend? I wasn't attracted to her at all. I'd never fantasize about her body like I have about yours. I'd never dream about falling asleep with my head against her breasts, but I sure have had that recurring dream about you."

I watch as a blush creeps up Audrey's neck, onto her cheeks, and her eyes darken almost imperceptibly. Her breathing has increased, and I wonder if her heart is beating as quickly as mine. I've never spoken to a woman like this. In all honesty, I've never had to. Being a professional athlete means women are all too eager to jump into bed with me, and I don't have to try very hard to get them on board.

But the thing is, I want to try with Audrey. I want her to know how desirable she is. How much I think about her. That I want to build up her confidence by worshiping every delectable inch of her body until she's screaming my name. I'm not sure if I've ever been as turned on like this. I'm almost vibrating with need.

"Jamie," she whispers, her eyes hooded and dark with lust. "Will you … please. I need you to kiss me."

I don't answer her. I don't have to. Grabbing hold of her wrist, I yank her forward until her body crashes against mine. A millisecond before my lips cover hers, I feel the relieved exhale from her, and I know I feel the same way. The moment our lips touch, I'm a goner. It's like I didn't know how much I needed this until right now. The room spins, and goosebumps erupt across my body.

Sliding an arm around Audrey's waist, I maneuver her into my lap, her legs straddling mine. As she sighs against me, I take the opportunity to slip my tongue into her mouth. Her taste explodes onto my tongue, and the velvety smoothness is a soothing balm on my soul. I skirt one hand under her shirt, up her spine, and the other slides into her hair at the base of her skull. She whimpers, her thighs clamping down as she searches for friction, and I groan as she provides perfect pressure against the length of my rigid cock.

I've never been huge into kissing. Maybe it's a sensory thing, or perhaps it's another random autistic characteristic where I can't enjoy the kiss because my mind whirls on about germs, tastes, and other ridiculous things. Right now, though, I feel like I could keep kissing Audrey forever. As her fingernails scratch my neck and scalp, I'm all too present and engaged in this kiss.

This isn't what I expected from Audrey. I only wanted her to hear me out, and state my case for why I think we should explore our connection. But this? This explosive chemistry? It's beyond anything I could have ever predicted. We have to explore this. I can't leave here with things up in the air. I have to convince Audrey to give me a chance.

A loud bark, and responding cacophony of squeaks, forces us to break apart. Both panting, Audrey rests her forehead against mine as we catch our breaths.

"Wow," we say simultaneously. I open my eyes to find hers glassy and unfocused, her lips swollen and rosy. I slide my hand from her hair, letting it drift across her neck. My thumb finds her bottom lip, stroking it softly.

Flash barks again from her bed in the corner, but I can't tear my eyes from Audrey's. She's so beautiful, and I need to tell her. Instead, what comes out is, "You have three freckles on the tip of your nose, and two under your left eye."

Her eyes widen. "I know. I just can't believe you noticed them."

I shrug. "I notice things like that."

"I never liked wearing sunscreen growing up. It's too sticky. While there's a genetic component to freckles, they are mostly due to UV exposure from the sun."

"I like them. Your freckles, I mean," I blurt out. My hand drags up and down her spine, and I find I enjoy the sensation against my fingers. "They make you unique. And I agree about sunscreen being sticky, but I'm in the sun too often during football season, so I have to wear it. I've found some that aren't as sticky. I can give you a recommendation, if you want."

She shudders. "I don't think I could do it. It's all I could think about the times I was forced to wear it. I had originally thought about working in a zoo or animal rehab facility, and I think part of the reason I went into veterinary medicine was because it would involve being indoors most of the time."

Flash barks again. "I got used to it. I'm sure I had a few melt-downs as a kid, though. It's tough getting over sensory challenges."

Audrey nods, and her eyes seem to change. Like our conversation is bringing forth a new dawn. Her lips hint at a smile, and she bites her bottom lip bashfully. The same lip I just stroked. "I have lots of sensory challenges."

"Me too," I answer tentatively. "I also struggle with saying things at the wrong time."

"Sometimes I can't read a room."

"Or see a social cue?"

"Yeah," she says, her eyes sharpening on mine. "And I'm really bad with confrontations."

"I don't do well with messes," I confess. "Things have a place, and if that gets messed up, I can't move on until I correct everything."

"I have areas that are really organized, then parts of my life are in complete disarray. I can ignore a huge pile of crap, but the placemat being crooked on the table will set me off."

"I don't like to be touched," I blurt out. Audrey's eyes widen in horror as she attempts to scurry out of my lap. "No! Wait. I didn't explain that correctly. I don't like it when people touch me without knowing if I want to be touched. Or without my consent. I very much want you on me right now, Doc, so don't you dare move."

The relieved smile that covers her face is blinding. "Will you tell me if I ever step over one of your boundaries? Sometimes I struggle to read body language, so I hope you'll trust that you can be honest with me."

"Will it hurt your feelings if I ever say I need some space? Sometimes I need a moment to reset." I wait with bated breath for her response, fearful of her answer.

"I'm not sure. I've never been in a similar situation, so I don't know how I'll feel. I might be hurt initially, Jamie, but I hope I'll be able to see things from your perspective too. When you need space, is it due to certain things? Like overstimulation?" she asks quietly.

I nod. "Yes. Also when I'm overly exhausted, or really stressed."

She takes a deep breath, her eyes dropping to my neck. "I want to ask you a question, and I hope you know I'm genuinely interested in the answer. Okay?"

Before she asks, I know. I see it in her eyes. She's asking me the big question. My hands drop to her waist, gripping her tightly, both excited and fearful of her response. "Ask away."

"Jamie, are you autistic?" Her eyes are focused on mine, zeroed in on my reaction, and I can't find the words to answer. Instead, I just nod. I expect quiet reflection, or an attempt to dislodge herself from my grip. I definitely never thought she'd grin widely as she says, "I thought so. I'm autistic, too."

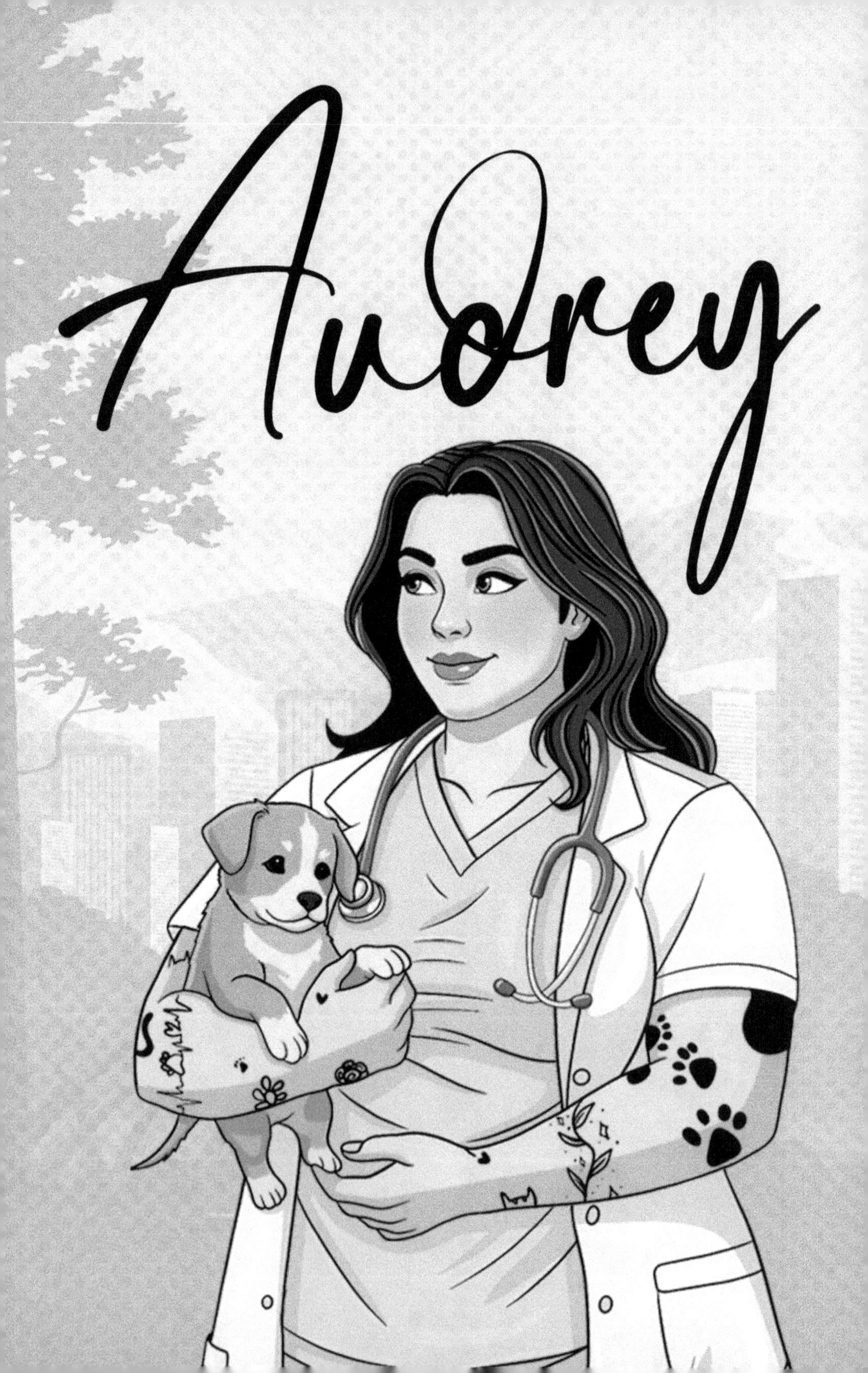

Audrey

CHAPTER 14

It's possible I've never been as happy as I am at this very moment.

I knew something seemed familiar about Jamie, but I couldn't put my finger on it. As a neurodiverse woman, sometimes I can see people who have similar personalities, or traits that I recognize. But other times, I'm so in my own head that I can't recognize anything outside of my tiny bubble.

I've never heard a word about Jamie being autistic. Neurodiversity is almost a four-letter word in professional sports, it seems. Hardly anyone talks about it. I'm sure there are other autistic men in sports, simply from a data perspective. I'd Googled it once out of curiosity. The CDC estimates under four percent of men are autistic. With almost seventeen hundred men on NFL rosters across the country, that means an average of fifty men are autistic, give or take. When adding in the number of coaches, trainers, medical professionals, and management, that number is bound to increase.

Honestly, I felt a connection to Jamie from our first interaction. Now knowing he's autistic, it explains why I thought all of his media interviews were too perfect. He probably memorizes most of what he says. It's somewhat refreshing to know that some of the same strategies I use in my everyday life, Jamie uses in his, even if our careers are nothing alike. I imagine the media are given a set list of questions they're allowed to ask as well.

As I look at Jamie now, sheer terror is evident in his eyes, and I can feel his heart beating incredibly fast against my chest. I'm sitting in his lap, refusing to move, and I've never felt more at home before.

"Not many people know, do they?" I ask quietly, and he shakes his head. "Why?"

Jamie sighs. "I've never liked talking about my personal life. Telling the world I'm neurodiverse is definitely a massive step into my private life. And my agent thinks it'll impact my reach everywhere else. He thinks it'll snowball into my charity not getting as many donations, and it'll scare away potential brand deals."

"Do you care about the brand deals?" I ask warily. I don't like that he's hiding his true self because of money, but I bite my tongue.

"No, I couldn't care less about them. But I donate a ton of that income to a variety of charities, as well as school districts in Oregon, Florida, and here. I have ownership in a variety of things, courtesy of my brand and sponsorship deals over the past fifteen years as well. Any leftover income goes into investments that I'll use down the road for donating to charities and shelters."

I stare at him in shock, my mouth slightly open. "Does anyone know you do that? I've never heard about you donating to schools."

He shrugs. "I keep all of it private. Even my foundation is under a different name, and the website keeps it all very hush-hush."

"Your agent is listed as a donor, too. Am I really the only one who has figured it out?"

He nods. "I'm not sure I even realized my agent is listed on the website as a donor. But anyone can donate, so it's surprising how you put it all together."

"I like doing research, and I can easily get pulled down a rabbit hole. Plus the comment you made during an interview I found on Google."

A slow smile spreads on his face. "Were you Googling me? Before we met this year?"

I feel the blush cascade over my skin. "Does it make you think less of me to say yes? In hindsight, I wonder if it's because I saw something in you that I recognized. I didn't Google you with the intent of looking at your private life, or seeing what your football stats were. I solely wanted to see if there was a connection between you and Playful Paws."

"If it were anyone else, I'd be freaked out," he says, grinning widely. "But knowing you Googled me is actually pretty cool."

"Why aren't you freaked? I can imagine that it must feel like an invasion of privacy," I comment as his hands skate up and down my arm, goosebumps erupting in their wake.

"Because it's you. And I trust you more than most people," he says simply.

"Why?" I breathe.

He smiles again, dragging a finger down my hairline from my forehead to behind my ear. "I felt like I could trust you from our first meeting, and I didn't know why. I knew I wanted to learn more about you. I felt a kinship with you immediately. I guess my brain recognized a like-minded woman, and wanted me to keep you in my life."

"It's hard for me to trust people," I admit. "Once they find out I'm autistic, they typically run for the hills."

"You tell a lot of people?" Jamie asks, and I nod.

"I'd rather people learn it early on and leave, instead of bolting when we've gotten closer. I am who I am. Get used to it, because I'm not going to change," I say surely. I know my brain works differently than most, but I like who I am. I'd rather have one, or a couple, of really close friends than a huge circle of acquaintances anyway. The only time I hide my autism is when I'm at events with my parents. It's not because I'm embarrassed or lacking confidence.

It's because they make awful comments about it, and I don't want to deal with that.

"I only have a couple of people who know," Jamie confesses, his hands settling on my waist. He squeezes gently, like he's grounding himself, his thumbs absentmindedly stroking up and down.

"How does it impact your job?" I ask. "We've discussed some sensory things, but it must be overwhelming at a football game."

"I'm usually okay because I know what to expect, and I have a variety of masking techniques I can use to get through the game. I struggle more in the post-game interviews, and when I'm doing any kind of public appearance. I don't know what it is about athletes, but people assume it's okay to touch me. I don't like that. Just because I'm a man doesn't mean I'm okay with that."

I'm sitting in his lap. Is he uncomfortable right now, and doesn't feel confident enough to tell me? He's said he'll tell me, but my anxiety is arguing that he might change his mind. "Are you sure it's okay if I'm in your lap? This is definitely touching you."

He chuckles. "Yeah, this is fine. Great, in fact. It's different in a romantic setting. I *want* you to touch me. And honestly, I love that you haven't moved."

"I don't want you to feel like you have to do something for my benefit. I know how important boundaries are. Obviously. Is there anything you're definitely opposed to? Parts of your body you don't want me to touch, or areas you're a little unsure of?"

"I don't like feet," he blurts out with a laugh. "I don't like mine, and I really don't want to touch other feet. But I also don't like looking at nasty feet. Is that weird?"

I burst into laughter. "I'm that way with facial hair! I don't understand how some men let it get so out of control, and it makes me feel itchy when I look at out of control beards or mustaches. How do they eat if hair hangs over their lips? All that rogue hair on their necks, that has to feel just awful!"

Jamie runs a hand over his scruff. "Does this bother you?"

"No," I answer, shyly. "It's a great length. Not too long, but long enough that I can feel it. It makes me wonder what …"

His eyes darken almost imperceptibly. "You're wondering what it'll feel like on other parts of your body."

I nod. But I'm not ready to find out yet. How do I explain that? Suddenly, I'm so nervous about taking the next step with Jamie. "But —"

"But you're not ready for that," he supplies. "Neither am I, truthfully. I'd like to take you on a date first. Maybe a few dates. Quiet dates, just the two of us."

My heart drops. "Quiet dates? Is this a way of hiding me? I've had that happen before, and I don't like it, Jamie. I don't want to be hidden."

He takes my face in his hands, thumbs stroking my cheeks. "I'm not hiding you. I'm more concerned with me, and what reaction the public will have that might scare you off. It's exhausting dealing with fans and paparazzi, and I want to shield you from that as much as I can. Be in our own little bubble while we get to know each other better."

"Okay," I say, somewhat warily. His response makes sense, but I'm a little too paranoid about previous relationships.

"Trust me, Doc," he says tenderly, leaning in to kiss my lips quickly, "I will proudly have you by my side to show you off, but it'll be when *we* decide. Not outsiders."

"Show me off?" I ask with a breathy giggle.

"Yup. Once we're public, all bets are off. I'm gonna want you at every event, and I'll plan to be with you for any stupid things your parents make you do. We'll be a team. But for now, I'm kinda liking the thought of having you all to myself," he says, a small smirk covering his face as he kisses me again.

"Do you think anyone will suspect something?"

Jamie laughs. "Not even a little bit. I'm known as the team hermit. It's rare that I'm out at clubs or anything like that. They think it's because I'm grumpy and don't like anyone, but in reality, I'm incredibly private and don't like when people I don't know disrespect my carefully constructed boundaries."

"And you promise you'll tell me if I ever accidentally cross a boundary?"

"I promise. Boundaries with you will be different, though. My inner circle has a lot more flexibility because I know you're trustworthy."

"Good to know," I say with a yawn.

"What time do you have to be at work?" Jamie asks.

I turn my head to glance over at my clock. "In about three hours. And no, I can't call in. I have two surgeries today."

"I wasn't going to suggest that. I know you're passionate about your job. You'd never call in because your clients would be the ones who suffer."

"Exactly. It may seem silly to say a dog would suffer if I don't spay her, but I know that dog's owners have fixed their schedule to be here today. And my second surgery is a dental cleaning and lipoma excision. For all I know, that dog actually is suffering. I could make a big difference today."

Jamie yawns. "Any chance I could take a power nap on your couch? I've got a workout mid-morning with a few teammates, and a meeting with my agent at lunch. I could use an hour to recharge."

"Can we both nap for an hour? I didn't sleep well last night. Or the previous night, honestly," I admit. Jamie bends to rest his forehead against my shoulder. "If it's alright, we can nap in my bed. No funny business, though."

Jamie chuckles. "Absolutely not. There's one thing you should absolutely know about me, Doc. I don't mess around when it comes to sleep."

My phone rings as I'm climbing out of Jamie's lap, and I point toward the hallway leading to my bedroom. Seeing that it's Chelsea, I pick up. "Hey. What's up?"

"Your surgery this morning has been canceled."

"Oh. Why?" I ask.

"Stomach bug ransacked their house last night. The mom said she doesn't think she can make it to the clinic without pooping her pants or puking."

I grimace. "Yuck. Alright. Don't charge her a cancellation fee. I'll be in for the second procedure around lunchtime."

"I figured you'd be thrilled you can take a nap," Chelsea says with a laugh.

"I'm very thrilled with napping." Ending the call, I look up to find Jamie watching me with an amused expression. "Why are you looking at me like that?"

"Your friend even knows how much you like to nap?"

I nod. "I also value sleep over most things. And now I don't have to be at work until lunchtime."

"You cool if I grab a change of clothes from my car? I was afraid to leave, so I know I must smell."

"Of course. Would you like to shower?"

He lets out a long exhale. "A shower sounds perfect."

"Let me go get my things out of the shower, and then it's all yours. Just come in when you're back." I need to go hide my vibrator, which I usually only use in the shower. Since no one comes into my house besides Chelsea, it's taken up residence on the side of my tub. I'd prefer he *not* see that.

Jamie extends a hand to me, pulling me up. "I've never looked forward to a nap more."

Two and a half hours later, I wake up sprawled across Jamie, apparently having no concept of personal space. Head on his chest and one leg over his pelvis, I try to carefully slide my body off of his, but his arm immediately tightens around me. That's when I feel his opposite hand grasping my hair, which is no longer in a messy bun. Jamie's body is turned slightly toward me, his nose against my hair, and a large chunk of it is wrapped around his fist. "I've never been attracted to hair before, but I'm absolutely obsessed with yours."

I can't help the giddy smile that covers my face as I snuggle deeper into his chest. My hair is almost always in a bun. My mother forced me to keep it shoulder-length all throughout childhood, and once I was able to control its length, I rarely cut it. It's down to my waist, but I obviously have to keep it up at work. I choose to wear it up whenever I'm around my parents, because it's easier than fighting all the time about it. Apparently, according to my mother, respectable women don't have super long hair.

It seems that I'm uncovering more and more trauma, courtesy of my upbringing, as I get older. I only recently realized painting my nails anything other than pastel pinks, shades of white, or a 'classic' style like a French manicure wasn't really a sign that I was a whore. Lipsticks were to be in neutral shades, and definitely never 'whore red.' All skirts and shorts were to be longer than the tips of my fingers when my arms were hanging straight, and no heels over two-point-five inches. Three inch heels were only allowed if I happened to be escorted by a man over six feet tall. Other than that, I'd be called a whore. A whore, for three inch heels and red lipstick. It appears my mother's favorite word for explaining anything about womanhood was the word 'whore.'

And my mother wonders why I stopped allowing her to play matchmaker. I quickly learned her ideals were virtually interchangeable with those of her friends, which meant any of the men they'd match with me would expect the same thing. No, thank you.

"My mother hates long hair," I murmur as I trace the letters of his Colorado Coyotes tee shirt.

"And since she hated it, you rebelled," he muses.

"There wasn't much I could have power over when I was in college, because I was still living at home part of the year. But I could definitely control the length of my hair."

"Your parents sound like they're barrels of fun."

"Not by a long shot. It might have been nice to have a closer family, but I don't regret growing up like I did. They paid for my college, even though they hated my major. They put up with some of my more unique extracurricular activities. It could have been so much worse."

"That's how I view my parents as well. I know everything they did was out of love for me, but they began living vicariously through me. They wanted me to go to the same university as they did, and pushed for me to look at the same fraternity my dad was in. I didn't even want to be in a fraternity! So I picked the farthest college I could go to that wanted me for their football team."

"That's how you ended up at Oregon?"

He nods. "They wanted me to stay in Florida. I knew it would mean they'd show up every weekend. They'd want to tailgate, push me into that fraternity, and hover over everything that I did. It wasn't that I wanted independence so I could party or be out of control. I just wanted to get out from under their thumbs."

"Did it work?"

"For the most part, yeah. My dad had an epiphany my freshman year of college, but my mom took much longer to understand. It became a really big sore point between the three of us. My dad cheated on her a lot, and I think she threw herself into raising me as a coping mechanism. It all became too much. So much so, in fact, they ended up getting a divorce. My junior year, my mom showed up in Oregon right before the second game of the year, and told me she was moving there."

"What?" I gasp, tilting my head up to gaze at him. "I hope she didn't!"

He shakes his head sadly. "She did. I was in an off-campus apartment, and she slept on the couch for a few weeks. I didn't have the heart to kick her out. But then she began showing up at practices, and the coaching staff was pissed. They encouraged me to kick her out, and if she didn't leave, they wanted me to file a restraining order against her."

"Oh, wow," I say quietly. "I can't imagine how hard that must have been for you to think about. Regardless of her actions, she's your mom. It's difficult to view a parent-child relationship objectively when you're one of the participants."

Jamie is quiet for a moment, twirling a lock of my hair around his finger. "I think I'm the opposite. It wasn't difficult for me to comprehend *why* my mom was struggling. I'm their only child, and I'd moved three thousand miles away. She'd been a housewife for my entire childhood, and didn't know how to remove that aspect of her life. She had no career aspirations, and didn't know how to survive without depending on someone else. She took her dependence on my dad and transferred it to me."

I don't reply. In some ways, our moms are similar. My mother certainly has no professional skills to speak of, unless you count designing floral centerpieces, setting an extravagant table full of fine china, or convincing rich people to bid on absurd items at a silent auction. She still won't tell me who donated the full-size taxidermy black bear, and what stupidly rich person won it.

"My mom had an affair with one of my coaches," Jamie blurts out suddenly. "Broke up a family. I cut all ties with her after that."

"When you were in college?"

"Yeah. It was a big story because the wife of my coach was previously an athlete herself, and she wasn't shy about telling everyone what happened. I still get tagged occasionally in some text message screenshots." His face is devoid of any emotion. "I haven't spoken to her in close to fifteen years. I don't even know if she's still alive."

"Do you want to talk to her?" I ask carefully.

He sighs. "No. I spent a lot of time in therapy after college, and it helped me to realize what a toxic person she is. When I told her about my autism diagnosis, because I wasn't actually diagnosed until I was twenty, she made it about her. Honestly, I'm surprised my dad didn't leave years before he finally did. I think me being away at college forced him to see her for what she truly was, because I wasn't there as a buffer."

"Do you still talk to your dad?"

"Occasionally. He comes out once a year for a home game, and we always have a game somewhere near him, so I usually see him then as well. I've talked him into coming out for Christmas once or twice, but he doesn't like to travel. The apple doesn't fall far from the tree, I guess. He has his area that he's happy in, and he doesn't enjoy deviating from it."

"I'm the same way. I like schedules. Expectations. I know what I want, what I like, and I don't go off to do things differently. The only thing I do enjoy is trying new food, but even that is within limits."

"Oh yeah? What are your limits for food?" Jamie asks as he pushes up onto his side. Removing his arm from around me, he props his head on his hand and looks at me.

"I don't want to see it alive before I eat it."

"I support this," he says with an exaggerated shudder. "Did you know when you boil a lobster, it screams?"

"I would scream, too, if you shoved me in boiling water!"

"Valid," he says with a laugh. "What else?"

"If I associate an animal with any kind of children's movie, cartoon, or television show, I can't eat it."

"Give me an example."

"Ever seen the movie *Babe*?"

His mouth drops open in horror. "You don't eat *bacon*? What kind of sick and twisted person are you?"

"There's an entire religion that doesn't eat bacon, Jamie. Or any pig for that matter. I assure you, I'm surviving just fine without it," I say with a giggle. "I had a much harder time giving up marshmallows than bacon."

"Why marshmallows?"

"Gelatin."

He looks confused. "So?"

"Gelatin is made from pork collagen. There are Vegan marshmallows, but they aren't the same. I really only miss them in Rice Krispie Treats."

Jamie grips the bridge of his nose. "I don't know which thing horrifies me more: you not eating bacon, or the fact that gelatin is actually pig collagen. This is a lot to process on a Monday morning."

I gasp. "Shit! It's almost noon! I have to get to work. Didn't you have a practice or workout this morning?"

I roll over and jump up from the bed. Jamie stretches, his long legs over the edge of my mattress, as his hands touch the headboard. "No, as soon as you fell asleep, I texted my teammates and told them I wouldn't be there. I needed the sleep too. Besides, you're much prettier than they are."

I giggle as I frantically get myself organized and ready for work. Jamie leaves the bedroom as I get changed, and when I walk into my living room, I find him carefully setting Flash into her wheelchair. He's mumbling to himself about the contraption as Flash faithfully licks his face. "There! Got it!"

"You should know that Flash hates just about everyone," I comment. "She wasn't even that fond of Chelsea when they first met, but Chelsea just smothered her and wore her down."

He chuckles as Flash licks him again. "I don't know Chelsea well, but that sounds about right."

Jamie looks up at me triumphantly as he attaches the last strap, and Flash gives him an excited bark. Grabbing my bag, I motion for him to walk to the front door. "I have an attached garage, so I go out through the kitchen. I need to lock up after you leave."

Jamie turns and gives me a shy smile. "Are you busy tomorrow night? I thought maybe I could bring over some dinner, and we could watch a movie or something."

I nod eagerly. "I'd like that."

He bends down to apply a soft kiss to my lips. "Good. I'll call you later, Doc. Bye, Flash."

After he leaves, I look down at my dog, and I swear she nods at me. "I know. I like him too."

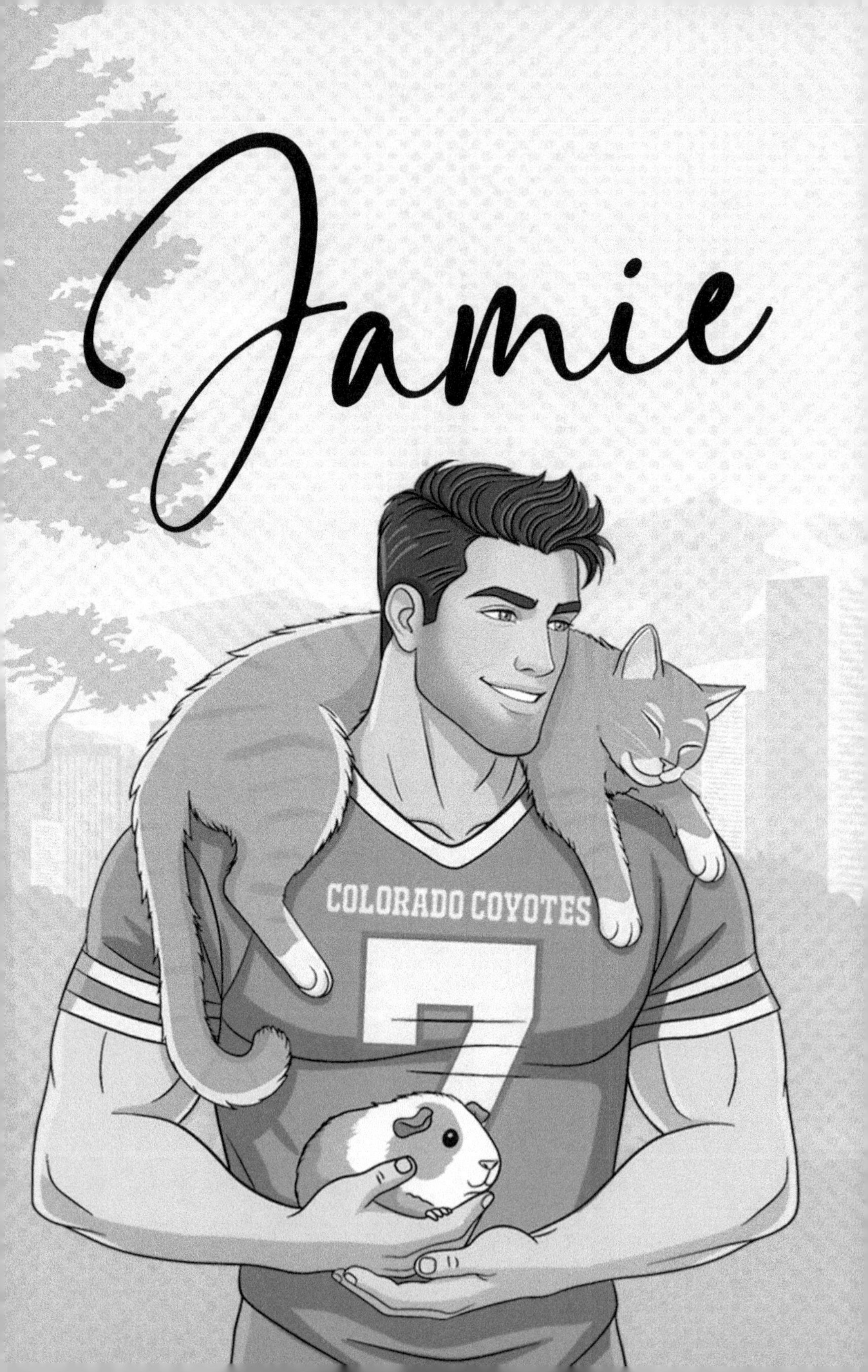

Jamie

CHAPTER 15

I didn't expect the morning to go as it did, but I'm not complaining. Not only for the amazing kiss, but for the much needed nap afterward. I'm usually someone who likes his own space. I'll have my arm around a girl for a moment as we get settled, but then I'm doing the 'hug and roll' a la Ross Gellar in *Friends*. But with Audrey, I couldn't get close enough. I wanted to wrap myself around her, where every inch of me touched her skin.

I've never needed a pre-game nap, always chalking it up to adrenaline and anxiety. Many of my teammates swear by them for late games, but I've always thought it was dumb. On the rare times I nap, I wake groggy, disoriented, and sluggish. How could that help me be at the top of my game?

But this morning changed my view on naps. Because if this is what my teammates experience, I'm all for naps now. I feel like I'm more alert than I've ever been. Walking on clouds. Happy as a clam. All the stupid sayings.

"Your happiness is weirding me out," Troy says over his salad. "You've never been this happy."

"That's not true," I reply with a chuckle. "Dramatic much?"

Max Callahan is having lunch with us, since we share Troy as our agent, and he raises an eyebrow. "I don't know you very well yet, QB, but you are more cheerful than I've experienced. Especially after that shitshow on Saturday night."

I shrug, failing to wipe the grin off my face. "It all worked out."

"For you, maybe. Not for the Coyotes," Troy responds. "I got a pretty nastily-worded email from the owner bright and early yesterday morning. And a phone call from your coach this morning before I'd even had my coffee."

Dread fills my stomach, and I'm immediately somber. "It was a series of misunderstandings. They know that, right?"

"I explained it as best I could. But you've got some groveling in your future."

I sigh. "Great. What do they want me to do?"

"Well," Troy says, as he opens his phone, "Martin Sanderson said you're going to be personally greeting his VIPs for the first month of the season, and he expects you to take any and all endorsement deals he sends our way. Oh, and he wants you at his beck and call for a couple of events this summer. The PR team worked nonstop getting footage removed from multiple sites, so you lucked out there."

"Those aren't too bad," I say slowly. "I'm assuming the ones from Coach are worse, since you led with Mr. Sanderson's things."

Troy shrugs. "It's hard to tell sometimes if he's really mad about something, since he's so damn grumpy, but I felt like I had to talk Coach off the damn ledge, man. He's furious about you bringing a bad name to the team, as well as screwing up his professional relationship with the owner. He was relieved there's no evidence online, but he's even more upset about his niece's spectacle. Says he blatantly told you not to let her drink."

"I didn't *let* her drink," I say exasperatedly, throwing up my hands in frustration. "I don't know how, or when, she got the booze. She ran off with a couple of friends. Was I supposed to chase after her? I figured since we both had told her not to drink, she wouldn't."

"Is the chick a teenager or something?" Max asks.

"No, Coach said she's twenty-seven," I reply.

"Jesus. You'd think a woman of that age wouldn't get so shit-faced she embarrasses herself, her date, and everyone around her," Max replies, disgust evident in his tone.

"Exactly!" I yell, only somewhat aware of how loud I've gotten. "I was only supposed to escort her and tell her not to drink. Oh, and he told me not to sleep with her. At least I didn't do that."

Troy coughs. "Lower your voice, Jamie. You're getting really loud."

"Sorry," I say quietly. "What does Coach want me to do since I clearly didn't do a good job babysitting his adult niece?"

"No one could have babysat her," Max adds in. "The girl was pretty out of control from the moment I saw her. She was hanging onto any athlete she could find. I bet she was determined to go home with one, and she didn't care which one."

"She made a pass at me before we even got to the venue, and I shut that shit down immediately. I wasn't interested, and I've got something going on with someone anyway."

"Well, this is news to me," Troy says, interest sparking in his eyes. "The entire time I've known you, I don't think you've had a serious girlfriend."

"Never met someone I thought was worth it," I confess.

"Are you wanting advice and a strategy for going public? What do you need me to do?" Troy asks.

"Don't do it, man," Max says with an exaggerated cough. "Hide that shit as long as possible. The press absolutely ruined my last relationship."

"I'm not announcing anything just yet. Gonna enjoy living in my little bubble for a while longer, and give her time to acclimate to what it will be like dating me. She's not in our world, and I'm afraid it'll spook her if she knows how much people will invade her space once they find out who she is."

"I don't get why women give up on relationships because of the press. Work schedules I understand. I can even sympathize with a woman hating that she can't trust her man out of town. But the press? Such a minor thing," Troy says. Max and I both glare at him.

"That's because you didn't make it big out of college," I blurt out. Troy played football in college, and could have gone pro as a running back, if it weren't for one play that completely blew out his knee, tearing his ACL, MCL, and meniscus. After over a year in recovery, his game wasn't the same, and he gave up playing.

"Yeah, and you're single," Max pipes up. "It's different when you're in our shoes. No offense."

"I guess," Troy says, frowning. "To me, it seems like it's worth it if you love someone."

"No. It's not as easy as that. We're talking about every last bit of your life under a microscope. The press will look under every rock. They'll interview people from your high school. Previous romantic partners. Anyone who has rubbed shoulders with you. They'll camp out around the corner from your house, or sneak up to your window and try to snap a picture. They have no shame in trying to deliver anything that will bring people to their websites. Some will even unabashedly make things up." I can feel my blood pressure increasing as I continue. "And I know what you're going to say next. You'll say that some women can handle it all. Well, I don't want some women. I only want one, and I'm going to give her every last bit of freedom I can before she gets a miserable taste of what I live every day."

"Damn, QB," Max comments. "I'd hide her away too."

Troy clears his throat. "No matter how much you prepare her, or how much time you give to hopefully let things die down, your girl may not handle it well, Jamie. You have to understand that."

I nod sullenly. "I know. But it won't be for lack of trying on my part. If, or when, I need you to step in, I'll let you know. For now, the topic is tabled."

"Can you at least tell me her name? I can run a background check, make sure she's in it for the right reasons —" I throw up a hand, making Troy immediately stop.

"No. Absolutely not. I may not be good at a lot of things, Troy, but one thing I excel at is judging character. There will be no background check. I don't want you butting in at all. I'm handling this my way."

He looks warily at me. "I don't think that's a good idea."

"It's not your decision to make. Now, tell me what Coach wants me to do for what happened this weekend."

Troy sighs. "He wants you to coach a peewee team, and said you're doing interviews twice a week until training camp."

"Fine. I sure do hope Coach laid into his niece and has some kind of consequence for her actions," I say pointedly.

"Oh, he does. Told me she'll be putting in a ton of effort with a charity that works with people struggling with addiction."

"Good."

"I still think you should give me the name of the girl ..." Troy trails off, before looking at me. "Shit. Dude, you better not be hooking up with that chick you're planning the foundation event with."

I keep my face devoid of emotion as I carefully ask, "Why?"

"Because this event is too big for you to fuck it up because of a little pussy."

I roll my eyes. "Give me the benefit of the doubt, please. But — wait. How did you know I was planning the event with a woman?"

Troy looks confused. "Because the veterinarian is a woman?"

"I never told you that."

He shrugs. "When the contact info came through, I saw her name is Audrey. I doubt that's a gender-neutral name, but I could be wrong. Whatever the case, don't fuck her."

"Jesus, Troy. A little tact would be nice," I reply, choosing not to acknowledge his overall fear of me sleeping with Audrey, because I'd really like to do just that in the near future.

"Tact is overrated," he says with a laugh. "Just keep your head on straight. I want to ensure you're protected at all times."

"Can't have your biggest client losing out on brand deals, because then you don't get a commission, right?" I snap, aggravation clear in my tone. I know Troy. There are a lot of sleazy agents out there, and Troy has never been like that. I could give him Audrey's name, and he wouldn't leak it. But I want to protect *her*, so his interest is rubbing me the wrong way.

"Your deals have nothing to do with this," Troy replies. "You've always been like a brother to me, man. When I say I want to protect you, it has nothing to do with football, and everything to do with you as a person. I don't want to see anyone take advantage of you."

I smile weakly with a tense nod, but I don't respond. This conversation has given me one heck of a tension headache.

ME

I learned a new word today.

AUDREY

Me too! What's yours?

ME

Twattle.

AUDREY

That sounds like a derogatory word for someone. "That little twattle!"

ME

Nope, but I have heard "twatwaffle" used as a derogatory name for someone, so I can see why you'd think that.

AUDREY

adds twatwaffle to memory for future use

ME

Twattle means to gossip.

AUDREY

Somehow that makes sense. I learned where the word "cocky" comes from.

ME

It doesn't come from cock?

AUDREY

No, surprisingly. It comes from the word "cockalorum."

Well, that's not entirely correct. Cocky and cockalorum both mean a boastful and self-important person, but cockalorum is derived from an old Flemish word.

ME

Now I'm going down a rabbit hole learning how the word cock came to be.

AUDREY

I assume it is connected to a rooster and how he struts around. Hence the word cocky.

ME

It also goes back to the thirteen hundreds, believe it or not.

ME

Woah, at one point, cock was a personal name!

AUDREY

I'm oddly relieved that it's no longer used as a first name, I guess.

ME

What, you wouldn't want to date me if my name was Cock? Cock Wahlberg does have a nice ring to it.

AUDREY

It does, actually.

Please don't change your name.

Jamie suits you.

So does Jameson for that matter.

I have a feeling you're researching how to change your name.

ME

Sorry. Went down another rabbit hole learning about how cock is sometimes used as a term of endearment in parts of Great Britain.

AUDREY

I am not using that.

ME

It's okay. You can call me Daddy.

How do I unsend a text?

Seriously. Ignore the last two texts from me.

Possibly this entire exchange. I'll have to scroll back to see where else I possibly forgot to filter my thoughts.

Jesus. Now I sound like I really DO want you to call me Daddy, but just didn't want to say it out loud, but that's not the case.

Sometimes my sense of humor skews a little offside.

I bet you don't even know what offside means.

Have I been blocked?

Googling how to figure out if I've been blocked ...

Well, shit. It says you're reading the texts, so you haven't blocked me. But I'm literally having a one-sided conversation here.

AUDREY

I. AM. DYING.

ME

Literally or figuratively?

AUDREY

Figuratively. I'm literally crying because I'm laughing so hard right now. That just made my entire day.

ME

Really? I would have thought the excellent kiss and amazing nap would score a little higher on the charts, Aud. I'm hurt.

AUDREY

You're right. It made my evening.

Believe it or not, I needed that. I had to euthanize a little girl's dog today. I can typically hold it together, but when she cried, I cried. It's not a good look to sob with a client while putting their dog down.

ME

Oh fuck. I'm sorry, Doc. What can I do to make you feel better?

AUDREY

This conversation is helping immensely. Thank you.

ME

I'm glad.

Whenever I'm really sad, I put on my favorite movie.

AUDREY

For someone else, I'd assume their favorites would be football movies like Rudy or Remember the Titans. But for you, I'm assuming it's completely unrelated.

ME

You are correct.

AUDREY

Can you give me a hint?

ME

A cult classic movie with a gangster twist.

AUDREY

According to Google, it's Scarface.

I can't believe that's it. You don't seem like the type who would find joy in a movie like that.

ME

It's not. It's Home Alone.

AUDREY

Oh, a gangster twist. "Keep the change, you filthy idiot."

ME

YA. Not you. YA. Sounds better that way. And it's ya filthy ANIMAL, not idiot.

AUDREY

My mistake.

ME

Well, what's your favorite movie?

AUDREY

Not sure if I have a favorite movie, but I definitely have comfort television shows. I tend to gravitate toward shows that have humor as the focus. The Good Place, Schitt's Creek, Brooklyn Nine-Nine.

AUDREY

But when I'm really in a sad place, I eat ice cream.

ME

Oh yeah? What's your favorite?

AUDREY

I love this one called Amaretto Cherry Cordial. I can only find it at some grocery stores. It's my absolute favorite. Other than that, I'm pretty plain, and enjoy a good homemade vanilla ice cream. I'm picky about brands, though.

ME

As you should be. Ice cream is important.

AUDREY

Did you seriously send me ice cream???

ME

I would have brought it myself, but both of my cats are laying on me, so I'm not allowed to move.

AUDREY

That is a rule. Thank you, Jamie. That was incredibly sweet of you.

ME

Promise to save me a bite? I need to know how good this flavor is.

AUDREY

You sent me two half gallons. I highly doubt I'll eat them both in the next twenty-four hours.

Jeez, how many toppings are in here?

ME

It's possible I may have gone overboard. It's entirely too easy to add things to an online cart.

AUDREY

I haven't had magic shell topping in years!

Oh, Ghirardelli has a fudge topping? YUM.

Wow, there's a cupcake flavor of magic shell! And how many containers of sprinkles did you SEND?

ME

I lost track.

AUDREY

This poor shopper must have been incredibly concerned.

ME

Why do you think that?

AUDREY

She hand wrote a note that says "He's not worth it. All men are pigs."

ME

Ouch.

I can message her and tell her you don't eat pig. Maybe that'll make her feel like you're doing okay.

AUDREY

I guess it's a good thing that all men aren't
pigs, then.

Because now I can still eat you.

ME

Hold on, I'm moving these cats
RIGHT NOW.

AUDREY

Leave them alone! It's fun like this.

Can I confide in you about something?

ME

Of course.

AUDREY

I've trained myself to hold in a lot of my
thoughts. Inside thoughts versus outside
thoughts. Never in a million years would I
have said that to you a week ago. But now,
I guess I feel like you'll be more
understanding and accepting of my inside
thoughts showing up on the outside.

ME

Obviously I have my own challenges with
inside thoughts, so I'm no judge on that.
But I'm glad you trust me.

AUDREY

I've had a lot of people give up on me
because I lack social skills at times, and on
occasion, I'll forget to put on my filter.

ME

Me too. That's part of the reason why I keep
to myself, and why only a handful of people
know I'm autistic.

AUDREY

Do you think people wouldn't be accepting
of you if they knew your diagnosis?

ME

I don't know, which is why I don't tell
anyone. I've never felt that I needed a huge
circle of friends. I have a core group I know
I can trust who I depend on, and I'm good
with that.

AUDREY

I'm the same way, but I don't hide that I'm
autistic either. Not that I'm out shouting it
around, but if someone asks, or if it comes
up in conversation, I'm upfront about it. I'm
autistic. This is me. Take it or leave it.

ME

They better take it, because you're fucking
amazing.

AUDREY

Thank you. I think you're pretty amazing
too.

And maybe it's the optimist in me, but I
have to think more people would be proud
of you for embracing your neurodiversity,
and owning it. Plus, you have such a
platform. I think you could help a
tremendous number of people, especially
children, who think they're not up to snuff
because of autism.

ME

Maybe.

I'm not ready to tackle that.

AUDREY

That's fair.

I'm proud of you for telling me.

ME

You asked me point-blank.

AUDREY

You could have lied. Or gaslit me. But you were honest. That takes courage, Jamie.

Thanks for all the ice cream goodies. I'm going to make myself a huge sundae and watch Home Alone.

ME

A woman after my own heart.

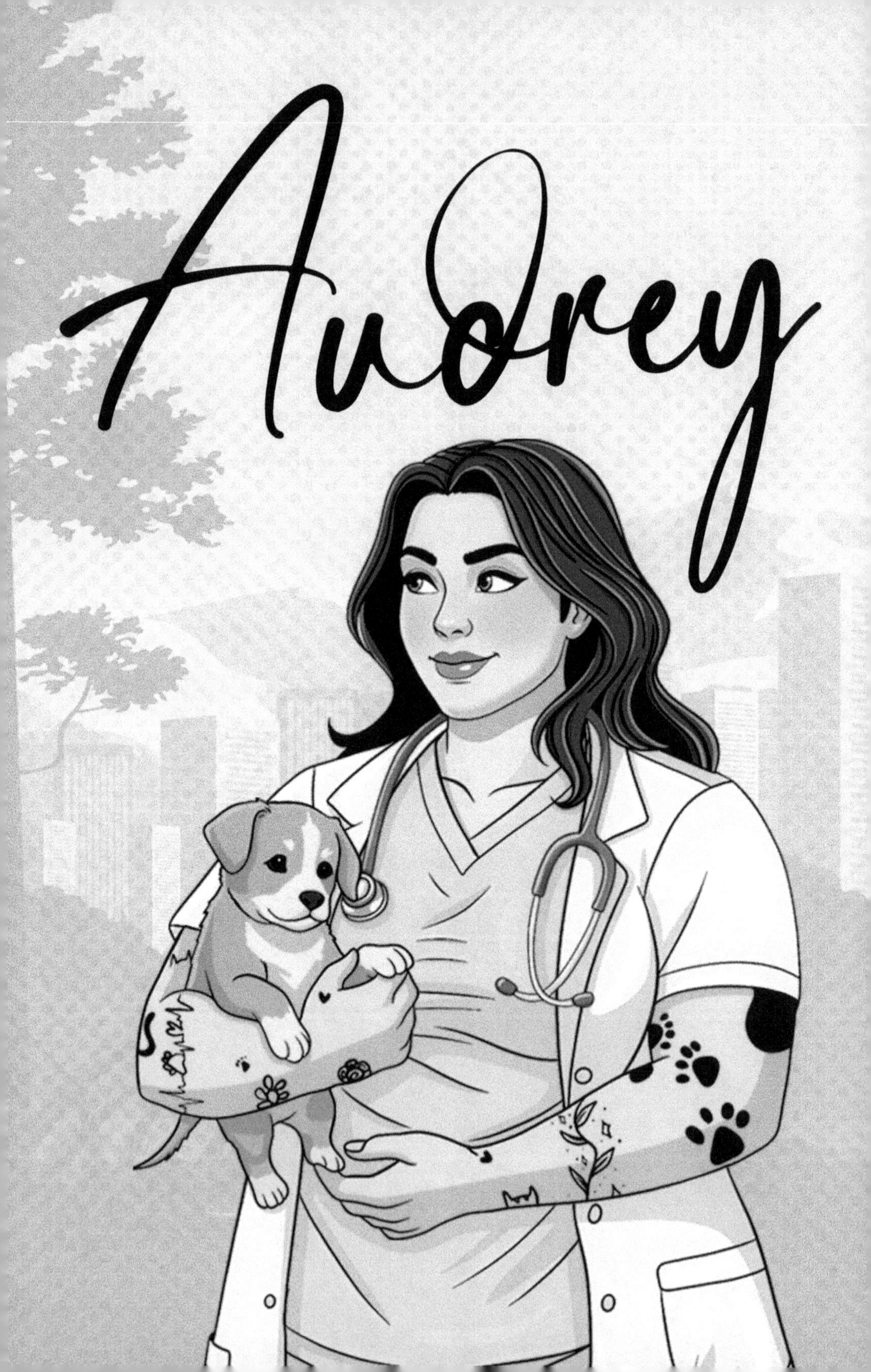

Audrey

CHAPTER 16

I have a date tonight, and it's safe to say I was a little unhinged at work the entire day because of it. I'm fairly certain Chelsea was ready to muzzle me more than once. I couldn't stop talking about Jamie, or asking her questions about dating etiquette.

I've dated before. I've even had sex … although not that much. I've never felt comfortable with giving it up to someone I barely knew, so one night stands were off the table. And a lot of guys expect it after a certain number of dates. Jamie is an NFL superstar. I'm sure he's had countless one night stands. He's probably slept with dozens and dozens of women. Maybe triple digits. Gross. God, I really hope he hasn't slept with *that* many women, but I'm not asking for a number.

That thought occurred to me at lunch today, and I had a full panic attack. I began thinking back to the last time I had sex, and I can't remember. I actually cannot remember the last time I slept with a man. That kiss with Jamie was the first bit of action I've had in well over a year, but I know it's been longer than that since I had sex.

The entirety of my sexual history fits on one hand, and the thought of doing anything with Jamie gave me one hell of a reality check. What if he expects a confident, sexual woman in the bedroom? A take-charge partner? Someone who has no problem telling her partner exactly what she wants and needs?

That is not me.

I can barely tell the Starbucks barista what kind of milk I want in my latte.

I'd almost talked myself into canceling the dinner tonight when I received a package at work. I was stunned to find oversized guinea pig slippers, and a coffee mug that says 'world's best guinea pig mom' on it. He attached a simple handwritten note that said:

Looking forward to our dinner and a movie date. I'll wear my slippers too.

-J

Now I simply have to go through with the date, if only for the purpose of seeing his slippers.

At six o'clock on the dot, my doorbell rings, and I have the sudden urge to puke, just like he did weeks ago. I open the door to find him grinning widely, a far cry from how he looked that first time when he barely made it to the bathroom.

I let out a loud burst of laughter when I see that his slippers are the cat version of mine. "Do they match your cats?"

"Who are you kidding? They won't let me put theirs on them," he says with a wink. "I wish I was kidding. But yes, my slippers match them. I have two tuxedo cats."

"Maverick and Goose, right?" I ask as I motion for him to come inside. Flash yips in greeting, and the pigs down the hall let out a crescendo of squeaks.

"Yeah. They're quite the pair. I brought a bag of food for the pigs, too."

My eyes pop to his in shock. "You didn't have to do that."

He shrugs. "I brought dinner for everyone. Even Flash."

Good God. I might cry. "What did you bring for Flash?"

"Well," Jamie says as he walks into the kitchen, depositing a bag and a cooler onto the counter, "I wasn't fully sure what her diet allowed, so I did some research."

"You know, you could have called her veterinarian to check," I murmur, watching as he pulls out a stainless steel container.

"Har-har. Everything I saw online said boiled chicken and plain steamed rice were good for dogs, so I brought that. Oh, and pumpkin puree. The unsweetened kind, which I didn't even know was a thing."

As he removes the top of the stainless steel box, I stare in shock. "Did you … did you *make* the food for Flash?"

"Yeah," he says quietly. "I mean, I made food for us, too."

I'm speechless. I've never had a man make me food. This is basically our first date, and he's pulling out the big guns. "What did you make?"

He scratches at the back of his neck, giving me a sheepish grin. "I wanted to surprise you, but I should have clarified on your food aversions. So I kept it pretty basic. It's also a simple chicken dish, but a variety of sautéed vegetables and a seasoned rice. I like to cook."

Wow. Emotion clogs my throat. How on earth has no one scooped this man up yet? "That's — wow. I've never had someone make me dinner before. That's incredibly sweet, Jamie. Thank you."

He nods shyly, his eyes drifting down to his bags. "It's nice taking care of someone, I guess. I don't get the opportunity to do it. Well, I will only cook for someone I care for, and someone I trust. It's a pretty small list."

"I don't think it's ever occurred to me to cook for someone," I muse. "I suppose everyone shows their feelings in different ways, although I'm not sure what mine is."

Jamie pulls more containers out of his bags, piling them up on top of one another. "Yours is words of affirmation."

"What?" I ask, choking back a breathy laugh.

He cocks an eyebrow at me. "You show everyone you care for

them by using your words. You just told me how sweet it was that I cooked for us. You've encouraged me to share more about my autism diagnosis, and as soon as I told you about my sensory issues, you flat out told me I had to be honest about them with you, because you didn't want to overstep. That tells me you care. I bet you're constantly telling people you're proud of them, or how inspired they made you feel. Some people may not recognize that, but I do. It speaks volumes about your character."

Mouth agape, I'm stunned. I've never felt so seen in my entire life. I can remember the first time I spoke to my family like that, when I was around ten. I'd witnessed my parents fawning over my brother and sister, and I attempted to recreate their compliments. I thought maybe they weren't encouraging me because I wasn't reciprocating. Unfortunately, I was wrong. My mother laughed at my attempt, and my father told me to be quiet. Afterward, my sister sneered at me, and told me I'd never be her, so I should quit trying.

All I wanted was to feel like I was an equal part of my family. It was a mask I'd put on, hoping to receive the affection I craved from my parents. I continued to try, and the mask became more permanent. Seeing it through Jamie's eyes, I understand why he viewed it that way.

"Do you know about love languages?" he asks as he begins rifling through cabinets. I point to the one with plates, and he pulls two down.

"Some, but not a lot," I confess. "I haven't done any tests for myself."

"Well, there are five. Words of affirmation, physical touch, quality time, receiving gifts, and acts of service. But what most people don't know, is you can have a love language that you want to receive, but also one you want to give. So the love language you excel at is very clearly words of affirmation. But that isn't necessarily the one you want to experience."

"Actually, I think words of affirmation is just one that I'm good at. It isn't what I want to give to my loved ones."

"Oh?" Jamie asks, cocking a brow at me as he plates a variety of roasted vegetables. "What do you think yours are?"

"Acts of service," I answer quickly.

"I can see that," he replies. "Like taking in the guinea pigs. I bet you watch all kinds of pets for friends too."

"I do," I say sheepishly, feeling a blush creep onto my neck. Biting my lip, I continue as I watch him carefully pile chicken onto our plates. "Well, I don't have a lot of good friends. Basically just Chelsea. But I'll petsit for anyone. Honestly, I like doing things for others. Sometimes it's watching a pet while they're on vacation, but it can also be dropping off a container of soup when they're sick, or going out of my way to meet someone who's going through a tough time. To me, acts of service are a perfect nonverbal way to tell everyone that I care about them."

"Let me get Flash's food so she can eat with us, then we can feed the guinea pigs after dinner." he says, handing me both plates. "And what love language do you want to receive?"

I sigh, suddenly feeling self-conscious. "Words of affirmation. My parents were never vocal about things with me. Nothing like they were with my brother and sister, and I think I always really wanted that. I had to ask if they loved me, and … it just sucked. Hearing someone tell me the reasons they care for me, it affirms so much for me."

Jamie is quiet as he follows me to the table. As I place each plate onto the surface, he lets out a curse. "I fucking hate your parents. I'm sorry if that angers or offends you, but I really hate them, Aud. They're vile people. No kid should have to ask their parents to love them."

I sit quietly, offering a nonchalant shrug. "It's fine. It is what it is."

His hand covers mine, surprising us both. It's as if he moved without thought, but before I can pull my hand out, he squeezes it reassuringly. "No, it's not fine. It's not fine for parents to so cruelly disregard one of their children. They're lucky I didn't know any of this Saturday night, or I would have …"

"What?" I ask, intrigued. "What would you have done?"

He chuckles. "Pretty sure I would have done nothing, but I'd have seethed silently, wished hellfire upon them, and then made sure I never donated to anything they're involved with again."

I let out a loud laugh. "You'd have done nothing? No fighting for my honor?"

Jamie smiles. "Can I blame two decades of media training on this? I'm so used to never making a scene, and always saying the right things. I don't know how to be confrontational. That's probably part of the reason why I stood there, staring at you like a deer in headlights, and couldn't even move. I'm never in contentious situations unless it's on a football field."

"You did look like a deer caught in headlights at the gala," I confess. "But I can understand where you're coming from. There's a lot of fear associated with confrontations. Never knowing how the other person will react, and how it will impact your life moving forward. So I get it."

"I hate it," Jamie blurts out, seemingly surprised at his own words. "It's kind of dishonest. I don't like playing a role. I hate feeling like I need to be perfect. Like the team depends on me, and a leader can't be a human being who makes mistakes. The stupid shit they're making me do because of the coach's niece Saturday night is frustrating."

"What do you mean? What are they making you do?"

He exhales in frustration. "Media stuff. I got roped into coaching a peewee football team for the summer, and attending more events than I'd been tasked with for the summer. Personally escorting VIPs. Stupid stuff."

"All because a woman had too much to drink and caused a scene?" I ask, flabbergasted.

"Yup. Evidently, I was supposed to control her every move, including policing every drop of liquid she put into her mouth. I was basically forced into taking her, and now I'm forced into all kinds of other shit because of her behavior."

"That's absurd!" I shout, and Flash barks in agreement. "If you hate my parents, can I hate your coaches?"

"Sure," he says with a chuckle.

"I can't believe you're being penalized for someone else's decisions. It's one thing to try and teach a child this way, but grown adults? It makes me assume your date —"

"Not my date." Jamie's interruption is quick, and I bite my lip to keep from smiling. "I see that grin trying to pop out, Doc. It's okay. You can be excited or relieved that it was absolutely not a date."

I grin. "It's not like I have a claim on you, so if it was a date, I wouldn't have any reason to be truly upset."

"While we may not have discussed logistics of our situation yet, I feel like maybe we should have a few ground rules," he says, his face serious.

"Alright." I stare at him, waiting for him to start, while he seems to be waiting for me. "Jamie, I don't know what rules we should set up. My dating history is pretty sparse, so I think you have to take the lead here."

His eyes widen. "Oh. I wasn't insinuating — I mean, I didn't think — crap."

I drop my hands into my lap, turning my napkin until a sharp point forms, and I rub it against the pads of my fingers. It's a weird stim I started in high school, and it helps to calm me. Right now, my nerves are through the roof. I'm debating on how I need to go about asking him some questions, when he suddenly blurts out, "I don't fucking share."

"What?" I ask with a laugh.

"Exclusivity. That's what I mean. If we're dating, then it's just us. I don't want to hear or see you with someone else."

"Well, I'm fine with that, because I did see you with someone else, and it really sucked. So I'm fine with being exclusive. What's next?" I'm absolutely delighted by the first rule. "Oh. Does this mean you're my boyfriend?"

He smiles. "Yeah, Aud. It means I'm your boyfriend."

I'm giddy with happiness as I reply, "I'm glad. Next rule?"

Jamie's brow furrows with concentration. I can see the wheels turning as he attempts to work out what he wants to say, and I patiently wait. Everything he's said leads me to believe he's very nervous about saying the wrong thing in all aspects of his life, and until he's feeling more confident to say whatever he wants in my presence, I'll give him the space he needs.

"As our relationship becomes more physical," he finally says, clearing his throat as his eyes dance between the wall behind me and the floor under our feet, "I think we should both commit to being honest with each other. If we're uncomfortable with something, we need to have a safe space for that."

"I don't like kissing after oral. For either of us. It's just … gross," I confess with a grimace. My sexual history is nothing to write home about, but I've had sex. Kissing a man after he's had his mouth on my vagina is such a turn off.

"Honestly, I don't like it either," Jamie says with a lighthearted laugh. His eyes meet mine, and I see a confident sparkle in them. "I have a problem with eye contact."

"In that you want me to keep my eyes closed?"

"No, I want them open. It helps to ground me, believe it or not. I want to be in every moment with you, and know you're feeling the same as me. I need to know that you feel it all."

The temperature in the room seems to have risen a good ten degrees. "I ca — I can do that. You may have to remind me to keep them open on occasion, though. I imagine I'll close them when something feels really good. Or if I'm about to … to …"

"To come?" he supplies, his eyes suddenly hooded. "How do you feel about dirty talk? Or any conversation at all during sex?"

Holy hell. "I've never experienced it, so I don't know if I'm for or against it."

"If I were to experiment with some things, do you promise you'll tell me if you don't like it?" he asks, and I nod eagerly. "Good girl."

I whimper, and he smiles wolfishly. Only moments ago, Jamie couldn't look me in the eyes while we started this discussion, and now he's done a complete one-eighty. Confidence in spades, and he's exuding alpha male energy. "This is not what I expected from dinner."

"From dinner, or from me?" he asks.

"Both, I guess? You seemed to flip a switch a few minutes ago, and it surprised me a little."

Jamie scoots his chair closer to me, so my legs are between his. He squeezes his knees together, effectively trapping me, and puts both hands on my thighs. I'm glad I'm wearing jeans, because goosebumps are erupting up and down my legs. "There's a lot in life that I'm not comfortable doing, Doc. I don't like talking in front of crowds, and I hate when people I don't know try to hug me. I know what I'm doing in bed, and I'm not afraid to tell you that. Maybe that makes me a cocky motherfucker, but I doubt you'll complain about it after I make you come a few times."

"Jesus," I breathe. This is so completely unexpected, but I'm not complaining. With only his hands on my legs, I'm more turned on now than I think I've ever been. But I'm also overwhelmed, self-conscious, and unsure. "This is a lot for me to process. I'm not sure if I'm ready for all of that just yet."

"I'd never expect you to do something you aren't completely ready for, but I'm really glad you know you can trust me enough to tell me when you're feeling overwhelmed. I like to take the lead in the bedroom, but I also know this is a partnership. I always want you to feel comfortable."

"Okay," I whisper, my head dropping as I look at his hands. I watch as he lifts one to grab my chin between his thumb and fore-finger, raising it up so he can see my eyes again.

"Is it alright if I kiss you?" he asks quietly, and I nod. He gives me a relieved smile as he pulls me closer, pressing his lips gently to mine. It's soft and sweet, and very unlike our first kiss. It's roman-tic, but I can tell he's holding back, as if he's scared I might get spooked.

Our first kiss rocked me to my core. It was passion personified, and I didn't feel like I could get close enough to him. I wanted to wrap myself around Jamie's body. Cover him in my scent. Make him forget that any other woman ever existed before me. While tonight's kiss is sweet, it doesn't feel like Jamie. The collected and calculated quarterback isn't the Jamie I'm falling for, and I want to experience him losing a little bit more control.

While his lips move carefully over mine, I rest my hands on his knees, pushing to a standing position. Jamie breaks off the kiss to look up at me. "What are you doing?"

With Jamie still sitting, I'm not that much taller than him, but I revel in the feeling of him looking up at me. I let a hand drift through his hair, allowing my fingernails to scratch along his scalp, and his eyes flutter closed.

"Eyes on me," I command, though my voice waivers slightly. His eyes pop open, pupils blown out with lust, as he watches me through hooded lids. "I — I think I need eye contact too."

Jamie's hands find my waist, sliding around to cup my ass, as he pulls me closer to his body. "Absolutely love that, baby."

Oh my. I've never been called baby before. I had a brief boyfriend in college who called me babe, and a guy I dated after vet school who called me hun. I hated both nicknames, but, like Jamie, I was never comfortable with confrontation, and didn't tell either man my feelings. But baby? I'm so here for this. Somehow, it gives me a boost of confidence to say what I'm thinking. "Kiss me like you really mean it."

He gives me a confused look, shaking his head. "What do you mean? I did kiss you like I meant it."

"No, you kissed me how you thought I wanted to be kissed. You figured I was overwhelmed, so you dialed it down a bunch. I don't want quarterback Jamie, the one who says what everyone expects, and does what everyone wants. I want *my* Jamie."

"*Fuck me,*" he says hoarsely, yanking me against his body as he crashes his lips to mine. As he thrusts his tongue into my mouth, he stands, unexpectedly picking me up, and I shriek against him. He manhandles me so my legs are wrapped around his waist, then sets off down the hall and into my bedroom. I'm tossed unceremoniously onto my bed with Jamie following me a split second later. I gasp when his length hits my core perfectly, then immediately moan when he reaches a hand up to wind my hair around his fist, pulling it at just the right amount of tension. He breaks off the kiss to slide his tongue down my neck, briefly nibbling on my collarbone, before sucking on my pulse point. "You're so fucking sexy, Audrey."

I'm about to reciprocate the compliment, when multiple things happen simultaneously: Jamie's phone rings, Flash begins to bark incessantly, and my quintuplet of guinea pigs screech horrifyingly loudly. Jamie raises his head to look at me, a look of disbelief on his gorgeous face. "Can't say I've ever been cockblocked by a guinea pig before, but I guess there's a first time for everything."

Jamie
COLORADO COYOTES
7

CHAPTER 17

IN HINDSIGHT, IT WAS GOOD THAT HELL BROKE LOOSE BEFORE THINGS went too far with Audrey. My phone call was Maddox checking in on me, wanting to be sure things were going well with Audrey. I sent him a quick text telling him that everything is great, and that he needs to kindly fuck off, because I'm with my girl. He respectfully doesn't respond.

Flash barked because she needed to go out. While Audrey got her hooked into her wheelchair, I checked on the guinea pigs. While getting everything plated for me, Audrey, and Flash, I'd forgotten to feed the pigs, and evidently, that was unacceptable. As soon as I dished out the array of fruits and vegetables, all five pigs happily gnawed away on their dinner.

I busied myself cleaning up after our meal, glad to have a moment to decompress while reviewing everything we discussed tonight. I know I surprised Audrey with a few things I said, and honestly, it was slightly shocking to me as well. I've never been so brash with a woman in bed. Yes, I've said things from time to time where I lacked a filter, but never in this way. Never a conscious choice where I finally allowed myself to speak freely. I trust Audrey more than any woman I've ever been with, and I know that's why I confidently asked her what I did. I'd always wanted to have a relationship where I could spice things up in the bedroom, but never felt comfortable with anyone before. I think Audrey is the first woman who knows so much about me, and it's given me a confidence I never thought I'd crave.

Our kisses alone are explosive, and it makes me wonder what everything will be like with her. And what she'll want or need from me. I'm confident in the bedroom, but this is the first time where I've been this damn excited about experiencing everything with a woman.

Because it's Audrey.

I jolt when I hear a scream, recognizing Audrey's voice from outside, and I sprint to the door. Throwing it open, I find a trembling Audrey carrying Flash in her arms, the poor pup whimpering. "What happened?"

"A bobcat ran out from under a bush," Audrey cries, rushing in to place Flash on the table. Quickly unstrapping her from her wheelchair, she pats over Flash's fur, looking for injuries. "The bobcat snapped at Flash, but I don't know if it got her."

Fuck. "Is the bobcat still out there?"

She shakes her head. "No, it took off. I don't know why it went after Flash! It was double the size of my poor puppy."

"Probably just a defensive maneuver," I murmur. "It didn't notice the size, just a threat."

I place my hands on Audrey's shoulders, not sure how to help. She shrugs off my hands, making me step back. "I'm sorry."

She shakes her head. "No, it's me. I need a minute. I can't be touched right now. It's an overstimulation thing."

"I understand. I get that way too." After incredibly intense games, especially when I'm unable to shut off the noise of the fans, I need time to decompress before I can speak to the media. Times when I'm out and get mobbed by fans I have an even worse time recentering myself. It's a relief to know that I can step back in this moment, give Audrey her space, and know that I'm not offending her. Plus, when I undoubtedly have a case of overstimulation in the future, Audrey will respect my boundaries as well.

Stepping back, I sit on the couch as I watch as Audrey frets over her dog. It's fascinating to see her transform from a pet owner to a veterinarian. I watch, captivated, as she murmurs quietly to herself, and I assume she's going through some kind of injury checklist. When she seems satisfied that Flash isn't injured, she lets out a relieved breath, closing her eyes. A minute or two later, she carefully picks Flash up, and places her onto her dog bed by the couch. Then she turns to me, and I can see the despair in her eyes. I don't approach her, waiting to see what she does. I'll only move when I know she's regulated and comfortable.

"Flash is all I have," she whispers. "Obviously the relationship I have with my family is contentious at best. I don't have a lot of girl-friends. Flash became like a child for me, and the thought that something might happen to her …"

"I know," I say quietly, then I confess something I've only told my therapist. "I watched a neighbor kill my dog when I was a kid."

Audrey gasps, coming to sit beside me. Her hands cover mine in a move I'm learning is subconscious, but it's comforting all the same. "That's awful! I'm so sorry, Jamie. Why?"

I shrug. "I never knew the reason. My dog got out, which he'd been known to do from time to time. My parents didn't have the best relationship with the neighbor, who was an old man, very set in his ways. There was a spot between our fences that Brody liked to dig through, and I tried to catch him before he made it into the guy's yard. As soon as I followed him under, I heard the shot."

"How old were you?" Audrey asks softly, her eyes brimming with tears.

"Nine."

She gasps again, covering her mouth with her hands. "You were so little! What did your parents do?"

"Nothing."

"What?" she cries. "How could they do nothing?"

"Neighbor said he thought it was a cougar, and that it was an accident. But I saw the look in his eyes. It was intentional. My parents offered to get me another dog, but I said no. I didn't want to experience the pain of losing another dog. I've never owned a dog again."

"Is that why you have cats?"

"I guess so. My cats are solely indoor cats, so I can control their environment, and what people they come into contact with. It's also why I started my foundation. We provide trap-neuter-release programs, training for both professionals and new pet owners, and work with shelters and rescues on ensuring pets are placed in good homes. I can't prevent another dog from being shot by a neighbor, but I can make sure that training is accessible to families. If we'd had training, I could have shouted a one-word command that Brody immediately followed."

"I saw most of what your foundation offers on the website, but I had no idea how personal it is for you. I'm so sorry, Jamie," she says, her voice soft, and filled with pain. "I've worked with a local trainer who teaches her clients to pick a specific recall word for emergency situations, like running into the road. I'm sure it could have been beneficial for your dog, but it sounds like your neighbor had a vendetta against you and your dog anyway."

"Possibly. But I understand what happened tonight. How you feared for her life, and how you immediately thought losing her would impact your world. I get it."

"Thank you for being so understanding," she whispers. "About her and about how I reacted."

"Of course. That jump in adrenaline put your senses into over-drive. I know how to handle some of it, but there are times when I'm hit with something unexpected. Game days I have everything down to the minute. I've been playing long enough that I can even handle kinks in my schedule. But sometimes, I get thrown such a massive curveball that my body almost seizes up. If my anxiety gets too high, I'll have a panic attack, or I might throw up, like I did the first night I came here. Typically afterwards, I feel an equal sense of relief and guilt over how my body seemed to take control however it wanted."

Her smile is slightly wobbly as she responds. "I have an adrenaline crash. Right now, I'm suddenly so unbelievably exhausted, but at the same time, I want to curl myself around Flash and count how many times she breathes per minute."

"How can I help? If the best thing I can do is leave, feel free to tell me. If you'd like me to count her breaths while you sleep, I can do that as well. Give me my marching orders, Doc."

Her mouth opens and closes a couple of times before she finally answers. "I know that some cats can be left alone for days at a time. Is that true with yours?"

"Yeah, I guess," I say with a confused laugh. Audrey gives me a shy look, clearly hesitant to say what she wants. "I have a pet sitter check on them when I'm out of town, but they've been left alone for a night or two without any issues. What's going on in that head of yours?"

"It's just …" she trails off, closing her eyes as she takes a deep breath. "I thought maybe you could sleep over tonight. I don't want to be alone."

"Of course I'll stay," I reply, pulling her into my arms. She comes willingly, fitting perfectly as her legs straddle mine, and we both sigh. This woman is quickly becoming a safe zone for me, and I can only hope she feels the same way about me.

Audrey lets out a relieved exhale as she gives me a genuine smile. "Okay. Good. I'll get Flash all situated in her kennel, then meet you in the bedroom."

She pecks my lips quickly before jumping out of my lap. Scooping Flash up, she murmurs quietly into Flash's ear, giving me a moment to adjust myself. My body responds to Audrey's nearness, regardless of the circumstances. Tonight is not the night for any bedroom activities, and I mentally tell my cock to simmer the hell down.

Standing, I quietly walk past Audrey as she places Flash in her cage, then stop when Audrey speaks up. "I have extra toothbrushes under the sink in my attached bathroom. Probably anything else you might need as well."

I laugh as I enter her bedroom, the familiar scent of her filling my nostrils. It's a mixture of lavender and rose, and I imagine the lavender is from her shampoo or conditioner, as I recognize it after waking up with my face buried in her hair. Walking into the bathroom, I open the cabinet to locate a new toothbrush, chuckling as I notice the same setup as her guest bathroom, with each item categorized by type and size. The rose smell is stronger in here, and I peek into her shower, trying to locate the possible culprit.

And that's when I notice her vibrator.

It sits on the ledge of her bathtub, bright pink against the white porcelain, and the erection I just willed into submission is fighting a winning battle against the fabric of my boxer briefs and jeans. My vision becomes tunneled as all I can see is the vibrator. All I can hear are the sounds my mind conjures up that Audrey might make, and I can almost taste her skin.

As I hear her pad into the room, I make a split second decision, calling out, "You cool if I take a quick shower? I sleep better if I feel, um, clean."

"Oh, sure. Use whatever you need," she says, and I shut the door without hesitation. Immediately unbuttoning my jeans, I hiss as I yank my cock out, looking at the angry, red, and engorged head. I quickly strip, turning on the faucet in the shower-tub combo as I step inside. Even the cold water doesn't curb my erection, and as soon as the water warms up, I grab the bottle with a rose emblem on it, filling my palm. As the aroma emanates in the humid air, I grip my cock tightly at the base, groaning as I take a long stroke all the way to the tip. I'm so turned on I think it'll be a minute or less until I come.

So, of course, Audrey crashes into the bathroom. Before I have time to realize what she's doing, she throws open the shower curtain, shouting, "Oh my God!"

As she frantically grabs her vibrator, her eyes dart to my groin, where they widen comically. I'm mid-stroke, and it's the only part of my body covered in soap. She has to know what I'm doing.

"That's — yo — you're …" she stammers, her eyes zeroed in on my dick. She seems unable to look away, just as I'm unable to let go of myself. It's then that I notice her legs shift, almost imperceptibly, as she's trying to provide some friction for herself. I think of what I can say at this moment. Ignore it all? Continue like it's totally normal? Ask if she wants to watch? But since all of the blood in my body is currently running to the organ she can't look away from, my brain and mouth are not on the same page.

"You get off in the shower, Audrey?" I blurt out, staring at the hand that fails to hide her pink vibrator. I expect a rebuttal, or a flat out denial, instead, Audrey nods, and I have to brace a hand on the wall to keep myself upright. I squeeze myself tightly, hitting the underside of my cock where it feels the best, and watch as her nipples pebble against her tee shirt. It's only now that I notice she's taken off her bra and pants, and I want nothing more than to drag my tongue along every perfect inch of her creamy thighs. "The thought of you playing with yourself is really fucking hot, Doc."

She doesn't reply, but the lust in her eyes as she watches me slowly jack myself is answer enough. I've never had someone watch me masturbate, and I'm finding it incredibly erotic. But I'd like it more if I get a show as well.

"Show me, baby," I say huskily. Her eyes pop to mine, and I see the confusion there. "Show me how you touch yourself. If you're going to watch, I think I need to as well."

I wait with bated breath as she nervously bites her lip. I assume I've surprised her, and honestly, I'm surprised myself. Not only that I asked her to touch herself, but how turned on it made me to think about her doing it. I squeeze the base of my cock again, harder this time, in an attempt to hold off my impending orgasm.

"Have you thought of me?" I ask, nodding at the vibrator. "When using that, have you thought of me?"

"Yes," she whispers, her voice much higher than I've ever heard it. I expect her to open the shower curtain, maybe move to the other side of the bathroom, but she surprises me by stepping into the shower, right under the cascade of water. Her tee shirt is immediately plastered to her skin, and I let out a loud groan as her perfect breasts are molded to the fabric. Large tits that I can't wait to get into my hands. Tits I want to fuck.

Audrey takes a step toward me, but I put up a hand to stop her. "No. I want to watch. If I get my hands on you, all bets are off. One time won't be enough, and I'll keep you up all night. But you've had a rough night, and you need sleep. Tonight you'll get yourself off, with my words, and then when I finally have an entire night to have you the way I want, I'll know exactly how you need to be touched."

I hear a muted buzzing as Audrey turns on her vibrator, then slips it between her wet panties and her skin. Jesus Christ, I can see the outline of her pussy, and the dark hair covering it. I want to drop to my knees and worship directly at her altar, but I force myself to stay upright. Touching herself in front of me is more than enough. She's trusting me with a part I'm willing to bet no one has ever witnessed before.

I don't have to see the vibrator hit her clit, I know when it does. Her sharp intake of breath tells me. "Jamie ..."

"Eyes on me," I command harshly as her eyes flutter closed. They pop open, glazed with lust. "If I touched you right now, what would I do?"

"What?" she asks, the word attached to a long moan.

"Where would you want me to touch you? Right now, Doc. Do you want my fingers circling your clit? Or deep inside you, feeling you pulsate around me? What about your breasts? I want to know how sensitive they are. Do you like having your nipples sucked?"

"Jamie," she moans, her head thrashing around as her hips rhythmically undulate against the vibrator.

"Words, baby. Tell me what you want," I reply as I give myself a long stroke.

"You — your mouth," she stutters. "I want your mouth."

"Where?"

"My nipples. And then my clit."

"Fuck," I groan, quickening my pace. I see Audrey's finger move, as she presses a button on the vibrator, and I hear the corresponding speed amp up on the toy. I feel the tingling at the base of my spine, the telltale sign my orgasm is mere moments away, and I'm determined to bring Audrey with me. "This is the hottest thing I've ever done, Audrey. Without a doubt. I barely made it into the shower without coming, just at the thought of you touching yourself. I can't wait to taste you. To fuck you. To make you mine. Marking you."

I see the moment the words take hold, and her eyes roll back as her back arches in bliss. She lets out the most beautifully guttural moan I've ever heard, and that sound sets off my orgasm. The first rope of cum hits her wet tee shirt across her breasts, and the second across her abdomen. Gasping for breath, I miss her tiny hand reaching out to grasp my dick, and it sucks the air out of the room. Her thumb tenderly rubs a final drop around the crown, and I watch as she brings her thumb to her lips, licking my release off her skin. "Jesus Christ, baby."

Wide brown eyes peer up at me as her hand drops from her mouth. "I'll let you finish up in here."

Audrey steps out of the shower, and after wrapping herself in a thick towel I noticed hanging from the back of the door, she quietly lets herself out of the bathroom. It's only then that I allow my legs to relax, sliding down the wall until I'm lying in the tub.

Who the hell is this vixen?

Audrey

CHAPTER 18

Who the hell am I?

That was the most brazen thing I've ever done. Hell, more than one brazen thing. What was I thinking, barging in there to grab my vibrator? I knew the probability of him finding it was high, but at that moment, it was like my body operated on its own accord. I should have grabbed the vibrator and bolted, but once I saw Jamie was masturbating, I couldn't move. I was completely spellbound. Captivated.

When he began talking, telling me how he would touch me, I was a ticking time bomb. The grittiness of his voice was like sandpaper against my skin. I could *feel* what he wanted to do to me. My body reacted viscerally to his words, and my orgasm almost knocked me over.

But me reaching out to touch him, and then licking off the last bit of his release? I have no idea what came over me. That act should have made me incredibly uncomfortable. All of my sexual experiences thus far have been incredibly tame. Tonight, however, I immediately knew he was thinking about me, and I was emboldened for the first time in my life. Feminine confidence and sensuality. It was like my orgasm gave me an even bigger high, and I had to capitalize on it.

Now, though, I'm shaken and feeling quite raw. When I hear the water turn off in the shower, I frantically strip out of my wet clothes, rushing into my closet to get appropriately dressed. Should I get into bed and fake sleep? Act like nothing happened? Shit. I'm overthinking this.

As I exit my closet, the bathroom door opens. Wearing only his boxers, Jamie strides toward me, and before I can say a word, he takes me into his arms, kissing me deeply. I sigh into his mouth as I wind my arms around his neck. The kiss isn't passionate, but it's exactly what I need while my mind is working overtime to mess with my emotions. It feels like Jamie is claiming me. Telling me it's okay, that nothing has changed in our dynamic.

Breaking off the kiss, he rests his forehead against mine. "You still okay if I spend the night?"

I let out a relieved breath as I nod. He could have asked if I still wanted him to stay, but by specifically stating it the way he did, he put the decision with me, as if *he* needs *me* instead of the other way around.

"Good," he whispers, placing a tender kiss on the tip of my nose. "I think I need a cuddle after that. You kinda rocked my world, Doctor Carrington."

I snort as he lets go, heading to the side of the bed where he napped yesterday. I turn off the lights, close the door, and round the bed to my side. We both get under the covers, facing each other.

"Can I tell you a secret?" he says quietly.

"Yes."

"I've never done anything like that before."

"Really?"

"Yeah. That was incredibly hot."

"I'm surprised. I'd have thought you had all kinds of experiences like that," I tell him, shyly.

He's quiet for a moment before he speaks. "I don't think I've ever felt comfortable enough with a woman to ask her to do something like that. And as cocky as this sounds, most women who want to sleep with a football player aren't in it for the experience. Once they realize I'm not the stereotypical athlete, they want to get off and get the hell out of there."

"But you feel comfortable with me," I state softly, almost to myself, then yelp as he grabs my arm, yanking me against him so my head is on his chest.

"Yeah, Doc. You make me feel like no other woman has."

"What?"

He sighs as he kisses the top of my head. "You make me feel normal."

As the first ray of light courses between the wood blinds of my bedroom window, I know I'm alone. What is most surprising is how sad I feel that I'm alone.

Before we fell asleep, Jamie told me he had an early workout with a couple of the guys from his offensive line, and said he'd be quiet. Knowing how lightly I sleep, I assumed I'd still wake up. Either he is a ninja, or that orgasm put me into a coma.

Honestly, I'm not sure which reason I think is more accurate. In any case, I'm slightly bummed I didn't wake up, because I know he's going out of town for the rest of the week.

Reaching over to pick up my phone, my hand hits a piece of paper.

> *Aud,*
>
> *You're cute when you snore.*
>
> *In case you've forgotten, I'm headed out of town until Friday for a brand marketing thing. I'd love to have you and Flash over for dinner at my place Friday night. We*

need to finalize the menu and place setting for the event, and I really want to have you in my space.

I've never invited a woman to my home before. Do with that what you will.

If you were to bring an overnight bag, I wouldn't object. Will the pigs be okay for twelve hours? If not, bring them. I'll buy another cage.

Already missing you.

-J

I hold the paper to my chest and squeal. It still makes no sense to me that this man isn't taken. What woman in her right mind wouldn't see the remarkable man that he is? He's ready to buy another behemoth cage on the off chance I want to spend the night at his place. I bet he'll also get a dog bed, dog bowls, and the whole nine yards if I don't stop him.

Grabbing my phone, I fire off a text, expecting he won't reply until later. He, of course, responds immediately.

ME

Do NOT buy another massive cage. The pigs will be fine.

QB

If a cage were to miraculously appear, would it be like we share custody of them? A single man to a dad of eight. What a story.

ME

Five guinea pigs, Jamie. Five.

QB

Plus Maverick, Goose, and Flash.

ME

You counted my dog in your new fatherhood experience?

QB

Of course. I was ready to go murder a bobcat, so I think that qualifies as a father figure.

ME

I don't have any weapons in my apartment, so I'm honestly intrigued with how you intended to murder it.

QB

It's at this moment I realize I don't know how big bobcats are. In my head they're the size of my cats, but more attitude and clearly feral.

Oh shit.

I Googled them. Nope, disregard. I love Flash, but I'm not equipped to take on a bobcat unless you have a crossbow, a set of carving knives, or a variety of grenades lying around.

ME

You know what? I JUST gave out my last grenade as a Halloween treat to a kid down the block last year. Bummer.

QB

Weirdly disappointed, Aud. But, courtesy of Amazon, I can get a variety of throwing knives, axes, or even steel spikes delivered by lunchtime tomorrow.

ME

What can't you buy on Amazon?

QB

Apparently nothing if you search for "things
to kill a bobcat with."

ME

Your search history is so screwed now.

QB

All in the name of Flash's honor.

I can't help the laughter that bursts from me as I toss my phone onto the bed next to me. I'm not sure I've ever felt this happy or content. All because of the hot professional quarterback who searches for how to murder bobcats.

Before I know it, it's Friday evening. Jamie texted me all week while he was in California, meeting with the team from some kind of shoe deal he has. He filmed a commercial, and said it'll start airing right at the start of football season.

My boyfriend has his own shoe commercial.

How is this real life?

After nervously packing an overnight bag, I pack everyone in the car — because I truly know Jamie will have a cage for the pigs — and set off to his neighborhood. While we don't live too far from one another, Denver traffic can be abysmal at best, and Friday night at rush hour is heinous no matter where I'm going. The typical drive should take no more than twenty or thirty minutes, but takes me over an hour.

When I pull into his gated community, I have a moment of panic. It reminds me of where I grew up. While the houses are newer, a wave of anxiety and PTSD makes my heart rate spike. What are his neighbors like? Do my parents know anyone here? Probably not. They'd consider this area to be 'new money' and wouldn't want to associate themselves with anyone they deemed less than. After witnessing their distaste of Jamie last weekend, I can only assume they'll be horrified at my relationship.

Ten years ago, I'd have ended things with a man my parents disapproved of. Even knowing I'd never gain their unconditional love and trust like my brother and sister have, I wouldn't have chosen to rock the boat. I smile to myself as I drive slowly through Jamie's neighborhood, realizing just how much I've grown in the last decade. While my family is still in my life, and there are times they control situations or attendance at events, I've stood up for myself more times than I can count. My confidence has grown leaps and bounds, and I can only hope having Jamie in my life will continue that.

"Holy shit," I breathe, as I pull up to another gate at the top of a very long driveway. I can't see the entire home yet, just the roof, as it's built beyond a hill. Jamie has a gated home within a gated community. What does he go through that he feels he needs this kind of protection? Am I getting in over my head?

I pull up to a control box with a camera, prepared to push the button, when a loud buzz sounds. I watch as the gate begins to open, and more of the palatial home comes into view.

"Doc."

"Hmm?"

Jamie chuckles through the speaker. "You can drive in. The door won't bite you."

"Uh-huh," I murmur.

"I might, though."

"What?"

Loud laughter answers me. "Just pull in, baby. Garage is open, so pull in the open spot. I'll come help you unload."

I don't answer as I take my foot off the brake, inching forward at a glacial pace. As I slowly move down the driveway, my mouth drops open at the scope of the home. The magnitude is astounding. It's at least double the size of my parents' house. The palatial estate has cream stucco, and oak shutters frame every window. Even with the sun setting, I can tell the windows are tinted, and they mirror the sky as it darkens. A two-story entry with double oak doors is highlighted by large stone pillars, and modern lighting accents the entire front.

As I pull around the side to the attached four-car garage, I find Jamie waving eagerly, pointing to one empty bay. I creep into the space slowly, my eyes dancing around to notice the phenomenal view of the Rockies from the rear of the home, and Jamie's three cars parked in a perfect line in the other garage spots. So perfect, in fact, I bet I could pull out a measuring tape to find they are all parked at the exact same distance from the wall. As someone who loves good organization and patterns, I appreciate this, and attempt to match his depth.

I barely have the car in park before Jamie opens the passenger door to grab Flash. He gives me a huge grin as he nods his head toward the carrier in the back seat. "Knew you'd bring 'em."

I shrug. "I knew you'd have a cage, whether I told you to or not."

"I do."

"Is it the same one you got me?"

He puts Flash down on the concrete pad as he hits the remote button to close the door, then scratches the back of his neck sheepishly. "It might be a little bigger than yours."

I don't even know why I'm surprised. I shut my door, then round the car to meet him by the trunk. "If you spoil them, they won't want to go home."

He kisses me quickly, then winks. "Maybe that's the plan. Did you, uh, bring an overnight bag?"

I'm tempted to lie. Tease him mercilessly. But he looks so hopeful, so excited, that I can't bring myself to do it. "It's in the trunk."

Jamie's answering grin is instant. "Hell yeah. Which is heavier, your bag or the pig carrier?"

"The carrier, definitely. I travel light when I don't have pets," I answer. I'm nowhere near as vain as most women my age. I don't wear a lot of makeup, I rarely purchase shoes, and I'd rather be comfortable than stylish any day. Honestly, the only thing that I spend money on that goes on my body are my tattoos.

Opening the trunk, I grab my bag, as well as a bag of supplies for Flash, but now I'm assuming Jamie also has stuff for her in his house. He ushers me to the door, and I follow him into a massive mud room. I toe my shoes off, leaving them next to his, then continue into one of the largest kitchens I've ever seen.

"No wonder you like to cook," I murmur, surveying the beautiful space. "I would too, if I had this kitchen."

Two parallel islands move into a stunning two-story great room. White quartz with light gray marbled throughout, the counters are empty of clutter, except for perfectly placed decorative pieces. A giant range sits beside a double oven, and through a doorway, I can see a gigantic fridge. "Why is the fridge back in there?"

"It's a butlers' pantry. Or at least that's what my realtor said when I asked about it. A giant fridge takes away from the clean lines of the kitchen. We can't let anyone know we actually eat, you know," Jamie says sarcastically.

Turning, I stare in awe at the floor-to-ceiling windows that cover the entirety of the back of the house, giving me a stunning view of sunset behind the Rocky Mountains. "Wow. That is spectacular."

"Big selling point for me. I wanted a view. Plus the land behind me is a federally protected reserve, so I know no one can build back there."

"What's the deal with the double gate situation?" I ask, watching as he bends down to give Flash a bone.

"I've had some overzealous fans in the past who've managed to get right to my front door. I'm a private guy, and my house is my safe space. I don't want anyone here unless I personally invite them."

"So you've had stalkers?"

"I wouldn't go that far," he says hesitantly.

I walk to him slowly. "Okay. Define 'overzealous' for me, then."

He exhales. "One particular person —"

I interrupt him. "Male or female?"

"It was a woman." Of course it was.

"What did she do?"

"She turned up at my apartment downtown. I moved out to the suburbs, and she turned up there, too. So when I found this place, I bought it under the foundation's name, and had everything moved while we were playing one Sunday afternoon. I had a private investigator who tracked her to the game, and that allowed my agent to spearhead a moving team. They had me packed and out of there in three hours."

"Jesus, Jamie," I whisper. "She was stalking you. That's not okay. Does she still live here?"

"According to my PI, no. She moved out of the state a year or two ago. You want to help me get the pigs set up?" He grabs the carrier again, motioning for me to follow him.

"Nice change of topic," I comment. "Do you think she's someone I should be worried about?"

"No, especially since we aren't public yet. I'd occasionally get a DM from her here or there, but I haven't gotten anything since she moved. I really think she gave up." I follow him down a hallway, past a guest room, and into a large office. Inside, I find a wooden cage at least twice the size of mine.

"Seriously?" I screech, pointing at it. "What the hell is that?"

He laughs. "It's possible I misjudged the measurements. Jax enabled it, though. He wanted to buy one as well, but Becca said no."

"At least one of you is smart," I mumble, standing beside him in front of the behemoth cage. I reach out to touch a material covering the cage, similar to window screening. "Is this a net?"

"Kind of. It's the thickest screening I could find. I don't think my cats can claw through it, but I wanted to take every precaution necessary." As if summoned by a beacon, a loud yowl sounds from behind me, then I hear Flash's front paws trying to gain traction on the wood floors. A cat tears by me, soundlessly jumping onto the top of the enclosure, as Flash wheels furiously down the hallway. She attempts to turn the corner into the office, but a wheel gets stuck on the transition to carpet, and she thunks into the wall. "Well, shit. I didn't think Flash would be involved in antagonizing the cats, too. This one is Maverick. He's a little too curious for his own good, and I'm fairly sure he's gone through a couple of his nine lives so far."

"I don't know if Flash has ever seen a cat up close," I muse, righting her wheelchair and scratching behind her ears. "Whenever she's at my clinic, I keep her sequestered behind the desk so she can't get into any scuffles. She's a scrappy little thing."

"Just like her mom, I suspect," Jamie says warmly, and I roll my eyes.

"No. Confrontations are not my thing. Flash has more balls than me." As Jamie opens one of the enclosure doors, I quietly hand him each guinea pig, watching as he carefully places each one at varying spots. Bill takes off to hide in a little hut, with only his tush showing. Desmond proudly poses at the top of a staircase, twitching his nose in every direction. Frank and Norm attack a plate of fresh hay, while Burt goes right for a large carrot dangling from a rope. I scope out a large plastic bin next to the enclosure, assuming Jamie has lots of other supplies inside, and also notice a supersized bag of hay. "They don't go through that much hay in a night, Jamie."

"Wishful thinking, Doc," he says, giving me a lopsided smile. "I'm hoping this isn't the only night you stay over. Now let's go find my other troublemaker for an introduction … well, never mind."

A blur of black and white jumps soundlessly onto the guinea pig cage, right next to his brother, and stares down his nose at me. "I take it this is the grumpy one."

Jamie nods with a chuckle. "Don't take it personally if Goose doesn't want anything to do with you yet. He's anti-social."

I guess I identify as a cat, because anti-social is a huge part of my personality too.

Jamie
COLORADO COYOTES
7

CHAPTER 19

Audrey doesn't reply, but pink covers her cheeks as she bites her lip. I'm taking it as a good sign, but I don't want Audrey to feel like I'm pressuring her. I can be patient.

Grabbing both cats off the enclosure, I secure them against my chest before placing one hand on Audrey's back, and lightly push her toward the doorway. "I'm going to close the door so the pigs can get acclimated without Maverick or Goose bothering them."

"Probably wise," Audrey says quietly, allowing me to guide her out of the room. Flash follows, her eyes zeroed in on Goose in my arms, occasionally growling at my angry cat. I toss Goose onto the stairs right as the oven timer goes off. "Did you cook?"

"No, I put our dinner in there to stay warm."

"What are we having?" Audrey asks as she follows me into the kitchen.

"I had the event caterers send us two of everything they offer so we can finalize the menu. So it's pretty much a smorgasbord."

"Wait!" she shouts, and I turn to find a horrified expression on her face. "They have seafood on their menu! You can't have anything!"

"I can't believe you remembered that," I murmur.

She huffs. "Of course I remember! I could have poisoned you with clam chowder!"

I chuckle. "Poison is a little bit of a stretch, and usually I ask what something is before I put it in my mouth. The caterers know. They assured me everything was prepared separately from any seafood dishes, and also said we can have a gluten-free area for the event. Their head chef has a child with celiac, and he takes food preparation very seriously."

"Oh, that's good. We should include that option on the RSVPs so we know how much to request."

Putting oven mitts on my hands, I carefully remove the large aluminum pan, placing it on the island. "Would you prefer to plate things and eat in the dining room, or —"

Audrey pulls the foil off the top of the pan, immediately grabbing a roasted potato and popping it into her mouth. "We can eat here. Why dirty up plates?"

This woman is perfect. "Sounds good to me. Pull up a stool."

And this is how I have my first meal with my girlfriend in my home, hovering over a disposable pan full of twenty different foods.

"So," I say, chewing on the top of my pen, "I have beef tenderloin, chicken Provençal, and mushroom risotto. Sides are roasted potatoes, a vegetable mix, and a side salad with a vinaigrette dressing. Servers will have trays of hors d'oeuvres including a potato pastry puff, bacon wrapped beef, chicken bruschetta, and hummus-filled phyllo cups. Should we have more sides at dinner?"

"No," Audrey answers confidently. "I've been to enough of these events. I can guarantee most people will barely eat anyway. As long as we have an open bar, they won't complain."

"I was thinking a cash bar," I admit. "We've made a lot of money that way in the past."

"Rich drunks spend more money on things, especially when the alcohol is free. Why do you think casinos in Vegas offer free drinks to gamblers?"

Well, I feel stupid. "That makes a lot of sense, and I feel like an idiot. No one on the board has argued with me over it."

"You're the owner. You're intimidating. While it's possible the board doesn't know about casinos, I know I'd be intimidated by you if I had to disagree with something like that."

"Oh yeah?" I murmur, pulling her stool closer to mine so I can wrap my arms around her. I glance quickly at Flash, zonked out on the new dog bed I purchased today, her wheelchair perched next to her. Evidently, chasing after a curious cat is exhausting. "Am I intimidating now?"

She giggles, the sound melodious and phenomenal. "Not especially, no. Do you *want* me to be intimidated by you?"

"No. I like you in my space. I don't want to scare you away."

"It's not like I can get out of here without your permission," she jokes. "I'm not scaling the fence, and frankly, your driveway is too long. If I'm running, I can assure you that something is chasing me."

"What if I'm the one chasing you?" I ask softly, leaning forward to suckle on the spot where her neck meets her shoulder.

Her quick intake of breath, followed by the tiniest of whimpers, is music to my ears. "I've never been chased before. Literally or metaphorically."

"Metaphorically?"

"Yeah. Like when a man puts in the effort to win a woman's heart," she says breathlessly as I nibble lightly on her collarbone. Her words make my head whip up to stare at her incredulously.

"No man has ever tried to win you? No courting, nothing?"

She shakes her head shyly. "I've mentioned before that my dating experience is pretty lackluster. I've been fine with that. Then you sort of steamrolled in, and took me completely by surprise."

Stunned speechless, my eyes dart between hers. How is this possible? Audrey is the sweetest and most genuine woman I've ever met. No one has ever been as compassionate with me before. I find it hard to believe that any guy she's come into contact with has seen this side of her still chose to bolt.

"I think, maybe, I've been waiting for you," Audrey blurts out, and a lump forms in my throat. Maybe she's right. Maybe that's why I've never felt the inclination to get serious with another woman. I suppose I may have been waiting for her too. But the words don't seem to come out. Instead, I lean forward to kiss her deeply.

I try to pace myself. Focus on breathing. Try to read every nonverbal signal Audrey sends my way. The sounds she makes, if she touches me, and how she kisses me back. But honestly, I'm shit at reading signs like this, and I send up a mental thank you to the man upstairs when Audrey climbs into my lap. That's a signal I understand.

"Jamie," she whispers against my lips. "Take me to bed."

"Yes, ma'am," I mutter, putting my hands under her ass to lift her. She wraps her legs around my waist, and I vaguely think about how perfect she feels like this as I quickly stride to the stairs.

"Will Flash be alright down here for a bit? My bedroom is upstairs," I explain.

"She'll be fine. She's a heavy sleeper," Audrey answers, her voice sultry and husky as she applies a light kiss to my neck. The sensation sends a shiver down my spine, and I almost drop her as I stalk into my bedroom. Noting Maverick on the large cat tree in the corner, I unceremoniously drop Audrey onto the bed, then grab Maverick, evicting him from my room. Closing the door quickly, I rip off my shirt as I cover Audrey's body with my own. She sighs happily into my mouth as my tongue circles hers, and wraps all of her limbs around me.

I pepper kisses down her neck, pulling her shirt up to expose her stomach and chest. Tonguing her nipple through her lace bra, I revel in how quickly it pebbles against the fabric. Audrey's hands latch in my hair, holding my head in place. I move to her other nipple, applying the same technique, listening to Audrey's quiet moans of pleasure. "Is this okay?"

"Uh-huh," she replies.

"You'll tell me if you don't like something? If you want me to stop?"

"Oh God, please don't stop," she whimpers, pushing my head down against her breast, making me chuckle against her skin.

"I don't plan on stopping, baby, unless you tell me to. As soon as you say the word, I stop." I pull her shirt all the way up, over her head, and she frantically removes it.

"I got it. Consent, good. Words, good. Jamie, good. Get back at it," she says, motioning for me to continue.

"You cool if I take off your leggings?" The thin fabric that seems painted on, covering her delectable ass that I want to bury my face in.

"Uh-huh. You cool if we nix the constant questions, and you just get to removing my clothes, please?" I see the passion in her eyes, and the slight bite of impatience in her tone makes me smile.

"I like this side of you, Doc. Not shy or reserved. You gonna give me lip the whole time, or do you think I can shut you up with my mouth?" I ask cheerfully as I pull her leggings and panties off simultaneously.

"Well at least if your mouth is occupied, you can't keep asking me ques — oh Godddddddd," she moans, as I dive right in, latching onto her clit. Yeah, that's what I thought.

Eyes closed, Audrey looks breathtaking as she moans and thrashes against me. One hand grabs a handful of my hair, while the other pinches her nipple. I had told her I needed eye contact, but right now, unabashedly watching her as I bring her closer to climax, I'm in awe. She's just so fucking beautiful.

Sliding my middle finger into her pussy, I begin manipulating her to determine what spot feels the best. Finding her G-spot, I apply minimal pressure, feeling her clench in response. When I slide the tip of my tongue under the hood of her clit, her entire body tightens unlike anything I've ever felt before. I dance around it, dragging my tongue up and down, close but never close enough, until Audrey yanks me by the hair and puts me where she wants me.

"Jamie, please. I need to come," she whimpers.

I apply a quick flick to her clit, then add a finger to rub against her G-spot. "Did you think I'd get you this turned on and not bring you all the way?"

Her head thrashes against the comforter. "I'm impatient. And it's been so long since someone has gone down on me. Please. I forgot how good an oral orgasm is. *Please*, baby."

Fucking hell. How could I say no to that? I squeeze another finger inside her channel, then clamp down on her clit, sucking hard as my tongue flicks under the hood. Audrey cries in a crescendo as she peaks, her body seizing as she comes. I patiently leave my tongue against her as shudders wrack her body, and as soon as her hand loosens its grip on my hair, I attack again. The second orgasm is much quicker than the first, and I don't give her even a moment before I build her up for a third. I'm ready to push her into a fourth, but she shoves me away with a foot against my shoulder.

Licking my lips, I revel in her taste as I grin at her. Audrey breathes heavily, hair in complete disarray, and her skin is a perfect shade of pink. "You okay, Doc?"

"Mmhmm," she hums, a tired smile on her face. "I forgot how much I like that."

"Oral?"

"No," she replies. "A man making me come. Well, in all honesty, I'm not sure if I've ever come that hard. You have a talented tongue, Mr. Wahlberg."

Somehow slightly embarrassed, I don't reply. I know what I'm doing in the bedroom, mostly because a girl in high school made fun of me, and a buddy sat me down to watch porn videos with me so I could learn technique. But hearing Audrey compliment me on it somehow makes me feel dirty. I don't like it.

"Have I embarrassed you?" she asks softly. Not wanting to lie, or stretch the truth in any way, I nod. "I'm sorry. That wasn't my intention."

"I know. I told you I'm confident in bed, but hearing you agree with me, kind of makes me feel skanky." My answer makes Audrey cackle, which lessens the feeling of embarrassment.

"And here I am, worried that my experience is so small compared to yours, and you're thinking you're a skank!" she says with a giggle. "Aren't we a pair. But in all honesty, does it bother you that I have virtually no experience?"

"No, of course not," I answer honestly.

"It doesn't bother me that you *do* have experience, Jamie. Neither one of us should be blamed for what we've done before we met. I'm really only concerned with what we're doing right now."

"I already know you're going to be the best I've ever had," I admit.

A soft smile graces her face. "Yeah?"

"Yeah."

"Me too," she says quietly, then laughs. "And a full disclaimer: that's not just the orgasm stupor talking. I thought that beforehand."

I chuckle, then stand up. "Do you remember that talk we had about things we like and dislike about sex?"

She nods, her smile widening. "You need to brush your teeth."

"Yeah. And mouthwash. I really need to kiss you after this."

"Hurry up, then." Grinning, I jog into my en suite, quickly brushing and swishing mouthwash. When I walk back into the bedroom, Audrey sits up, leaning back on her elbows, waiting for me. "Lose the pants, QB."

"Yes, ma'am," I murmur, pulling my joggers off. "Think you could help me with the rest?"

Audrey beckons me forward with a crook of her finger, and my dick twitches in response. Only a small section of her hair still sits in her bun, while the rest falls in glorious waves around her shoulders. I can't wait to see how spectacular she looks when I'm done fucking her.

Her hands find the waistband of my boxer briefs, and I hold my breath as one finger traces my bulge. She watches, entranced, as my cock twitches again, then slowly pulls down on the waist band. I can't take my eyes off of her. She licks her lips as my cock comes into view, and I see what she wants to do a half-second before she does it. Reaching out, I trap her chin in my hand. "No, baby. Not this time."

"But I want to repay the favor," she says with a pout.

"Another time. Right now, I need to be inside you. I've been dreaming about this for two months, and if you put your mouth on me, I'll come. I'm an old man. My rebound isn't as quick as it used to be."

"You're only a year older than me," she retorts. I swallow the laugh bubbling at the surface. Audrey looks genuinely pissed that I won't let her suck my cock.

"I'm holding on by a string, Aud. I need you. Right now, I'm the impatient one. I'm not willing to wait even an hour to have you. Please."

I'm trembling with a mixture of adrenaline and arousal. I need this woman in the most biblical sense there is. I know with every fiber of my being that this is the last first time I'll ever have, and I can't wait one more minute to bury myself inside of her.

"God, you're so sexy, Jamie," she pants as she grabs my head and pulls me toward her. Our lips crash together in passion, and I groan as I fall against her, my cock fitting between her legs perfectly. The heat from her core feels so fucking perfect. I'm two seconds away from sliding inside her, when I have a reality check.

"Wait. Condom," I rasp, sitting up to grab the brand new box of condoms I placed in my nightstand. Audrey doesn't speak, she just watches as I open the box, and rip an individual pouch out. She wordlessly takes the pouch out of my hands, tearing it open with her teeth.

"Which way does it go?" she whispers, shocking me. Her eyes are training on the latex as she slowly twirls it between her fingers.

"You've never put one on?"

"No. They've always unnerved me. But you make me feel ..." she trails off.

"What?" I whisper, encouraging her to continue.

Her eyes flick to mine. "You make me feel confident, and I know I can trust you. You won't make me feel stupid when I ask questions."

Emotion clogs my throat. I fucking hate that people in her life have made her feel inept. Audrey is the smartest person I know. She's beautiful, compassionate, talented, and such a genuine human being. I'm stunned that people in her life don't recognize that. Clearing my throat, I take the condom from her hands. "I'll never make you feel stupid. You can tell which way the condom goes by how it rolls on."

Taking her hand, I cover it with mine. We place the condom on my cock together, rolling it down. Somehow, the moment is pure, erotic, and emotional. Knowing Audrey trusts me like this is incredibly poignant.

As Audrey lays back on the bed, I cover her with my body. She bites her lip, then says, "I haven't had sex in a while. Go a little slow, okay?"

"Of course," I say hoarsely. Notched at her opening, I take her lips in a deep kiss as I inch slowly inside her. God, she feels incredible. Her tight heat surrounds me, squeezing me perfectly, and I'm forced to mentally chant a variety of play calls to keep from coming. "God, you feel so good."

She moans in reply, her nails scratching against my back. I continue slowly, achingly slow, until I'm bottomed out. "You good, baby?"

She smiles, nodding. "I'm good. You can go faster now."

Thank fuck. I kiss her breathlessly as I begin moving, forcing myself to keep a steady pace. I'm determined to make this good for Audrey. Her whines and moans are definitely stroking more than just my ego. And when I look in Audrey's eyes, I see every emotion I'm feeling. Lust. Contentment. Connection. Passion and affection. Love. Soulmate. My partner.

"Audrey," I stammer, overcome as I quicken the pace. "I've never — this is —"

She slides one hand up into my hair, holding my head against hers. "Me too."

The room shifts. It's no longer sex or fucking. It's not about an orgasm. This is about becoming one with the woman who I'm falling for. The one who has seen more of my soul than any other person. The only woman for me. I lose sight of my steady pace as emotion and passion overtake me. Audrey's eyes glaze over as she cries out. "Jamie, I'm coming!"

When her walls flutter around me, I'm right behind her. The tingling starts at my toes, crashing over the length of my body as I have the most intense orgasm of my life. Forgetting to breathe, my vision wanes, and I collapse on top of Audrey as I try to catch my breath. Holy shit.

It takes a few moments for me to regain my composure, and when I manage to raise my head from where I'd been against her neck, I find Audrey's eyes sparkling with mirth. "What on earth are you thinking?"

She smiles devilishly. "Did you say your rebound is an hour? A whole hour? That's disappointing, QB."

"I believe I meant that as an average."

"We're gonna need to work on improving that."

I smile as I bend down to kiss her lips. "I'm okay with that."

Audrey

CHAPTER 20

It's not an hour. Thirty minutes maybe. I asked Jamie if it was an athlete thing, that men like him could be predisposed to excellent rebound time because of their physical fitness. He assured me it's really due to me, and how badly he wants to have me, over and over again.

I am absolutely not complaining, but my vagina finally had to wave the white flag after Jamie woke me up an hour before sunrise. Why? Because he also woke me up around three, and slightly after midnight as well. We'd even had sex before going to sleep Friday night. Five times in twelve hours, after not having sex in quite some time, means my poor little pussy is sore beyond comprehension.

I felt bad turning him down Saturday morning after breakfast, but he took it all in stride. Made us pancakes, then threw me up onto one of the islands and devoured me. I lost track of how many orgasms I had, each one as intense as the last. It was like he studied me, learning each tiny area that pleasured me the most, and capitalized on it. I felt seen, but also used. Cherished, and exhausted.

I made an excuse about needing to pay a house visit to a client, and tore out of there mid-afternoon on Saturday. Well, tore out of there as quickly as a woman with a paralyzed dog and a carrier of six guinea pigs can. Jamie was bummed, but also said he had plans for dinner with a couple of teammates. When I got back to my quiet townhouse, I thought I'd feel relieved. That time with Jamie was pleasure unlike anything I could have imagined, but also overwhelming. Yet being alone in my home wasn't filling my cup like it always has.

After putting the pigs away in their enclosure, and settling Flash on her bed with an enrichment toy where pieces of kibble are hidden throughout the fabric of the toy, I sit on the couch, determined to learn some new ways I can enhance my time with Jamie.

I wasn't lying about anything I told Jamie last night. My past experiences are few and far between, and I don't hold it against him that he has a much larger history than I do. But it's difficult not to play a comparison game. If he's had amazing partners, where do I stack up? I have no doubt, if I asked, that he'd say it's different with me, and nothing compares. But does it really?

I'm a smart woman. I know how to research, study, and learn. So what if I don't have a lot of experience now? I can change that. Sitting down on my couch, I open up my browser. The Internet is a vast place, and one search for porn brings up a gazillion pages. I click on the top link, and — "Oh my *GOD*! They don't even ask my *age* or anything?"

Woah. The teaser image is two guys with a very well-endowed woman. Damn. Her boobs are even bigger than mine, but perky and jiggly. Probably fake. Intrigued, I click on the video. I've heard some terminology for a threesome before, but I've never tried to research it. When would there ever be an opportunity for me to be with two men at the same time? But I have questions. Where do the guys go? Lots of orifices to choose from. "Oh, so that's what DP looks like."

It's not turning me on … for the most part. It's all for science. I find myself tilting my head to the side as the gal does some kind of backbend with a split so she can suck one guy off while getting banged by the other. "How is that even possible?"

"Holy shit, Aud!" Chelsea shouts from the doorway. I yelp in shock, tossing my laptop into the air. "What the hell are you doing?"

"Research!" I yell frantically, catching my laptop as Chelsea steps into my townhouse. My hand hits some buttons as I catch it, and somehow I turn the volume on full blast.

"Yeah, Daddy, fuck our baby girl with your big cock," comes screaming out of the speakers, and Chelsea covers her face as she cackles.

I furiously tap all the buttons on my computer to no avail. "Why won't it quiet down?"

"I'm gonna suck you so hard while she watches."

Chelsea hoots as she drops a bag on the floor. "Oh my fucking God, I'm laughing so hard I might pee."

"Don't you dare! And close the damn door!"

"I'm coming! I'm coming! Aaahhhhhh —" Silence as I slam the computer shut, then turn my murderous eyes on Chelsea, who stands innocently by the still open door.

"I have clients in this neighborhood, Chelsea."

"I know," she replies, a wicked grin on her face. "Not my fault you were getting your kicks that loudly."

"I wasn't! It was for research!"

"Oh?" she asks. "You plan on getting banged by a father-son duo?"

"No, but —" I look down at my laptop. "It was father-son?"

Chelsea shrugs. "I don't know. I sure as fuck hope not. I'm not one to yuck someone's yum, but incest sex just ain't it."

I grimace. "That's incredibly gross. And illegal everywhere, I think."

She plops down next to me on the couch. "Wanna explain to me how you ended up watching some porn at four in the afternoon?"

Suddenly shy, I avoid her pointed gaze. "I told you. Research."

"Hmm," she hums, tapping a pointed nail on her chin. "I'm going to assume you and Jamie finally did the deed, and now you're spiraling because you're assuming you aren't the best he's ever had, so you're going to try and rock his world the next time."

"That's not exactly true," I mutter. It's pretty close, but I'm not telling her that.

"Audrey. You can't watch this kind of porn and think it'll make you suddenly a better lover. These are professionals, first off. But what did you think you'd learn?"

"I didn't intend to watch it. I was just curious for a second." God, my face must be beet-red.

"Alright. What were you hoping to find?" Chelsea asks gently.

Okay. I can admit this. I can tell her. She's my best friend. She won't judge me. She'll probably make fun of me for a bit, but I know it's in jest. She'd never be consciously hurtful. "I wanted to learn more about blow jobs."

"Ahh. Why is that?"

This is the part that hurts. "The guy I dated after vet school said I was really bad at them."

"Did he come each time?" Chelsea asks pointedly.

My cheeks burn. "He usually stopped me before it got that far. Said he wanted to come inside me instead. When he told me I was bad at them when we broke up, I didn't know what to believe."

"How difficult could it be? I wouldn't know. Been enjoying the taco for as long as I can remember."

"Enjoying the taco," I snicker.

"You got any bananas? We can practice. I'm all for learning new tricks. If anything, it'll be great for scaring the hell out of my super conservative and religious neighbor," she says with a laugh as she jumps up to go search in my kitchen. Flash lifts her head, looks between the two of us, sighs, then puts her head back down. She startles when Chelsea hoots. "Score! Found the naners!"

"Give part of one to Flash, or she won't leave us alone," I say absentmindedly. Flash loves bananas.

"Obviously. You think I'd leave her out of this chaos? Never." Chelsea dutifully feeds my dog on her way back to my couch. Clapping her hands together gleefully, she pats my knee. "Alright. Bring on the porn!"

For the next thirty minutes, we flip between a variety of videos.

We steer clear of the lesbian ones, much to Chelsea's chagrin. It turns out she's very particular about all porn, and I finally had to tell her to shut up when she critiqued one of the storylines. It's porn. I'm not expecting it to win an Academy Award. Yeah, I know getting my dishwasher fixed isn't going to result in me being railed against the sink. Chelsea grumbles her thoughts occasionally, but for the most part, stays blissfully silent.

When I happen upon an actual instructional video, we're both glued to the screen. This time, it isn't Chelsea who can't stay quiet. I have lots of questions.

"How is she not gagging?"

"Does the piercing get caught? Remember that one movie with Cameron Diaz and Christina Applegate where it got caught in Selma Blair's mouth?"

"She keeps focusing on that one spot. I wonder if it's super sensitive on all men, or just that guy."

"What's the normal size of a penis?"

"He sounds like he's in pain."

"Jamie wants eye contact, but I don't think I can do *that* while looking him in the eye."

"Does anyone ever vomit?"

"Do their lips and tongue fall asleep?"

"How do they breathe normally?"

"How long is this going to take?" That question makes me giggle, as I say it very closely resembling King Julian in the animated *Madagascar* movie.

When Chelsea growls at me, I look over to find her glaring as she pauses the video. "You can't learn anything because you won't shut the hell up."

"Don't you have questions?"

"No, because I'm not fucking a man!" she yells. "How hard can it be? Put it in, suck, see how far you can get it down your throat. Jesus. It's not rocket science."

"Evidently it's more involved than that, or my ex wouldn't have said I'm awful at it." The more I think about it, the more pissed I get at OJ for telling me. He could have just broken it off and walked away. But no, he had to get one final dig in. Honestly, it's my own fault by dating someone who chose to go by OJ, when his given name is Owen. Who chooses that? Dumbass.

"Fine. Then let's give these puppies a go," Chelsea says, twirling a banana between her fingers, while handing me one. "How's your gag reflex?"

"Well, I don't barf when I deal with abscesses or parasitic worms, and I pretty much get marked by an animal every day without me puking in return."

"But how is the physical aspect of it? Can you touch the back of your tongue without gagging?" Chelsea asks, sticking her finger in her mouth, immediately gagging.

"I don't know. I've never forced myself to try," I tell her.

"Go ahead then. You know what? Use the banana. That's what it's there for anyway."

"Alright. Wait. Let me get a trash can, as a precaution." I run to the bathroom, grabbing the small trash receptacle I keep in there. "It already has a bag, so if needed, it's an easy cleanup."

"Good call," she says with a laugh, wiping a tear from her eye. "Man, it's a good thing I'm a lesbian. No way could I give a blow job without hurling."

"I honestly want to know the first man who thought about this, and who he convinced to try it out."

"I would like to know how many decades, if not *centuries*, it was before a woman realized she could have a similar experience," Chelsea says with a huff. "Because we both know a man did not decide to go down on a woman on his own."

I chortle. "Knowing men, they were probably more willing to suck each other off before they even thought about reciprocating on their wives."

"Probably a true story," Chelsea jokes, then points at me. "Let's get this going, ma'am. You're the one with something to prove. Hollow out them cheeks and suck that 'naner."

I furrow my brows, staring at the banana. "Should I peel it? This can't be a good sensation on my tongue, and it certainly won't taste good."

Chelsea shakes her head. "I have to assume the real thing is also both of those qualifiers, and if you remove the peel, you could choke on part of the banana."

"Alright," I sigh. I guess she's right. "Here goes nothing."

I take a deep breath, placing the banana at the tip of my tongue. So far so good. Not a great sensation, but I'm not feeling the need to barf, so I'm chalking it up as a good thing.

"You can go further than that," Chelsea urges. "Swirl your tongue around it too."

"Wut?" I mumble, inching the banana backward into my mouth.

Chelsea shrugs. "I don't know. Any porn I watch when an unfortunate male is involved usually has tongue swirling."

"Wike wis?" I ask, then loudly laugh when I realize the banana is too far back for Chelsea to comprehend anything I'm saying, and I can't do a thing with my tongue anyway.

I'm still cackling when I hear her say, "Oh, take it out, I'm gonna answer this for you," but I don't fully understand what she's talking about until I look at her to find her horrified gaze.

"Wut?" I ask. Chelsea doesn't respond verbally; instead, she points to the computer screen. On it, I see my own reflection, with half the banana into my mouth.

Right next to Jamie's open-mouthed face.

"He FaceTimed you, didn't you hear it ringing?" Chelsea hisses, but I'm completely frozen. Frozen in fear, but my skin is burning with the heat of humiliation. That is, until I see the naked lust covering Jamie's face. He's looking at me with a completely feral expression, like he'd attack me through the screen if he could.

I don't know what to do. I'm literally unable to move. Slam the laptop shut? Wave like a weirdo? Slowly remove the banana? Run out of the room, screaming, and immediately move to a foreign country?

Chelsea reaches up, grabbing the top stem of the banana, pulling it from my mouth. "Um, I'm gonna go home now."

She quietly collects her things, pats Flash on the head, pantomimes "call me" to me, and walks out the front door. I slowly turn my head back to Jamie, and find him moving swiftly throughout his house.

"I'll be there in twenty minutes. Don't even think about moving a muscle, Audrey."

Oh shit.

I hear tires squeal a little over fifteen minutes later. I've mapped the route between our homes, and I know it takes longer than fifteen. Even making all the lights, I believe it takes longer than twenty. I wonder how fast he went to get here this quickly, but before I can think to ask, Jamie bursts through the door. I'm still sitting exactly where I was, the banana in my lap, and my laptop on the table in front of me. The screen has gone dark, but one quick touch of a key, and Jamie will see exactly what I was doing.

"Didn't you have plans with your friends?" I finally ask, as Jamie stares at me without speaking.

"It ended early," he finally answers, then toes off his shoes, kicking them to the side. He steps toward me, then detours over to scratch Flash behind her ears. When he comes to sit beside me, he notices the laptop screen. He taps on the touchpad, illuminating the paused video. "Were you watching porn and sucking on a banana?"

A high-pitched and nervous laugh erupts from my windpipe. "When you put it that way, it sounds really creepy."

"I don't think it was creepy. Your best friend was here, and it looks like you were watching an instructional video," he says as he reaches out to press play on the screen. "Were you trying to learn more about giving head?"

I really wish a hole would suddenly form in my house and swallow me right up. God, the embarrassment. "If I were, would you think less of me?"

I hear a strangled noise come from Jamie, but peeking out from under my lashes tells me he's remarkably composed. "No. I'm intrigued to learn why you're suddenly wanting to know more, though."

"Just curious, I guess," I lie.

Jamie grabs my chin, turning my head so I'm forced to look at him. "I've told you before that I'm not a good liar, but it is also worth mentioning that I don't like being lied to. You might consider this instance to be you stretching the truth, or you hiding something from me, but it's still dishonest. I'll always tell you the truth, Audrey, and I really hope you want to give me the same respect."

Now I feel even worse. I close my eyes, take a deep breath, and spew out everything. "Okay. Last night was great. Intense, but so great. And it got me thinking. I said I didn't care about your history. And I don't! I swear, I don't. But my lack of history means there are things I don't know how to do really well, and so I decided to do some research. Well, one guy said I didn't do something well, and I like to learn, so I figured the Internet could teach me a thing or two. Chelsea showed up completely coincidentally, and I was so focused on the porn video that I threw my computer. It went full volume, so I'm sure my neighbors hate me, and I'll have to move. Then she decided we should practice on bananas because she's a lesbian, and she's never sucked a dick before. All this because a mean boy in my past said I'm bad at it, and now I want to disappear for a few years."

Jamie is quiet, but I don't open my eyes. My heart is beating faster than I can ever remember, and my stomach feels like it's two somersaults away from some pyrotechnics. How did I get from a billion amazing orgasms to admitting I sucked a banana?

"Am I correct in assuming that you did this because you think I won't enjoy a blow job from you?" Jamie asks, his voice even, but somehow sharper than I've heard it before.

"Yes. And before you say anything, I know you'd tell me it's different because it's me."

"Yep." He takes the banana from my lap, placing it next to the laptop, then shuts the screen.

I scoff. "You can't actually know that."

Jamie grabs my hand, placing it in his lap. In his very hard and firm lap. "Do you feel that, baby? Really feel it. Wrap your hand around it and squeeze. That's what the sheer thought of your mouth on me does to me. I'm two seconds away from coming, Doc. It will not matter what experience you do or don't have. The moment I see you on your knees for me? That's it. It won't fucking matter."

His entire body is tense as I do as he asked, squeezing him gently. He puts his hand over mine, putting pressure on his cock.

"Take it out," he says finally, his voice gruff. It's now that I notice he's in nice jeans, a henley, and white sneakers. He looks incredibly handsome, and it gives me a sense of power that I'm bringing this beautiful man such pleasure. I gingerly undo his jeans, helping him pull them down slightly, then move his boxer briefs so his cock can stand fully erected. "On your knees."

A gush of wetness floods my panties as I slowly sink to my knees in front of Jamie. This controlling and dominating side of him is insanely attractive. "Will you tell me what to do?"

He nods. "I'm going to tell you exactly what I want you to do. You learn with me. You want to watch porn? Fine. But you only get off with me."

"Aren't you gone for days at a time during the season? That doesn't seem really fair —" I stop when he sticks two fingers into my mouth, sliding them along my tongue.

"With me, Audrey. In person, on the phone, or FaceTime. With me. Not alone." His fingers hit the back of my tongue, and he growls. "Jesus, woman. I can tell you right now that whoever told you something about blow jobs was being petty and spiteful. No fucking way you weren't built for this. You're going to look so beautiful with my cock buried in your throat, baby."

I moan around his fingers. The times I've given head before were out of duty, not because I felt I wanted to. But right now? I think I might die if I don't get his dick in my mouth right this very moment. "Please, Jamie."

"Please, what?" He removes his fingers, dragging the wet digits across my cheek and into my hair.

"Please let me suck your cock."

He smiles devilishly. "Since you asked so nicely."

Jamie guides my head right to the tip of his cock, gripping my hair tightly. "Lick the tip. Slide your tongue around it. Yeah, just like that. Now suck on the head. Nothing more, just the head. Fuck, yeah, baby. Now drag your tongue down to the base. Fuck, that feels so good. Back up. Suck the head again. Now slide down a little, Jesussssss ..."

While I appreciate the instruction, I'm too keyed up to continue listening. Hollowing my cheeks, I take him as deep into my mouth as possible, sucking hard. Then, remembering a bit from the instructional video, I reach up to cup his balls. Jamie hisses, groans, then begins to move my head up and down his shaft.

A couple of times he hits the back of my throat, making me slightly gag, and tears fill my eyes. But I look up at Jamie to find him intently watching me, his face full of lust and tension. Each time he hits my throat, his moans grow louder, and I happily continue. I want — no, I need — to watch him unravel. I want to witness him completely lose control, and know that it's because of me. I feel when he's close, as his words grow stuttered and border-line nonsensical.

"You're so fucking beautiful like this. My sweet and dirty girl. Bet you're soaked. Gonna get you to sit on my face and cover me in your cum. Best ever — you thought I'd have better — nothing better than you. Gonna fucking mark you so everyone knows you're mine. My ... perfect ... little ... slut ..."

With a roar, he comes down my throat, the hot and salty ropes coating my mouth as he holds my head against him. I dutifully swallow every bit, surprising even myself at how much I enjoy it. Jamie falls back onto the couch as he catches his breath, his eyes finally closing.

I rest my head against his knee, watching him. That was intense. For me, at least. Did he really mean he intends to have me sit on his face? And why should him calling me his perfect little slut be so hot?

"Gimme a minute," he murmurs with a smile. "Wow. That was … wow."

I can't help the smile that covers my face. "I did okay?"

"Yeah, baby. That was way better than okay, though. Did I call you a slut?"

I giggle. "You did."

He opens one eye. "You know I don't actually think that about you, right? I got a little in the moment."

"I found it hot, actually. I've never thought that about myself, but maybe I could just be your slut?"

He chuckles. "I'm cool with that."

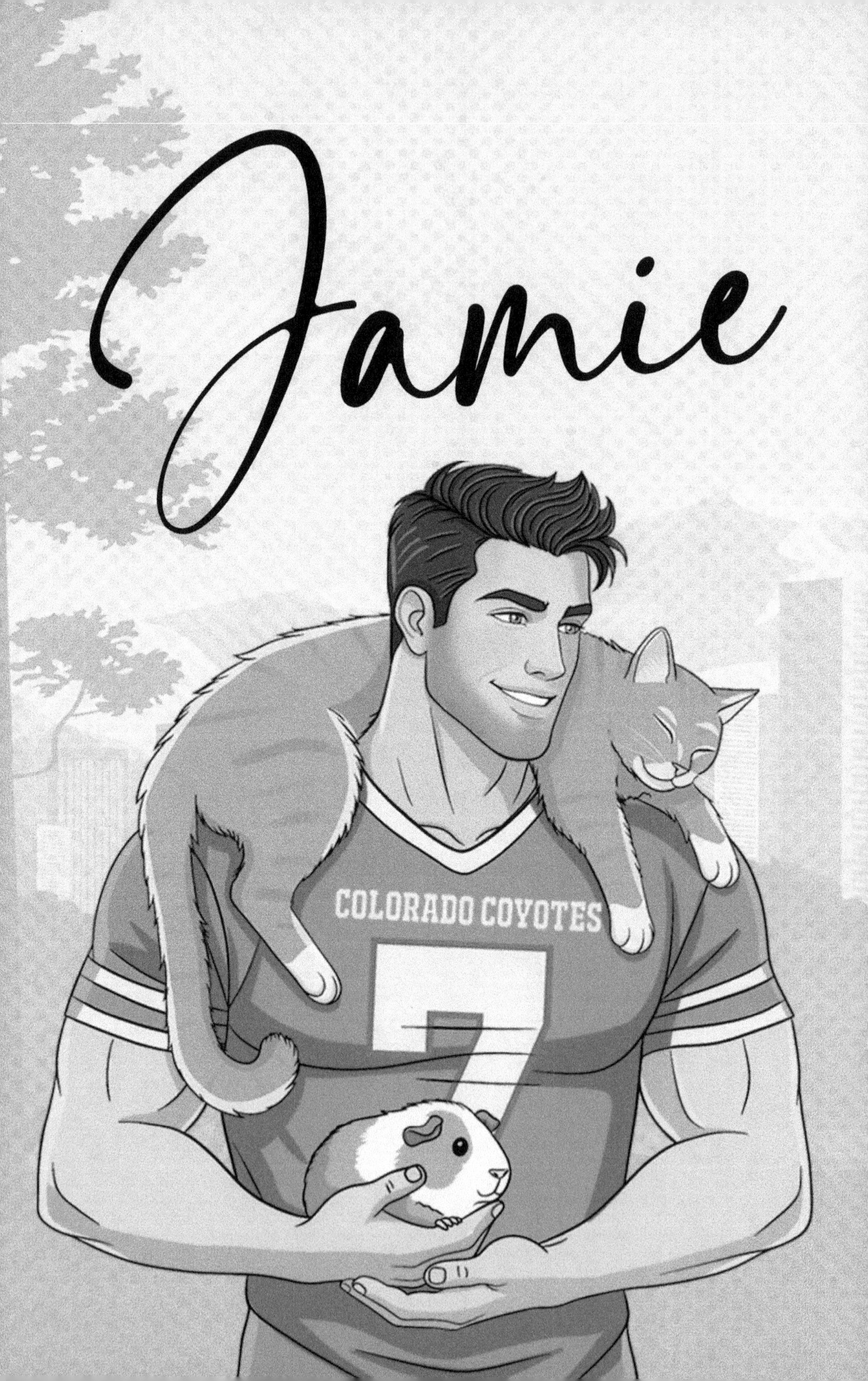

Jamie

CHAPTER 21

Audrey excuses herself to brush her teeth, and I let out one hell of a relieved exhale. I didn't know what exactly to think when I FaceTimed her to find an entire unpeeled banana buried into the back of her throat. I think I blacked out driving over here. I didn't expect to get the best blow job of my entire fucking life once I got here, but I certainly wasn't going to let her try to figure it all out alone.

I know she doesn't have as much experience as me. If I wasn't a professional athlete, I wouldn't either. And I know a good chunk of the women I've slept with only did it because they wanted the notch on their bedpost. Hardly any women I meet are interested in dating me. They want money or sex, and sometimes both.

But then I met Audrey, and she turned everything I thought I knew about the female species upside down. When she said she knew I'd say every experience I have with her will be different because of her, it's fucking true. When she smiles, my heart skips a beat. When she unconsciously reaches out to touch me, I feel like I'm flying. I think about her every moment I'm awake, and she infiltrates all of my dreams. So, yeah, I knew my dick in her mouth would be life-changing.

A current of air rushes across my dick, and I tuck it back inside my boxers without opening my eyes. I know Audrey is in the room, though, and I hold out a hand for her to join me. As soon as her fingers touch mine, I yank her into my lap. She squeals, landing with a jolt, then laughs as her hair surrounds us. I open my eyes to find she's let her hair down, and it quite literally takes my breath away. She smiles sweetly at me, her beautiful eyes sparkling, and I'm acutely aware of the fact that I'm falling in love with her.

"Hi," she says innocently, with a giggle. Quite the juxtaposition to her devilish attitude from only a few moments ago, where she took complete control over me.

"Hi," I reply, my voice raspy and deep. I reach up, hooking my hand around her neck, and pull her down for a kiss. It's a languid kiss, where we aren't worried about time. I slowly devour her. As I slide a hand around to meander up her spine, I realize she's changed. Instead of the comfortable loungewear she had been wearing when I arrived, she's in a frilly tank that reaches mid-thigh, with ruffles along the seams, and a deep v-neck dipping between her phenomenal tits. My hand drifts down, finding the edge of the tank, and I find a set of shorts with the same ruffles. I quickly break off the kiss, grabbing the hem of her shirt so I can see the shorts.

"What are you doing?" she giggles.

"I have to see these," I murmur. The view is awesome. Cupping her ass so perfectly, the cherry design featured is both innocent and alluring. "God damn, baby. I can honestly say this is the first time I've ever been turned on by cherries."

Audrey bites her lip, offering me a shy smile. "I like pretty things for sleeping. There's something very sexy about silky lingerie, or girlie sets like this."

"I will love whatever you wear," I tell her honestly. "As long as I get to take it off you, I'm going to find it sexy."

She rolls her eyes. "Medical scrubs are not sexy."

"The hell they aren't! Do you have any idea what they do to your ass?" I ask as I grab handfuls of each cheek. "You're lucky I didn't bend down to bite you when I was there helping you move boxes."

"You know Chelsea set that up, right? She got there early and moved the boxes off the shelves first."

"I figured as much," I tell her with a smile. "All the box-shaped dust marks on the shelves were a dead giveaway. Not that I mind having a wing-woman, though."

"She'll love hearing that you called her that. I don't date often, so she'll be pretty happy knowing she was part of pushing us together."

I pull her down for another kiss, loving how she sighs into my mouth. I'm torn with wanting to dial up the heat a little, but also really enjoying how sensual it feels to slowly kiss her. I massage her ass lightly, and feel her start to shimmy in my lap. When she lightly scrapes her fingernails along my scalp, I groan, feeling tingles shoot down my arms. I grip her ass tighter, my tongue stroking hers a little harder, and she pushes her core against mine.

"Jamie," she whispers against my lips.

"Hmm?"

"I don't want to sit on your face," she blurts out. Opening my eyes, I find her staring intently at me. She doesn't look shy or apprehensive. I don't detect one ounce of self-consciousness in her gaze. Instead, she looks tightly coiled, turned on as hell, and a fucking vision.

"Okay? Do you want to tell me what you *do* want?" I ask tentatively.

Audrey bites her lip again, a move I'm noticing is her go-to for when she wants to speak her mind, but is afraid to. "I've never been on top before. I want to ride you. Just like this."

Holy fucking hell. "What else do you want, baby?"

Her eyes become more hooded. "I want you to suck on my breasts while I ride you."

"I want that too," I tell her honestly.

"And I want to ride you bare," she finishes, her eyes dancing between my eyes and lips.

I'm not going to need that full thirty minute rebound now. I'll be lucky if I last thirty seconds buried inside her raw. "Are you sure, Aud?"

"Yes," she says, nodding affirmatively. "I'm on the pill. I take it religiously. I really want to feel you, and —"

I cut her off by crashing our lips together. Say no more, Doc. I'm not turning this down. There's even a tiny voice in the back of my head whispering how amazing it would be to create a baby with Audrey, so evidently, I'm even more on board with this than I would have thought.

Audrey inches my shirt up my abs, and I lean forward, reaching over my shoulder to rip it off. I then grab the hem of her frilly shirt, pulling it off slowly, watching as every creamy inch of skin becomes visible. As soon as her breasts are free, I lean forward to suck a tip deep into my mouth. Audrey's moan is instant and guttural as she holds my head against her. "You're so good at that, Jamie."

I don't answer, only because I refuse to remove her breast from my mouth. Slipping a hand between her thighs, I find the seam of her shorts hot and damp, the fabric sinking deliciously into her pussy. I rub the fabric, feeling it become much wetter, and love the sounds Audrey makes as I continue my ministrations. Pushing it aside, I easily push two fingers into her channel. Her walls flutter around me, and I wonder if she's close to coming. Letting her breast pop out of my mouth, I look up to find her gaze unfocused and lust-filled. "Are you about to come, Doc?"

She nods, then uses a hand to push her breast back into my mouth. As soon as I nibble on the tip, her orgasm crashes over her. I watch, utterly captivated, as she capitulates, thrashing around through aftershocks, her walls tightly clamped onto my fingers. A beautiful rosy hue covers her body as she catches her breath. I wait patiently, alternating between each nipple, tonguing them gently, as my fingers slide painstakingly slow through her wetness. When her eyes open, I can see a much clearer gaze. "Stand up."

Audrey stands, her legs shaky and unstable, and I remove her shorts before pulling her back into my lap. A quick shuffle as I pull my cock out, running it through her pussy. Notching it at her opening, I say, "Eyes on me."

She dutifully gazes at me, placing her hands behind my head, as I grip her hips. I slowly pull her down, filling her painstakingly slowly, but I know this is going to be exceptionally quick. She feels incomparable. When she's fully seated against me, I look at where we're joined, and I can't focus enough to find where she ends and I begin. I want to live right here. Where this perfect woman completes me so flawlessly.

"This is gonna be quick, Aud," I finally rasp, my voice strained with need and tension. "Gonna need you to touch yourself to help me out. Get yourself there."

"Okay," she whispers as I pick her back up, where I almost slide completely out of her, then slam her back down. "Oh, God, Jamie, it won't take me very long."

Thank fuck for that. I'm a half-second away from coming. I can barely see straight as pleasure zings through every nerve in my body. I quicken the pace, white spots dancing in the corners of my vision, and Audrey rests her forehead against mine. Her moans are getting louder, and I feel her walls begin to clamp down on me, but I can tell she's not quite there yet. I lean down, latching onto her nipple, and slide one hand around to press my thumb against her back hole, and that combination does the trick. We come together, our slick bodies moving as one, and I've never had a better orgasm. Audrey collapses against my shoulder, her hair tickling my sweaty skin along my side and abdomen, and I wrap my arms tightly around her.

"You good?" I whisper breathlessly, placing an absentminded kiss against her shoulder.

"So good," she murmurs.

I've always been partial to schedules. I'm not a man who thrives in an environment of chaos and inconsistency. So, it's not only an absolute relief to find that Audrey likes schedules as much as I do, but that she also needs the safety of it. However, blending our schedules together is more difficult than I'd anticipated.

As I get closer to training camp, I'm in the gym more, meeting with trainers and coaching staff, and finishing up any sponsorship deals I have. Adding in all the punishment tasks I'm still completing means my schedule is jam-packed.

The month of June has me out of town three times, and the only thing that keeps me from losing my mind is video calling with Audrey every night. Sometimes it's while I eat a very late dinner, and more than once we've talked while she's been in bed. Audrey explained to me that she extends her hours every summer, because many pet owners have more time to schedule yearly checkups when their kids aren't super busy with school, sports, and extracurricular activities. She's as tired as I am.

The few nights we're able to see each other, it involves take out, a movie — which usually leads to sex — and sleep. I have more restful sleep when she's by my side than I do when I'm alone, that's for sure. More often than not, we're at her townhouse, only because it's easier. Packing up five guinea pigs and a handicapped corgi is involved. My cats definitely bitch when they see me the following morning, but they don't care about being alone for a night.

Any extra time I've had has been helping Audrey coordinate everything for our event. I know I haven't been as hands-on as I'd like, and that's completely my fault. My schedule is nuts, and any time I have with Audrey I obviously want to just enjoy spending time with her. But Audrey keeps a smile on her face, never once telling me to do a fair amount of work. Even Maverick and Goose are voicing their own frustration at feeling left out and alone.

That changes for my next trip, however.

Due to my pet sitter being on vacation, Audrey volunteered to come stay at my house while I'm gone for three days. We figure the cats would severely object to being moved to her townhouse, so it's less painless to bring the pigs and dog to my house. I can tell Audrey is nervous, but I think it'll be fine. It's the first time I've given someone a key to my home, and I try to downplay it. But deep in the recesses of my heart, I know it means something more to me. It means forever.

The first day I'm in Miami, it's nonstop chaos. After seeing the success a couple of Canadian companies have had featuring ads with famous Canadian NHL players, the NFL stepped up, trying to create the same thing. A handful of current quarterbacks are participating in a series of commercials. It's all guys I know, but I'm not close with any of them. It's a struggle to keep my breathing slow, and my nonchalant mask in place, as we film take after take.

When I finally grab food to take to my hotel room, I'm so relieved to call Audrey. She answers in my kitchen, and I can't help the huge smile that covers my face.

"Is that my shirt, Doc?" I tease. She's wearing an old Oregon shirt of mine, and it's never looked better. Hair in a messy bun, and not a speck of makeup on her perfect face, she's an absolute vision.

Audrey giggles. "I hope you aren't mad. It's so soft, and I kind of wanted to wear something of yours while you're gone."

"Not mad at all. It looks so much better on you anyway."

She sighs. "I feel like I've barely seen you this month, so this helps a little. Sleeping in your bed will be nice too."

My grin fades. "It won't get much better once training camp starts, Aud. I don't want to be a downer, but you need to be prepared for that. I'd rather mentally prepare you now, than have you be really upset in a couple of months."

"I don't think there's a way to mentally prepare myself for the NFL. Especially once anyone knows about me ..." she trails off. We talked in depth about what we want to do in terms of a public announcement. Troy has always said athletes should be proactive, and control the narrative. But I know how vicious the public can be, and I don't want that for Audrey. I'm petrified she'll end this because of things people say while hiding behind a computer screen.

"Are you still on board with waiting until the fall?" I ask tentatively. We discussed attending our event together. Walking the red carpet and everything. When Audrey expressed hesitation, I immediately stopped the conversation. I'm not forcing her to announce it until she's ready. Plus, our event is the week after training camp begins. I need to be focused on my job.

"If that's what you feel is best, I'm fine with that," Audrey answers, her eyes shrouded in sadness.

"I can tell you're sad, but I can't tell why. Is it just loneliness, or something else?"

She hesitates, chewing on her lip. That damn lip, telling me Audrey has something she's afraid to say. This time, I'm pretty certain I know it before she speaks. "It's hard not to feel like I'm being hidden for a reason, Jamie. I know we've talked about it, and I understand your reasons. But my own insecurities are rearing their ugly heads."

Fuck. "I know. I'm struggling too."

"Why?" she asks.

I close my eyes, taking a deep breath. "I'm afraid the public will be awful, and you'll end things because you don't want to deal with it. You won't think I'm worth it."

"Oh, Jamie," she whispers. "I wish I could give you a big hug right now. I hate that you think I'd give you up that easily."

I chuckle bitterly. "The media is ruthless, Doc. If it gets them a scoop, or an article goes viral, they don't care who they hurt. I'm worried it'll impact your job, and how your family will react. I don't want you to realize I'm not worth the trouble."

"I don't care what my family thinks. There may be things I do to pacify them, like letting my mother pick out my dress for a family event, but they don't get to have an opinion about who I date. My parents have incredibly poor taste in men, so I don't trust their suggestions anyway. My sister married someone my parents approved of, and I've lost track of the number of affairs they've each had. It's appalling."

I screw up my face in distaste. "I don't get why people cheat. Just end the relationship, for fuck's sake."

Audrey shrugs. "I'm pretty sure my sister and her husband have an agreement. Quiet affairs are fine, but they aren't allowed to embarrass the other publicly. She's comfortable with the lifestyle, and even though my parents have money she can fall back on, she knows if she leans on them in any way, they'll begin controlling her life again. It's easier to stay married, and keep my parents at arm's length."

"We both came from some messed up situations," I comment, feeling slightly better as I scarf down my cheeseburger and salad. Normally, the month leading up to training camp, I'm very conscientious about the kinds of food I eat, as well as calorie intake. Frankly, I survived today without making a fool out of myself, so I deserve this cheeseburger in all of its greasy goodness.

"I like that we're both still optimistic about finding someone, though. Well," she giggles, "for the most part. We'll just ignore the whole convo about the media, and focus on the good things. Goose made biscuits on me this morning before I left for work."

"Seriously?" I ask, impressed. "He never does that with me. Maverick won't leave me alone when I'm home, though, so maybe Goose figures you're his human now."

"Maverick is too intrigued with the guinea pig enclosure. He sits outside the door, meowing to be let inside. Flash chases him away, though."

"She can really get going with those wheels."

"Oh, no. This was without the wheelchair. She just took off, dragging her legs behind her, barking incessantly at Maverick."

"No shit?" I laugh. "We certainly have an eclectic bunch of animals."

Audrey smiles softly, and I love how her eyes have lost the pained look from before. Now they shine with contentment and comfort.

Audrey

CHAPTER 22

While it hasn't been completely smooth sailing staying at Jamie's house, I can't say I've hated it either. I've taken advantage of his massive steam shower, and doing my weekly meal prep in his dream of a kitchen was a highlight for the week. Chelsea came over one night to enjoy a bottle of wine in his large backyard, filled to the brim with every item made to entertain. An enormous covered porch with wrought-iron furniture faces a large brick wall where a television hangs over a fireplace. There's a massive built-in grilling station, including a sink and small fridge, off to the side. Beyond the porch, an in-ground jacuzzi and lap pool sit, surrounded by a good sized area of grass. Colorado is known for packing homes in where there are hardly any backyards to speak of, but Jamie's is well above average. Beyond the yard, a sweeping view of the Rockies to watch the sunset behind.

I grew up in wealth, but our house was slammed on a tiny lot in a Denver suburb. Nothing like this. We always had our curtains and blinds closed, because any of the neighbors could look right in from their lots. Nothing like this, where half the windows face onto an open space. Jamie's bedroom has a balcony with even better views, and I've taken to opening the door each evening to allow fresh air in, as well as admire the mountains as I fall asleep.

The final morning of Jamie's trip, I struggle to determine if I should pack everything up now, or wait until he gets home. It's possible he'll want his space to unwind, and I'd hate to feel like I'm encroaching on him. But, he may also hope that I'm here.

Packing my things will take a bit, especially getting the pigs settled in the carrier, and Jamie won't get in until well after dinnertime. It's an almost five hour flight from Miami to Denver, but courtesy of the time change, he makes up two hours in flight.

Still, I'm not quite sure what he may want, so I decide to call him and bluntly ask. Jamie has assured me on more than one occasion that he wants me to be honest with him, so that's what I'm going to do.

When the call connects, but no one speaks, I pull my phone away from my ear to see if we're still connected. I can hear some background noise, but nothing else. "Jamie?"

"Look, I don't know what you expect from me right now, Troy."

"I asked for clarification. I need to know what to expect." It takes me a moment to remember that Troy is Jamie's sports agent. He's spoken highly of Troy, but he never mentioned Troy would also be in Miami.

"No, you're being nosy as fuck. There's nothing to tell."

"You suck at lying, man. And I've known you too long for you to pull off an acceptable fib. I need to know if you're with the vet or not."

Jamie sighs loudly, and I wonder where his phone is that I can hear it so clearly. My heart beat quickens, waiting with bated breath for his response. "There's nothing to tell, Troy."

"Yet she's watching your cats right now," Troy comments.

"And? We fucked a few times. That's it." Ouch. That's one way of keeping our relationship secret. Unless ... what if it really is the case?

"Dammit, Jamie, I told you not to shit where you eat. Your

fucking charity event is in two weeks. How are you going to handle that?"

"I have it handled. I've got it under control."

"Oh, yeah? How so?" Troy says, a challenge clear in his tone.

"I told her we have to keep our relationship a secret. She's fine with it."

"And you're gonna keep her on the line until after the event? That's surprising, actually. Pretty cold-blooded for you. Wait. Is this the girl you told me about? The one you were interested in?"

"No, no. Different girl. Same timeline, different girl."

And it's as if the bottom drops out on my life.

I should have known. I should have fucking known.

In what world would a superstar athlete ever want me? Of course he was just using me for his own benefit. I've been doing most of the heavy lifting for his event, since he's been so busy this summer. I've finalized the linens, the guest list, all of the bachelors for the auction, and the centerpieces. I worked with the live band on a list of approved songs, and the venue staff on the overall schedule. In fact, looking back, I don't think Jamie made one decision since we agreed on the menu so many weeks ago. He's agreed with my choices, but hasn't really participated.

I pull the phone from my ear, bringing a shaky hand to touch the screen and end the call. It was all too good to be true. I should have trusted my gut, and never let myself fall for him. But I guess I didn't fall for him. I fell for the mask he put on for me. The role he decided to play. Hell, maybe he isn't even autistic. Maybe everything has been a game to him, including crushing my heart.

In an almost zombie-like state, I float around Jamie's massive home, removing every element of my existence. One of my favorite blankets ended up here two weekends ago, and a coffee mug sits next to an espresso machine. He'd added another reading chair in his office for me, so I could sit and watch the guinea pigs, but he paid for it, so it stays. I pack up the pigs, being careful to leave any of the items he bought. I make a mental note to add up everything he purchased at my townhouse. I'll have to go with a ballpark number, but I refuse to feel like I owe him even one cent.

I load up my car, being sure to take out his garage door opener, and remove his key from my keyring. Ripping a piece of paper from one of the notebooks on his desk, I write him a goodbye note, and let him know any and all communication about the event will be made through the foundation. Then I block his number.

I pick up Maverick and Goose separately, giving each cat a cuddle and chin scratch, telling them I love them so much, but their Daddy is a dumbass and heartbreaker, so it's his fault I'm leaving. I have no shame in admitting who's at fault here.

Taking one last, longing look at his home, I pick up Flash, then leave for the final time.

Upon arriving home, I get every animal situated, then collapse onto my couch. I can't go into my bedroom yet. My last night in that bed, I spent wrapped up in Jamie, feeling like I was on top of the world. Like I'd met my match. The partner who would conquer life with me. I thought we complemented each other so well, and I loved how he comprehended my struggles with everyday life.

How am I supposed to find someone who gets me?

Overstimulation.

Inability to recognize social cues.

An apparent lack of a filter in certain situations.

Hardly any friendships because women don't accept me.

Texture and taste issues.

Married to my job.

Will I ever find a partner who loves me for me?

Who doesn't use me as a placeholder, or hide me away while trying to find someone better?

Curling up in a ball, I begin to cry.

My brother and sister couldn't care less about me.

My parents only put up with me if it benefits them.

None of them support me, or accept me for who I am.

I have one friend. One.

It's only a matter of time before she realizes I'm not worth the trouble.

I'm alone.

So fucking alone.

After crying for an inordinate amount of time, I text Chelsea and ask if she can come watch my animals for the night. She responds with a joke about how much noise I'll make with Jamie when he gets home, and how innocent animal ears shouldn't hear it. I don't correct her.

I stalk quickly into my room, grabbing an empty bag and a change of clothes. Back in the living room, I remove my necessities from the bag I had at Jamie's, then go to my car. Once I get to where I'm going, I'll contact Chelsea. But not now. She'll talk me out of it, but I need to leave. I can't be in the same city as Jamie right now.

Jax's wife, Becca, told me about a boutique hotel in a small town called Eternity Springs, about an hour west of Denver, and it sounded like a great place to take a vacation. A quick check online found an open room, and I scooped it up for the week. Everlasting Inn and Spa has a restaurant, spa, hot springs, and free Wi-Fi, so I can handle any official business from there.

I have the radio turned off on the drive. Complete silence, except for the sound of traffic on the interstate. I turned my phone off quite some time ago, not that anyone will call me. Chelsea thinks I'm getting banged six ways to Sunday, and Jamie isn't in Colorado yet. But I can't take the chance that anyone might call me. If I speak a word, I'll begin to sob.

Driving the main road in Eternity Springs, I'm greeted by an adorable town full of touristy shops, a large town center with a playground, and a huge hotel that looms in the distance. Pulling onto the Everlasting property, I stare slack-jawed at the hotel. It's absolutely gorgeous. Four stories, with bay windows on the ends, it somehow appears both quaint and awe-inspiring. I could see having a large, grand wedding here, but also a brunch with friends.

After parking, I slowly walk into the grand foyer to the concierge. A woman smiles pleasantly at me. "How may I help you?"

"Uh, hi," I answer, my voice instantly unsteady. "I just reserved a room about an hour ago. It should be under Audrey Carrington."

"Oh, yes. Are you by any chance related to Paige Carrington? I can't remember her married last name, though."

Great. Even an hour away from home, my last name makes things difficult. "She's my sister."

The woman's face screws up in immediate distaste, but she schools her expression instantly. "Oh, how lovely. I've interacted with Paige on a variety of events in Denver."

"What events?" I ask, hoping it isn't the main one my family does. If she knows Paige, she may know my parents.

"Mostly for Children's Hospital of Colorado. I don't think Paige was super involved with the events for the hospital, but I usually saw her in passing."

"Oh, I believe her husband works for Children's, or their parent hospital company. So it explains why she was there. She doesn't really like kids, though, so I'm betting her husband made her go," I blurt out.

The woman lets out a loud laugh. "I take it you and your sister don't get along too well?"

"No, not really. We're very different people," I answer honestly. "And her husband is a jerk."

"Oh, thank God," the woman admits, letting out a long exhale. "I worried I'd put my foot in it. I'm Arianna, by the way."

"Hi, I'm Audrey."

"How did you hear about Everlasting?" she asks, as she types something on her computer.

"A friend had great things to say about it. I think her husband used to play hockey with someone who worked here?"

Arianna beams. "That's my brother, Luca! Our family owns the hotel. Which of his old teammates?"

"Jax Mitchell?"

"Ahh. You're friends with his amazing wife Becca, then."

"Sort of. We were introduced by a mutual friend … actually, no longer mutual. We were introduced by someone no longer part of my life because he's a lying, cheating asshole and I hope his life on the football field is paved with only green LEGOS," I state, not realizing my voice has risen remarkably quickly.

"Okay," Arianna says hesitantly. "And you're here to avoid him?"

I nod sullenly.

"Do you want to talk about it?"

"No. Well, yes. No. Not now. Maybe later. I don't know?" I say, my tone as confused as me.

Arianna laughs. "I get it. Men are complicated. Give me your number, and we can touch base once you're settled. I can give you the lay of the land and tell you which places to avoid in town."

I rattle off my number, surprised at how quickly Arianna has gone from a nobody to a potential friend. "Okay."

"Check your phone. Did the text go through?" she asks.

"My phone is off. I didn't want to talk to … anyone," I admit.

"Right. Well, I'm here until six, so if you need anything, call down."

"Are you always at the concierge desk?" I inquire.

Arianna smiles. "No. I'm hardly ever up here, but the concierge we've had for years needed the day off. I said I'd fill in. I oversee the spa and hot springs, but in all honesty, I'm mostly home with my kids."

"How many kids?"

"Four."

"Four!" I shout incredulously. Jesus, I need to work on my volume level.

"The last one was a buy one, get one free sale, so I said fine. What's one more when you're already outnumbered anyway?"

"Buy one, get one free?" I stare at her, confused, until it makes sense. "Oh. Twins."

Arianna giggles. "Yeah. I have three girls, and one boy."

"Sounds like your house is full."

"It is," she answers cheerfully. "Full of toys, noise, and chaos."

I sigh. "And love, laughter, and family."

Arianna tilts her head to the side as she studies me. "Oh, girl. We're definitely having drinks this week. You'll fit right in with my sisters and sisters-in-law."

I'm not sure about that. Groups of women tend to avoid me.

Once in my room, I unpack, then sit quietly on the bed. I pull out my phone, hesitantly turning it on. As soon as it connects, I get a handful of texts from Chelsea, a text from an unknown number that I assume is Arianna, but nothing else. But before I can respond to Chelsea, she calls me.

"Hey."

"Why are you in Eternity Springs?" she demands.

"How did you — I know you track my location, but I literally just turned on my phone."

"There's a setting where I can ask for a notification once you've moved. I figured you had your phone turned off, but didn't know why. Your zoo of animals is fine, by the way."

"Oh. Well, that's at least good."

"Now explain why you're running."

"Running is a harsh word, Chelsea."

"Not in this instance. What did he do? I know this has to involve Jamie."

I sigh, try to control my breathing, and then blurt out the entire story to her. Chelsea is quiet for a moment, before she growls, "I will fucking kill him."

I can't help the loud, sputtering laugh that bursts from my lungs. "I don't think it's *that* serious, Chels."

"I think it *is* that serious. This is the first man you've been interested in in I don't know how long. He almost systematically got you to lower all your defenses. You've planned the entire event, and he's had you watching his cats. It's all bullshit, and he deserves to pay."

"I don't want revenge. I want to move on with my life, and forget he ever existed." Heated emotion simmers at the base of my throat, making my eyes water, and my nose run. I hate this. I don't like showing emotion.

"When are you coming back?" Chelsea asks.

"I reserved a room up here for a week. I don't intend to stay that long, I don't think. And I certainly don't expect you to keep Flash that entire time."

"Oh, shut it. You know it's fine. Flash loves me more than you anyway. Are we closing the clinic, or should I call that weird guy?" The weird guy, otherwise known as Doctor Noah Pratt, is a travel veterinarian. He roams around the Front Range of Colorado, filling in where needed. His personality is well past quirky, but he's efficient, inexpensive, and almost always available on short notice.

"Call Doctor Pratt, but also go through the appointments this week and reschedule any you think will be upset if they don't see me. And can you watch Flash and the pigs? I'll probably come home earlier than a week. I just needed to get away from Denver, and away from … Jamie." My voice cracks on his name, like even acknowledging his existence hurts my heart.

"Got it. Do me a favor and let me know if you're coming home early. That way I can be ready," Chelsea says, her demeanor odd.

"Why?"

"No reason. Uh oh, the pigs are squealing. I guess it's veggie time. Gotta go! Text me later. Or call me. Whatever. I'll be here!" Chelsea ends the call, and I'm left wondering what trouble she'll get into without me there to reel her in.

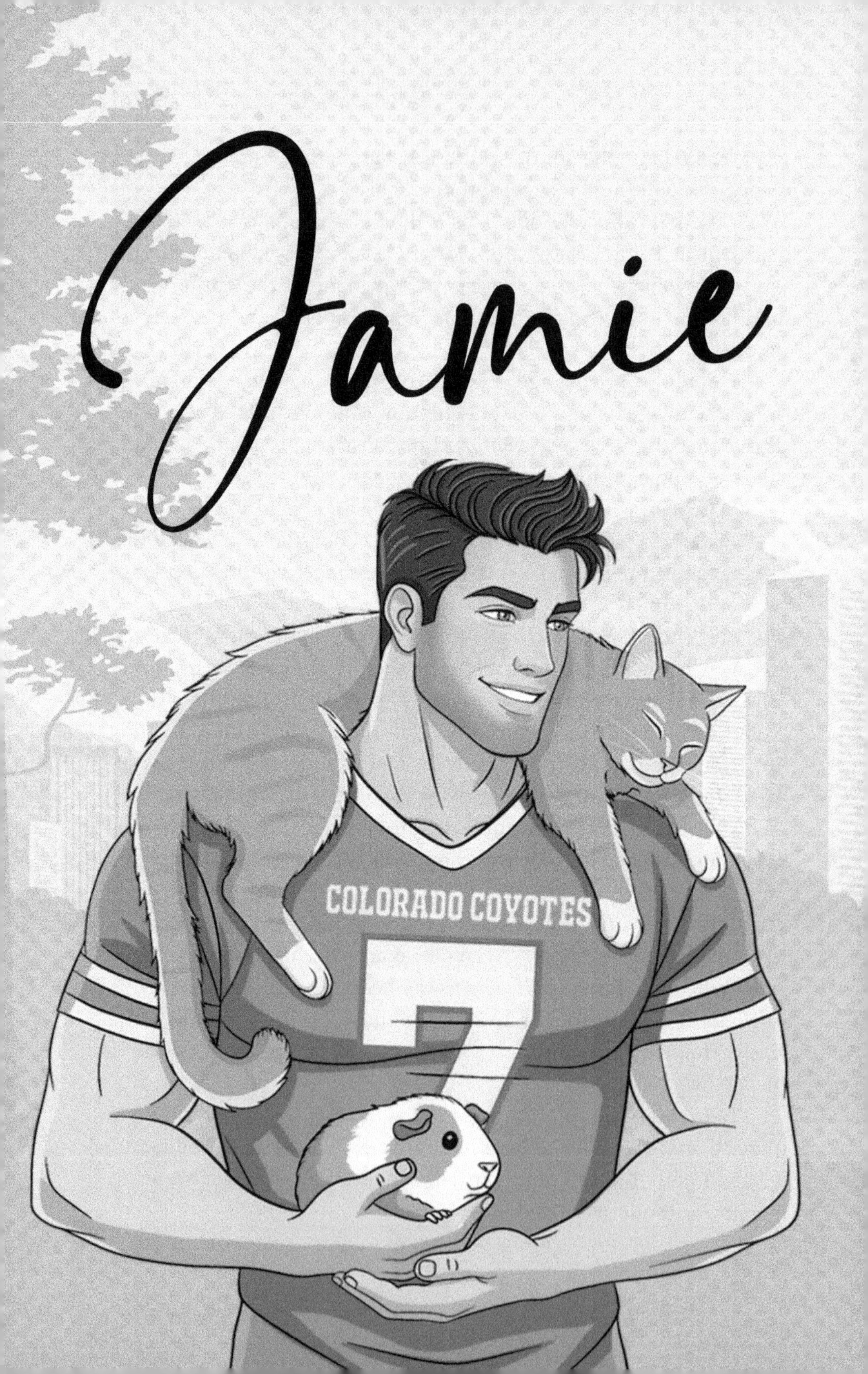

Jamie

CHAPTER 23

WHAT THE HELL?

"You okay?" Troy asks as we're taxiing down the runway at Denver's Centennial Airport.

"I got a pretty threatening text from an unknown number," I murmur, showing Troy my phone.

"Woah. You want me to track the person down?" he asks.

Another text comes through.

A foreboding sensation wafts over me, sending chills down my spine. *Who* trusted me?

I think back to any interactions I've had over the past six

months that someone might misconstrue as misleading. Granted, my ability to recognize normal social cues is nonexistent, so I don't come up with any winners.

"Jesus," Troy says, reading the second text. "Who the fuck did you piss off?"

"I have no idea. The only woman I met recently was a woman from my night out with Jax, and then Audrey and her best friend. It can't be the first woman. I don't even remember her name, so there were no walls to break down. We didn't even have sex, because she kicked me out beforehand. So that leaves Audrey and her best friend."

"Who is Audrey? Oh, the vet." His eyes narrow. "What the actual fuck, Jamie? You said it was nothing! She's the one you've been with this entire time. Am I right? It was more serious than you've led on."

I sigh, resting my head against the seat. "We made a deal to keep things private until after the event. I want to protect her as much as I can, Troy. I've never had a truly public relationship, and the fans are going to go nuts. She's not ready for that."

As the flight attendant motions for us that we're able to get up, Troy grabs my arm. "You should have told me. I have to protect you, which means her as well. I can't get in front of things I don't know about. I should have asked more questions. I fucking knew you weren't being completely truthful about this."

"I hate lying. You know that. But I'll do anything for Audrey." I look at Troy, then say the thing I've barely admitted to myself. "I'm in love with her, man. She's the one."

He nods, giving me a grin. "Okay. I'd like to meet her, and then we can all work out a plan to protect both of you."

"I need to call her and tell her you know," I say cheerfully, pulling out my phone. Bringing up her contact, I'm confused when it immediately goes to voicemail. "That's odd. It's going straight to voicemail."

"Maybe she was making a call," Troy suggests. "Text her so she knows to call you back."

I fire off a "can't wait to see you" text, which comes back as undeliverable. This can't mean what I think it means, can it?

"What the fuck?" I breathe, my blood pressure rising. I feel anger, terror, and hysteria beginning to boil in my stomach. What happened? Is Audrey okay? Is this a mistake, or is it intentional? How did the bottom drop out after a phenomenal night together? "Isn't this what happens when you're blocked by someone? Did she block me? Did my girlfriend fucking block me?"

"Alright, buddy, I'm gonna need you to breathe," Troy says, as I jump to my feet and begin stalking up and down the small aisle of the private plane. It only takes a few strides to go from the front to the back, but my adrenaline is pumping too much for me to sit down. "Give me your phone. I'll see if I can call her from mine."

I watch as he copies Audrey's number from my phone, then listen as it rings. He hangs up after two rings, then calls it again from my phone. Straight to voicemail. "What the fuck!"

Troy stands up, placing his hands on my shoulders. Squeezing, he gives me a little bit of the pressure that I need to maintain a semblance of composure. "Breathe. In-two-three-four-five. Hold it-two-three-four-five. And out-two-three-four-five. We're going to get to the bottom of this, Jamie. Repeat the breathing. Sit down for a moment. What's Audrey's friends name?"

"Chelsea," I mutter, closing my eyes as I feel panic clawing at my chest. What the hell happened? I spoke to her last night, and things were fine. We talked about the event. Granted, I haven't been as hands-on as I'd liked to have been, but Audrey didn't seem to mind.

"To ensure you have plausible deniability, don't ask how I tracked the unknown phone number down, but it's a registered cell for Precious Paws Veterinary Clinic, owned by Doctor Audrey Carrington."

My heart falls into my stomach, and I drop my head into my hands. What the hell happened? "You have any kind of tracking software that can track someone's location without them knowing? Because I guarantee she's nowhere I'd find her."

"It seems like she doesn't want to talk to you," he says nonchalantly.

"Well, that's not really an option," I snap. "I deserve an explanation, and we have a major event in two weeks. She can't just cut me out without telling me."

He hands me my phone. "Then call her friend."

I scoff. "She probably won't answer the phone."

Troy shrugs. "You don't know unless you try. Call the number. If she won't help, then we'll come up with some other kind of plan."

The unknown number stares at me, daunting me. I hate confrontations. It's partially the reason why I'm so even-keeled in press conferences, and I let reporters speak to me however they want. The thought of Chelsea yelling at me makes me feel like puking. But I can't give up on Audrey. I need any information Chelsea is willing to give to me.

I call the number, and Chelsea answers after one ring. "You have a lot of nerve calling me, asshole."

"Chelsea, what the hell happened? Is she okay? Where is she? I don't understand. I spoke to her last night and things were fine. Perfect, even."

"Well, isn't that the way you set it up to be?" she sneers. "Keeping Audrey safe at home, doing all your bidding, taking care of your pets, and warming your bed, while you're out there doing who the hell knows what."

"That's not — that's not how it is at all," I sputter. "Doing who the hell knows what? That's not me. She knows me."

"She doesn't know you at all. Actually, forget that. She knew who you painted yourself to be, but now she knows the real you."

"What the hell are you talking about?" I yell. "She does know the real me! She knows me better than anyone on this planet!"

"She knows you're cheating on her, you philandering asshat. So fucking typical! The athlete getting his kicks while his woman is at home. You disgust me," she snaps.

I feel sick. "I am not cheating on Audrey. I would never do that.

I can't stand cheaters. I haven't spoken to my mom in years because she had an affair with my married college coach, and broke up a marriage. I would never do that to Audrey."

"Then why did you admit it to your agent, Jamie? She literally heard it straight from your mouth. You can say all you want to me, but the only one to blame here is you. You lost the best thing that's ever happened to you. Don't call this number again, and don't even think about showing up at the clinic. Audrey took the week off anyway, and she's out of town, so don't sit outside her place like a lovesick puppy either."

The call ends without a response from me. Confused, I pull up my call log. "Chelsea said Audrey heard me say I was cheating on her. The only time I've even insinuated that was during our conversation this morning, and — oh, my God. There's a call from her. It was a couple of minutes long."

"So she overheard our conversation, and you said something about how you'd fucked Audrey a few times, but the real woman you wanted was … how did you put it? Same timeline, different girl."

Nausea overtakes me. "There's no other girl, Troy. I swear. Audrey is it. She's the only woman that has ever mattered to me."

"Fucking hell, man." Troy sighs, leaning back against the seat and propping his foot on a table. "I'm at a loss here. Let's meet in the morning and we'll figure out a plan."

"Chelsea said Audrey went out of town for the week," I murmur sullenly, dropping my face into my hands. It's remarkable how much a mood can change in twenty minutes.

"Well, we can concoct a plan for the event. She has to be there. We'll get your girl back, Jamie. I know we will," Troy says assuredly, but I don't get my hopes up. If Audrey overheard me lying to Troy, then she had every reason to block me. I would have done the same thing.

An hour later, I slowly walk into my empty house, knowing it's devoid of the only person I want to see. I knew she wouldn't be here, but it was still like a knife to the heart when I saw her empty garage spot. Walking through the house, I see she's cleared everything out. Not even a hair on the shower wall has been left behind.

Back in the kitchen, I spot a paper on the counter, next to her garage opener and my spare key. Fuck.

> *Jameson,*
>
> *I should have known better. Shame on me, I guess. Same timeline, different girl. I should have known a guy like you would never go for a girl like me.*
>
> *All future event correspondence will go through the foundation board. At the event, do not speak to me. I want nothing to do with you. Congratulations on breaking my heart. I hope the event will be worth it to you.*
>
> *Doctor Audrey Carrington*

She called me Jameson.

The handwritten note gives me an immediate migraine. I don't deserve her. To know that I've hurt her this way? God. I feel like such a fucking failure. I wish I wasn't blocked, so I could tell her how sorry I am. How I'll never forgive myself for causing her even a moment of pain. And that I'd do whatever she asked for if she'd give me another chance.

But, knowing that she probably won't ever unblock me, I decide to get the words out on paper. A therapist during the first few years of my NFL career suggested that I write things down. He said that sometimes the words need to come out of our heads. It's a quiet and simple way to get the release I need. I've done it before, and it's helped.

I walk into my office, staring at the empty guinea pig enclosure. Sitting in the chair I bought for Audrey, I grab a notebook from the table and get to work.

Doc,

I have a million things to say, yet I can't figure out a way to start saying them. I hate knowing you're somewhere alone, hurting. That I can't be there for you. That I'm the reason WHY you're hurting. I'm such an idiot.

There's no other woman. There never was. Same time-line, different girl? No. A complete lie. I was trying to buy us some time. I hadn't fully admitted to my agent about our relationship, and I thought it was better if I kept him in the dark. You know how much I hate lying, and he does too. He even called me out on it, saying he knew something was up. But I just doubled down, instead of fessing up to my feelings for you.

I wasn't hiding you for the reasons I'm sure you've conjured up in your mind. I think it was twofold: (1) I was so fucking scared you'd take one look at what I deal with every day of my life, and you'd run as far away from me as possible, and (2) I liked having you all to myself. We were in our own little bubble, and I didn't want to burst it. But I fucked it up, and you ran anyway. Not that I blame you.

I don't trust a lot of people. I've learned to keep my circle small and tight. Bringing you into my heart was so easy it scared me. Loving you has been like breathing. That's what this is: love. I love you. I'm beyond love, honestly. I'm borderline obsessed with you. I'd go to the ends of the earth to bring you what you need or want.

I will regret that stupid conversation with Troy for the rest of my miserable life, but I won't regret the brief time I had the privilege of loving you.

Love always,

Your Jamie

That one letter opens a gaping wound in my heart, and I begin writing to Audrey whenever I fancy. In between workouts, before I go to sleep, every night at dinner. A full week has passed since my world imploded, and I've yet to run out of things to say.

Aud,

My word for the day is flibbertigibbet. It's a flighty person. For some reason, I always thought it was a noun for a tangible object, not like a personality trait. I guess I was addlepated, which means confused. That was yesterday's word.

Your pillow doesn't smell like your shampoo anymore, and I've never been this upset about a pillow. I spent an ungodly amount of time at the store today, smelling every shampoo, trying to find it. I've been holding your pillow to sleep every night, as if it's somehow a suitable alternative to the real thing (newsflash: it isn't). I haven't slept well since the last time I held you in my arms. On one hand, I hope you're sleeping well. But on the other, I hope your sleep is just as shitty as mine. Because maybe, it'll mean you'll come back to me. And then I can get on my knees to grovel, and beg you to forgive me.

Please come back to me, baby.

I talked to my dad today. He said my mom has been in contact with him. She has cancer, and it doesn't look good. He encouraged me to forgive her, and wants me to see her. I don't know what to do, Audrey. I still have a lot of anger about how she treated me growing up. Trying to force me into certain things so she could live vicariously through me. But if she dies, will I regret not saying goodbye? I wish I could talk to you. I know you'd see things from my perspective, and how even talking about my mom makes me feel out of control. It throws a massive kink in my life that I don't like. You'd understand. God, I miss you so much it hurts.

I heard from the board today. They said you're having each bachelor showcase an adoptable animal from a variety of shelters around Denver. That is so phenomenal, Doc. If you ever decide to give up your day job, you'd be an excellent event planner. Or a foundation board member. I'm in awe of you every day. I wish I could tell you that.

Training Camp started today. I'm hopeful for this team. It's a good group of guys, and we're already gelling quite nicely. But deep down, I hate knowing you won't be there to cheer me on. And that's not a guilt trip. I know this is absolutely my fault. I only want you to know that I'm always thinking of you.

Aud,

You'll love knowing I learned a new word outside of my word-a-day calendar. As part of my penance for what happened with the Coach's niece, I have to do more interviews than ever. Some guy came over from England, and he referenced our "smashmouth" offense. Evidently it means being brought by brute force. I thought he was referencing the band! No one on the team knew what he meant either, because I went around to ask everyone.

I love you. I wish I'd told you that. I wish you knew how much I crave you. How you've made such an impact on my life, and how I'll never be the same man because of you. I want to do better. Be greater. Do all the things you've inspired me to do.

In another one of my punishments, I'm coaching a peewee football team. There's this kid. Emmett. He's quiet. Really introverted. But I can see the wheels turning in his head as he watches our plays. He's soaking it all in. After four weeks of practice and games, he told me this week that he's autistic. And Aud, I told him I am as well. You should have seen the look that came over his face.

You were right. I have a platform I'm not using.

And that changes now.

Audrey

CHAPTER 24

"Oh my God! Audrey!" Chelsea screams from my living room.

I've been home from Eternity Springs for a week. I didn't know how desperately I needed the vacation. It's been a few years since I took any significant amount of time off, and I know I can't keep going like that. Arianna Santo Dixon pulled me into her girl squad, throwing me into the most chaotic group chat ever, possibly in the history of mankind. These ladies accepted me with no expectations. Then, as soon as I explained Chelsea, they popped her into the chat too.

I have girlfriends.

While sad to leave the denial bubble I created in the mountains, I had to come home. The on-call vet hadn't killed any of my clients, but Chelsea reported more than one aggravated regular who didn't like his table-side manner. Plus, I had a handful of last-minute tasks to get done for the auction.

Which is tonight.

And I'll have to see Jamie.

Excuse me while I go hyperventilate a little.

So, Chelsea came over to get ready with me. I voluntold her she'd be attending as my plus one. She is my platonic lesbian life partner, after all, so it's fitting. We shared a bottle of wine while doing our hair and makeup, and it did a great job of relaxing me.

"Audrey! Get in here!"

As I walk into the living room, I hear someone on the television say, "This is such a big development for the sport of football. What a platform he now has."

"Who?" I ask.

Chelsea shushes me as the announcer continues. "Boy, I gotta say, I'm surprised we're only now finding out about this."

A woman pipes up. "From a female perspective, I can relate. We are told to be careful how we act, what we say, and anything we do in this male-dominated world of sports broadcasting. I have to assume that Wahlberg kept his diagnosis to himself as a precaution. He protected himself and his emotional well-being. I can't find fault in that."

"And Shara, do you think his announcement will help, or hinder, the Coyotes quarterback?"

"I think it'll be twofold. On one side, you'll have hundreds, if not thousands, of kids who now want to learn from him. Who see him as an even bigger role model than before. But, there will be old school fans who turn on him, because he's tainted that picture-perfect image they concocted in their own minds."

"Did he —" I stop, swallowing hard, as I stare at a gorgeous picture of Jamie transposed in the upper right corner of my television. "Did he announce he's autistic?"

Chelsea's head whips to stare at me. "You fucking knew, and you didn't tell me?"

"It's not my secret to tell. And honestly, the only reason I know is because I asked him if he was. I doubt he would have told me. Although, after everything that happened recently, I wasn't sure if I believed he was autistic."

"Why not?"

I struggle to keep emotion off my face, and my voice even. "I thought maybe he used my diagnosis to get close to me. That if he acted throughout the entirety of our short relationship, then maybe that was an act too."

"Oh, Aud," Chelsea whispers. Her expression is pained as she stands, giving me a hug. "Don't think that. Besides, he's not that good of an actor. I saw the way he looked at you when he was here. The man was smitten."

"Maybe there was interest, but he didn't see it going long-term. It's fine. I'm glad I found out before I fell even harder." I sniff, failing to keep the single tear from dribbling down my cheek. "Alright. We need to go. You remember your one task, right?"

Chelsea nods. "I'm never to leave your side, and I play man-to-man defense if Jamie approaches you. Do fouls count in a charity benefit? Like, if I kneed him in the balls, would I get kicked out? Does he get a free shot on me?"

"You're mixing your sports metaphors, but let's not have any violence, okay? Bad publicity could impact our business. Leave Jamie out of it." I get an alert telling me our rideshare is here. "We need to go. I really hope this night flies past so I can move on."

Chelsea doesn't respond as we walk to the car. I requested a large SUV, because both of us are wearing dresses that need a little bit of breathing room. My A-line champagne dress with sheer sleeves is embroidered with floral lace featuring green stems and every shade of pink imaginable. The deep V-neck on the front and back highlights my chest and shoulder blades. It's the dress of my dreams. My gorgeous best friend is adorned in a baby pink fit-and-flare sequin dress with a small train. She will be the interest of many men tonight. And probably a few women.

I'm silent on the way to the downtown hotel, focusing on my breathing and some personal mantras I like to repeat to myself when I'm really struggling to feel overstimulated and out of control. *I am not defined by anyone else's expectations. I am beautifully unique. My voice matters. I deserve love and respect. I learn and grow from every experience. I make my own joy. I don't need a man to have a fulfilling life.* I may have to repeat that last one over and over again tonight, because the thought of Jamie in a tux is probably going to do me in.

"You ready?" Chelsea whispers, squeezing my hand in encouragement. I didn't realize I'd grabbed her hand at some point, but I'm appreciative of the support.

"No, but I don't have a choice. Let's get this over with." Stepping out of the rideshare about a football field length away from a large contingent of press — and no, the irony isn't lost on me — Chelsea and I walk swiftly up the red carpet and into the hotel lobby. I met with the florist yesterday, and memorized the layout of the hotel, so I'm able to pull Chelsea right into the ballroom.

Where, of course, I run right into Jamie.

I let out an oomph at the collision, and his hands immediately come to my arms, holding me upright. The delicious smell of his cologne wafts over me, and I'm suddenly right back in his bedroom, safe in the confines of his bed. Wrapped in his embrace. Tears fill my eyes as I look up to find a stricken Jamie.

"Audrey," he breathes.

"No," Chelsea snaps. "Let go."

"Doc, please," he pleads, but acquiesces by letting go of my arms. The loss of his touch is almost painful. It's only been two and a half weeks since we were together, but it feels like an eternity. I hate this.

"I can't," I whisper brokenly. Turning away, I allow Chelsea to take my hand, but as we step away, Jamie grabs my other one. "Wha — what are you doing?"

He gives me a sad smile. "You look exquisite tonight, Audrey. I can't let you walk away without telling you that."

My breath catches as I stare at him, but Chelsea yanks my arm. He looked genuinely broken. But what can I believe? Chelsea pulls me out the side door of the ballroom, and into a long hallway. She doesn't stop until we're safely in the confines of the women's restroom. I take in a shaky breath as I brace my hands on the counter. "Chels, am I just love-drunk? He looked so sad. Was that acting?"

"I don't know. I'm so confused right now," she murmurs, placing her small clutch next to my hands. "Your boy sure does clean up well, though."

I let out a snort. "Not my boy, but yes. He definitely does."

She catches my gaze in the mirror. "You'd make an insanely striking couple on the red carpet."

That comment hits me where it hurts, and she knows it. "It's moot. He didn't want to be seen in public with me. I refuse to be someone's dirty secret."

"'Atta girl," Chelsea says with a swift nod. "Keep that attitude the whole night, and you may just make it out of here without mounting his leg."

She's not that far off from the truth. I know how amazing his thighs are.

"Are your parents coming tonight?" Chelsea asks.

"I don't know. They're on the guest list, but they didn't RSVP. That didn't surprise me, though. They like to make an entrance."

"They wouldn't come just to support you?" Chelsea says, then laughs. "I can't believe I actually said that with a straight face. Of course, they wouldn't."

I chuckle, the sound awkward and off-key. "Right? They'd be more likely to come to this because of the guest list. Certainly not me."

"I don't know," she muses. "Half of Denver's professional athletes are coming. This is well below their pay grade."

"Plus, they really despise Jamie. They probably won't forgive him after the bullshit at the gala." My phone dings with a timer, letting me know guests are due to arrive any moment. "Alright. Let's go check with the hotel staff on dinner, and make sure the band is setting up. Then we should be able to hide in a corner with a bottle of some kind of alcohol."

Two hours later, I can barely feel my feet.

As someone who literally stands most of the day, every day, that's saying something. But women's shoes are made directly by Satan himself. Granted, I love how powerful and beautiful the Christian Louboutin shoes make me feel. The four inch stiletto suggested I was a force to be reckoned with. Maybe I should have chosen a smaller heel.

I ran into Claire, one of the women in the crazy group chat. She never talked much, and as soon as I met her, I understood why. Claire is quiet and introverted, just like me. She's an accountant, has a type-A personality with an analytical brain, and I can tell we'll gel right away. She tells me about a run-in with a man outside the bathrooms who infuriated her.

"He was loud, brash, and completely out of line!" she huffs.

"How so?"

She is simmering with tension and anger. "He suggested we have a quickie in the bathroom. I didn't even know his name! Drunk I might do that, but sober? No."

"But you would drunk?" I ask, completely amused at the dichotomy between our conversation and Claire's very detail-oriented and meticulous personality.

She shrugs. "I have been known to make some rather question-able decisions when drunk. But still! The audacity!"

"What else did he say?" I ask.

"He commented on my dress, and that I was the most beautiful woman he'd ever seen." Claire's ice-blue strapless dress fits her thin body beautifully, an almost perfect match for her eyes.

"Well, you look amazing, so you can't fault him for that."

"Audrey!" Chelsea hisses from behind a pillar. Claire says goodbye as I turn to Chelsea. She motions me to approach, then looks around to see if anyone is listening. "Did you mess with the seating chart?"

"No. Why? I finalized it two days ago and sent it to the hotel. Is there an issue?" My mind whirls with possible problems. Did I acci-dentally put sports rivals at the same table, or a man and his current girlfriend next to his ex wife and her date, who just so happens to be his ex-best friend?

"Dude," Chelsea says, her eyes wide. "We've both been moved."

"What?" I explode. "That's preposterous! Who wou —"

"Oh, I think you know exactly who did. And now we're stuck, because I certainly can't switch with you. He's at the head table, and you're the only one who hasn't sat down yet."

I close my eyes, willing the emotion clogging my throat to settle down. "This can't be happening."

Her eyes are full of sympathy. "My guess is he planned this, because he knew you would avoid him."

I laugh bitterly. "Well, he's right."

Chelsea sighs. "I figure this can go a few ways. You can sit politely, wait until the auction begins, and then we can go hide again. Or, you could light into him as soon as you sit down, so all of his buddies know what happened."

"They don't even know he was hiding me, so I'd look like a psycho," I tell her. "Any other ideas?"

She gives me a small smile. "You listen to him. Hear what he has to say. Then either forgive him and move on, or forgive him and move toward him."

I gasp. "Move toward him? I don't want to get back with him! I deserve a man who wants me beside him, not one who thinks he's better than me."

"Like I said, listen to him. He may have a valid reason for what you heard. He's looking for you. Go," she says, pointing toward Jamie's table. She pats me on the shoulder, then walks off toward the furthest back table. The table I was also supposed to sit at. I take a deep, shuddering breath, then walk slowly toward the head table. Jamie immediately stands, smoothing a hand over the front of his gorgeous tuxedo, and I force my eyes to look away.

"Everyone, this is Audrey. She spearheaded this event. Audrey, you remember Jax and his wife, Becca. Then we have ..." Jamie says, pointing to all the men sitting around the circular table,

"Maddox, who plays football with me, and Troy, my agent. Lastly, Max, who plays baseball for the Rocky Mountain Raptors. And I apologize, I already forgot the names of your dates. I'm awful with names."

Everyone laughs as Jamie pulls out my chair. I reluctantly sit, as I had intended to come up with some excuse as to why I couldn't sit for dinner. But I see the relief on Jamie's face, and I'm reminded that he also struggles in social situations. Regardless of our relationship, I assume he needs all the support he can get. Directly to my right, Becca leans in. "Are you okay? I know something happened between you two, but I don't know what. Jacob sucks at giving details."

I love how Becca only refers to Jax by his full name of Jacob, but smile sadly as I shake my head. "No, nothing to report. I'm fine. Just tired, and my feet are killing me."

She lets out a breathy giggle. "Women's shoes are the worst! But you look absolutely amazing tonight. Jamie hasn't been able to tear his eyes off of you."

I stiffen slightly, biting my lip. That was all I wanted. To be the object of a man's devotion and love. I didn't expect my partner to shower me with gifts, or love bomb me. I can appreciate the quiet ways love shines through. Like getting my favorite candy, and having the only coffee I'll drink stocked in his kitchen. I'd rather have that kind of love any day of the week. "I'm not comfortable talking about this right now. I may never be ready."

Becca nods. "I get it. Do you want to grab coffee this week? Or a quick lunch? Even if we don't talk about the heathens around this table, I can be a friend."

I smile gratefully at her. "I'd like that."

Dinner is served, and it looks outstanding. Due to the large brick currently rolling around in my stomach, I fake eating, spending the entirety of the dinner portion of the schedule pushing food around on my plate. As we get closer to the auction, Jamie's leg begins to shake. Then I notice him rubbing the pads of two fingers together. Back and forth. Back and forth. He's no longer conversing with anyone, and when I look out of the corner of my eye, I see his face has paled considerably. Without thinking, I rest a hand on his arm. "Are you okay?"

His body stills as he stares at my hand. Before I can react, he reaches up, grabbing it tightly. "No. No, I'm not okay. Audrey, I'm fucking *lost* without you."

Tears fill my eyes. "Maybe you should have thought about that months ago, Jameson."

He winces. "Don't call me that. I'm not Jameson to you."

"I don't think I really know who you are," I whisper, watching as his eyes screw shut in pain. He lets go of my hand, then reaches into his tuxedo coat. Pulling out a small notebook, he hands it to me. "What's this?"

"It's me. It's everything I should have said weeks ago. I think you'll find that you've always known the real me, Doc. I just forgot for a moment." Jamie stands, buttoning his coat. "If you'll excuse me, I have a speech to make, and an auction to MC. Audrey, please read it. Please."

I watch as he strides away, out a side door. Knowing my own challenges with overstimulation, I assume he's off to get himself centered and in control. I bet he uses the same techniques he's used when on the football field. I watch his retreating back before someone drops unceremoniously into Jamie's vacant seat. I look to find his agent, Troy, studying me. "How much did you hear that morning?"

"Enough," I snap.

"Did you give him a chance to explain?" he asks, but before I can reply, he continues. "No. You assumed the worst and blocked him. He's a shell of his former self, barely surviving, and he's in training camp. He might lose the starting position, did you know that?"

"Woah," Maddox says, standing. "It's not her fault, man."

"Oh?" Troy replies, his eyebrows raised defiantly. "It sure seems like she's the catalyst. My guy was doing fine until she rolled into his life like a fucking wrecking ball."

"I didn't ask for any of this," I tell him defensively. "I didn't ask to be hidden like I'm an embarrassment. To be made to feel like I'm less than. To second-guess my entire existence because a man was embarrassed by me. I certainly didn't ask to fall in love with him, yet here we are."

Troy laughs sardonically. "You know, for someone so smart, you're really fucking stupid."

"Cool it, Troy," Max says rigidly. "You're only saying this because Jamie isn't here."

"Well, someone has to!" he explodes. "He told me about you weeks ago. He wouldn't tell me your name, but I knew it was you. Then, when I began questioning him that morning you somehow overheard our conversation, I second-guessed myself. Jamie isn't a liar. He despises liars, frankly. So for him to lie to me, I just couldn't believe it."

"Maybe he didn't lie," I whisper hesitantly.

Troy rolls his eyes. "He fucking lied, Audrey. You're the only woman. There hasn't been a woman in his life in years. He lied because he's so petrified you'll run when you see what his life really is like. How he can never be himself. How he has two gates to go through at home, because people don't leave him alone. He thought he'd finally found his match. You accepted him, exactly as he is. Hell, he fucking told the entire world he's autistic because of you. No way in hell he would have done that six months ago. He's in love with you."

I shake my head as tears fall freely. "I'm not to blame for him announcing he's autistic. No way you're gonna fault me for that one."

"Jesus, you're as stubborn as he is," Troy mutters. "I wasn't blaming you. I've been telling him for years he didn't need to hide. He's a brilliant quarterback, and I believe it's partially due to how his brain works. There's a misconception that autistic individuals can't do certain things, like professional sports, and he's proof that they can. He's going to bring so much hope to a new generation of kids. That is largely due to your support of him. You showed him that he can be accepted exactly as he is. No woman has ever shown him that, not even his own mom. You are the sole reason for him finally having the confidence to stand proudly as himself. But if you don't give him another chance, I'm not sure how he'll handle it."

"I don't — I mean, I can't —" I stammer, then stop when I see Jamie walking on stage. Troy quickly slides into his own seat, acting as if he hasn't been berating me since Jamie stepped away. I look up to find Jamie's intense gaze solely on me, and we both take deep inhales. Simultaneously. Exhale. Inhale. Exhale. I laugh at the absurdity of it all, and Jamie smiles. A genuine smile so perfect it makes my heart ache.

"May I have your attention please. If you are participating in the bachelor auction, please make your way to the front of the stage. You'll be directed where to go. I have a bunch of rules to go over with all the prospective bidders, so be sure to listen. But before we get started, I have some things I'd like to say."

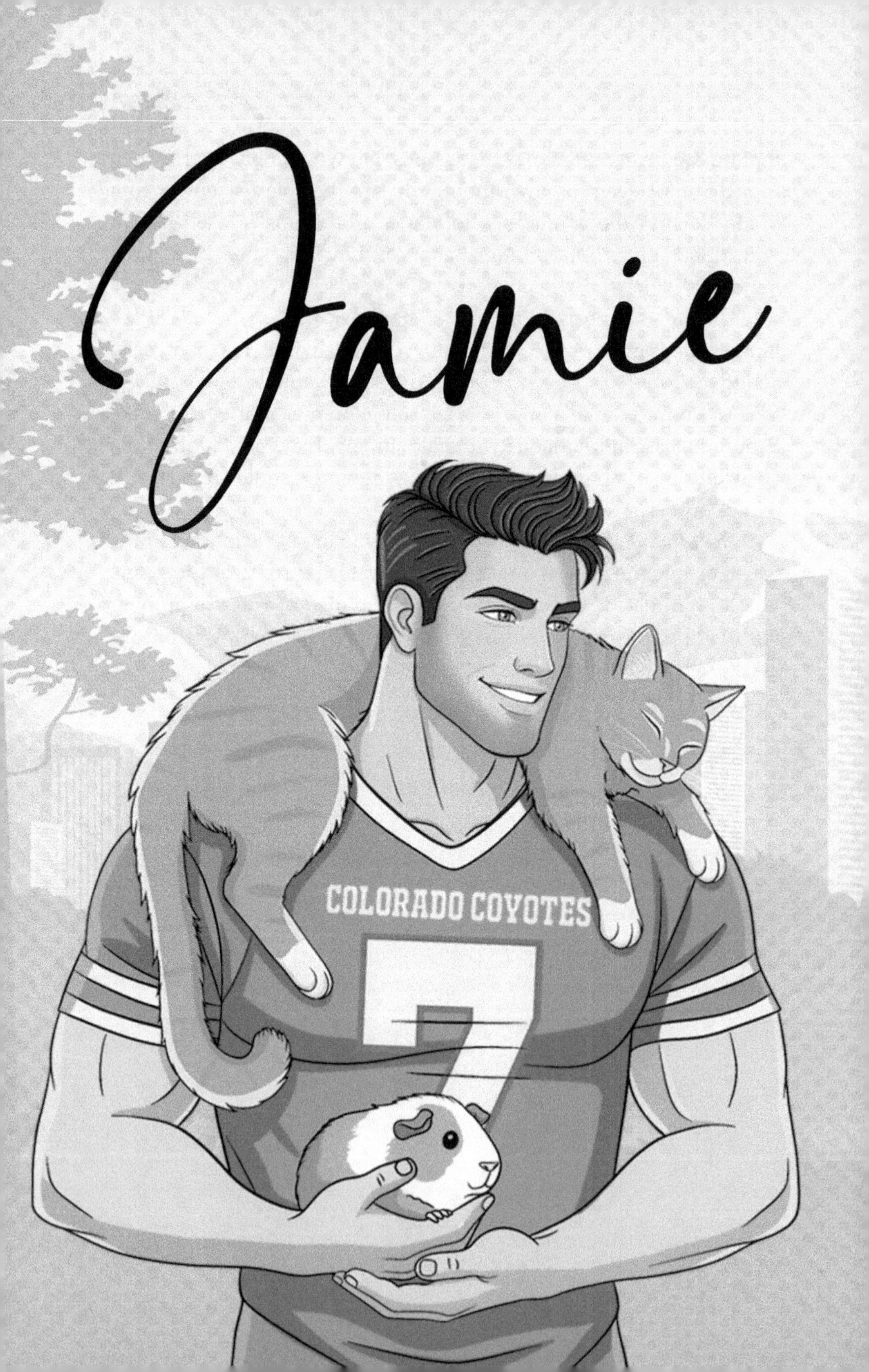

Jamie

CHAPTER 25

Audrey's beautiful gaze is locked on mine. I don't look down at the stack of cards at the podium, as none of this is planned. I need to say all of this directly from my heart.

"Around five months ago, I was tasked with MC-ing this event, and told by the board of the foundation that I needed to help a local veterinarian plan it. Known only as Doctor A, I assumed the vet was a guy. Luckily, I was wrong. " A wave of pleasant laughter fills the ballroom as I continue. "I was matched with Doctor Audrey Carrington, a brilliant veterinarian with one of the kindest hearts I've ever had the privilege to meet. While I had looked forward to planning this event about as much as someone looks forward to a root canal, I found my time with Audrey to be so unexpectedly enjoyable. And that even includes our first night planning this event, when I got so anxious I threw up as soon as I walked in her front door."

Hushed gasps fill the air. "That's right, folks. I barfed. Hard. I'm not sure of many things in the world that could be any more emasculating than that. But Audrey took it all in stride, never once making me feel embarrassed. And that's the thing: Audrey is the most genuine person I've ever met."

I see Becca and Jax nodding their heads in my periphery, but my eyes don't leave Audrey's. Her face is devoid of expression, but a constant stream of tears cascades down her face. I wish I could go to her. Promise to take away every bit of pain I know I'm responsible for delivering. "You may think I'm making that up, but a few days after that night, while texting back and forth, Audrey ghosted me. But not for a reason you might think. She found a box of guinea pigs dropped off at her vet clinic, immediately fell in love with all five of them, and is now raising them herself. Along with her handicapped dog, conveniently named Flash. Audrey is a single mom of six, I guess."

Louder laughter breaks out, and I notice Audrey's lips twitch. I'm taking that as a good sign. "I should have known I was in trouble — or, at the very least, my heart was — when she point-blank asked me if I'm autistic. And she didn't bat an eyelash. In fact, I think my admission may have worked in my favor. She saw something in me that so few have ever seen. I've hidden the real me, choosing to use a variety of masks I've taught myself how to use, and act like real Jamie isn't worthy. Or lovable. But Audrey proved me wrong. She patiently taught me that I'm enough. And then I went and fucked it all up."

A crescendo of gasps fill the air, but I wave for everyone to stop. "Even though I had gained a tremendous amount of confidence from Audrey, I was still broken in one sore area. I was convinced that, if Audrey were to be introduced to the public as mine, she'd be so freaked out that she'd leave. She'd want nothing to do with me, because what self-respecting woman wants her entire life to be under a microscope? So, when my agent pressed me about any budding romance between me and Audrey, I lied. And I'm an awful liar. He saw right through me, but unbeknownst to me, Audrey was listening through my phone. I'd accidentally connected an incoming call from her, and she heard me lie to my agent. But she didn't know I was lying."

Emotion fills my eyes as I look down on her. "I'm so sorry, Doc. I'm so sorry that you thought for a second I'd want anyone but you. It was an awful attempt to protect you. As misguided as I was, I wanted to give you time to come to terms with what life would be like with me. I wanted you to be certain that you thought I was worth it. I didn't want to force your hand, or feel like the media outed you when you weren't ready. And now," I say with a watery laugh, "I've outed you in front of a thousand or so people, and a ton of media outlets. I'm really batting a thousand here."

Many laugh, but my attention is only focused on Audrey. She swipes at a tear, but her gaze doesn't leave mine. My notebook, which became a diary over the past two weeks, is held tightly to her chest. "Audrey, you've taught me so much. I'm a better man because of you. I'm begging you to give me another chance. Let me grovel, and beg, and do everything within my power to convince you that you are a fucking goddess. I need to be in your orbit."

Someone in the back of the room shouts, "One thousand dollars for Jameson Wahlberg!"

I chuckle awkwardly. "Uh, I'm not up for auction."

"Five thousand dollars!" Another woman shouts.

"Six thousand!" A guy yells, making everyone laugh.

"No, seriously. I'm not part of the auction, and I just laid my heart out here. I'm not going out with someone else," I say.

"Ten thousand!"

"Come on, Wahlberg! I'll make it worth your time."

Jesus. This is proving why I didn't want Audrey to experience my life. I basically just told the love of my life that I'm nothing without her, and multiple women are getting in line. Who does that?

Before I can say anything, Audrey stands, still gripping my journal. Her face serious, she holds up one of the bidding paddles from the table.

Everyone waits, on bated breath, as she smiles.

"One hundred thousand dollars."

I smile so hard my lips might rip open. Thank fuck. This has to mean she forgives me.

I point to her. "Sold."

Jumping off the stage, I'm in front of Audrey in two strides, and crash my lips to hers. It's like coming home. Her arms sneak around my waist, her hands tight against my back, and I shudder against her. I can't hold her close enough. Reaching down, I put an arm around her ass, lifting her, laughing as she squeals in shock. I stalk toward the closest door, taking us into a hallway as thunderous applause fills the ballroom.

"Jamie," she breathes against my lips, and the dam breaks.

"I'm sorry. I'm so fucking sorry. I hurt you, and I know I'll be a dumbass again at some point, but please, let me love you. It's the only thing in this entire world I want to be good at. You deserve everything, and I swear if you give me another chance, I will spend every day of the rest of our life together proving to you how perfect you are." I can't remember the last time I cried. A few years ago, maybe, when we lost in the AFC Championship game. But here I am, close to sobbing, because this woman needs to know how much she means to me.

"You love me?" she whispers, her eyes shining.

"Of course, I do! That's all you got out of that?"

She laughs, the sound so perfect it makes me cry harder. I press my back against the closest wall, sliding down until I'm on the floor, and Audrey is straddling my lap. She wipes my cheeks with her thumbs. "You know how you said you need my eyes open? That it's important to you?"

I nod.

"I need to hear the words, Jamie." Her eyes are full of uncertainty, and I realize how much she's suffered because of never hearing how important she is.

"Audrey Carrington," I begin, dragging a lock of hair and tucking it behind her ear, "I am so desperately in love with you. I didn't know how a relationship could be until meeting you. Until I barfed in your bathroom, and found my perfect match had toiletries categorized alphabetically and in order of height."

A burst of laughter leaves her lips as more tears fall, and I continue. "I love your heart. How much you do for the animal population of Denver. How supportive you are of me, and how you make me want to be a better man because of you. You deserve the best, Doc. And there's nothing I want more in life than to prove to you that I can be the man for you."

"I love you too," she whispers. "I've barely survived this week. Up in the mountains, I could live in denial. Act like you didn't exist. But when I came home, all I wanted to do was find you and demand answers. I was so heartbroken."

I rest my forehead against hers, taking a moment to breathe her in. As my body begins to relax, I realize the tension I've been carrying the last two weeks. "You're my home, Doc. You're every-thing. I've been lost without you. My life isn't complete unless you're in it. I need to know you're here. My safe space. And I want to be that for you."

Audrey sniffles. "I want all of that. Please. When can we go home?"

I laugh as I kiss her again. "I'm supposed to MC this damn event. I can't leave yet."

"Damn. So at least another hour?"

"At least. But you planned this, so you know the schedule better than I do." I watch as Audrey's eyes drift off to the side, and I can tell she's doing math in her head.

"Probably two hours. I'll need to make sure everyone stays on track. And every minute you aren't MC-ing the event, I guess that extends the time until we can leave."

"You that impatient to get me alone, Doc?" I tease. She rests her hands on the back of my neck, lightly scratching through my hair, making me shudder.

"And you aren't?" she asks, one eyebrow cocked. The light is back in her eyes, and I grin widely. "What's that look for?"

I shake my head with a shrug. "I'm just so damn happy. I love you."

Audrey giggles lightly. "I love you too. Now hop to it, QB. Let's get this auction over with."

She stands, and I marvel at how beautiful she is. "This dress was made for you. It's stunning."

"Thank you," she says quietly as I get to my feet. Leaning in, I kiss her again, then we're interrupted when she's yanked away from me. "What? Mom! What the heck are you doing?"

Her mother is trembling with anger, an expression of sheer violence covering her tight face. "Do you have any idea what our friends are saying about you, Audrey? You have made this family a laughing stock again!"

Audrey puts her hands on her hips, rolling her eyes. "Please. Preston got a DUI last week, and Paige's husband got another woman pregnant. Me kissing a quarterback in public is the least of your worries."

Mrs. Carrington gasps in horror, throwing a hand up to cover her mouth. I see when her eyes change, a calculated and savage look filling her gaze. Her hand flies forward, striking Audrey's cheek quicker than I can step in to block.

"You deceitful cow. You are a disgrace, Audrey Michelle. The only one in our family we're disappointed in is you," she growls. The hatred emanating from this woman is appalling, and I step forward, pushing Audrey behind me.

"That's enough."

Mrs. Carrington laughs haughtily. "I don't think so. An athlete won't tell me how to treat my daughter. Do you have any idea who you're dealing with?"

I raise an eyebrow at her. "Do you have any idea who I am?"

"Does it really matter? A quarterback. A nothing. My family could destroy you."

I chuckle. "So you don't know who I am. Cool."

She scoffs, and Audrey peeks around my side. "Don't antagonize her. It's not worth it. My mother is petty and cruel, and she'll try to take you down."

"She couldn't if she tried." I look at Audrey's mother with a sinister grin. "Keep your friends close, but keep your enemies closer. Audrey, did you know your parent's company was just part-nered with another real estate firm?"

"Uh, I didn't know that."

I watch as Mrs. Carrington begins to put two-and-two together as I continue. "I may be 'just an athlete,' but this athlete happens to own multiple businesses across the country, one of which is Pinnacle Asset Management. You see, Audrey, Real Estate Consul-tants hasn't been doing well for quite some time. And since they've regularly had to bail your brother out of a variety of bad decisions, REC is losing money fast. It was mere coincidence that my team began speaking to them about working together to salvage REC around the same time I met you. And as soon as you began to tell me about how awful your parents are, my plans for REC changed."

"What are you planning to do?" her mother whispers.

I sigh cheerfully. "Systematically disassemble your precious company until there's nothing left, of course. It's already in motion."

"What about all the employees? You'll put that many people out of jobs for some personal vendetta? Audrey, how can you allow this to happen?" Mrs. Carrington's voice has risen comically, like a bad cartoon villain who struggles when they're caught.

"Mother, you would throw every single person under the boat if it kept you afloat. And I didn't let anything happen. This is the first time I'm hearing anything about Jamie's business ventures." Audrey's voice is calm, but when she peers up at me, I see her eyes are sparkling with mirth. "And here I thought you were only good at doing two things."

"Jack of all trades," I answer. "But I'm intrigued. What are the two things?"

"Well, football, of course."

"Obviously," I reply, chuckling as I pull her into my side. "And the other thing I'm good at doing?"

She smiles devilishly. "Me."

I lean down and kiss her cheek gently, right over the reddening skin. I wish I'd realized what Mrs. Carrington planned to do ten seconds quicker than I did, so I could have protected Audrey. "That is my favorite thing to do. It turns out, I'm proficient at quite a few things, and one of them is making money. Did you know I'm actually a billionaire?"

Her eyes widen. "You're joking."

"Nope."

Audrey taps her lips as we walk past her mother, who is crying quietly. "How does one become a billionaire? Is it by dismantling companies run by awful parents?"

"Usually, no. Destroying your parents was just a lovely side gig this year. I've gotten my hands into quite a few pots over the years. Got some minority stakes in a few sports teams, and I've invested in a production company in LA. But mostly it's making excellent decisions in stocks and investment properties. If you ever want to vacation somewhere, I probably have a property there, or I know someone who does."

"Good to know. But last week was the first vacation I've taken in quite a few years, so it's safe to say I don't leave town too often."

"That's going to change, Doc."

"It is?"

"Yes. I'm making it my mission to show you the world."

Her arm tightens around my waist. "As long as I'm with you, I don't care where we are. I think my favorite place to be will always be right next to you."

I kiss the top of her head, loving how her hair tickles my nose. "You have your hair down tonight."

"I've been leaving it down more often," she says quietly. "Because I know it's your favorite."

It absolutely is.

As we walk back into the ballroom, I'm surprised to find Chelsea at the podium, handling the auction with ease. Maddox is up, arms crossed over his chest, as he glares at someone in the audience. He's holding a whining puppy that looks very confused by its surroundings, and Maddox absentmindedly scratches its neck.

"Ladies, remember your date can be anything you want! Dinner and a movie, picnic in the park. Or make them take you up in a private jet and join the mile high club! There is no limit. Use your imagination! The last bid was five thousand dollars, going once … going twice …"

"Ten thousand dollars!"

Audrey gasps, her body stiffening. Turning to her, I ask, "What's wrong?"

"That's Claire!" The woman stalking to the front looks furious, and taking a quick glance at Maddox shows me he isn't thrilled with the turn of events either. Audrey steps forward from where we're hidden off to the side of the stage, but I pull her back into my arms. I want to see how this plays out.

Claire stops before the stage, positively fuming, as Maddox squats down so they're eye-to-eye. "You want that quickie now, don't you, Sunshine?"

"No way," Audrey hisses. "He tried to proposition her earlier tonight!"

The grin Claire gives Maddox is menacing. "I'm going to make your life a living hell."

Maddox chuckles, then stands upright. "You'll be begging for my cock before we even get to the main course."

Claire laughs. "That little thing? Doubtful. I will, however, place a friendly wager with you."

"Oh yeah? I like winning. What are the stakes?"

"Whoever gives in first."

"And what do you get if you somehow manage to win?" Maddox asks boastfully.

"You donate one million dollars to wherever I tell you to."

Maddox whistles. "Jesus, Sunshine. A million? That's a hefty sum."

"I looked up your most recent contract. I know you can afford it."

"Alright. And when I win?"

Claire crosses her arms, forcing Maddox's gaze to dip. *"When?"*

He gives a feral smile. "Oh yeah, Sunshine. When I win. You're mine for a month, to do with how I please."

Claire holds out her hand, which Maddox takes. They shake, and then Claire turns, stalking away. I turn to Audrey. "What the hell was that?"

"I don't know, but I think it'll be fun to watch whatever happens with them."

Out of the corner of my eye, I see my coach stalk onto the stage, holding a leash with an absolutely massive puppy attached, clearly angry he is forced to participate. "Speaking of bets, my coach is up next, because he lost a bet to Jax's coach."

"Up next, we have Colorado Coyotes head coach, Silas Youngstown! At a whopping six - five, Coach Youngstown is starting his second season with the Coyotes. He's still got a lot of years left, at only forty-eight years old. He's accompanied by Winston Furchill, a six-month old mastiff and Labrador mix. You'll definitely need a large yard to train this one … and the puppy, too. Coach, you want to strut your stuff?"

"No."

"Alright then," Chelsea says nonchalantly. "He's a growly one, ladies. It says here that, in his spare time, Coach likes long walks on the beach, braiding a woman's hair, and writing a sonnet or two."

"The fuck I do!" Coach yells, turning to where I stand with Audrey. She's standing with her back resting against me, and I've got my arms wrapped around her with my chin resting on top of her head. "Guess you're wanting a lot of footwork drills this week. That about right, asshole?"

I attempt to hide my smile against Audrey's hair, but I see Coach's eyes narrow. "Totally worth it!"

"Okay. Let's start the bidding at five hundred dollars."

Coach rubs the bridge of his nose with one hand as bids come in. A group of women outbid each other until the bids stop at fifteen thousand dollars. Coach's face rivals a tomato, until one voice clearly rises above the rest.

"One hundred thousand dollars." I watch as a pretty, young

thing walks toward the stage. Not rail-thin, but not plus size either, with light brown hair and blue eyes, she strides toward Coach with confidence. She can't be more than thirty, and Coach's mouth drops open. She peers up at Coach with a smile. "Surprised to see me, Silas?"

He only nods, his mouth open in shock. Their gazes don't break as Chelsea announces Coach has been sold, but then I hear a voice I absolutely *do* recognize shout, "Motherfucker, did you sleep with my granddaughter?"

Oh shit.

Audrey

CHAPTER 26

I barely get my front door unlocked before my back is against the wall and Jamie is devouring my mouth. I feel his hard length jut against me through every layer of my dress, and I'm desperate to get it into my body somehow. Honestly, I don't care how. Anywhere.

I only vaguely register hearing Flash's excited barks, but Jamie breaks off the kiss. "I guess my other girl is happy to see me, too."

He crouches in front of her kennel, carefully pulling her out, and straps her wheelchair on. He then bends down so she can give him kisses. Standing, he points to me. "You. Get that dress unbuttoned, or unzipped, or whatever needs to happen so that I don't rip it off. I'll take Flash out."

I giddily pass by him, then yelp as he slaps my ass. Stunned, I turn to him. "Jamie?"

"Too much?" he asks.

"I'm not sure."

"Something you may want to revisit?"

"Yes?"

He steps into me, wrapping his arms around my hips. "You're allowed not to like something. Just tell me, and I won't do it again.

You never have to feel self-conscious telling me what you like or don't like, Doc."

"It's just …" I trail off in hesitation, but when he gives me a patient smile, I continue. "If I liked that, it doesn't mean I'll like other violent things."

Jamie shudders. "Good, because spanking is as far into the S of BDSM as I'm willing to go. And something tells me you're not a masochist, so I doubt you'd like anything worse than spanking."

I let out a relieved breath. "Okay, good. But can you undo the top couple of buttons before you go outside? It's hard for me to reach them."

I turn, pulling my hair over my shoulder. Jamie's breathing quickens slightly as he drags a finger down my spine. "There aren't any buttons here, minx."

"I know." I don't look as I walk confidently down the hall. I hear him laugh all the way out the front door.

The day before Jamie returned from his road trip, I quietly went on a lingerie buying binge. I almost threw it all away. Almost. I chose not to, because I felt beautiful in every item. Yes, I bought them for Jamie. But I realized I wanted them for me as well. Right now, I'm thankful I didn't toss them, as I quickly grab my favorite piece. Unzipping the dress, I step out of it, leaving it in a heap on the floor, then run into my attached bathroom. I close the door as I hear Jamie come back inside. He murmurs to Flash, then goes into the kitchen. I assume he's getting a puzzle ready for her, which gives me extra time to put myself into this getup. The deep purple corset is a striking color against my pale skin, and fortunately the front lacing allows me to strap it on without help. I quickly put on black stockings, attaching them to the garter belt, and leave my black panties on. I'm hoping Jamie is so overcome with lust that he rips them right off. They were cheap, so I don't care if I have to replace them.

I hear the bedroom door quietly close before Jamie speaks. "Doc? You okay?"

"I'll be out in a sec," I reply, checking myself out in the mirror one last time. I look damn good. There's something so inherently feminine and powerful about wrapping myself in lingerie. I've never felt this good about myself, and I think it's partially to do with the man standing on the other side of the door. But mostly, it's me. I'm brilliant, caring, loving, and just plain amazing. I don't care what anyone else thinks about me, other than Jamie and my close friends. This is me. If someone doesn't like it, they can fuck right off.

Fluffing my hair one last time, I open the door with a flourish, watching as Jamie's mouth drops open, and then he drops his tuxedo coat. "Holy fuck."

"You like?" I ask, twirling a lock of hair around my finger while biting my lower lip.

"Yes," he replies, his voice strangled and high. He clears his throat as he removes his cufflinks, setting them on the nightstand. "I don't even know how to explain what I'm thinking. You look … Jesus, Aud. You're my wet dream, come to life."

I preen at his words, and he smiles. I guess he was correct, that words of affirmation really are my love language. After going so long with virtually no positive encouragement or unconditional love from my parents, I crave it. And I love that Jamie recognizes that, and gives it to me selflessly.

I take a step into the bedroom, then hesitate. I'd only thought as far as putting on the lingerie, not about what I should do next. Jamie's smile widens as he beckons me forward with a slow crook of his finger. As I glide toward him, he stares at me unabashedly, his gaze sending heat across my skin. Eyes now hooded, he takes his time, lasciviously devouring me with his gaze. "I should take my time with you, Doc. Taste every decadent inch of your skin. Take you to the edge again and again, until you're trembling with so much need you can't do anything but beg me to let you come. But, truth be told, I'm so fucking desperate to be inside you that I don't think I can wait. And I know once I'm inside you, I'll come in a minute or two because you look like *that* and my willpower is dangling by the tiniest string."

"I can't wait either," I gush. "I've missed you too much."

"Thank fuck," he mutters, grabbing my hand and yanking me against his body. His lips cover mine in a desperate kiss, and I moan into his mouth. His hand finds my hair, grabbing a handful, and manhandles me into the position he wants so he can deepen the kiss. His velvety smooth tongue glides over mine perfectly as his other hand grabs a handful of my ass. He groans deeply, kneading me, then reaches between my cheeks to rub against the tiny scrap of fabric covering my pussy. I gasp at the exquisite friction, but before I can circle my hips to gain traction, he removes his hand. I don't have time to complain before he drops to his knees, throws one leg over a shoulder, and attacks my pussy with a vengeance. I let out a loud, guttural moan as pleasure fills my veins. The friction of his finger is nothing compared to his tongue, but I need more.

"Rip them off," I moan.

"My pleasure." I feel a tiny sting against my skin as he rips the fabric from my core, but then his mouth soothes the pain away. I latch both hands in his hair as I hold on for balance.

Almost every time Jamie has gone down on me, he's meandered around. He'd switch things up so I never knew the pattern, building me up so perfectly that when I finally shattered, it was mind-blowing. Tonight, his need is outweighing his quest for orgasm control, and I love that I'm responsible for his desire. He suctions onto my clit, flicking it quickly with his tongue, then slides two fingers inside to hit my G-spot. My orgasm hits out of nowhere, robbing me of the ability to breathe as the wave of pleasure overtakes me. I'm barely done before Jamie stands, manhandles me against the wall, rips open his pants, and buries himself inside me. "Fuck, yes. Fuck. Give me your eyes, Doc."

So overcome with sensation I didn't realize I'd closed them, I open my eyes to find Jamie staring intensely at me. I can barely focus, but manage to lift a leg higher to give him more room to work. He immediately grabs my other leg, wrapping both around his waist, then intertwines our fingers together on one hand, placing them above our heads. His movement is slow. Measured. Calculated and ridiculously erotic. "I love you so fucking much, Audrey."

"I love you too," I whisper, tears filling my eyes as I recognize how poignant this moment truly is. He's making love to me. We're connecting on a different level that I haven't experienced before, and I hope he hasn't either. "Jamie …"

"I know," he says quietly. "Me too."

His gaze doesn't waver as he builds me back up. The world falls away until it's only the two of us, connected in this perfect way.

"Promise me," he whispers, his voice deep and husky with lust. "Promise me this is it. You and me. Always, Doc."

"Always," I repeat. He leans in to kiss me, and I wrap my arm tightly around his neck. He slides his free hand between our bodies to find my clit, and my core clenches around him. One pinch and my back arches off the wall. My orgasm triggers his, and he roars his release as he shudders against me. We stay against the wall as we catch our breaths.

"I can't feel one foot," he mumbles, dropping his head to my shoulder and nuzzling against my neck.

I snort. "If you let go of me, I'll get down."

"No."

"I don't have any sympathy for your foot."

"I wasn't asking for sympathy. I was stating a fact. I can't feel one foot. Do I regret what caused it? Nope. Was it worth it? Fuck yes."

Laughter gurgles out of my throat. "Your feet are more important than any part of my body, Jamie. Put me down."

His head pops up. "That's actually wrong."

I raise an eyebrow, disbelief evident on my face. "Seriously? How are you going to tell me that? You must make ten million a year. Clearly that means your body parts are worth more than mine."

"Technically that's not what you said. And I make forty million a year."

"Forty?" I yell, making him laugh.

"I love that you have no idea how much money I have."

"Well, I had no idea you're a billionaire. But what do you mean about the technicality?"

"You said my feet are more important than any of your body parts. Not worth. Importance."

"Same thing," I huff.

He shakes his head with a grin. "Not even close. Your heart is priceless. My feet are nothing compared to that."

The breath is sucked from my lungs. "Jamie."

He leans down to give me a soft kiss. "I can survive without football. But these last couple of weeks have proven to me that I won't survive without you. Maddox had to pick me up every morning for training camp, or I wouldn't have gone. My house is a disaster. The only thing I did was play football, sleep, and write in that journal I gave you."

I gasp. "The journal! I haven't had a chance to read it yet! Put me down! Put me down!"

Jamie chuckles as he lets go, but as soon as my feet hit the ground and his cock slides out of me, my face screws up in disgust. He bursts into laughter. "I could have walked us into the bathroom."

Keeping my knees together, I waddle over to grab a towel. "It's fine. I want to read the journal."

"Are you sure?" he asks hesitantly. "I know how I am with stuff touching me, so I really won't judge you if you want to take a shower."

I sigh. "It's not fine. I'll be right back. I'd invite you to join me, but I don't think we'd actually shower, and I really want to read the journal!"

"I know. Go," he says, pointing toward the bathroom as he kicks off his pants and tucks his cock back into his boxer briefs. Standing here like this, knowing he just annihilated me against a wall, is one hell of a feeling. "Baby. Go take a shower!"

"Alright," I mutter, untying the corset as I walk. I dispose of the ripped panties, then strip out of the corset. Somehow one of the stockings has a run, but I don't care. I quickly pull them off and step into the shower. Piling my hair on top of my head, I take an incredibly cold, but fast, shower, then wrap myself in a thick fleece robe. "Done."

"Damn," Jamie says with a laugh, then pats the bed next to him. He's already under the covers, and he's moved Flash into her kennel in my room. Climbing into bed, I grab the journal to begin reading.

Within a minute, I'm crying. I flip between laughing tears and straight sobbing as I read so many pages about his thoughts over the past two weeks.

"Did you make a decision about your mom?" I ask quietly.

"I don't want to see her," he says bluntly. "That much I know. But I'm debating on calling her. If I did, would you sit with me when I do it? I don't think I want to do that alone."

"Of course," I whisper. I continue reading to hear about how his cats miss me, a new restaurant he thinks I would enjoy, and all the reasons why I've made his life better just be being me. When I finish, I turn to Jamie as I wipe the last of my tears away. "Can I implement a rule for when you're out of town?"

"Sure, but I'm honestly hoping I can sweet-talk you into traveling with me on occasion," he says with a laugh.

"On occasion, maybe. But I can't close my clinic every week for a couple of days. That's not fair to my patients and their parents."

He smiles at me sweetly. "I know, Doc. I'd never expect you to do that. If we make it to the AFC Championship, and then the Super Bowl, I'll probably beg you, so be prepared."

"Noted. So, when you're out of town, I think we should write letters like this to each other. It will be a way we can stay connected, and a keepsake for us to look through in the future. This journal," I say, squeezing it against my chest, "will be something I cherish. I want you to have that as well."

"I love that idea," he says huskily, sliding his arms around me.

"Can I write about all the things I'm going to do to you when I get home?"

"You better. And don't skimp on the details."

"I'm *very* good at being graphic."

A little over a month later, I'm in a suite at Rocky Mountain Stadium, watching my hot boyfriend battle against the Nashville Tigers. Jamie told me to invite anyone I wanted, so I decided to invite pretty much everyone I know. Chelsea, Jax, and Becca are here. Arianna from Eternity Springs drove down with her husband, Stone, and her brother, Luca, brought his wife, Hannah. Claire is here with another gal from the crazy group chat, Natalie, and one of Arianna's other brothers, Dominic, brought his wife, Kate. The suite came with a catered meal, and the thick glass partition separating us from the rabid fans is perfect for limiting the amount of noise we hear. While I don't always have an issue with overstimulation due to loud sounds, I really don't want today to be a day for that.

"Your boy is looking good," Jax says from beside me.

"He is." Whoever created football pants is an angel.

"He mentioned the fans have been a little … overzealous with wanting details about you." Overzealous is a politically correct way of saying psychotic, it seems. I've come home to people rifling through my mailbox, fans scheduling new appointments at my clinic when they don't have pets, and tailing me on the highway.

"He moved me into his house while I was at work this week," I confess with a giggle. "He said it stresses him out too much knowing I'm alone at my townhouse. I'll be putting it up on the market next week."

"Moving pretty fast," he muses, right as his wife walks up.

"You better not grill this poor woman about her intentions,

Jacob Mitchell! You married me before we'd even had a proper date." Hands on her hips, Becca Stephens-Mitchell looks stern, but her eyes are sparkling. "Ignore him, Audrey. You're moving at the perfect pace for you and Jamie. No one else is allowed to have an opinion on the matter."

Jax puts up his hands in mock surrender. "I wasn't saying it was too fast! Just commenting. That's all. I'm in full support of Jamie and Audrey. I don't want to sleep on the couch, Darlin'. The pigs make too much noise, and Thunder farts a lot."

"Oh shit," Dominic shouts. "He's got a window!"

I take my attention away from Jax to look out onto the field. Jamie has the ball, and he's able to run straight through the middle at the twenty yard line, right into the end zone for a touchdown.

"You guys gotta watch the replay," Dominic says. "That was amazing. Dude has phenomenal footwork."

I look up to the large screen in the corner, listening as the analysts dissect the play. "Wahlberg is typically a passer. Look where the wide receiver is here," a player is circled in red, "and the running back here," another circled in blue. "He drops back, fakes to the running back, but Diamante on the Tigers read the play, running perfectly with the wide receiver so Wahlberg can't throw. A window opened up and he took off. Now look at his face when he gets into the end zone." The camera zooms in on Jamie, with a massive grin on his face. "He may not be known for running the ball, and he's currently one of the oldest quarterbacks in the league, but Jameson Wahlberg just proved why he's an MVP candidate year after year."

I then notice Jamie looking up, over the crowd, and run to the window. I see his grin from here, and he points to me, then makes a heart with his hands, and points to me again. Jax chuckles beside me. "Never thought I'd see the day when he'd be as gone for a woman as I am for my wife. But damn, it's good to see it happen."

Epilogue

EPILOGUE

Four years later

"It's your fortieth birthday. It's monumental," Audrey says. "We should do something special."

"You know birthdays have never been a big thing to me. Well, except for his," I say tenderly, looking down at my two-year-old son, currently building an elaborate tower of magnetic blocks on the floor of our kitchen.

I didn't know what happiness was until Audrey walked into my life, and the bliss I feel being a dad is indescribable. Brooks Jameson Wahlberg was born almost two years to the day from when I met Audrey.

"What if," Audrey says softly as she sits in my lap, "I were to tell you a secret?"

I rest my hand on her very swollen belly, full of our daughter.

"A secret? Is this a secret you think I'll be happy about, mad about, or one you feel I need to prepare myself for?"

"A little of all three, I think," she says with a nervous giggle. "Maddox and the O-Line are planning a surprise birthday party for you, and they asked me to get you to pick out a restaurant for it. Then they'd do the rest."

"Baby," I sigh. "My birthday is too close to your due date. I don't want to risk something happening to you."

"I figured you'd say as much, which is why I have compiled a list of suitable restaurants we both like that are within five minutes of the birthing center."

I stare at her incredulously, then throw my head back in raucous laughter. "I will never not be surprised by how well you know me."

"That's my job as your wife," she replies.

I proposed to Audrey one year after we met, at the exact restaurant. In the same booth. With the same server. Was it the most romantic proposal out there? No. But it was poignant and so special to us. I proposed with a simple three carat solitaire ring, because I knew Audrey's tastes. She'd never want something outlandish or blingy. She attaches moments to physical things, and she finds joy in small details. A diamond the size of her knuckle would overstimulate her, and a band with tiny diamonds would scratch her skin. So the simple diamond on a thin platinum band was perfect.

We had a small ceremony in our home, with only a handful of friends in attendance. Flash was our flower girl, and the five guinea pigs were ring bearers. Weird? Maybe. But very much us. We did invite my dad, but he'd been unable to attend. We did not invite anyone from Audrey's family. They were furious when she 'purchased' me at the auction, saying she shouldn't have access to the one hundred thousand she bid on me. Audrey very firmly told them to fuck off, and reminded them that her trust was hers to do with as she pleased. Since I wasn't actually up for auction, I said she didn't have to pay, but she vehemently argued that it was the best thing she'd ever purchased, and the money went to a good cause anyway.

I can't fault that reasoning, especially when I know I'd have dropped well over a million if the roles were reversed.

We've run into the Carringtons a couple of times in the last four years, but my beautiful wife walks past them with her head held high. She doesn't give them the time of day, and it makes me so proud of her. There have been rumblings that her father may have tried to blackmail an elected official in Douglas County, but no arrests have been made.

I meant what I said about the Carrington family business. I pushed them out, then broke apart the business, piece by piece. I interviewed every single employee personally, finding suitable jobs for them at a variety of other businesses I own. In the end, fewer than fifteen employees were furloughed without a new job. All of those individuals were tied to the Carrington family by blood or marriage, and none of them deserved the jobs they had. I fucking hate nepotism.

Audrey's sister, Paige, was divorced by her husband a year ago. It turns out he wasn't having affairs *all* the time. He was working nonstop to pay for all of her expenses. He knew she was sleeping with more than one man, though, and he strategized his divorce to coincide with the demise of REC. He immediately married the woman he got pregnant, telling Paige he'd wanted to be a father more than he wanted her family's connections. Audrey's brother, Preston, was arrested for trying to orchestrate a Ponzi scheme, which was absurd because the dumbass had zero experience with investments. He'd basically been told his entire life that he was God's gift to business and real estate, so he thought he could get away with anything. As soon as REC was under my control, everyone in the commercial real estate world began to recognize the Carrington family for what they were. Preston was dead in the water before he even stuck his toe in the tide.

A few weeks after Audrey and I got back together, I called my mom. She was in the end stages of her cancer fight. Breast cancer had metastasized into her lungs, kidneys, and spine. She apologized for all the things she'd done, admitting she had lived vicariously through me in high school and college. She'd gotten divorced again, and remarried a man from Portland. They lived a modest life up until her death, only days after we spoke.

I struggled with my decision to call instead of visiting her, but Audrey wisely reminded me that I'd been so used to being disrespected by my mother. She never honored my very clear boundaries. I didn't owe her anything during the final days of her life just because she was dying. It may seem cruel, but it was what I needed to hear. I spent my childhood dealing with toxicity from her, and when I finally went no-contact, I had an immediate sense of relief. Throughout those years, my mother didn't love me for me. She loved me for what I could do for her. Hearing her apologize was closure that I needed, and I was able to move on without any guilt.

"Daddy."

I look down at my son, with his cherubic face and eyes the exact shade of his mother's, and smile. "Yes, Brooks?"

"Bay boot ball today?"

I chuckle. "No, I'm not playing football today. We played Thursday night. Remember?"

"Bay boot ball." I will honestly be sad when he figures out how to pronounce sounds correctly, because 'bay boot ball' sounds so much better than 'play football.'

"Okay, I've picked a restaurant," Audrey says, putting her phone down on the counter. "I figured you weren't going to settle on one, so I chose what I'm craving most."

"As if I'd say anything against that," I chuckle. "What my pregnant wife wants, my pregnant wife gets."

"It's wise of you to feel that way, QB." She stops suddenly, looking at me. "I only have a few more months where I get to call you that."

Standing, I stride to her and pull her into my arms. "You can call me QB anytime you want."

After winning the Super Bowl, and the MVP, last season, I made the decision to retire at the end of this year. I'm not getting any younger. I love the sport, and I'll miss it dearly, but it's time for me to hang up my cleats.

After more than a few run-ins with fans at her clinic, Audrey made the decision to sell it to another veterinarian. She didn't leave the veterinary world, however. She now does veterinary work for a handful of shelters and rescues around the Denver metropolitan area, and she's taken on the role of CEO of my foundation. When she was announced as CEO, people finally realized it was my organization. I'd gone well over a decade incognito, and had managed to donate millions to Denver humane societies and shelters during that time.

We managed to pull Chelsea into the foundation as well. She's still Audrey's right-hand woman, and also takes on quite a bit of the donation portion of what we do.

I notice Audrey biting her lip, which is always a clue that she has something she's struggling to say. "What's on your mind, Doc?"

"It's just …" she trails off, sighing. "I picked that Mexican restaurant we like for your surprise party. But now I can't stop thinking about the queso. Oh, and the fajitas. God, those sound so good. And Brooks loves their homemade tortillas."

I'm already putting on my shoes. "Call it in. I'll go pick it up."

Audrey beams at me. "You're the best baby daddy in the whole world."

I kiss her softly, rub Brooks' head, then stride out the door.

Thirty minutes later, I'm surrounded by my teammates. "How the hell did you pull this off?"

Maddox slaps my back. "Aud had her list, and we told her to pick by four o'clock today. So we all just hung out in a Target parking lot until she told us what she wanted to eat."

"Not where she wanted to go?" I ask, amused.

Maddox shrugs. "I'm not dumb. She's a billion months pregnant, and the two of you are already pretty particular about food. I knew it would end up where she wanted to eat tonight. Ask her yourself."

He points behind me, and I find Audrey slowly walking in, with Brooks by her side. "So not a surprise party, but kind of one?"

She smiles sheepishly. "It's fun to surprise you every now and again. But seriously, I did order food on the way over here. Move, or I'm eating you. And not in a good way, QB."

Our favorite server waves to my wife, then immediately puts a heaping bowl of queso in front of her. I feel someone slap my back again, and I turn to find Chelsea. "You're here too?"

"Aud called. Said there was food. I was thinking I'd steal Brooks for the night anyway. He hasn't had a sleepover at Aunt Chelsea's in a couple of weeks. We need our bonding time." Her eyes don't meet mine, but her gaze is trained on where Audrey sits with Brooks.

"She's in labor, isn't she?" I ask, stepping toward her, but Chelsea stops me.

"Listen. She's timing the contractions, and her water hasn't broken yet. Her bag is in the car. She knows they won't let her eat once she gets to the hospital, so please, let her eat. She made me promise not to tell you, but apparently, you've got some kind of mind reading bullshit going on, because I didn't say a word."

"You wouldn't look me in the eye, Chels. That's how I knew." I walk nonchalantly toward my wife and son, hoping to hell I can act like I don't know our lives are about to change.

"You rarely look me in the eye, QB! I guess turnabout is fair play!" Chelsea shouts, making me shake my head in disbelief. They're as different as night and day, but it makes me so happy to know Audrey has Chelsea in her corner.

Pulling out a chair at the table, Brooks clambers into my lap. Audrey looks at me with an adorable pout. "I tried to fit in a booth. These chairs are uncomfortable. It should be illegal for chairs to have odd wooden rods just haphazardly strewn throughout the back. No one can find this enjoyable."

"Mmhmm," I murmur, turning my hat around before scooping a pile of queso into my mouth.

"Jamie," Audrey snaps.

"What?"

Her eyes are murderous. "You will not force me out of here until I'm done eating. Do you understand me?"

"What are you talking about?" I mumble around a tortilla chip.

"Oh, don't give me that. I know you know. You are the worst liar. Promise me you'll let me eat."

"How far apart are the contractions?" I ask.

"Nine minutes apart."

"Do you promise to tell me when they're coming closer together?"

"Only if I get my fajitas."

"Audrey," I sigh.

Her eyes narrow. "No. You listen here, Jameson."

Uh-oh. The government name. Audrey is serious now.

"I was in labor with your son for twenty-eight hours. Well over an entire day! And since the epidural wore off, I experienced pain like you will never truly comprehend. I had a second degree perineal tear because you have an enormous head, so naturally, so does your son. And for that labor, you took me to the hospital when I had my first contraction, and I was already hungry when I got there. They wouldn't let me eat. If you attempt to abduct me and force me to leave before I've filled my stomach, I'm filing for divorce."

I chuckle, which only aggravates her more. I stifle my laughter and regain a stoic expression. "I promise I won't force you out of here until you've had your fajitas."

"Thank you," she says, beaming, but then she gasps. Her eyes dip to the ground, and I know.

"Your water broke."

"It did. Please let me eat."

"Baby —"

"Divorce, Wahlberg. Divorce. Let. Me. Eat."

"Fine. But I'm timing the contractions." I pull out my phone, where I've installed the same app as Audrey. A plate of sizzling fajitas is set in front of her, and I breathe a sigh of relief. We're that much closer to leaving. Once I get her to the birthing center, I'll feel even better. While I don't bring this up to Audrey, I'm pretty freaked out about all the complications that can happen during childbirth, especially to mothers' of 'advanced maternal age.' I also haven't told her I have two OB's on call for if they're needed. I'm not taking any chances. She's my life.

"Oh my God," Audrey moans, her eyes closed.

"What?" I shout. "Is it the baby?"

One eye opens. "You seriously need to relax a little. We're one-point-seven miles from the birthing center. I moaned because this tastes so good. Brooks is going to stay with Chelsea tonight, and you don't play until next Monday night. Honestly, this little girl must be as Type-A as you, because she's timing this perfectly."

I can't help but smile at the thought. My little girl already has me wrapped around her finger, and she isn't even born yet.

Twelve hours later, after my rock star wife pushed twice, Magnolia Elise Wahlberg made her debut.

And just like that, my family grew by two perfect feet.

Want to read Jax and Becca's story? Grab Forecasting the Forward on ebook and audiobook today!

Interested in Arianna Santo and her cantankerous set of meddling siblings? Start Worth the Risk, Arianna's brother AND Jax's teammate, Luca's book today!

Pre-Order Max Callahan's book, Cooking Up a Curveball, coming Summer 2026!

· · ·

Want to learn more about Max's previous team, the Bridge Point Bears? Go check out my friend A.R. Rose's book, Stealing Forever!

Want to find out what happens between Maddox and Claire? Sign up for my newsletter to get release information on The Calculated Catch, coming in 2026!

Acknowledgment

This book was so incredibly hard for me to write, not only because it occurred during one of the busiest times of my life, but also because I was so scared about messing it up. I'm about 90% sure I'm autistic, I know my husband is, and one of my kids is. I needed this to be as close of a representation to how neurodiversity can impact a budding relationship because it's something ND individuals have to deal with, and I want my kids to see that their brains may work a little differently than some of their peers, but they are still worthy of love and acceptance. But man, I struggled with this one … until I didn't.

It was like pulling teeth at the beginning. I could barely write a couple hundred words a day. Then suddenly, a light flipped on, and the words just poured out of me. 75,000 words in three weeks. I think I could have kept writing. Seeing Jamie, the NFL superstar who didn't trust that anyone would ever love him for him, gain confidence because of Audrey? Chef's kiss. And Audrey, recognizing that her body is beautiful? Yes, please!

I'd like to thank my beta team of Morgan, Daisy, Heather, Anna, and Valerie, for dissecting every word. I'm so fortunate to have all of you, and your backgrounds, to help me navigate such a sensitive topic. To the remainder of my arc team, thank you for always getting so excited about my characters, and sending me all the amazing voice messages as you read.

To my editor, Brenda, for now recognizing which Oxford commas I'm unwilling to budge on, and leaving them out of her edits.

To my PA, Morgan, for continuing to put up with me for God knows what reason, even remaining optimistic when she asks me questions like, "are you ready to send out the arc?" No, Morgan, the answer is almost always no. But I appreciate your enthusiasm. And I love you for putting up with me.

And finally, I want to acknowledge every neurodiverse reader out there. You, the reader who knows every technique under the sun to help with panic attacks. And you, the reader who only reads by vibes, whether the cover is pretty, and if you like the name of the

MMC. The readers who hear all sounds at the same decibel, won't eat a specific food because of one bad experience twenty years ago, or buying ten of the same bra because it doesn't itch, and is needed in every color. I see you. I am you. You're perfect in your uniqueness, and you deserve a Jamie Wahlberg in your life. So what if you eat things in even numbers, because you don't want the item to be lonely in your digestive tract? And it's no big deal that you sometimes lack a filter in social situations when you're uncomfortable. Be you. Fuck everyone who says otherwise.

-Jen

Also by
JENNIFER J. WILLIAMS

About the Author

Jennifer was born and raised in Ohio, but currently calls Colorado home. A lifelong lover of romance books, Jen felt pulled to write stories with older characters, because "old farts" deserve love too. Jen prides herself on delivering realistic characters that struggle with normal problems. She spends most of her free time within her zoo: two kids, two dogs, and two cats! When not containing the chaos, Jen can be found lounging on her covered porch devouring books on her Kindle.